To Manong ~~, This will help you go to sleep!

Garry

In The Shadow of La Generala

A Novel

By

M. A. ADRIATICO

For Adriana, the little Generala,
And her Lola Erna, the big Generala.

4

Prologue

Was it love?

He didn't know then, and over the better part of two decades later, he still has no clue.

For what did a twelve year old boy know about love? Or a full-grown man for that matter, who, although feared and respected by his peers, flounders helplessly around women?

He didn't know then and nothing has changed.

But one thing he knows for sure. He could not get her out of his mind. Her memory still haunts him almost every day like a persistent dream that came at odd moments. Perhaps that was what she had become, just a dream.

Or perhaps he indeed was in love. And maybe he still is.

For after all these years he still remembers clearly the day she left as if it only happened a few days ago.

He ran as fast as he could.

He was the swiftest runner among the boys in the village but it seemed that he was not moving fast enough. He silently cursed himself for going up the mountain so early in the morning to check on his bird traps. But he had not known.

If not for his friend Akash who had followed him later that morning, he wouldn't have known that she was leaving.

The trail going down the mountain was still slippery with the night's dew and he had a rough time going down the steep inclines. The branches of the small trees and shrubs that crowded the trail left welts on his bare legs. His arms too were marked with gashes as he used them to protect his face and upper body from the slashing branches. But he did not slow down his furious pace. He was oblivious to the pain. He would feel it later but not at the moment, for his thoughts were focused on reaching the village as fast as he could and nothing else.

He wanted to see her one more time, even just to say good-bye.

He rounded a bend and he finally saw the river that meandered by the village, shimmering in the distance as the morning sun rose quietly beyond it. He scanned the bank on the side of the village for the sign of the raft that would take her down to the lowlands and saw nothing there. He stopped suddenly, stumbling as his left foot skidded in the mud, but he caught a branch hanging over the trail and steadied himself.

She's gone, he thought, catching his breath. His chest was heaving painfully from his run but he realized the pain was coming from someplace else deeper, closer to his heart. He felt his throat and eyes burning but he fought the urge to cry. He lowered his head, a feeling of great loss beginning to envelope him.

He clenched his teeth and raised his head, his eyes lighting up as he noted a movement from behind Apo Allak's hut that abutted the riverbank. The old man's hut was built so close to the river that he used its posts to tie down his rafts, one that was used for long trips and another shorter one that he used for fishing by the village. Every year when the long days of rains came and the river crested, the hut got swept away. But every year, like the wild grass returning after the first rain at the end of a long dry summer, Apo Allak kept rebuilding on the same spot. It was a running joke in the village that Apo Allak considered the river an extension of his hut. Apo Allak waved the jokes off by claiming he was the only man in the village with a new hut every year.

He started running again as he realized it was the longer raft used for long trips that was pulling away, and on it he vaguely saw her, hunched between her mother and her older Uncle Allong. He saw Apo Allak heft the long bamboo pole and thrust it expertly into the water, and the raft silently glided away from the bank and floated downriver. There was no way he could get there in time to say goodbye.

"Ilang!!!" he shouted with all his might although he was too far for her to hear him. But his voice must have been carried by the wind and somehow reached her for she abruptly raised her head and looked back at the village and up the trail. She may just had been taking a final look but he knew in his heart that she heard him for she raised a hand in farewell, then she looked downriver and held her gaze there. She didn't look back, even when he finally reached the riverbank, but by then the raft was just a faint speck of a shadow away. He watched solemnly until the raft finally rounded a bend in the river then vanished in a hazy blur that he realized with a start was caused by the tears gradually forming in his eyes.

He slowly walked into the river, unaware that the water was still cold at that time of the day. "I'll come for you, Ilang," he said softly. "I'll come for you, I promise."

Then he plunged headlong into the water as he felt his eyes swelling with tears and knew he could no longer hold them from flowing. His body was jolted by the coldness of the water, but he swam vigorously beneath the surface and the chill went away. He stayed underwater until he felt his lungs seemed to burst for want of air. When he came up, he found himself in the middle of the river. His tears came then uncontrollably, mixing with the cold *rivulets of water running down his face, and it took all his resolve not to sob loudly.*

He trod water for a while, looking downriver for the raft that was no longer there. He raised an arm and waved anyway.

Then he turned and swam toward the opposite bank not knowing exactly what to do once he got there. He lay on his back in the sand as soon as he got to the other side, breathing in short bursts, not bothering to wipe the tears that still flowed freely down his face. He stayed in that position for a long time, even after he had calmed down, staring blankly at the cloudless sky until his eyes hurt from the glare of the morning sun.

He must have fallen asleep for the shadows were short and the sun was burning brightly and hot in the mid-sky when he finally moved and swam back across the river to the village.

"I'll come for you, Ilang," he said again as he climbed out of the water and headed back up the trail to find solace among the trees. "I'll come for you someday, I promise."

Chapter One

He loved this time of the day when the night birds had gone home to roost but the day birds had not ventured out yet for the dawn was still a few hours away. It was the time when the mountain was most calm, silent like a giant child in deep slumber. There was stillness so profound that made the moment seem so spiritually sublime. Sometimes he felt that somehow he was intruding into something so sacred where no mortals should dare tread.

And that feeling of intrusion was intensified when the fog was so thick but he had no choice but to go through it, and more so when there was no moon like now. Yet at the same time he felt like he was meant to be here at this precise moment, to absorb the mystery it possessed, whatever it might be. It was a mystery, he knew, that was not meant to be solved nor understood, but simply to be felt and experienced. Seeking for an answer was futile and meaningless.

And there was the fog now silently rolling and gliding among the bushes like an apparition, beckoning mesmerically as if luring and daring him to discover the mysteries hidden in the recesses of the mountain.

He was certain in his belief that the spirits of his ancestors and unseen dwellers of the forest hid and played in their shadows.

And out of respect, not of fear, he trod carefully.

He had always felt a special sense of communion with the spirits of the ancients and the unseen dwellers of the forest and he tried to seek them out as often as he could. He had yet to see them but he always felt their presence, as he did now, for he felt the goose bumps cover his arms, and ran up his shoulders and nape. He nodded his head to no one in particular, just a general acknowledgment that he was aware of the presence of whoever were out there.

"Just passing through, *Apo*," he whispered softly, using the word of reverence accorded to elders and respected people. He felt a cold breeze gently caress his back as if in response and he shivered slightly. Then the moment passed, the goose bumps went away, and he felt a sense of peace.

He had lowered his eyes as he spoke, but now as he felt his body warming up, his eyes darted back to the shadows among the trees. He was not expecting to see anything in particular but he could not resist the urge and the chance perhaps to witness something that could not be explained. But as in the past, all he could see was the fog shifting in the dark, drifting lazily toward the deeper contours of the mountain as if looking for a place to escape from its eventual demise by the coming of the sun.

Perhaps it is true that things of importance are just meant to be felt and not seen, he thought and he moved on.

The grass beneath his bare feet was wet with the night's dew and the air was cold and damp, heavy with mist, but he liked the coldness of it against his bare chest and broad shoulders.

There were just his bow and a quiver full of arrows slung across his back and with them he felt warm and comfortable enough despite the fact that he wore nothing else but his *ba-ag*, his loin cloth. He carried his wooden spear in his right arm, its iron tip pointed upward. Every now and then he used it for a staff.

He had been up and walking at a brisk pace for at least a good hour now, having left the village as soon as he heard the first crow of *Apo* Kagaid's roosters. They would start crowing again closer to dawn which would still be another good hour or so away.

Everyone was still asleep when he left. He heard no one stir as he made his way among the huts. Even the dogs were too sleepy or too lazy to get up and bark. Perhaps they smelled him and knew he was no threat to them. He knew the village dogs would bark at an approaching stranger even from a good distance away.

He looked back once he got to the foothills yet he did not see any movement below in the village, not even a flicker of a lamp in *Apo* Basig's hut. The old woman was usually the first to get up as far as he knew. When he was growing up, it seemed to him that the old woman never slept.

He trod more carefully now as he veered off the trail when he reached the bend by the huge boulder just past the foothills, and he could no longer see the village below. It was his habit not to follow any trail when he went up the mountain to hunt or just to wander about, and he usually took off to any direction once he passed the boulder. He preferred to walk where there was no apparent path hoping to discover something new although he did not expect any. He had been walking all over this mountain since he was a little boy and he knew it intimately like he knew his own backyard. He knew where the cold springs and ponds were where wild game gathered to drink and wallow. For unlike most of the boys in the village who preferred swimming and fishing in the river by the village, he sought and found refuge in the shadows of the forest, discovering its secrets and its bounty. He felt at home among the trees and the caves and the cold springs they hid. He knew where there was water where there seemed to be none, even the underground spring inside a cave that nobody knew about, of this he was certain.

He found the cave by accident when he was still a young boy, led to it by a wounded deer that refused to go down after he had put his arrow into its side. He tracked the deer and found it dead by the spring inside the cave. He had not seen any sign that any other human had been there before him. There were small animal droppings and bones, but not much else. No sign of a fire that could have been built a long time ago or any indication that anyone had been there before him.

It was a good sized cave, big and high enough for at least three or four evenly spaced huts. And in its far corner to the right bubbled a cold, clear spring that probably seeped its way through some crags beneath the rocks. As he grew up, he had gone back many times to the place, staying there for a few days at a time, making it his home away from the village.

And that was where he hoped he would be when the sun went down for the night.

He had not taken a wife even while his two much older brothers and his boyhood friends had started raising families of their own, so he came and went as he pleased. The folks in the village had become accustomed to his wanderings and they did not mind for they knew that he could take care of himself. Much more, they appreciated that every time he returned he always brought game, mostly deer or boar or a string of wild chicken, or sometimes birds and fish to be shared, especially with the older folks who no longer hunted or did not have anyone to hunt for them.

Besides, they only had to sound the hollowed-out wood drums at the center of the village to signal for an emergency gathering of the men and he would be there. As had happened a few times before when there were troubles with the other mountain tribes. He had always listened to that insistent beating of the drums and came down running every time to lead the men, for when trouble came and there was fighting to be done, the men in the village followed him and his brothers. For they were noted fighting men, just like their ancestors, the renowned warrior brothers, Lam-ag and Lagam.

But he had noticed that ever since they took wives and had children, his two older brothers, Ittok and Ayong, had deferred to him when it came to fighting despite the fact that he was almost ten years younger than Ayong, the middle son. He did not mind for he'd rather die in battle than see his nephews become orphans.

His senses were acutely developed from tracking and hunting prey that he knew when he heard a sound that did not belong to his surroundings. Like the sound of wooden drums in the forest. And their distinct sound carried far into the stillness of the mountains. But he did not expect to hear them today nor anytime soon for there had been peace among the tribes for some time now. And the lowlanders had learned not to venture up into the mountains to hunt or to cut trees for their houses. But somehow he had a lingering feeling that the drums would not be silent for much longer. He had been hearing troubling words from his friend Akash who made frequent trips to the lowlands and they may get dragged into the troubles of the Ilocanos.

Because of Ilang and her mother.

And it worried him for there were hot blooded young men in his village as well as in the other mountain tribes that were part of the *budong*, the inter-tribal pact of mutual protection and cooperation, who sometimes did not think right and were too eager to prove their manhood. Especially when they were emboldened and fueled with *tapuy*, the potent fermented rice wine.

He never had a taste for it. The one time he tried, it gave him such a headache the following day that he could not get rid of even after a cold swim in the river. He shook his head in disgust at the thought. He had not touched the stuff since, despite the teasing of his friends who seemed not to be able to gather together and talk without sharing a mug or two.

And then there was that sugar cane wine, the *basi*, from the lowlands. It had a sweeter taste but gave one an even worse headache than the *tapuy*!

He never understood why anyone of sane mind would resort to drinking such awful concoctions. He found himself shaking his head and started to jog, and after a while, eased fluidly into a steady run, subconsciously trying to leave the thought of drinking wine of any kind behind. He had no trouble running; he could run all day if needed.

Perspiration had begun to trickle down his bare back despite the cold and he felt invigorated by it. The night fog still hovered among the trees, clinging stubbornly underneath their crowns, shrouding the shrubs growing in their shadows. There was a faint grey in the east portending the approach of dawn.

He made his way among the trees and the undergrowth, carefully avoiding the thorny bushes along his path. He looked up at the sky when he reached a small clearing, providing a break from the covering of the trees. His eyes searched for the big star in the north, which wasn't hard to do since it seemed it was the only one left as the grey light of dawn gently pushed back the blackness of the night and with it the lesser stars.

He lowered his gaze and glanced around taking in his surroundings with a brief sweep of his head. Nothing moved, not even the leaves among the trees. There were no animals or birds lurking in the shadows. He moved across the small clearing silently like a ghost, quickening his pace, as he stepped into a gap among the trees. He wanted to be at the twin pines halfway up the mountain when the sun came out. Soon, he thought, glancing up once again at the sky through the covering of the trees.

He would be there as the sun rose over the horizon. He always did, regardless of the path he took. He quickened his steps and broke into a run, his bare feet flattening the wet grass with abandon.

The east was awash in the color of fire as the sun was about to break through the grey of dawn when he finally sat underneath the southern pine, his back snuggly resting on its majestic trunk that rose, tapering to a point, about a hundred feet up. Its twin stood a few paces to the north, matching it regally limb by limb. He faced east toward the rising sun which was now peeking through the fog and the low-lying clouds floating atop the trees and valleys. He took a deep breath and contentedly welcomed the new day, awed once again at the magnificence of the view from where he sat.

He had witnessed so many sunrises from this vantage point, ever since his grandfather first brought him up here as a little boy of ten, yet he never tired of watching the sun come up, finding the experience refreshing and inspiring every time. It was a beautiful spot, a favorite of his grandfather, and no doubt his father and his own grandfather and their fathers before them. This was a sacred place where they could be one with nature and the spirits of their ancestors. There was an eerie tranquility in the place that made one feel at absolute peace with the earth.

He waited and watched patiently and calmly as the sun cleared the far horizon. He closed his eyes and whispered a soft prayer of thanks for no particular reason to the ancient spirits. He listened carefully, feeling their presence in the now soft rustling of the leaves as a gentle breeze passed by. And he felt the breeze briefly caress his face like a whisper, then as quickly, it passed and he felt his face growing warmer from the sun floating now against a clear sky. Somehow the low lying clouds had disappeared leaving it alone to shine in its entire splendor.

For a long while he sat motionless, his eyes closed, his mind wandering on its own, unguided by any single thought, floating like a wisp of smoke from a dying fire, his body glowing effervescently in the soft warmth of the morning.

Finally he let out a deep sigh and opened his eyes. It's a beautiful day, he thought, would today be the day for him to go down to the lowlands? But he dismissed the idea as fast as it came, as he always did in the past, for how long now he couldn't remember. Fifteen, twenty summers? More? He was not sure, the years having tumbled over each other as they passed. Perhaps subconsciously, he had willed himself not to remember. But how could he forget? He had tried countless of times but that day a long time ago clung stubbornly in his mind. And with it the memory of the promise he made that he had yet to fulfill.

Some days the memory faded especially when he was up here in the mountain stalking an elusive prey. But like a pestering wound it always came back, especially at odd moments. Like now, as he watched the sun come up.

"Someday perhaps," he whispered to the wind. "Someday, but not today..."

But like the countless whispers in the past that it had become ritual in this place, there was no conviction in his voice. For again the idea that she had but all forgotten him and the village nagged at him. He closed his eyes once again and felt the comforting warmth of the sun once more on his face. He tried to force his mind not to think of anything as before, letting it float softly into the blank universe in his head, but he could not banish her from his thoughts. After a while he gave up, opened his eyes and slowly arose, taking his time like an old man.

He picked up his quiver and slung it across his back, the string that held it resting snuggly on his bare chest, the arrows within easy reach off his right shoulder. He held the bow in his left hand and with his right, he grabbed the spear that was leaning against the trunk of the pine. He did not figure on using the spear to hunt but it would be useful to finish off game if it was not killed outright by an arrow after it fell. He hated using a rock to bash off the head of a dying deer or a wild boar like some of the hunters did. The practice was brutal. A quick thrust to the heart with a spear was kinder, and that was what he always did.

Up in the trees, the day birds had begun to stir, breaking sporadically into sing-song whistles that were answered and echoed farther down into the deeper woods. Then they would erupt simultaneously into such a melodious harmony that made it seem the whole forest had decided to burst up into a song.

Every now and then he could also hear the animated chattering of the monkeys starting their day in their usual garrulous manner. He could hunt down some if the deer and wild pigs were scarce, he thought, although he was not too keen to the idea. He did not like hunting monkeys. They seemed all too human especially when they cried.

He looked at the sun once more then he turned away and walked deeper into the forest.

He was more than halfway up the mountain when he spotted the faint trail of deer by the side of a small ravine, its bottom holding some water that had pooled into a basin. He stealthily followed the trail, watching for the telltale depressions in the grass and the bent boughs of the bushes where the tracks were not apparent. There were four of them, he figured. One was a big buck based on the set of a wide and long-gaited track, one slightly smaller, a mature doe, while the other two sets were probably yearlings or younger. The tracks veered off the ravine then followed the shoulder of the mountain, headed, he was sure of it, to a wide clearing on the southern side where there was a small spring where game usually gathered to drink and bathe.

He quickened his pace yet only a faint whisper marked his passing, his feet soft and light on the grass, instinctively avoiding the dry twigs. Then he saw them as he rounded a corner, a six-pointer buck and three good-sized does. He stopped so suddenly that for a while he thought the herd had sensed his presence. He uttered a soft thanks to the spirits as the deer did not seem to be spooked, noting with relief that he was downwind from them.

They had stopped to graze, munching contentedly on the green grass and the low lying lush branches of the trees by the trail. The does were close to one another, the buck was off by itself to the far side, reaching for the leaves of a *camachile* tree.

Quietly he crouched closer to the herd, stopping briefly as the buck paused from pulling down a branch, angling its head as if listening for something. The does also stopped grazing for a while, lifting their heads momentarily. He stopped and held his breath, immobile, not moving a muscle, his bare brown skin blending inconspicuously with the brown trunks of the trees and bushes around him. The big buck stretched its neck farther up, bit and pulled down another branch. The does followed suit and complacently went back likewise to their grazing.

He finally exhaled softly as he was sure the deer had their full attention back to their feeding. He was perhaps a little more than thirty paces away from the herd. Close enough, he decided. He did not want to scare them now and spend the rest of the day tracking them down. He concentrated on the buck, certain that it would be the most vigilant as protector of the herd.

He put his spear down on the ground and slowly raised his right hand over his shoulder and pulled out an arrow from the quiver. His motions were fluid and deliberate, nothing wasted. Slowly he rose up on his left knee, planting it firmly on the soft ground, his right leg stretched at an angle to the side for support, giving him the balance he favored while shooting from a low position. He nocked the arrow and pulled the string all the way back until the guiding feathers gently brushed against his chin like a soft whisper. He held his breath and looked intently at the buck, his eyes fixed on the base of its stretched neck. He was so focused that nothing else existed except him and the buck.

Then the buck stopped tugging at the branch, let it go, and started backing down and looking up at the same time. He exhaled softly but held from releasing his arrow, his eyes drifting up to the tree, following and searching for the cause of the buck's concern. He saw an eagle about to light on a branch of the *camachile*, its imposing wings spread regally to slow its descent, then folded briskly with a final flutter as it sat on the branch, unconcerned with the herd grazing below.

As the eagle settled above, the buck started to lower its head to nibble at the grass by its feet then suddenly lifted it right back up. Its neck stretched to its full length and the head swiveled around scanning the area as if sensing something else other than the bird above. It again canted its head and stood at attention, its eyes now locked at where Kulas crouched, motionless, with his bow fully drawn, his head and shoulders well above the covering of the grass. Their eyes met and held, man and beast, hunter and prey coldly sizing each other up.

The buck met the hunter's eyes unflinchingly as if daring him to make the first move. At that instant, the hunter made a decision. With his eyes still locked on the buck, he slightly raised his left arm holding the bow and released the arrow, his peripheral vision tracking the arrow's flight as it headed toward the buck and way over its head, ending in a soft thud as it hit the breast of the stunned eagle, catapulting it up and away from the branch. The buck and the does vanished into the brush before the eagle hit the ground. He stood up from where he crouched and let out a monstrous laugh.

"It's your lucky day, big buck," he yelled after the herd. "I am not ready to go back down to the village yet, perhaps in five more days! Pray that we shall not meet before then!"

He walked toward the tree and picked up his arrow that was firmly embedded in the dead eagle, its eyes gazing unseeingly at the sky. "As for you, my dear eagle," he whispered. "I am sorry but I thank you. You're all I need for lunch right now."

His steps were light as he headed toward the cave, planning on cleaning and cooking the bird when he got there. He took his time walking. There was no need to hurry. The cave was just less than an hour walk away.

Then suddenly he stopped and silently glided into the cover of the nearest pine tree. He had felt another presence and it was not that of a spirit or game. He put down the bird and stood quietly behind the tree and listened, his eyes scanning his surroundings with barely a perceptible movement of his head. Then he saw a shadow emerging from the trail.

He hefted his spear, but stopped and lowered it back to the ground as he recognized the familiar gait of Dagyo, one of his friends from the village. He bent down slowly and found a small rock. He picked it up and with a quick flip of his wrist, threw it at the other side of the trail where it made a sudden crashing sound in the morning silence. He stifled a laugh as Dagyo jumped and quickly drew his long knife, looking around and all too ready to fight. The man did not talk much but he was always quick and ready, he thought in appreciation. He half-expected Dagyo to run or at least move back a bit but instead he saw him cautiously yet fearlessly walk towards the noise.

He found another small rock and threw it behind Dagyo who again jumped at the sound, frowning when he did not find anyone or any game that may have caused it. Dagyo scratched his head then suddenly, he yelled. "Kulas? *Si ano tuwe?* Is that you?"

He did not answer, silently grinning at his friend.

"I saw your trail, you fool! I thought I heard you laughing and shouting too a while back!" Dagyo said. "Show yourself up. I have something to tell you."

He remained still. Then silently he moved behind the trunk of another tree, picked up a handful of small stones and threw them one after the other, each one falling farther away from the previous, the clattering sounds simulating the noise of a small animal running away. But Dagyo was not fooled.

"You can do better than that, you dumb monkey," Dagyo said. He put his knife back in its wooden sheath then he took off the bow that was slung on his back. He fitted an arrow, and walked toward a copse of pines overlooking the valley below. Then suddenly he pivoted, pulled and released his arrow in one fluid motion, watching with a big grin on his face as the arrow quivered ominously when it hit the tree trunk where his tormentor was hiding. "Your trail could be seen by a blind old woman, you fool. Stop playing around and come out. And get that arrow out for me. Thank you."

"I could have put one through your big rump as soon as you appeared down the trail, you dog!" Kulas finally said as he stepped out behind the tree. He reached up and pulled Dagyo's arrow out from the trunk. It was aimed a good foot over his head. He knew Dagyo did that on purpose. He was one of the better shooters in the village and he could put an arrow in most anyplace he wished. Kulas turned around and nodded his appreciation of his friend's good sense but Dagyo was already sitting under a pine a little off the trail. He was looking down at the valley below, his face toward the morning sun.

"Akash is going down to the lowlands today," Dagyo said, raising his head as Kulas stood beside him. "I think you and I may need to go down, too."

"Why?" Kulas said, frowning.

"Just to make sure he's safe."

Kulas raised an eyebrow. Akash could take care of himself. "Safe? What harm could possibly happen to Akash? He had been going down to the Ilocos for so long that he could pass for an Ilocano!"

16

Dagyo did not answer, but the worried look did not leave his face.

"What's going on?" Kulas finally said, sensing his friend's concern.

"Listen," Dagyo said gravely. And Kulas listened as his friend who was mostly silent at village gatherings talked at length. It was the longest time he had ever heard Dagyo speak and he let his friend talk without interruption. He had heard about the troubles between the Spanish and the Ilocanos and Ilang and her husband's involvement but he had not heard about this latest trouble. Ilang was a widow again. Her husband, Diego, had been killed, betrayed by his friends. Kulas did not know if he was glad. He felt ambivalent toward the news but what bothered him was the thought of Akash going down to the lowlands to avenge Diego's death, if Dagyo's suspicions were correct. Akash was fond of Diego so Kulas was not really surprised if such was the case. But perhaps Akash just went down there to make sure Awad and Ilang were alright. He hoped that such was the real reason and there was no need for worry.

"*Agudongkan*. Go back home. We're not following Akash," he said.

"Why not?" Dagyo said. "He would get in trouble."

"He'll be alright. He can take care of himself."

"You don't understand," Dagyo said. "I think he went down there looking for trouble."

"And he went alone, by himself? C'mon, Dagyo, he's not that stupid! Maybe he was just checking on Awad and Ilang."

"Perhaps, but I saw and talked with him last night. There's something off in his demeanor that bothers me. I'm worried, that's why I came looking for you. You know how Akash is when he gets mad but he'll listen to you."

Kulas did not say anything for a moment. He knew that Akash had a temper and could be stubborn once he made up his mind. He looked at Dagyo and asked the first question that came to him.

"How'd you know I was up here anyway?" he said.

"I couldn't sleep. I saw you when you left the village."

Kulas nodded. He should have known. Dagyo was the best guard and lookout in the village. Nothing got past him. And like old *Apo* Basig, he did not seem to sleep. He morosely looked down the mountain at the dense valley below without saying a word, his expression not lost on Dagyo.

"You don't want to go," Dagyo said softly after a while. "Is it because of Ilang?" They had teased Kulas from time to time about Ilang when they were growing up. They knew that Kulas was fond of her.

"It's not what you think, Dagyo," Kulas said with a sigh. "The soldiers and the Ilocanos may see us as threat if they saw more of us down there."

"We'll stay out of sight. They wouldn't even know we're there." Dagyo looked up at Kulas with a smug smile on his face. "We'll just be around to make sure Akash is alright."

"How? We'll stick out like sore thumbs among the Ilocanos." Kulas met his friend's gaze and shook his head.

"We'll dress like them, like Akash does when he goes down there. Pull up our hair under that hard-shelled squash hat that they wear, the *kattokong*. And there are too many people down there, nobody would notice us."

"Trust me, they will," Kulas said. "It's not a good idea. We may just be walking ourselves into trouble. And you know we drag the whole village along when that happens."

Dagyo did not answer. Kulas was right. If something happened to them the whole tribe will be involved and other tribes as well. It was the law of the *budong*. He turned his gaze back to the valley below, thinking.

"But maybe I can follow him and talk to him before he gets to the town," Kulas said softly after a moment as if he was simply voicing a thought. He followed Dagyo's gaze, scanning the magnificent view of the valley below them.

"Alone," he added.

"I'll go with you." Dagyo said, looking back up at Kulas. Then with feigned irritation in his voice, said, "Can you sit down so I don't have to keep looking up? You're giving me a crick on my neck." He patted the ground by his side.

"No, alone," Kulas said, shaking his head as he sat down. "Go back to Immil and your kids. It's best if I go alone. Perhaps I could catch up to him before he gets to the town and try to talk him out of going down there."

"Well, maybe you still can catch him on the trail. He may just have left the village," Dagyo said. "I don't know if you could talk him out of going down to the lowlands though."

"He'll listen. Don't worry, there will be no trouble. If I can't catch up to him, I'll follow him down to town."

He wished he believed his own words as soon as he said them.

"But.." Dagyo started to say but stopped when Kulas raised his hand.

"Trust me, my friend," Kulas said. "Go home." He stood up and patted Dagyo's shoulders.

Dagyo looked at him with a question on his face but he did not say anything.

"Rest a while, or find game to bring down and go back home. No need to make Immil worry," Kulas said, referring again to Dagyo's lovely wife who was heavy with her third child.

Dagyo frowned and lowered his face. "Alright," he finally said softly without looking at Kulas.

18

"Be careful," he added as he sensed Kulas move away.

He did not hear Kulas respond. He turned around and caught a glimpse of his friend's back as it melded and vanished among the trees.

"T-t-that's not the way to the town," Dagyo stuttered shaking his head. He never did understand his friend. Well, he thought, nobody did for that matter.

At least, as far as he knew.

Then Kulas reappeared from behind the tree holding the dead eagle in his hand. He tossed it to the startled Dagyo. The bird fell a short distance away, rolling stiffly as it hit the ground.

"Bring it down to Immil or to *Apo* Basig," Kulas said. "It's fresh."

He turned around and went back into the trees before Dagyo could say anything.

Dagyo watched his friend go deeper then vanished into the woods. Then slowly he stood up, picked up the dead eagle, examining it briefly, noting the well-centered arrow wound that killed it. "The man can shoot," he said to himself.

Then he turned around and started back toward the village.

Chapter Two

Don Manuel woke up with the sun on his face and the sound of garbled voices and laughter pushing through the fog in his mind. He reluctantly opened an eye and tried to determine where the voices were coming from, feeling a little disoriented. He opened the other eye and looked around until his attention focused on the window that he had left open the night before as was his habit when he was in town. He uttered a curse as his surroundings became familiar and it occurred to him that it was Sunday and the plaza by his house turned into a busy *mercado*, a big marketplace.

He had been sleeping out in the open too many times lately. Damn those *rebeldes*, he cursed again under his breath.

He groaned and continued his string of curses as he realized he had overslept. He had wanted to get up before the sun was up and take a quick walk to the slaughterhouse for an early breakfast with the *matadores,* the butchers, before they moved the fresh meat to the stalls in the plaza, but he must have been more tired than he thought. He had returned with his troop late yesterday afternoon from a fruitless foray to the south, by the coastal *pueblos* of Santiago and Santa Maria, looking for the rebels led by the Silang widow, Maria Josefa Gabriela, now called *La Generala*, based on information that turned out to be false. There were no signs of the rebels, but he knew now that they had gone deep into the mountains of Abra. This latest information was from a most reliable source.

He should have had hunted and hanged the *hijo de puta* who had sent them on a wild goose chase instead, he thought, as he rose with great effort and let his feet searched for the *chinelas,* the slippers, that he kept by his bed. He found them without looking down and he stretched lazily as he walked toward the window that faced the *plaza mayor*. Below in the plaza, the vendors were almost done setting up their stalls for the Sunday market.

"Damn," he said again as he realized he had also slept through the ruckus the vendors must have created when they put their make-shift stalls together. He looked down at the plaza below, stifling a yawn, ignoring the glances thrown his way. His upper body was bare for he slept only in his underpants. He had yet to get accustomed to the heat of the damn place. He would not have stayed long and would have asked for a new command somewhere else if this godforsaken place had not reminded him so much of his rugged boyhood village of Grazalema in Andalusia.

"Except for this damn humid heat," he muttered under his breath.

It must be close to eight o'clock, he thought. The bells of the nearby church of San Pablo right across the plaza started ringing as if in affirmation, summoning the faithful to the second and final Mass of the day.

"Damn!" he said again as he realized he had also slept through the ringing of the bells for the dawn Mass at four o'clock. And there was just the plaza that separated his *casa* from the church. He shook his head in disgust, and he called himself a soldier? He must be getting old, but *caramba*, he was not even thirty years old!

He looked up at the sun, cupping his left hand, palm outward, over his eyes to ward off the glare. It was an unusual way to shade the eyes for most men cupped their palms downward with the back of the thumb, not the knuckles, anchored to the forehead.

But *Don* Manuel, the *Señor Capitán* of His Majesty's army in the north of *Las Islas Filipinas*, the soldier people respectfully and fearfully called *El Niño*, was an unusual man.

The young Manuel had joined the King's army when he was barely fifteen, lying about his age.

He was a tall, broad-shouldered young man even at that early age, a lot bigger than most mature men, but it still took the word of an old drunken soldier, Tiago, to convince the hesitant Sargento Arseño Mata de Beneza to take him.

"I swear on your mother's grave, Sargento," Tiago had declared, his breath emitting the fetid vapors of the previous night's ale. "This boy, I mean this man is eighteen years old to the day. Why, I have known him since he was knee-high." He held his left hand, palm down by his waist. Manuel had just met Tiago the night before and it took all his self-restraint not to smile and his face remain impassive as the old soldier lied like only a man who had seen most of everything and not bothered by any of it, could.

"Leave my mother out of this, Tiago. She's very much alive in Burgos," Don Arseño de Beneza gruffly waved Tiago off. He had known the old soldier for a long time. If he wasn't such a good soldier, sober or not, he would have kicked him out of the force a long time ago. And the man could fight, drunk or sober, it did not matter. He was a born fighter, if there ever was one.

He turned to the young Manuel. "Can you fight, boy?"

"If I have to, sir." Manuel was respectful. He wanted so much to get into the King's army and get out of España, like his great uncle Hernán did years ago, and he did not want to give the Sargento any reason to dislike and reject him.

Besides, he was telling the truth. His father and his colorful friends who had visited their Rancheria in the northern tip of the province of Cadiz in

21

Andalusia had taught him and his brothers the fighting arts. It was known in the region that all of Don Marcelo's six sons could fight as well as any other man, with the pistol, the fusil, the sword and dagger, or with any other weapon. And perhaps, better, a lot better than most men. And that went for bare knuckles, rough and tumbles fighting as well. This was not far from the truth for their teachers were all renowned fighting men, respected experts in different martial arts, despite their shady backgrounds.

"That, I can honestly vouch for, Sargento," Tiago had added promptly. Manuel had come to the old soldier's aid at a tavern by the waterfront in the city of Cadiz the previous night. There were now five local troublemakers being treated somewhere for various wounds and broken bones for erroneously assuming that Manuel was just a harmless country boy and Tiago a defenseless drunk. To return the favor, although he vehemently claimed that he had not needed Manuel's help, the old soldier had promised Manuel to help him enlist when he found out about the boy's desire to serve the King.

"If they are able and if they were not such disreputable men, I would gather five ruffians who'd swear on their mothers' graves and even to their abuelas that this boy, I mean, this man has no equal when it comes to fighting." Suddenly Tiago had become eloquent. "But, alas, Señor, the five unfortunate ruffians are currently indisposed after meeting with me and the boy here last night."

"Shut up, Tiago." Sargento de Beneza paused for a moment and gave Manuel another appraising look then his eyes hovered at the quill sitting by the inkwell at the side of his desk. He reached out slowly and picked up the quill, dipped it in the ink, then wrote with flourish on the open ledger before him. He replaced the quill in its holder and studied his handwriting for a moment, blowing at it gently to dry. Satisfied, he pushed the ledger and an ink pad toward the boy. "Put your mark there, hombre." He pointed to a blank space halfway down the bottom part of the page where he had elegantly written Manuel's name.

Above Manuel's name, the page was filled with a long list of names beside most of which were thumbprints that went all the way to the top. To the Sargento's surprise, Manuel grabbed the quill, dipped its point in the inkwell, let the excess drip, and after brushing the tip slightly against the well's mouth, proceeded to write his name in deliberate strokes.

"Ahh, a fighting man who can write," Sargento Arseño de Beneza beamed. "I assume you can read as well?"

"I have read Cervantes, Cortazar, and the great Catalán poet, Lutgardo Queppet, Señor, among others. My mother was an educated woman and she instilled in us the love for the written word."

"¡Bueno!" Sargento de Beneza slapped his hands together in a single clap that boomed in the room. "Perhaps we could make an officer and a gentleman out of you, then you can have Tiago under your command. You may be able to make a soldier of him yet."

"Ahh, Sargento, I am a soldier!" Tiago protested half-heartedly, but there was a big grin on his face as he winked at Manuel.

That had seemed a long time ago, but Sargento de Beneza was prescient. Tiago had been with Manuel since and he was now his Sargento, relying on the veteran soldier for sage advice on his decisions as commander of the King's army out here in the northern provinces of King Felipe's islands.

He had learned also that Tiago was once a Sargento even before Sargento de Beneza became one, but it seemed that his love for the ale had become the old soldier's undoing, his major roadblock to getting up in the ranks, and losing them the few times he managed to get a promotion. But to Tiago, it did not matter. All that he cared for was that he was still in His Majesty's service. The man was happy being a soldier and he did not care much about ranks and titles. He knew his real worth.

"Sixteen years," Manuel hissed. He had been a soldier for sixteen years. He was an old man at almost thirty and he did not have any heir to his name. But then again, what would the poor boy inherit? He shook his head at the thought. Except for his command, he had nothing. No wife, no property except for his sword and saddle. Even his horse was His Majesty's horse for crying out loud. And surely, no money except for a few measly pesos he kept on the side for the occasional card game with the other officers. He had not even fallen in love yet, not that he knew what that would feel like anyway.

'What a life,' he thought. 'What a life...'

And what a life indeed.

They shipped out of the port of the great city of Cadiz on the feast day of La Nuestra Señora de La Victoria de Naval that commemorated the Holy League's decisive victory over the Ottoman navy in the battle of Lepanto, a most portentous day if there ever was one.

Barely a couple of weeks out in the open seas, they encountered a pirate ship but their superior firepower was too much for the battle-weary pirates. After a steady barrage of small cannon fires tore holes in the pirate ship's stern to the delight of the fresh crew, the pirates sailed off with their tails tucked between their legs. Manuel was dejected, as well as the other new recruits, that they were not able to board the pirate ship before it escaped. It seemed everyone was eager to fight and show their bravery to the older, veteran soldiers who were just contented at having driven the pirates away.

They had seen too much blood and the sight of it no longer brought much excitement to them anymore.

The deceptively soft-spoken Capitán, Don Godofredo Tuzon de Alvarez, was that rare antithetical combination of a very devoted and religious family man and yet a consummate soldier who was known for his courage, cunning and savagery in battle.

"More brutal than a beast, he is, the Capitán," Tiago had proclaimed to his young listeners as they were preparing to embark. He had served under the Capitán in two previous expeditions to the New World. Four months later, in Santo Domingo in the West Indies, Manuel was a witness to the Capitán's courage and savagery.

They had arrived at the settlement in Santo Domingo after over a month long passage on rough seas. Manuel was not bothered as much by it as most of the new men for he had sailed the seas by Cadiz since he was a little boy, with his brothers and their father, exploring nearby islands, and the waters there were not always pleasant. But he had not seen as big and rough waves as he had in the open Atlantic that despite his sailing experience, there were nights when he went down to his bunk queasy and weak kneed. Tiago's ribbing did not help, but the remedies he came up with for seasickness and the knowledge he got from him during their talks surely did. The old man had taken him under his wings, not that he needed any help from any man when it came to protecting himself, but that surely kept at bay the bored troublemakers who wanted to pick on the youngest recruit.

They found the settlement inside the fort in a state of disarray and in short supply of everything when they got there. The settlers could not get out far to hunt, or tend to the small plots they had cleared because a renegade band of Carib Indians had been on the warpath. A response to the perceived destruction of their forest and the violation of their hunting grounds as the settlers felled trees and cleared some areas for farming. And the rabble-rousers among them did not have to do much convincing to get some younger warriors to take arms despite the caution from the elders. The renegade band had struck several times at the settlement, killing two farming settlers and wounding another and that had kept the settlers inside the fort. Their raiding successes had made more young warriors join the ranks of the renegades.

Don Godofredo's timely return brought new hope to the settlers. They had resorted to killing their older oxen for food. But soon the little supply the new troops brought was getting low that they had to send hunters out with extra soldiers for protection. Manuel proved himself to be a superb hunter and exceptional tracker. But game had been scarce. The settlement needed to raise sustainable crops.

Patrols had also been sent out time and again since the new troops arrived, but the hostile Indians had been hard to pin down, despite Don Godofredo's hiring of some friendly Indian guides.

They were at the end of their second month at the settlement and the young soldiers had yet to engage the hostile band of Indians in combat. They were raring for a fight, but the Indians had been elusive and had not dared to come close to the fort since the arrival of the fresh troops.

The settlers welcomed the lull from the hostilities, but the young soldiers who were eager to prove their mettle were getting restless from inactivity and their futile efforts to hunt and engage the renegade Indians. To keep them occupied, Captain Godofredo Tuzon de Alvarez and Sergeant Arseño Mata de Beneza commanded them to train and practice under the tutelage of old Tiago whom they knew was a superb swordsman.

Besides, Tiago used to be a drill sergeant, and if there ever was one who could whip and keep the young soldiers into a ready, disciplined and capable force, it would be the old soldier, sober or not.

It had been said among the companies where he had served in his long military career that a sober Tiago was the best swordsman among the soldiers, including the officers. And it had also been said that Tiago was the second best swordsman when he was roaring drunk.

And Tiago took with relish and vigor this new task of assessing and honing the skills of the soldiers, particularly the new recruits who have yet to be tested in battle,.

The first day of training, Tiago challenged the young recruits, for anyone to engage him with the sword with the promise that if he got bested, the victorious soldier would be exempted from further training.

The big-muscled and more boisterous recruits readily volunteered and lined up to take on the old soldier's challenge, but as quickly the first ten were dispatched by Tiago in rapid succession, not anyone of them lasting a few minutes. Each of his opponents went back to join the ranks looking stunned and confused, still trying to understand what had just happened. They were holding a sword firmly and had ably exchanged a few brief thrusts and parries with the old soldier then in a flash, their sword was flying out of their hands.

And the old man did not even break a sweat, the young soldiers noted with growing admiration for the veteran soldier. This was the side of Tiago that they had been hearing about from the older soldiers which they thought were just tall tales but now every one of them was turning to be believers.

They had just witnessed the old, drunken Tiago, regardless he was sober at the moment, disarm ten able and strapping young men with various tricks that were executed so fast that they were hard to follow.

Except for someone who had been likewise adept and trained in swordsmanship practically all his life, like the young Manuel.

And he watched the old soldier from the back of the troop with great appreciation of Tiago's skills.

He had stayed back and did not volunteer to take Tiago's challenge for he had no intention of skipping the training. He had spent most of his life in martial training and he loved every moment of it, like his brothers who had treated the constant practice and training as play. And it kept them from working in the fields and looking after the animals. He felt most comfortable and relaxed when he was swinging a sword in his hand.

He smiled as he saw and recognized with affinity the various moves and tricks that Tiago had used against the novice soldiers. His face broke into a grin when he noticed that the rest of the group who had eagerly volunteered began to slowly ease themselves back into the ranks of the soldiers who had not stepped forward. Nobody else seemed to be willing to step up against Tiago and be subjected to certain humiliation and surely be the butt of jokes in the mess hall and barracks for days, if not months and years, to come.

"C'mon, muchachos, anybody else who wants to try his luck?" Tiago yelled."C'mon! Show this old man that you have balls at least! Is there any real soldier among you?"

But no one dared to move.

"Bunch of niñas!" Tiago spat derisively. He scanned the faces of the young recruits who tried vainly not to meet his gaze until his eyes caught the grinning face of Manuel.

"Ahah, Niño, you at the back, how about you?" Tiago pointed his sword at the direction of Manuel. "You're smiling. You think this is funny, eh? 'Want to come up front and show us what you got?"

Manuel quickly dropped the smile from his face and looked around him not certain if Tiago was addressing him. But everyone else had turned their heads and was looking at him, some of them sighing with relief at the diversion of Tiago's attention.

"W-w-who, me?" Manuel stammered, his thumb innocently pointing at his chest.

"Yes, you!" Tiago said, smiling openly now. "You were good with your hands that night first time I met you, but how are they with a sword?" Manuel now remembered that he did not draw out his sword that time despite the fact that their opponents did. There was no need against the ruffians who were already impaired by too much ale.

"Not as good as you, old man," Manuel said, smiling again briefly. "Besides, I don't want to miss the training and the opportunity to learn from you."

Tiago smiled. He already liked the boy and he liked him more after he spoke. He sure had a way with words, but his curiosity in finding out what the boy knew about sword fighting took the better of him.

"Old man?" Tiago said with false contempt. "C'mon, Niño, show this old man how a young man like you fights!"

The recruits in front of Manuel had parted now and a big soldier standing beside him nudged him forward. He stumbled into the open space, glaring at the big soldier, but by then the other soldiers started clapping and egging him on, some of them patting his back and pushing him forward, giving him lively encouragements.

Despite his reluctance, the love of the fight slowly came alive in his breast and Manuel stepped up warily to the front, swiftly noting the terrain of the open space where he and Tiago would likely do battle.

"Come, come," Tiago gestured with his left hand, the sword swaying playfully in his right but his eyes were expertly gauging Manuel's demeanor.

Manuel thought the old man was being comical and he grinned finally, shaking his head, and put his left hand on the hilt of his sword. He drew it out slowly with his left hand then turned his back and deliberately walked a few steps away from Tiago, the crowd opening up before him. He stopped after a dozen paces and turned around, his sword still in his left hand, now tilted upward in a salute to the old man.

"Oh, a lefty, eh?" Tiago's lips curled in an amused smile, but one of his eyebrows also lifted uncertainly. He had been around fighting men so long that he recognized a formally trained swordsman when he saw one with a sword in hand, lefty or not. And he believed he was seeing one now in Manuel. This should be interesting, he thought.

And a few moments later, he was proven right.

Tiago approached Manuel and he likewise poised his sword in a salute. Manuel was in the process of stepping back after acknowledging Tiago's salute when Tiago immediately attacked without warning. If not for his youthful dexterity and natural quick reflexes, Manuel would have been in trouble. He deftly parried Tiago's thrust with seemingly frantic swings of his sword that appeared to be luckily connecting with the old soldier's sword, redirecting the thrusts away from getting too close to his body. He finally was able to step far enough away from Tiago to seemingly regain his composure and balance. He shook his head as if to clear it from a fog.

Tiago likewise found himself shaking his head but in an amused kind of way. His curiosity was now totally aroused. He did not believe that the boy escaped his initial attack simply by pure luck. He backed down a bit and waited for the boy to initiate the attack, anxious to find out what the boy really knew about the art of the blade.

Manuel tentatively approached, his eyes on his opponent, visualizing in that few seconds every stroke and step he was going to take. Out of habit whenever he and his brothers engaged in friendly bouts with one another and before starting another series of engagement, he saluted with his sword. Their father and his friends, shady they may be, insisted in gentlemanly and noble gestures despite having taught them also of not so honorable ways of fighting.

Tiago smiled as he properly acknowledged the young soldier's salute this time. This kid is something else, he thought, and it occurred to him that the boy had really never talked about himself, where he came from, or his family, if he had any. A fleeting image of the boy in regal garments flashed across his mind. Perhaps somewhere, the boy had a tinge of the blue in him. He smiled. There was only one way to find out. He waited for Manuel to move.

Manuel initiated a few tentative thrusts that Tiago deflected easily. The old soldier counter-attacked likewise, but this time, Manuel had seemed to finally find his rhythm and parried fluidly, stepping back gracefully when needed. Once in a while, Tiago pressed on vigorously, employing a few of his tricks that he had previously used against the first group of recruits, but either the boy was a quick study and had been paying attention and now was just skillfully using what he learned or he was just plain lucky since he somehow was always able to get away and managed to cling on to his sword.

So they exchanged thrusts and parries, and the minutes stretched to almost half the hour and yet no one seemed to be at an advantage. The young recruits were now gaping in awe, not too few of them feeling relieved now that they had not picked a fight with the youngest recruit. Every now and then they uttered a howl of disbelief and wild clapping and yelling of appreciation when one of the combatants executed an incredible move or evasive parry.

By then, the swordplay had also attracted the attention of Sargento de Beneza and the veteran soldiers. In a moment, the rest of the officers including Don Godofredo Tuzon de Alvarez who had heard of the ongoing bout were also out and watched from a respectable distance. If they were not seeing it with their own eyes, they would not have believed that there was someone in the King's army in the New World who could have stood against Tiago for more than three minutes. And such a young lad at that!

Then someone yelled he was putting a bet on the young Manuel. This was readily taken on and the betting began. The group was almost equally divided as both of the combatants seemed to be holding up well against one another, no one with an obvious advantage.

Manuel was into the flow of the fight and he now used some of the tricks that he had learned from his father's friend and when Tiago successfully defended them, ended up wondering if somehow the old soldier learned from or perhaps was related to the same mentor who taught him and his brothers the art of the sword. He found himself shaking his head in wonder not a few times for it seemed such was the case.

Tiago had also been caught shaking his head a number of times in wonder and growing respect toward the young man. And he was beginning to enjoy the sparring; glad this time that finally there was someone who knew his way with the sword, however young he may be, who could give him a good workout. Somehow he was growing an affinity and fondness for the boy, not that he hadn't already since the night he came to his aid.

Then he had to scramble backwards hastily as Manuel came at him in another wave of furious attack. The boy did not seem to tire down, and Tiago realized he had been breathing hard for probably the best of the last five or so minutes. Age was most certainly catching up to him!

The spectators roared in a unified groan as Tiago seemed to have lost his balance. They collectively held their breaths when the old soldier wobbled as if he was about to fall down, but they were puzzled as they saw Manuel pause, hesitating to follow through on his apparent advantage.

Manuel was sure that his thrusts and swipes were not heavy and hard enough to cause Tiago to stagger the way he did, so he hesitated when Tiago went through his gyrations. Then a faint smile crossed his lips as he remembered his mentor, old Gustavo, the Gypsy friend of his father, who came as a guest at their Rancheria when he was about eight years old.

Gustavo, he and his brothers found out later, was on the run. The Gypsy was also a fighting man, adept with various weapons, but most of all he was a master with the sword and the dagger. Gustavo was not a coward, his father said, when the boys asked why he was running away from his enemies when he was such an accomplished fighting man. He was just prudent, their father averred, since his enemies were many in number, aside from the fact that they came from both sides of the law. So Gustavo sought the sanctuary of the Rancheria, as a guest, until things cooled down a bit, for he was a very dear friend. And stay he did, for five long summers. And during all those times, he taught the boys everything he knew about fighting especially the art of swordsmanship.

And among his many tricks and techniques was the move which he called the Art of the Tipsy Sword.

And Manuel saw it now as Tiago seemed to lose his balance and wondered again if Tiago and Gustavo's path had somehow crossed before.

Manuel hesitated a moment, then he quickly moved forward as if to take advantage over the tottering Tiago. He knew it was the wrong move but he wanted this to end for he saw the old soldier was really getting tired. And he has had enough workout for the day, so he pressed on despite knowing what would happen next, momentarily pausing at the exact moment when he expected Tiago's sword to meet his exposed breast as he executed a half-hearted thrust.

Sure enough, Tiago had a big grin on his face as he feinted and extended his arm at the same time, with his sword held firmly with nary a flutter as its tip rested commandingly on the young Manuel's breast. It would have gone directly into the heart in actual combat.

"Bravo!" Manuel said as he lowered his sword to his side acknowledging defeat. He stifled the smile that was again beginning to cross his face for he knew that with a quick pivot with his left foot and a slight roll of his shoulder, Tiago's sword would have harmlessly slid by and with a quick arm switch, his own sword would have found the old soldier's heart or wherever he had wanted it to go. He fought using his left arm. Tiago and the rest of the soldiers did not know that he was a natural righty, but he could fight as well with either hand thanks for the countless times that Gustavo had him and his brothers train with their dominant hands tied behind their backs until they could fight with either one with equal ease and skill. As Gustavo had said, they have two hands and might as well learn how to use either one equally in case one got hurt and rendered useless in a fight.

Manuel grinned at the remembrance of the lesson. He was glad he had not countered the move and resorted to using his right hand. It would be well to have something likewise hidden up his sleeves. He would surprise the old goat the next time.

"You have to show me that trick again sometime, Don Tiago," he said instead, throwing his sword to the ground in acknowledgement of defeat. He looked at Tiago with a sad look on his face as if he was dismayed that he had not gotten the exemption from training.

He heard the groan of the losers in the crowd and the tinkling of coins changing hands.

"The Art of the Tipsy Sword, Niño," Tiago said with pride, but in his eyes there was a hint of suspicion that the boy was not new to the trick. "I was keeping it from you in case we have to duel for the heart of a lovely señorita sometime. That was the last one in my sleeve. I was forced to bring it out now for a couple of minutes more, I would have dropped from exhaustion!"

He gestured with his sword for Manuel to pick up the sword that he dropped. Manuel reached down and picked it up, brushing the dust off the *blade with a sweat-soaked sleeve. He sheathed his sword and looked at Tiago.*

The old man indeed was catching his breath while Manuel breathed easily, his heartbeat now returning to normal. He always had that ability to recover fast. It was also another trick that he learned from Gustavo.

"I don't believe you, Viejo. I am sure you have more tricks in that shriveled mind of yours. As for the señorita, you have no cause to worry. The señoritas you like are not to my liking!" Manuel laughed. "But be aware, I'll get you next time."

Tiago laughed. "I'll look forward to it, Niño," he said truthfully.

As he sauntered back to join the troop, Manuel wondered again if Tiago somehow knew old Gustavo. He would not be surprised if he did. But he restrained himself from asking. There were after all things better kept to one self.

The soldiers gave him an appreciative applause and he got not a few friendly pats on the back as he found his place among them, but this time most of them stood behind him.

And all of them showed varying degrees of newfound respect in their eyes.

Chapter Three

Weeks later, Manuel was on another horse patrol, his fifth since they arrived. He had been assigned to a regular patrol since Sargento de Beneza had learned of his tracking skills, from a drunken Tiago no less, who had seemed to develop the habit of bragging now and again about his self-assigned protégé's various skills. Besides by then most of the soldiers at the fort knew how good the young man was with the sword, although the veteran soldiers were still divided in their opinion on how he would account for himself in real battle.

They were three days out of the fort, with old Tiago leading the troop, a last minute assignment from Sargento de Beneza who had wanted to get out himself but he was laid down with the crapping disease the night before they were set to leave. There were two dozen of them with a half dozen Indian guides walking and running, scouting ahead.

"Damn bastards are scared of horses," Sargento de Beneza had observed when they recruited the guides and they just stared in awe at the horses, not daring to get any closer. The horses in turn were skittish around them.

"It's their smell," Tiago had insisted, but one never knew if the old man was telling the truth or not. So the Indians stayed clear of the horses, running ahead of the troops instead. Manuel was very much impressed with their endurance. They did not seem to get tired. They could walk and run all day and would still be smiling at camp at night.

The previous patrols were usually out on a day's ride, two at the most. This was the farthest any patrol had ventured out. Tiago was persistent to engage the renegade band and get rid of the problem once and for all. Manuel and the rest of the young troop were of the same mind. This was what they signed up for anyway. They were confident that their body armors, sables and rifles, as well as their skills, were superior to these savages who had yet to learn the use of proper clothes.

Manuel had noticed it first. His awareness of his surroundings, especially in the deep woods during a hunt, was so keenly developed from the countless hunts he had as a boy with his brothers and father, and especially old man Salazar, his father's ancient friend and the best tracker Manuel had ever known, that he could feel instantly if something was amiss. And he felt it now. He did not exactly know what it was at first, but he felt that something was wrong. He reined up, gesturing to Tiago who was riding beside him in front of the troop.

"What are you stopping for, muchacho? Do you need to piss?" Tiago turned to him trying to sound annoyed but his expression turned serious when he saw Manuel's attention focus on the trees, his eyes intently scanning the shadows. He motioned for the troop to stop, looked around but he did not see anything that would cause concern. He looked back at Manuel who was straining to listen to something, ignoring Tiago and everything else around him.

"What is it?" Tiago whispered. He had learned to respect the boy's instincts.

Manuel listened again. Then he knew.

"Gather 'round and have your weapons ready," he whispered but loudly enough for the last man to hear.

"There's no one out there, Manuel."

"Tiago, the guides, they're gone. Listen."

"I don't hear anything."

"Exactly. No sound of birds either, nor anything. "

Tiago was not an old soldier who had survived numerous battles and encounters for nothing. "Dismount, and form a circle," he ordered.

The soldiers needed not to be told a second time. They have heard stories of the skill and brutality of the savage Indians. They quickly got off their horses and hastily formed a circle using their horses for shield and that probably saved most of them from sudden death, for it seemed that they had barely cleared their saddles when the trees spewed out deadly arrows from all directions. Manuel had his sword in his hand as soon as his feet touched the ground. A quick glance showed him that at least four soldiers were down, arrows sticking from parts of their unshielded bodies. But miraculously, it looked like everyone else was unharmed, and had their rifles and swords out and ready. But they lost a couple of horses and two more had ran off, the injured soldiers unable to hold on to their mounts.

Then the place erupted with eerie cawing and yelling as half-naked, painted Indians yielding clubs, hatchets and spears burst forth from behind the trees, rushing at the surviving soldiers who were crouched behind the horses that were still standing. A horse reared on its feet and fell as it was struck by a spear, and two more bolted leaving a gap in the circle where now the battle mad Indians rushed. Three of them had fallen beyond the circle, felled by bullets, the sound of which had momentarily halted some of the attacking braves, but the others had not stopped, and blindly poured through the gap, yelling and furiously hacking at anyone in their path.

Manuel saw a soldier by the gap go down, his head tilted in a crazy angle, his metal helmet dented by a savage blow from a club of hardened wood, its rounded end gleaming like a small polished leather ball. Another one followed with a spear sticking from his neck. Some soldiers let go of their mounts that had been rearing on their hind legs all spooked from the noise and blood. The ones who had fired their rifles and were unable to reload dropped their guns and drew their swords and engaged the oncoming Indians in a bloody hand to hand combat.

Manuel deftly pushed aside a spear aimed at his belly and cut down the yelling Indian behind it with a quick thrust of his sword. He pulled it out in one fluid motion and buried it deeply in the breast of another Indian who blindly rushed into it. He braced his left foot against the dead Indian and pushed him back against another who was running behind him, and saw him fall against the other brave, both of them tumbling over backwards in a heap. Manuel rushed on and buried his sword into the other Indian who was trying to push off the dead Indian who fell on top of him. He moved forward, thrusting, parrying and slashing to his left and right, Indians falling at his wake. He was oblivious of anything else. He felt something cut into his arms and legs almost causing him to fall but he regained his balance and moved on until he found himself alone with his back behind a solid trunk of a tree. He warded off a thrust of a spear from the remaining persistent Indian who had hounded him under the tree and with a quick flick of his wrist thrust his sword into the Indian's open mouth, and watched its tip come out from behind the warrior's neck, his eyes open in shocked surprise. Manuel quickly drew his sword out before the Indian started to fall.

Manuel lowered his sword and leaned back against the tree and noted for the first time the blood flowing from his arms and legs. His body underneath his tunic and armor was also sticky, with blood or sweat, he was not sure which, probably both, and he did not have much time to dwell on it for he saw that there were just two of his troop left barely standing by the clearing, gallantly but futilely warding off a dozen Indians who had surrounded them.

Manuel glanced around and found no one else standing close to him. He sensed a movement behind the tree. He lifted his sword as he quickly pivoted to face whoever lurked behind the tree and sighed with relief as he saw one of the horses that did not stray far and was now nibbling at the green grass unmindful of the bloody fighting nearby. A veteran war horse no doubt, he thought as he slowly moved toward it. He looked back at the fighting men as he heard a sharp cry, noting that there was just one soldier left, swinging madly at the Indians who were now taunting and playing with him.

"Don Tiago," he whispered, and was not surprised that the old soldier was still standing and fighting. He looked with wonder as Tiago parried another thrust of a spear and quickly cut down another Indian who ventured too closely, but Manuel saw him wobble on his feet for a moment, fighting desperately not to fall down. Manuel swelled with pride as he saw the old man regain his balance with his sword up and ready, yelling loudly himself, daring the savages to get him.

The Indians warily circled Tiago but they kept their distance, fully aware now that they faced a skilled fighting man. Yet they knew too that he would fall shortly for blood was flowing freely from his wounds.

Manuel eyed the horse and went to it swiftly and softly whispering to it at the same time so as not to spook it. The horse raised its head and shied away at the smell of blood but it calmed down as Manuel soothed it with his soft gentle voice. He grabbed the reins dangling from the horse's neck as he got close enough, and mounted as fast as he could. He turned to the clearing, yelling with all his might as he spurred the horse forward toward Tiago and the Indians.

He must have been a sight, for his sudden yell and the rushing sound of hooves stopped the Indians from circling Tiago. They turned around in surprise, and tried to get out of the way as Manuel crashed through them, his sword cutting mercilessly anyone within reach.

"Grab my hand, Viejo!" Manuel yelled as he got through the circle, slowing down briefly and extending his left arm. To his credit, the old man was still alert and quickly grasped Manuel's arm and tightly clung on to it.

Manuel likewise gripped the old man's arm, his fingers trying desperately to squeeze through the slickness of the blood covering Tiago's arm. He found purchase and he kneed the horse to a gallop, half-dragging the wounded Tiago up behind him, who thankfully had enough strength left to haul himself up behind Manuel.

"I thought you were left-handed," Tiago said as he wrapped his weary arms around the young man's waist and hanged on for dear life praying that the Indians were too surprised to reach out for their bows. Manuel ignored him concentrating on where to point the horse for a successful escape.

The horse was swift and battle-tested, brought all the way from its native Andalusia. Cross-bred from the Spanish Vilano stock noted for its strength and the fleet Barb horse of the Mongols, the horse showed its superb breeding as it rushed through the trees, unmindful of the extra load, running easily from the surprised Indians and leaving them well behind before they realized what was going on. But the Indians quickly recovered and sprinted with enthusiasm after the fleeing soldiers, unable to use their arrows effectively as Manuel led them through the thick foliage, letting the horse sprint through open spaces as he found them.

They heard the Indians coming after them for a good half hour of steady running, but the horse was full of spirit and eager to run, but they knew that it could not keep the pace up with both of them on its back.

"Leave me be, Manuel. Save yourself. I'll hold the bastards back."

"We'll make it, old man. Don't worry."

"The horse can't run for three days, and you know it. It will go down before nightfall with both of us on it. Just put me down. Perhaps it's time for me to die."

"You're too ornery to die, old man. Just hang on. We'll make it together, or we'll die here together."

"You're a stubborn, bastard," Tiago mumbled then he fell silent. Manuel sensed the old man's arms slacken around his waist. He gathered the old man's arms and held them close and tight around his waist as he slowed down a bit. He glanced back and let out a relieved sigh as he noted that Tiago merely passed out from his wounds and he could hear the sound of the pursuing Indians fading out in the distance. He gripped Tiago's arms and spurred the horse on hoping that the old man would not fall off. Then it seemed that they were finally alone but Manuel did not stop.

They rode for a good part of the day and well into the night, slowing down and stopping briefly now and again to rest the horse when they reached the cover of denser trees or a canyon. Manuel finally stopped early the following day when they reached a spring hidden behind a clump of thickly crowned oak trees. Manuel was certain they were no longer pursued. He had taken care to cover their tracks, sometimes going around in a loop, through the creeks, over and back again, sometimes dismounting to sweep away their tracks. He used all the tricks he learned from old man Salazar who had the distinction of having never been caught by the authorities despite breaking every law there was, or so his Tió Macario said, and never left the province under pursuit.

Manuel dismounted and eased the old man down. Tiago had regained consciousness but was barely able to sit on his own. Manuel took the saddle off and let the horse drink its fill, then he rubbed its back with clumps of balled grass. He tethered it by the spring where the horse immediately proceeded to nibble at the green grass growing abundantly on its banks.

Manuel took off the old man's helmet and body armor as well as his own and washed them as best he could in the spring where it gently spilled down to a lower catch basin. He stood up after a while, took a few steps upstream and took a drink. He filled the old man's helmet with water and brought it to where Tiago laid on his back at the foot of an ancient oak. The old man was too weak to get up and rest his back against the trunk.

Manuel helped Tiago sat up and leaned him against the tree, balancing the helmet filled with water in one hand. When Tiago had settled down, Manuel handed the helmet and watched as the old man gratefully drank from it.

Manuel went back to the spring, tore a piece of his undershirt, and washed it thoroughly. He again filled his helmet with water and went back to the old man, who had put down his helmet upside down by his side, still half full of water. Tiago grinned weakly as Manuel approached.

"You keep saving my sorry arse, muchacho. Keep doing it and pretty soon I'd rely on you to breathe."

"Glad to see you're well, old man," Manuel said. "Perhaps you need to learn how to protect yourself and stay away from trouble so I can rest."

"Can't help it, but trouble follows me, m'boy." He raised a hand up feebly in protest as Manuel dropped down to his knees by his side and proceeded to wash the old man's wounds. "Don't you be doing that, Niño. You have done enough. Go wash and tend to your wounds and let me be."

"Shut your trap for once and let me do this, Tiago," Manuel said firmly. "I don't want you losing an arm and leave me to wipe your arse." He took off Tiago's leather guards and washed and dressed the old man's wounds as best as he could. Tiago whined in protest all the time, finally shutting up in surrender after Manuel returned for a third time from refilling his helmet with clean water. By the time Manuel was done, Tiago had fallen back to sleep.

Manuel stripped down and went into the spring, keeping his sword close at hand, although certain that they were safe for the time being. He was sure the Indians had cut off their pursuit to tend to their own dead and wounded companions.

The water was cold and it felt good. He dipped his head gratefully and filled his mouth, swishing the water around, gurgling softly, then spat it out. He stretched out in the shallow spring and gratefully let the water sooth his aching body. Then using the piece of tunic he had used on Tiago, he cleaned his own wounds. He was surprised to find little superficial wounds underneath all the blood that covered his body. Must not be mine, he thought. He uttered a silent prayer of thanks to San Miguel, his family's patron saint.

Finally he stood up, dried himself with his tunic and cursed silently as he noted his arms and body splotched with blood from the bloody tunic. He went back into the water with the tunic and washed it and himself again in the spring. He got out after some moment of wringing and re-wringing the tunic and he spread it to dry on the grass.

He looked at his other bloody garments and uniform and decided to wash them also. He bundled all of them together and dumped them into the spring, going in again and tried to take as much grime and blood off of them as best as he could. Then getting out of the water one more time, he spread the wet wash on the grass beside the tunic. And then he likewise gratefully lay down without drying himself off, soaking in contentedly the heat of the rising sun. It was summer and he knew the day got hot and dried everything fast in this part of the world.

He dozed off after a while and finally fatigue caught up with him and he was soon fast asleep. Then as if a moment had just gone by, he suddenly sat up with a start, his hands automatically searching for the sword by his side but they came up empty. Bewildered, he looked around and noted that he was naked, and nearby were his garments and uniform spread out, dried and relatively clean on the ground. He saw his sword by the spring, his helmet and breast plate, as well as Tiago's under the tree and the old soldier himself still sleeping peacefully.

Manuel silently stood up anxiously, puzzled at what woke him up and realized the sun was now past the zenith. He gathered his clothes and uniform and quickly put them on then he retrieved his sword. He went underneath the tree, put on the rest of his protective gears and strapped his sword on. He looked down at Tiago, debating whether to let the old man rest some more or wake him up. He decided to let the man rest but he remained standing himself, straining to listen, trying to catch the noise that jolted him up as he was dozing off. He heard the twitter of the birds, the soft gurgling of the spring, and the rustling of the leaves as a gentle breeze passed by, but there was nothing else. He heard nothing but the normal sounds of the jungle and the soft breathing of the sleeping Tiago.

Then after a lull, he heard a very distinct but faraway sound. He hastily walked toward the clearing by the spring and stopped, listening intently. He heard nothing out of the ordinary but he noted that the horse which was feeding nearby had stopped and raised its head, ears perking straight up. It must have heard something too. Then he heard it. He went to the horse and saddled it swiftly, pulling it gently toward the still sleeping Tiago.

"Tiago!" He shook the old man's shoulder. "Tiago, wake up."

Tiago groaned, but he opened his eyes. "W-what?" he asked.

"Wake up, we're moving," Manuel said. "Get ready. Get on the horse."

He helped the old man to sit up. He picked up Tiago's helmet and placed it on his head. Tiago slowly pulled himself up, using Manuel's strong arms for support. Manuel helped the old man put his armor and leather straps on and then Manuel lifted him up into the saddle.

"How about you?" Tiago asked.

"I'll walk. We'll meet them." Manuel pointed toward the settlement.

"Who?" Tiago asked with a puzzled expression on his face.

"Our men," Manuel said.

Tiago raised an eyebrow underneath his helmet. "It's still at least a couple of day's ride to the fort. What are you talking about?"

"I heard a horse, perhaps a kilometer away, maybe less."

"You're crazy. Heat's gone into your head, Niño. No one could hear that far, or you must have heard one of the horses that ran off."

"No, Tiago. Sound carries far in the forest if you haven't noticed before. And I heard metal on stone too. A patrol's out there. Let's go meet them." Manuel started off, pulling the horse behind him. It followed willingly and eventually walked beside him. Tiago merely shook his head and settled for the ride.

They heard them clearly after a few hundred meters and then Manuel stopped when they got to the edge of a clearing, their location protected from view behind a dense thicket. The old soldier was conscious enough to note what Manuel was doing and he smiled in appreciation at the cautiousness of the boy. They waited grimly and silently then after what seemed a long time, the horse patrol finally came noisily through the trees.

Tiago grinned for the first time and looked down at Manuel who seemed unaffected by the sight. The boy is something else, Tiago thought, nothing seemed to disturb him. He shook his head in wonder.

They stepped out into the open, the patrol galloping forward as they saw them. Sargento de Beneza himself was at the lead. He must have been feeling better, Manuel thought.

The Sargento looked at them with questioning eyes but did not need an explanation to know what happened.

"Damn guides led us into the ambush," Tiago said. "If not for the boy here, we would all be dead."

Sargento de Beneza looked at Manuel and nodded.

"You look all cleaned up," he said.

"We camped by a spring last night, sir." Manuel did not lower his gaze at the Sargento. He was grateful to see them, but he was tired and hungry and the last thing he wanted to hear was about the way he looked.

"Can you ride?" The Sargento's voice softened sensing Manuel's irritation. He knew what the boy can do with a sword yet he must have been through hell with his first battle. But by God, he came out alive and did not look the worse for it! Then he looked at Tiago and noted that the old man was barely hanging on. Now was not the time for talking, Sargento de Beneza decided. Tiago needed looking after right away and he, Sargento de Beneza, would get the whole story later on at the fort.

"Yes, sir." Foolish question, Manuel thought. He imagined taking the Sargento down and just grab his horse and let him walk, but he remained standing by Tiago. He relished the idea though.

"Garcia!" Sargento de Beneza barked. A hulking soldier riding a big, frisky chestnut came forward and saluted smartly.

"Take the boy with you. That horse of yours is the only one big enough to carry extra load."

"Yes, sir!" Garcia nudged his horse closer to Manuel and extended his left arm. Manuel gratefully grabbed it and hauled himself up behind the big soldier. As they rode, Garcia could not refrain from asking the boy what happened and Manuel answered as briefly yet truthfully as he could, leaving out details of what he had done.

They rode fast, adjusting their pace only by Tiago's condition, but the old man was game. He kept a steady stream of curses at anyone who asked if he was doing alright, including the Sargento, until everybody just rode on, each one eager to get back within the relative safety and comfort of the fort. They reached the fort by nightfall the following day. Don Godofredo de Alvarez himself was there to meet them at the gate.

"Just the two?" Capitán de Alvarez asked after returning the Sargento's salute.

"Si, Capitán," Sargento de Beneza replied, "Tiago's hurt bad and, the young lad, Manuel. The lad's well except for a few scratches."

"Put Tiago in the infirmary..."

"Ah, Capitán, I am alright. I just need a good rest and wine," Tiago protested before the Capitán could finish.

"Nonsense! Go to the infirmary and have Doctor Arturo tend to your wounds. And you," he pointed at Manuel, "follow me."

Manuel got off the horse, thanking Garcia who firmly held him until his feet touched the ground, and followed Capitán de Alvarez to his quarters. He heard Sargento de Beneza give the order for the troop to proceed to the livery then to the mess hall for supper after looking after their mounts, and Manuel felt his stomach growl, reminding him that he had not eaten much for the last two days. He hoped the Capitán would not ask too many questions.

Capitán de Alvarez was a man of few words. He let Manuel talk, asking a pertinent question every now and then. Manuel was likewise a quiet man who would rather have his actions speak. He went through his story directly, omitting the fact that he had to ride through a bunch of war-crazed warriors to help Tiago.

"Bueno," the Capitán finally said. "Go and have the medico look at your wounds also, take your supper and have a good night's rest."

"Gracias, Señor." Manuel bowed. He started to move back out to the door when Capitán de Alvarez raised his hand to stop him.

"I heard you can track," The Capitán said.

"A little, sir."

"If we go back to the place, can you track them down?"

"I will try, sir."

"Try is not good enough in the King's army, son."

"Yes, sir, I can," Manuel said tersely.

"Bueno," Capitán de Alvarez said. "Will you be able to ride by tomorrow?"

Manuel was about to say he could ride now, but it was pointless to go at night. Besides he needed to eat and rest.

"Yes, sir. I can ride tomorrow."

"Excellent! Report to me at five in the morning, we'll set out early. Go." He waved his hand in dismissal. "And tell Sargento de Beneza to come see me."

"Yes, sir." Manuel saluted and turned around quickly before the Capitán could think of something else. His stomach growled again as he reached the door. He headed straight to the mess hall. Doctor Arturo can wait. He would be busy with Tiago anyway.

By the time supper was finished, everyone at the fort knew what happened. Tiago had probably been talking, for from the tidbits he overheard, Manuel had appeared to have singlehandedly fought off the savages to help Tiago out after the rest of the troop went down.

He just shook his head and buried his face in his food, and promptly left as soon as he had his fill. Thank God the soldiers gave him some space, noting that he was not in the mood for useless talk.

They rode out at dawn, two hundred strong, each man loaded with enough provisions for two weeks, including Capitán de Alvarez who was leading them. Riding beside him was Sargento de Beneza.

The young Manuel, all rested and raring for battle, rode well ahead of the troop, slowing down now and then to look for signs and get proper orientation to where they were going. In his heart burned the fire of revenge for his comrades who were mercilessly ambushed. There was also the sense of guilt for having survived the encounter and he hoped to get rid of it by avenging their deaths. There was no small talk. Each man had seen the Capitán's face as he briefed them that morning and from his expression they knew he would not stop until he saw blood spilt.

Most of the men Sargento de Beneza picked were veteran soldiers who had ridden with the Capitán before in other missions. They left Tiago under the medico's care amidst his half-hearted yet loud and colorful protestations.

The day was clear and they made good time, stopping only to rest the horses and give them drink at the spring where Manuel and Tiago had rested.

Manuel silently thanked God and his family's patron saint, San Miguel, for the lack of rain last night and for the clear day. The tracks should still be fresh.

And then they reached the site of the encounter. Manuel did not have to speak and retell his story for the signs were there for everyone to see. The mutilated bodies of the dead soldiers, all stripped of protective gears and clothing, spoke loudly enough of the brutality they met there.

They buried the soldiers where they lay, with the Capitán saying a solemn prayer for all of them. He did not bring out his Bible. He spoke passages from memory. And at the end, he vowed to hunt and kill everyone responsible for the deed. Then he crossed himself.

The soldiers listened in somberly and made the sign of the Cross as Capitán de Alvarez did and each one left the clearing determined to carry out the Capitán's vow.

They rode out of there at a rapid pace, not needing to slow down for the signs were easy enough to read. The Indians had not bothered to cover their tracks and they had carried their dead with them.

"They went back to their village," Manuel said. "Shouldn't be that far from here, otherwise they would have gotten rid of the bodies."

The Capitán nodded and motioned Manuel to lead on.

Manuel saw the faint smoke before he saw the village. He raised his hand and pointed and the Capitán's brows furrowed for he could not initially see what Manuel was seeing, and then the brow cleared flat as he finally discerned the smoke.

"How far?" he asked.

"Half-hour if we ride hard," Manuel answered. Distances could be confusing in the forest. Perhaps they could get there in twenty minutes, less if he was riding by himself.

The Capitán looked up at the sun that was on its way down to the west. There should still be plenty of light in another hour.

"Let's rest," he said as he dismounted. "We move after an hour. Look after your weapons and horses."

There was no need for the reminder for he had veteran soldiers. They silently dismounted, watered and rubbed down their horses, took a cursory look at their swords and rifles that had been prepared for battle back at the fort, then stretched down or sat around on the ground to rest. They were up and ready in an hour.

"We ride in and kill all the bastards. I want no prisoners." Capitán de Alvarez looked each soldier in the eye as he rode down the ranks. The soldiers met his stare grimly. They had seen that look in their Capitán before.

Manuel sat uneasily on his horse, wondering at what was going on in the Capitán's head. He kept his silence and readied himself for battle. He now rode in front with Sargento de Beneza, the Capitán between them.

Manuel was surprised that the Indians did not post any guard as they approached the village. When they rode down from the hills, he saw that most of the villagers, men, women and children, were gathered at a wide open space in the middle of the village, surrounding a fire, as if there was a ceremony going on.

They must be honoring their dead, Manuel thought. Then he saw the Capitán put a knee to his horses, moving up ahead. He had his sword out and was shouting as he sped up and charged.

"San Tiago!!!" He yelled as he raced forward, waving his sword, invoking the protection of his homeland's patron saint.

"San Tiago!!!" The soldiers echoed his cry, their swords, rifles and lances on the ready as they followed the Capitán and Manuel who now rode by his side toward the center of the village.

And the massacre began.

The attack came as a complete surprise. The Indian warriors never had a chance to regroup and defend their village in a concerted effort. The few warriors who were able to get to their weapons were mercilessly cut down, as were the others, armed or not, including the women and children. And in the middle of it all, was the Capitán, wielding his bloodied sword, cutting and thrusting at anything that moved, be it a man, woman, or child, his eyes glazed like a mad man.

And beside him, striking fear to the Caribs was the young Manuel of Andalusia, who matched his Capitán's rampage strike by strike. They were a sight to behold, the gentleman officer and the young soldier by his side, both crazed with battle, skillfully mowing down anyone that stood and moved before them. They were terrifying apparitions to the cowering natives for they were covered with blood not of their own, yet their swords were real enough and they brought horrifying death to anyone within their reach.

And when they saw no Indian left standing, they burned the village.

The natives who made it to the shelter of the forest and survived the massacre retold their story later on to the other tribes. And the word spread everywhere throughout the island. The white foreigners were devils incarnate and it was not wise to fight against them. There were no more troubles afterward. The colonization and conversion of Santo Domingo and the whole island followed soon without much trouble.

And Capitán Godofredo Tuzon de Alvarez did not forget the lad who skillfully and valiantly fought by his side. Sargento de Beneza was promoted to Teniente and the young Manuel became the Sargento, the youngest ever in the King's army for he was barely in his teens. And when Señor Arseño Mata de Beneza retired a few years later and went back to raise sheep in Burgos, Manuel became the youngest Lieutenant in the King's army.

By the time he reached his twentieth birthday, he had led forays through most of the islands in the Caribbean, sowing terror and planting the Cross along his path. He was sent to Mexico to befriend the Aztecs as his exploits were known and he became a Capitán there on his twenty fourth birthday.

And everywhere he went, he took Tiago with him, all the way to these Islas de Filipinas where Capitán Manuel volunteered to come when the word about the Indios causing problems to his majesty's army reached his ears.

"*Pro Deo et patria,*" Manuel sighed as he remembered. "For God and country." Yes, indeed. Sometimes he wondered if it was all worth it.

He looked down at the plaza below and found himself considering doing the same thing they did in Santo Domingo here in this godforsaken place if these wretched Ilocano rebels kept trying his patience. And they were led by a woman at that! "*¡Que barbaridad!*" the *Capitán* huffed in disgust.

I must get ready for church, he thought as he moved away from the window, calming down a bit. *Padre* Joaquin would be on his back the whole time he was in town if he missed Sunday Mass. He rolled his eyes at the prospect of listening to the sermon of the long-winded priest. But, he reasoned out, that was a small thing to pay for the hearty breakfast that the *Padre* will surely invite him to share with if he saw him in church. He always did without fail and *Don* Manuel looked forward to it, as well as the lively conversation that would surely occur during and after the repast. No doubt the *Padre* would update him on what had been happening in the *pueblo* while he was away. The *Padre* seemed to possess the uncanny ability to know everything that went on in the town. That was one reason why he avoided the *Padre's* confessional.

Don Manuel crossed himself at the blasphemous thought. He cast another backward glance at the plaza and the church beyond.

Down below, some of the Indios who had missed the dawn Mass started trooping toward the church. Then out of the corner of his eye, the *Capitán* noticed a girl, barely a woman in his eyes, walking among the stalls, heading toward his villa, balancing a basket full of purple and green fruits on her head.

"*Caimitos,*" *Don* Manuel whispered the local name of the star apples that filled the girl's basket. But he was not looking at the fruits or at the basket that sat regally on the girl's head. He was curious and mesmerized by the girl, no, a woman, and he moved closer back to the window, intently looking and searching in the back of his mind where he had seen her before. She was every bit all woman, he was certain now as she passed by his window and more than ever he was convinced that he had seen her before and definitely not here in town.

He searched his memory but he came up blank. He tried to look at her face underneath the basket but he could not get a clear look from where he stood and the basket covered most of her features. He considered running down to the plaza to get a better look but he hesitated because he was not properly dressed. So he just watched as she went by, not across the plaza but down the side street below. He followed her every move until she disappeared underneath the overhang of the villa next door.

A *mestiza*, he thought as he noted that she was fairer and taller than most of the locals. He wondered why he had not noticed her before, here or any place else, although in the back of his mind, he felt he had seen her in the past. He shook his head as if the act might help clear and refresh his memory but nothing came back. He frowned, thinking deeply and hard.

Nothing.

He finally gave up as he saw the crowd trickling into the church had thinned down to a few late comers.

He hurriedly turned around, grabbed a towel off the headboard and went out to the well in the backyard and washed up. He returned to the house and gave a sigh of relief as he saw that Clara, his Ilocana housemaid, had already prepared his clothes and they were draped over the chair by his armoire.

He dressed up quickly and headed out to church, his eyes scanning the stalls and the plaza hoping to find the woman but it was in vain.

The woman had totally disappeared. He quickened his steps as it occurred to him that perhaps she may have also gone to church.

It was Sunday after all.

Chapter Four

Miguel Vicos was in a sour mood. And the fact that he had a terrible headache did not help his bitter disposition. After another night of hard drinking, he woke up with a throbbing hangover.

Like in the past, he failed yet again in his intent to drown his frustrations and anger with *basi,* that potent sugar cane wine. But what did he expect? Why would this morning be any different?

He needed another drink badly to make him feel better, he thought. Wash away the bitter taste in his mouth, the awful headache, and perhaps the anger in his heart. Yet he knew it was a hollow hope. Deep inside he knew he was going through the same stupid cycle all over again.

It seemed to be a daily occurrence now, at least for the past couple of months since Diego's death. He knew he was going nowhere, but what was the alternative in this hell-hole of a place? The Spanish *Dons* and the *Frayles* who were supposed to be his friends and *padrinos*, who promised to take good care of him, were useless and of no help. After what he had done for them, they had reneged on their promises. *Cabrónes* and *hijos-de-puta* the whole lot of them! May they rot in hell! He felt a surge of pleasure at the thought, but it did not last.

The feeling of hopelessness and desperation clung to him like a bloodsucking leech and was draining him physically and mentally. It seemed that the only thing that kept him going was the prospect of another day of drinking.

He dragged himself to the kitchen, grabbed a mug made out of coconut shell, dipped it in the water jar then proceeded to the *bangsal,* the all-purpose open air portion of the house that led to the stairs going down to the backyard, raising the mug to his lips as he walked, water dripping from his chin. He gurgled loudly, rinsing his mouth as thoroughly as he could and spat the water out over the *bangsal's* low partitioned-wall to the open ground below. His dog lying underneath yelped and growled, slinking away and shaking off the water that drenched it, looking up at his master and tormentor with annoyance in its eyes.

"Stupid dog never learns," Miguel hissed as he gulped another mouthful of water. Just like his master, he thought shaking his head. He contemptuously spat the water out, intentionally trying to hit the dog this time, but it scampered away out of reach. It glared up at Miguel then skulked towards the Tamarind tree, circled the trunk a couple of times then picked a spot to lie down, safe from its ill-tempered master.

Despite himself, Miguel chuckled. "At least the bitch has some sense," he mused, and then he grimaced as another wave of pain hit the side of his head. Instinctively, he poured the rest of the water over his head, wiping off his face with his free hand and shaking involuntarily like his dog. The cold water revived him momentarily, but his headache came back with a vengeance as he made his way back to the kitchen.

He had to do something different today, he resolved. But what, he had no idea. Maybe something will come up after breakfast. He scrounged around and found nothing good ready to eat.

He lived alone and he hated to cook so he decided to go over to the *garreta*, where the eateries, the *carinderias*, were located close to the slaughterhouse, and get breakfast there like he normally did most of the time anyway. His credit should still be good with *Apo* Andang. After all, he just paid off his outstanding dues a couple of weeks ago. He would have *longganiza*, the fatty and slightly acidic local sausage, and *kinirog*, the fried rice that the Tagalogs call *sinangag* and maybe a couple of eggs on the side. And definitely a bowl of hot *sinanglao*, the steaming soup made of cow's innards. That should make him feel better. There's nothing like a hot bowl of *sinanglao* to chase the hangover away, and perhaps give him a better start of the day. And maybe, just maybe, his luck would change today.

But truth be told, he doubted if any food could make him feel better at the moment. Or change his luck. He was not even sure if he could keep anything down. His stomach growled as if to answer his thoughts. Perhaps it may be up to the challenge after all.

He put on a clean shirt and used the same trousers he had the day before. He reminded himself to ask Mameng, the neighborhood *lavandera* who lived a couple of houses down the road to come over and get his laundry. He could not find a comb so he brushed his hair with his fingers, not even bothering to look in the mirror, and went out without locking the door. He did not have anything of value to be stolen anyway. Besides, nobody would dare steal from him.

After all he was Miguel Vicos, the liberator of the Ilocos from its deranged self-proclaimed president, Diego Silang. And besides, he was the son of a *Castilian*. Nobody would dare.

But deep inside, he knew his being a *mestizo* did not mean a rat's ass to anyone, not to the Ilocanos, and surely not to the Spaniards. Especially to the good-for-nothing Spaniards! And the fact that he got rid of Diego, who was beginning to be a royal pain in their sides on top of them dealing with the invading British, did not do anything to his social standing either. Ungrateful bastards all of them! And to the contrary, he felt more ostracized by the Ilocanos, if that was all possible. The deep hatred in his heart began to stir again at the thought.

He should be well-off, a respected gentleman, a Spanish *Don* in the town just like the other Spaniards, for after all he had their blood in his veins. Half maybe, but still it was there. He should be better off, at least, than the godforsaken, full blooded native Indios.

Like that damned Diego, the pretentious little twerp who deserved what he got. Or even the impertinent *Itneg* who was supposed to be his friend and *compadre*, Pedro Becbec, who for God's sake was given the esteemed office of a judge in Abra! Did he need to get stabbed like Pedro first to be properly rewarded? So nobody had gotten to him yet, but not for lack of trying. And what did he, Miguel Vicos, get so far? Practically nothing! Aside from a few bloody *pesos*, he was still a miserable and angry man with nothing to look forward to except for another bout with the *basi*. He had yet to receive the position he was promised at the *municipio*. They said he would eventually be the *Alcalde* of Bantay where he lived, because it was going to be a *municipio* instead of just a *sitio* of Vigan but when was it going to happen? He was no longer holding his breath on that one. But hell, it did not matter now. He would take the lowly position of a clerk if it was even offered.

Sure, Diego and Pedro were his friends but it grated against his craw that he played second fiddle to either one of them. He should be better than them, for crying out loud! He was taller and fairer, thanks to his Spanish blood, and because of his blood, partial it may be, he should command more respect.

But that was not the case. Not at the very least. Neither the Spaniards nor the Ilocanos accepted him as their equal. Much more as a superior even to the Indios! He knew that in truth he was an unwanted half-breed, regarded with suspicion and contempt by both the Ilocanos and the Spaniards. Respect? He did not get any respect!

So he bristled with hate and anger. And it grated and ate at him deep inside.

Yes, he thought betraying and killing Diego would change all that, but it didn't, he was aware of that now with not just a little feeling of regret.

But what he regretted more was the fact that he only created a martyr and a hero out of the little man. And made an improbable leader of the rebels out of his widow who was now known as *La Generala*! Hah! He, Miguel Vicos, should be leading the Ilocanos and not that usurper of a woman. '*La Generala*, my ass,' he thought. She could not even lead a bunch of children!

He hailed the first *calesa,* the horse drawn carriage that came his way and instructed *Mang* Doming, the *cuchero,* to take him to the *garreta.*

"Not the church?" *Mang* Doming said.

"What?" Miguel asked. His mind was still wandering someplace else and was not paying attention to the *cuchero.*

"The church," *Mang* Doming said. "It's Sunday."

"Ohh, yes, it's Sunday," Miguel said. Of course he forgot that it was Sunday and decent people go to church on Sundays. "I'll go after breakfast," he lied.

Mang Doming knew his passenger well and he did not say anything. He knew that Miguel would be at the *garreta* most of the day, drinking as usual. He exhaled deeply as he caught a whiff of the sour smell of *basi* from his passenger's breath. "Tsk, tsk," he said, shaking his head slightly in disgust covering the gesture with a quick tug of the reins to urge the horse forward in case Miguel noticed, but his passenger was out of it. Miguel had his head on the side of the *calesa* with his eyes closed.

Miguel was indeed oblivious as he instinctively closed his eyes to ward off another jolt of headache as the *calesa* jerked forward. He kept his eyes closed and the pain eased off finally, soothed down probably by the rhythmic trot of the horse. Perhaps he was lulled to sleep for they were at the *garreta* when he finally opened his eyes and he somehow felt the *calesa* come to a stop. He reluctantly paid his fare and got off slowly, fighting another wave of nausea in the process. He gripped the door jamb of the *calesa* tightly until the nausea went away. *Mang* Doming patiently waited while his passenger regained his composure.

Miguel headed towards *Apo* Andang's stall in measured steps, careful not to stumble and fall on his face as he felt the eyes of the early customers focused on him. He ignored them and gingerly moved on, then paused, momentarily surprised as he found Pedro Becbec seated at one of the five tables by *Apo* Andang's little *carinderia.* In front of Pedro was a steaming bowl of *sinanglao.* He did not know the judge from Abra was in town. The man must be feeling better after getting stabbed while they were paraded as heroes after killing Diego. Miguel wanted to turn around, but Pedro had lifted his face from slurping a spoonful of *sinanglao* and was now looking at him with a big grin.

"Ahh, Miguel! It's good to see you!" Pedro yelled, showing no effect from the wounds he sustained in the attempt on his life, some say for his role in betraying Diego. Rumor had it that Diego's widow herself had done the deed but other people were not convinced. Pedro would have been dead if she did. Pedro himself was not of any help saying he did not see his attacker. "Good morning, *Compadre!*"

49

Miguel winced inwardly but he tried not to break his stride and approached Pedro's table with as much dignity as he could muster. Despite his headache, he realized that everyone's eyes were on him, mostly with dagger looks and perhaps wishing for him to fall. He was not about to give them that satisfaction.

And Pedro's table was the only one left with a vacant chair.

"Good morning, *compadre!*" Pedro said, pushing his chair backward and started to rise but Miguel waved a hand, signaling him not to bother. Pedro obliged and waited for Miguel to reach his table.

"Good morning to you, too," Miguel mumbled as he took the empty chair facing Pedro.

"You don't look too good, *amigo*. A bowl of this should make you feel better." Pedro gestured toward the steaming bowl of *sinanglao*.

"A cup of *basi* instead would probably work better," Miguel said dourly.

"Uh-unh. Not without food in your stomach. Trust me, get some of this first," Pedro pointed to his bowl then waved at Gorio, *Apo* Andang's helper, to bring another bowl of *sinanglao*. The boy promptly brought a steaming bowl over, placing a spoon beside it.

"Thanks, Gorio," Miguel mumbled.

The boy left without saying anything. Miguel glared behind his back but the boy was off to get another bowl for another customer, oblivious of Miguel's annoyed stare.

Miguel picked up the spoon and mindlessly stirred his soup, watching impassively the pieces of meat and innards and blobs of fat swirl around.

"So what brought you to town?" he asked Pedro after a while without looking at him. "I thought you'd gone into hiding after that attempt on your life."

"I just want to visit you, my good friend, see how you are," Pedro said. "Aren't you glad to see me?"

"Cut the crap, Pedro," Miguel said wearily, glancing up at his friend. He turned his attention to his bowl, scooped a spoonful of *sinanglao*, blew on it momentarily, took a sip then slurped the rest of the food. It felt good going down, but he did not find much enjoyment as he looked back at Pedro. He knew in his gut that his presence was not good for either of them. "What's going on?" he said. "What made you come out in the open? Aren't you scared they'll make another try at you?"

Pedro sighed, the jolly grin vanishing from his face. He knew his friend and realized Miguel was not in the mood for small talk.

"Eat your soup," he said in a low voice, looking around as if anyone was listening to their conversation. "We'll take a walk later."

Miguel casually glanced at the other customers and found no one paying them any attention. Every one of them was busy eating whatever they ordered. The man's paranoid, he thought.

He had felt the same way after they killed Diego but he had learned to ignore the feeling. At least during the times he was under the comforts of the *basi*. Sure, he had some sleepless nights and perhaps the alcohol induced sleep helped control the rearing head of his conscience, and the fear of reprisal although the Spaniards had guaranteed their protection, which was not much considering the rebels were able to get to Pedro, but he was convinced he's gotten over it. Oddly enough, he felt the old feeling slowly creeping back as he turned his attention to Pedro who had resumed eating his *sinanglao*. He likewise took another scoop, the act more of a reflective action rather than the desire to satisfy taste or hunger. He was losing his appetite, yet he went through the motion of eating.

They ate in silence. Miguel finally pushed his bowl when he was halfway done. There was no need to order for the eggs or the fried rice. His stomach was holding out pretty well but he had entirely lost his appetite. He noticed that his companion had no such problem, paranoid or not. Pedro did not look up until his bowl was empty.

"That was good," Pedro straightened up, patting his stomach. "What's the matter?" he asked as he noted Miguel's unfinished soup. "Not feeling well?"

"I'm full," Miguel lied.

Pedro shrugged. "Coffee?" he signaled at Gorio before Miguel could respond.

"No, not for me. I'm good," Miguel said.

"Suit yourself, but I need one to chase away the fat from that *sinanglao*." Pedro said and turned to Gorio as the boy came up to their table. "Give me one coffee, please, and a piece of *suman* if you have any." Pedro had a sweet tooth and the *suman*, the steamed sweet rice mixed with molasses rolled in banana leaf that is a favorite dessert of the Ilocanos would go well with the coffee. His mouth watered in anticipation.

"Sure," Gorio said. "How about you, *Mang* Miguel?"

"No, nothing for me, Gorio. Thank you," Miguel mumbled.

Gorio left and promptly came back with Pedro's steaming coffee and a roll of *suman* which the latter devoured swiftly, finishing it off in a couple of bites before turning his attention to his coffee.

Damn, man has an appetite, Miguel thought as Pedro drank his coffee noisily. Miguel had the eerie feeling that the day would not be any better and he suddenly wanted to get away from the *carinderia*. Pedro finally noticed his companion's unease and beckoned Gorio to settle their account. Miguel let him pay the bill after putting up a half-hearted protest.

"I have a problem," Pedro said as they walked away from the *carinderia* towards the river that ran past the *garreta*.

Miguel remained silent. Deep inside he felt his anger stirring awake. He did not need Pedro's problem in addition to his own.

"I can't stay in Abra anymore," Pedro continued. "I am still getting death threats, more frequently now."

"I have one every day, Pedro," Miguel said. "There's nothing to it. It's all talk. I'm still here."

"They are serious, Miguel. They've tried before and they'll try again. People come around when the sun goes down. My dogs are up barking all night."

"So does mine. That's what dogs do. They bark at their own shadows."

"This is different, Miguel, believe me," Pedro said softly, with a little tremor in his voice. "I couldn't sleep. I'm scared for my family."

"It's just your nerves and imagination playing with you, Pedro. Perhaps you're just feeling guilty over what we did with Diego."

"No. I'm over that, believe me. We did the right thing," Pedro said with conviction. "But like I said I worry about my family."

For once, Miguel was glad he was not married and did not have any children.

"Nobody would dare touch them," he said with, he hoped, an assuring tone in his voice, but somehow it seemed to come out hollow. "You're a judge, for crying out loud," he added, a little forcefully than he intended.

"Yeah, yeah, I know. But still..." Pedro's voice did not seem assured.

"You worry too much. There's nothing to it." Miguel wanted to end the discussion. It was getting on his nerves.

Pedro didn't say anything. After a while he said softly, "I wish I have your confidence."

If you only knew you fool, Miguel thought with a smirk but tried to act composed. It was a good thing they were walking side by side and Pedro could not see his face.

"It's been two months, Pedro. If anything was going to happen, it would have happened by now."

"M-m-maybe. I-I, I hope you're right." Pedro stammered.

Miguel shrugged but did not answer. He hoped he was right also. But deep inside, the sliver of worry that bordered to fear that had stirred awhile ago fluttered back to life.

"I sent my wife and my children to go visit with her family, up in Isabela," Pedro glanced at Miguel. "They may be safer there when they are not around me. I was hoping I could stay with you for a while until this dies down."

Miguel knew that Pedro meant until the rebels would surrender or get captured. The man was not just paranoid but crazy too, he thought. The way things were going, it would be a long while before the soldiers could catch up with the rebels especially now that they are deep in the forests of Abra. And there was no way he would let the paranoid *pendejo* stay with him all that time. He barely had enough provisions for himself!

"You know my house is always open for you, Pedro, but I can't let you stay with me. What would the people think? That we are scared? Or worse, we're planning something else? Get a hold of yourself, my friend. You're worried about nothing." He stopped and looked at his friend and saw the fear in his face. Maybe this was more serious than he thought.

"Perhaps, you're right. I'm sorry to impose," Pedro said timidly, his head dropping like a prisoner who just heard a stiff sentence.

"No, no, no, no," Miguel said hastily. "Don't get me wrong. You're not imposing, you know that. It's just what I say it is. We have to show them that we are not scared and we did the right thing." Miguel wished he believed what he just said after he had a moment to think about it.

"I wish and hope you're right, Miguel," Pedro murmured softly after a while, but his voice did not evoke much conviction.

Miguel did not say anything more and turned back toward the river. Pedro slowly followed. They walked in silence until they reached the riverbank.

"You're not going back to Abra today, are you?" Miguel asked as they watched a family of ducks going up and down the river, staying close to the bank. The ducklings playfully snipped at one another while the mother duck hovered around, keeping a wary eye at the two people standing nearby. Her motherly instinct taking over, she swam farther upstream away from the two humans, her ducklings dutifully following behind in a disciplined file.

"I was not planning too," Pedro said as he turned his attention back to his *compadre*. "I told them I would be here for at least a couple of days on official business."

Miguel did not answer, his attention still on the ducks swimming away.

After a while he said, "Well, you can stay with me for a couple of days." He regretted it as soon as he said it but he softened a bit as he looked at Pedro and saw the faint relief on his face. "But you know I live alone so we have to cook our own food or come here to eat," he added then it occurred to him that he was running low on funds.

"Oh, thank you," Pedro said. "But don't worry, I brought some provisions and I can cook. But if you wish, we can always come here. My treat."

"No, no, no. You're my guest," Miguel said but in his heart he wished Pedro did not take his protestations seriously. He sighed with relief when Pedro said, "No, no, my friend. I insist. I brought some extra money too. Like I said, I don't want to impose."

"Well, if you say so, my friend," Miguel tried to put some emotion in his voice as if his feelings were hurt, but it was alright for a friend's sake. He took a deep breath and sighed loudly for effect. "Your presence is no imposition, don't ever forget that," he hoped his tone was not too dramatic but Pedro was feeling a great deal of gratitude to notice.

Well, maybe a company for a couple of days would not be too bad, Miguel thought. Perhaps a break in his routine would actually be good for him. "Besides," he murmured, more to himself, "we have lots to talk about."

Pedro bobbed his head, his face showing a trace of a smile. At least he could get a good rest for a couple of days, he hoped.

That night, over a number of mugs of *basi* that they had lost count after their third, they talked until they could no longer hear any dog barking or anyone else moving about in the night, two lonely souls commiserating in the soft glow of a solitary lamp.

The roosters had started their pre-dawn crowing when they finally went to bed.

Chapter Five

The Mass had started when *Don* Manuel walked into the church. He thanked God that *Padre* Joaquin was fervently praying loudly facing the altar, no doubt with eyes closed, so he would not know if the *Capitán* was late. Or so, he hoped, but with a nagging doubt in his heart because sometimes it seemed that the good *Padre* had eyes behind his head. Somehow he knew what was going on in the church even if he had his face turned away from the congregation. He only faced the people to give his homily which was always long and fiery, during communion and his final blessing at the end of the Mass.

Don Manuel walked softly up the aisle by the east wall, pausing now and then to look for the woman among the churchgoers and finally decided she was not there. He stopped as he reached a marble pillar that rose all the way up to the high ceiling of the church, surreptitiously noting who were sitting in the pews that were not fully occupied. He surely did not want to sit by people he was trying to avoid, who, he realized with chagrin, were mostly the people he knew and socialized with in the town. They were gossips all, and not just the women.

"God forgive me for having such thoughts in church," he prayed half-heartedly, grinning impishly as he saw *Señora* Carmen, the town's *numero uno chismosa*, the indisputable queen of gossips, eyeing him over her *abanico*, the small, lace-trimmed accordion fan, covering her no doubt smirking, overly rouged lips. He lowered his eyes and walked up and away from where the *Señora* and her hen-pecked husband, the merchant *Don* Andres, and their three children, sat.

He saw a space between two decent looking Indios whom he could not place at the moment. Perhaps visitors from nearby *pueblos* who came for the market after church, he thought. Silently he eased himself slowly into the pew, the Indios nervously moving and giving him ample space between them as they realized who he was. *Don* Manuel smiled and gestured with his hands benignly, nodding his head in gratitude to the men, putting them at ease. He was in church after all where everyone was most certainly equal in the eyes of the Lord. Outside was another matter.

Don Manuel is a believer. Indeed Spaniards and Indios, all people regardless of color, he believed, are all children of God. Nonetheless there is always a favorite even among God's children. And in the scheme of things, the Spaniards are God's special people, destined to spread his Word all over the world. *Don* Manuel bowed his head to hide the smile that crossed his

55

lips. He closed his eyes and tried to concentrate on the words intoned by *Padre* Joaquin. You have to give it to him, he thought, the *Padre* has a good voice.

The *Capitán* nodded paternally to the Indios around him as he caught their glimpses, extolling them quietly with a smile of camaraderie on his face to say their responses and prayers a little louder as he noticed that they became more tentative and nervous since he sat by them. Sensing his sincerity and goodwill, the Indios warmly responded, belting out their responses with renewed vigor and lustily joining the *Capitán* in the singing of the hymns.

They could sing, these Indios, the *Capitán* beamed in appreciation. Indeed if there was one thing these Indios were superior over most Europeans, the *Capitán* conceded, it was their singing. He looked around again hoping to find the woman he saw by his window but he still did not see her. Perhaps she would be at the *mercado* later on, he hoped as he tried to concentrate on the prayers instead.

During the homily, *Don* Manuel noticed that *Padre* Joaquin's eyes were roving around more than usual as if he was searching for someone. He had the uneasy feeling that the good *Padre* was looking for him since the priest's roaming eyes paused for a long time when he spied the *Capitán*. Damn, Manuel thought, crossing himself hurriedly for cursing in church albeit silently. The *Padre* knew that he was late, Manuel was sure of it. He stared back blankly at the *Padre*, trying to ignore the attention he was giving him. He finally gave out a relieved sigh when the *Padre*'s eyes went back around the church looking for new targets, his impassioned voice, all the while, never missing a beat.

In a moment, the *Capitán* was lost in thought, oblivious of the people around him and of what *Padre* Joaquin was talking about and trying lustily to expound and share with the people. His thoughts went to the rebels and the mountains of Abra and to what possibly would the *Padre* wanted to talk with him about for he surely had something in his mind the way he looked at him. And he thought of the woman, desperately trying to remember where he might have perhaps seen her but still nothing came up. He gave with a start as the Indios beside him stood up for another prayer. He did not even notice that *Padre* Joaquin had finished his homily and was now back facing the altar to resume the Holy Mass.

The *Capitán* tried to concentrate for the rest of the Mass, piously going up to the rails to receive Holy Communion when the time came, gently encouraging the Indios in his pew to go with him, which they timidly did, but accorded him a respectful distance.

After the final hymn, the church began to empty as the people ebulliently moved out toward the plaza to do their Sunday market. *Don* Manuel tarried in his pew after silently acknowledging the apologetic bows of the Indios around him as they moved out to join the rest of the people, his eyes scanning the faces of the women who passed by but the woman with the basket was not there. She would have stood out in the crowd.

He knelt down and closed his eyes as if in deep prayer so he did not have to acknowledge anyone who would nod at him in greeting. He let his mind go blank, ignoring the persistent soft greetings thrown his way but his ears were tuned to the bustling sound of the rest of the churchgoers going by in the aisles. The sound subsided eventually and *Don* Manuel sighed contentedly as the silence of the church enveloped him. He always loved this moment, him alone in the church, with just the sound now and then of the timbers and pews as they creaked and seemed to sigh as the temperature inside changed.

He had always found comfort and peace inside a church, and the feeling seemed more enhanced with the silence. Again he sighed contentedly, finally saying a silent prayer of thanks for no particular reason.

Then he heard the unmistakable sound of *Padre* Joaquin's sandals as he walked out of the sacristy into the altar. He heard it pause for a moment. No doubt in front of the altar, the *Capitán* thought as he kept his eyes closed, imagining the priest genuflecting before the tabernacle. Then he heard the footsteps resume, each step becoming louder as it approached the *Capitán's* pew.

Don Manuel counted the steps mentally, sensing before they finally stopped that the *Padre* had reached his pew. He kept his eyes closed as if in deep prayer as he felt the *Padre* eased himself down silently into the pew but with great difficulty for he was a man of wide girth. He almost smiled at the picture that crossed his mind.

Padre Joaquin likewise closed his eyes while he waited patiently for the *Capitán* to finish his prayers. As a man of the cloth, he appreciated holiness in lay people, especially soldiers.

Don Manuel finally opened his eyes. "*Buenos dias, Padre,*" he turned toward *Padre* Joaquin.

Padre Joaquin gave out an audible sigh and opened his eyes.

"*Buenos dias, Capitán.* It is great to see you back safely in town." The *Padre's* voice was somber belying his angelic smile. "I need to talk with you, if you have time to spare. I know you're a busy man."

"Of course, *Padre,*" he said. "I will see you at the convent after breakfast?" He wanted to get to the plaza first and perhaps find the woman.

But *Padre* Joaquin said, "Ah, no, *Capitán*. You will have breakfast with me, *ahora mismo*. I have asked Magda to cook extra for today. It is Sunday after all." He grabbed the top of the pew and hauled himself up noisily, motioning for Manuel to follow him, before the latter could say anything.

Don Manuel crossed himself piously as the *Padre* looked back to make sure he was going to follow. What could possibly be so important that the *Padre* would want to talk about, he thought, as he rose slowly and followed the *frayle* toward the side exit leading to the cobbled pathway that went behind the church and to the convent a few steps away.

"Nice day," *Don* Manuel tried to make small talk as he caught up with *Padre* Joaquin.

"Yes it is, but we need more rain," the *Padre* replied. "This place is going to be so dry if we don't get any rain. The wells are beginning to dry up."

"Just like home in Extremadura, *Padre*, just like home, so you would not get homesick." Manuel joked as he knew that *Padre* Joaquin was from that arid part of Spain.

"*Si*, and to think I had to travel across the earth to get away from it only to end up in a similar place!" *Padre* Joaquin gamely quipped. "But seriously, I am glad to see you safely back. I have heard nothing but disturbing news about these rebels."

"*Gracias, Padre*. I am glad to sleep in my own bed for a change. What news have you been hearing?"

"Your bed must be very comfortable, *Capitán*. You almost missed the Mass!" To his dismay, the *Padre* ignored Manuel's question as he hoped his being late to church would not be brought up.

"I apologize, *Padre*, I woke up late." The *Capitán* conceded. There was no way around it. The *Padre* was like a bulldog when he focused on a subject. "Yes, I almost missed your excellent homily. Thank God I caught all of it."

"You would not have missed much, *Capitán*. There was nothing you have not heard before."

True, the *Capitán* thought but he dared not voice his opinion. Instead he vigorously shook his head for emphasis as he replied, "Why, *Padre*, that was the most profound homily I have heard for a long time anywhere, and you know I go to Mass as often as I could, here or even back home in Spain. The Archbishop of Madrid himself could not have done any better!" *Don* Manuel could palaver with the best of them when necessary and he was into it now, intent on humoring the priest.

"You flatter me, *Capitán*," *Padre* Joaquin said trying to hide his satisfied smile, "but thanks anyway. I can only try my best every time I take to the pulpit."

"*Padre*, if I were the Pope I would make you the Cardinal of this whole archipelago!"

The *Padre* laughed wholeheartedly.

"You, the Pope! That's a sobering thought. No offense but I wait for an earthquake every time I see you in church!"

"I too am scared of that happening, so I try to stay away, but you know I could not miss to come in and give thanks to the Lord every time I get back safe from patrol."

"I am always glad to see you, *Capitán*. I would take it as a personal affront if you did not show up in church when you are in town."

"I'd be dying in bed if I don't come to church when I'm in town, *Padre*!" *Don* Manuel said. He hoped *Padre* Joaquin would not ask what he got from his homily because, for the love of God, he did not remember any word the good *Padre* said. Fortunately, *Padre* Joaquin changed the subject suddenly. *Capitán* Manuel sighed with relief.

"*Capitán*, I need to verify with you some rumors I heard, but I hope you take this in confidence and forget I ever brought it up if there was no truth to it."

"Surely, *Padre*. What is it?"

"We'll discuss it after breakfast, *Capitán*. Let us not destroy our appetites."

"By all means, *Padre*." *Capitán* Manuel always appreciated a person who knew his priorities as he gladly followed the *Padre* into the convent and on to the dining room where Magda, the *Padre*'s cook, was putting various dishes on the table. The room was redolent with the smell of fried *longganiza*, the famed pork sausage of the Ilocos, fried rice, eggs, fish and even *bagnet*, the local version of crispy *chicharon* made of pork belly, that reminded *Don* Manuel how he sorely missed good home cooking. He felt his mouth watering as he neared the table. The woman with the *caimitos* will have to wait.

Padre Joaquin talked incessantly throughout breakfast, falling silent only when he shoveled food in his mouth. The *Padre* had a great appetite as evidenced by his corpulence. The *Capitán* was also a man who appreciated good food and he showed it as he busied himself getting large portions of the various dishes. He listened with exaggerated attention to his host, acting the role of a captive audience, as he had his fill of the feast, but promising himself to get to the barracks and sweat it out with a little go at the swords with Tiago later on in the day. He could not afford to grow a belly like some of the older soldiers although the chance of that happening was pretty slim for he was an active man. Besides, he knew of no one in his family, both from his mother's and father's sides, who was fat. 'And how can one retain fat in this godforsaken heat?' he mused, wondering in passing how the good *Padre* could do so, with him swathed in thick robes all day as it was, and like most of the Spaniards, constantly perspired like pigs.

Don Manuel waited for the *Padre*'s important question but it seemed that he had forgotten or, he assumed, it was just a ruse on the *Padre*'s part to get his attention to keep him company for breakfast. He did not mind for he also hated eating alone. He did not remind the *Padre*, nor did he wish to know anything more as *Padre* Joaquin covered all the various rumors and news in town as well as in the neighboring parishes. Halfway through breakfast, *Don* Manuel had figured he had all the updated information on almost everyone of consequence, and some who were not, although he reminded himself to verify some issues the *Padre* brought up. He felt a twinge of remorse for doubting the words of a man of the cloth, but the *Padre* was known to embellish his stories sometimes.

Then out of the blue, the *Padre* asked, "*Capitán*, what's the word on Maria Josefa Gabriela, Diego's widow?" He lowered his fork and for the first time kept his mouth shut as he waited for *Don* Manuel to respond.

"Well, *Padre*," Manuel did not exactly wish to discuss their futile search for *La Generala* but he sensed that all the *Padre*'s updates were leading into this single question. The *Padre* was close to Diego and his wife, although he himself had no recollection of meeting her. "We followed her to Abra but she had vanished in the Cordilleras. We never saw her shadow or any of her men. I am afraid they had gone up deep into the mountains and God knows we would not be able to find her if she stayed there."

"I see. Would there be a possibility of them finally realizing the futility of their cause and they had perhaps disbanded?"

"I don't think so, *Padre*. On the contrary I have a feeling she's trying to regroup and get more men."

"That's a foolish thing to do. And where would she get more men? She's mad. How could she expect to succeed when her husband, who had much more men, failed? The woman is surely mad."

"Diego did not exactly fail, *Padre*. He took over Vigan, remember? We only took the city back when we got rid of him."

"He only took over for a little while, *Capitán*. He could not have held it for long even if he stayed alive."

Don Manuel did not agree with the *Padre* for he believed Diego and the Ilocanos would have had grown stronger the longer they stayed in power. He believed in the superiority of the Spanish army yet he was also a pragmatist. He briefly entertained the prospect of the rebels getting help from the *Itnegs* remembering that *La Generala's* mother was *Itneg* and he did not relish the idea, but he kept it to himself. Also he did not want the discussion to go any longer. The breakfast had stretched long enough. Besides, he wanted to visit the market and perhaps run into the *Señorita* who had passed by his window.

"Perhaps, *Padre*," he nodded his head instead, "perhaps. I hope the *Señora* Gabriela would reconsider her position and drop the whole thing. After all, she is still one of us."

"Half, *Capitán*, but yes, she is still of Spanish blood. I hope she would let it go for I don't want the dear child to suffer the same fate as her husband. I hope she surrenders."

Don Manuel did not answer. In his heart he knew that was not going to happen. This *La Generala*, according to the reports he received, was more resilient and stubborn than her late husband. Husbands, he corrected himself, as he remembered that the woman had been widowed twice.

"Would you pardon her if she surrenders, *Capitán*?" *Padre* Joaquin asked.

"She won't, *Padre*, and you know it. But since you asked, yes, I would but the Governor General may have a different idea," *Don* Manuel said truthfully.

The *Padre* paused from chewing, thinking over what the Capitán had just said and nodded his head but he remained silent.

Don Manuel waited patiently for the *Padre* to speak further but the priest was now silently looking out the window as if in a deep trance. The *Capitán* watched him for a while then finally decided it was time to go so he politely cleared his throat causing the *Padre* to turn his head toward him.

"Pardon me, *Padre*, but I have to visit the fort," *Don* Manuel said as soon as he had the *Padre*'s attention. "I thank you for a wonderful repast and a more wonderful conversation!"

He pushed back his chair and stood up before the *Padre* could respond.

Padre Joaquin likewise pushed back his chair rather hurriedly and tried to rise, talking at the same time. "Ahh, don't mention it, *Capitán*. It is my pleasure and my honor to have you for company. Of course, of course, duty calls even on Sundays. It doesn't have a day off."

"Surely you understand that better than I do," *Don* Manuel replied pushing his chair back in place into the table. "No need to stand up, *Padre*. I'll see myself out," he added pleasantly as he noted that the *Padre* had a little difficulty freeing his enormous frame from his chair, attempting to stand up. Besides, his plate still held quite a pile of food.

The *Padre* gratefully settled back in his chair.

"Promise to drop by before you go out again, *Capitán*?"

"Of course I will, *Padre*. Of course," *Don* Manuel nodded his head in emphasis. "*Gracias* again. *Adios*."

"Adios, Capitán," *Padre* Joaquin said to his back as the *Capitán* had already turned and headed to the door. He picked up his fork and stabbed at a piece of *longganiza*.

Don Manuel went directly to the plaza hoping that the *Señorita* had returned and was still there.

He walked around the market, exchanging pleasantries with the people who greeted him deferentially, his eyes constantly moving to the faces of every woman he met, searching for the *Señorita*, but she was nowhere to be found. After an hour, he finally gave up and left without buying anything, refusing civilly the offers of free produce and fruits from the locals.

He went up to his quarters and took his time to change from his Sunday clothes to his well worn practice suit, determined to sweat out the hearty breakfast from the *Padre*'s table. A bout with the sword against Tiago should take care of that, he thought, hoping that the old soldier was not yet drunk. It was after all a Sunday, and now as he thought of it, he had not seen the old soldier in church either.

Regardless, sober or not, Tiago was still the best swordsman among his soldiers.

Chapter Six

Don Manuel found Tiago furiously hacking at the straw dummy by the corral as he rode into the fort. He must have been at it for a while, he thought, as he noted the stain of perspiration on Tiago's suit, remembering also that the old soldier rose with the sun. Tiago was so engrossed with his thrusts and fluid swings at the dummy that he did not notice *Don* Manuel until the latter spoke.

"Don't you know that it is Sunday, you heathen, and you're supposed to go to Mass and rest? Even the good Lord Himself rested on the Sunday," *Don* Manuel said as he got off his horse.

Tiago stopped suddenly from pulling his sword from the straw dummy and turned to Manuel.

"Ahh Manuel, *Buenos dias*! So it is Sunday, God forbid!" He hit his brow with the palm of his left hand in mock repentance, the right hand still holding the hilt of his sword buried in the straw dummy.

Manuel shook his head in exaggerated sadness. "And to think that you used to live practically in the shadows of that great Cathedral in Compostela, that obviously had not made any impression on you."

"I have overslept, God forgive me, but I have said my prayers. This is my penance." Tiago grinned at *Don* Manuel who was still shaking his head, not believing a word.

"I would believe you if I didn't know better, you old goat. Why don't you find someone who could hit back?" Manuel looked at the dummy as Tiago pulled his sword from it.

"All those *bastardos* are still sleeping, except for the guards." Tiago slid the sword in his scabbard without glancing at it, his eyes locked on Manuel. "You're up early. I did not expect to see you here until perhaps late this afternoon. Aren't you tired?"

"It's Sunday, Tiago. There's a church in town and we decent Christians still attend Mass on Sundays, tired or not." Manuel did not want to admit that he also overslept. "I am rested enough. Besides, I just had a huge feast with the good *Padre* and I need to sweat it out. So take a break and rest for a while. I don't want you saying you're tired when I kick your arse." He led his horse toward the nearest stable before Tiago could answer.

"The day won't come when you can best me, *Niño*," Tiago laughed after him. "Except perhaps in your dreams so it's best you go back to sleep!"

"Get ready for a good whipping, *Viejo*," Manuel replied waving his free hand without looking back.

He and Tiago had been together for so long that they shared a familiarity that bordered to kinship. The old soldier had a genuine affection to Manuel like he was his own son. Likewise, Manuel considered Tiago as the only one true friend he had in the King's army.

Manuel had tried so many times to get the old man to talk about his family but Tiago always demurred, adroitly changing the conversation every time Manuel brought up the subject of family until the younger man finally gave up. It never occurred to him that Tiago had been trying to do likewise with the same results.

"If I had known that the *Padre* was giving free breakfast after Mass, I would have come to church," Tiago said as *Don* Manuel passed him by on his way from the stable to the armory. Tiago was fanning himself as he leaned under the huge Acacia tree that shaded the corral. His breathing did not show any sign of being tired, Manuel noticed in admiration. He had always wondered how someone at Tiago's age who also drank too much could recover so quickly after such a tiresome activity.

"I'm sure you would," Manuel replied. "I've never seen you decline an offer of free food."

"And I am glad you learned well from me, *muchacho!*" Tiago belted a good laugh. "I hope you ate enough for the two of us for you would need it to keep up with me!"

"I sure did," Manuel said and they both laughed as he added, "And *Padre* Joaquin ate enough for the whole fort! He was still eating when I left him!" May the Good Lord forgive me for the blasphemy, Manuel thought involuntarily. His mother did always tell her boys to respect the *frayles*. He turned around and hurried toward the armory. He never used his personal sword for practice, preferring instead a heavier piece made out also of pure Toledo steel that he kept in a special case in the armory. He needed the extra weight to counter Tiago's heavy hand.

Don Manuel picked up his practice sword from the armory then he went to the quarters he used when he stayed at the fort deciding to change to a well worn sleeveless undershirt he kept there as he felt the temperature rising. It was going to be another scorcher of a day. He would feel and move better with the old shirt instead of the heavier long-sleeved shirt he had on. He looked forward to these bouts with Tiago. He knew he needed every edge he can get for it seemed that the old soldier never ran out of tricks.

Manuel was sure he had seen all the tricks in swordplay for he and his brothers were trained in their boyhood by master swordsmen, including their own father and especially that Gypsy friend of his, Gustavo, who knew all the tricks and moves for some were named after him. Tiago would have been a worthy companion for anyone of them, Manuel thought, convinced that somehow Tiago did in his younger days, but the old soldier denied ever having heard of them. And then again, he never talked about his past.

He wondered what the old soldier had under his sleeves this time as he went to the courtyard and out back by the corral.

The sleeveless tunic hugged his trim body and accentuated his broad shoulders and toned biceps. *Don* Manuel cut a dashing figure but he seemed not to be aware of it. He had always been physically a big man, big boned and tall like his father, yet he moved nimbly like a big cat on the prowl when in a fight.

"Rested enough, *Viejo*, so I can kick your arse?" He asked Tiago who was now sitting on one of the big exposed roots of the Acacia tree.

"Ahh, *Niño*, I'd advise you to better go back to bed and sleep but it wouldn't help for you could not beat me even in your dreams." Tiago grinned, shaking his head.

"Are you ready?" The words had barely left Manuel's lips when he found himself parrying furiously the quick successive thrusts of Tiago. The wily old soldier had lunged forward suddenly from where he sat and attacked the *Capitán* with quick but controlled thrusts as he came within striking distance, expecting to talk first before they got into the bout.

"I was born ready, *Niño*, and don't you ever forget that!" Tiago yelled, grinning mirthfully at Manuel who was completely taken by surprise, but nevertheless still managed to successfully parry and evade the old soldier's initial surprise attack. Manuel should have known better for this sudden initial attack was Tiago's favorite. He was not thinking properly. Perhaps the *Señorita* was still in the back of his mind.

Tiago pressed his attack as Manuel tried desperately to move back to create a wider space between them so he can recover and counterattack.

But Tiago relentlessly followed, his thrusts swarming like bees all over *Don* Manuel, putting the younger man in full defensive mood. Manuel summoned all his skills and youthful dexterity to avoid the older man's furious attack.

In his haste to get away, Manuel lost his footing and fell on his butt to the delight of Tiago who belted out a hearty laugh, finally pulling back to let the younger man get up.

"Haven't I told you enough times, *Niño*, to protect yourself all the time and never ever trust anyone with a sword to act like a gentleman?" Tiago moved forward and extended his left arm to help pull Manuel up.

Manuel grasped Tiago's hand then pulled it down suddenly, tripping the old man with his left foot at the same time. Tiago lost his balance and found himself on the ground, and before he could move, Manuel was kneeling lightly on his chest with his sword pressed on his neck.

"And you better heed your counsel, old man," Manuel said as he stepped up quickly, moving away from Tiago, wary of another sneaky attack from the old man.

Tiago got up slowly, nodding his head in appreciation at what Manuel did. He dusted his pants, and faced Manuel with his sword up. Manuel likewise had his sword ready.

"I had you that first round, *Niño.*"

"Despite your trickery, your sword never got close to my body, *Viejo.*"

"Ahh, that's where you were wrong, *muchacho,*" Tiago smiled. "You would have bled to your death where you fell."

"*Bueno,*" Manuel said in agreement. He knew that what Tiago said was the truth. In a real fight, the old soldier would have had mercilessly cut down the fallen man. "The first round is yours then although you won it not as a gentleman."

"Bah, I never claimed to be a gentleman, *muchacho*, and I am proud of it!" Tiago said mockingly. "Many a gentleman had died needlessly because of their so-called gentlemen rules. It's pure rubbish. There's only one rule in a fight, and that is to stay alive at all cost, and don't you ever forget it!"

"There's such a thing as honor, *Viejo,*" Manuel said although he knew he might just as well talk to the wind. He slowly moved forward, with his sword poised for another encounter. "That, I am afraid, you will never understand."

He suddenly stepped to his left, then leapt forward quickly with his right foot extended forward, thrusting his sword at the same time. It was an easy feint, just an exploratory move Manuel knew, simply to gauge his opponent's reaction and state of his reflexes. But Tiago, despite his advancing age and having been up and practicing vigorously for the past two hours or so, was still quick and on top form.

"Honor is meaningless to a dead man," Tiago said as he parried the thrust easily. "As it is to a hungry man," he added, countering with a quick thrust of his own which was deftly deflected by Manuel.

"But remember, old man, that sometimes, honor is the only thing left that's there to keep us human and maintain our dignity, even in death." Manuel said as he jumped out of reach of Tiago's sudden swipe of his sword.

"Hah, you and your noble thoughts, *Niño!* Nonsense! That would be the death of you yet!" Tiago laughed as he momentarily stopped and waited for Manuel to regroup.

"Not for a long time yet, old man," Manuel said. "You might try it sometime, you may like it, although I believe that you are a man with honor yet I don't understand why you try so hard to hide it." He saluted briefly with his sword to acknowledge Tiago's courteous move.

The old soldier did not say anything but simply smiled, then he moved forward and their swords clanged together again in rhythm.

"Honor is in every man, *Niño*," Tiago said as their swords momentarily locked together. "Some live by it every day, and some keep it hidden inside and only draw it out when needed."

"Honor is never convenient, old man, and shown only when necessary. It should always be there in the open because it's what defines a man. Without honor, man is nothing."

"Whatever, *Niño*, you'd be a better swordsman if you didn't talk too much!" Tiago laughed as he stepped back then quickly attacked without any ceremony. Manuel easily deflected the thrusts.

After a few more mild thrash talking and tentative thrusts and counter-thrusts where no one was at a distinct advantage, they went at it with abandon, attacking and parrying recklessly, that to the untrained eye, it seemed that there was a deadly duel going on without the presence of seconds. Their swords clashed loudly and flashed swiftly with quick flicks of their wrists, their actions so fast, that it was hard to determine who was on the offensive, with their positions shifting in the blink of an eye. Their movements were so fast and furious yet so well coordinated and graceful that they seemed to be in a well synchronized dance, albeit deadly, yet beautiful to behold. The incessant and rapid clanging of their swords broke the stillness of the fort. So there they were, two men, both experts in the art of swordsmanship, displaying their unrivaled virtuosity to no one.

They were indeed a sight to behold, a magnificent pair, pushing and retreating, skillfully countering each other's moves in fluid precision, twisting and leaping in the air to press or escape an attack with no one appearing to best the other. It had been rumored about that nobody in the King's army could match old man Tiago with the sword until the young Manuel showed up. And there was no arguing that if anyone was there to witness them practice.

They were at it for almost an hour, yet neither was aware of the elapsed time. So engrossed were they at studying, learning and trying to predict each other's moves that they were not aware of the crowd of soldiers and Indio workers in the fort that had eventually gathered around them to watch, having been awakened and drawn to the sound of their swords.

The crowd at first silently watched the magnificent display of swordsmanship. It was not the first time they had seen this, but they never got tired of it, for somehow there was no predicting who would emerge as the eventual victor. And just like in the previous times, the spectators became more animated as the battle went on with neither of the combatants willing to give ground.

The dueling duo finally became aware of the crowd as the ohhs and ahhs in appreciation of a flashy move from either one grew louder and more frequent. A loud groan broke out every now and then as one of them seemed to be at a disadvantage, followed by the sound of sharp whistles and boisterous clapping after the execution of a skillfully maneuvered parry and escape.

The combatants ignored the crowd, focusing more intently at one another, yet both of them were fully aware that wagers had been made as to who would lose a sword, fall to the ground, or finally give up first. It was almost always an even bet in the crowd, for the soldiers had witnessed this exercise previously in numerous occasions, but each one with no certainty of the outcome since neither seemed to have a distinct superiority over the other. Most of the spectators thought that *Don* Manuel had an advantage over the older man because of his youth and tenacity, yet many also favored Tiago for his wiliness and inexhaustible bag of tricks. Regardless of their opinions, the spectators were always treated to a good show when Tiago and Manuel practiced. Winning a few pesos on the side added extra excitement to the event every time.

Then Tiago suddenly made three consecutive thrusts of his sword, the first two of which were deftly deflected by Manuel, and the third barely evaded by a quick arching of his body, keeping both feet on the ground as Tiago's sword swished by inches away from his stomach. Manuel's own sword came up from behind his back, switched hands with a quick cross-over throw and made two quick successive taps on Tiago's back as he leaned close to the *Capitán*.

Tiago gave out an appreciative laugh at what the *Capitán* did and he dropped his sword.

"That was a clever move, *Niño!*" Tiago bellowed. "My God, I haven't seen that trick for ages!"

"I have some tricks up my sleeve as well, *Viejo*, in case you have not noticed!" Manuel said with a satisfied smile. "You were tiring me out so I had to pull that one out."

"Tiring you out, me, an old man?" Tiago cried out incredulously as groans, insults and coins were exchanged among the soldiers in the background. They dispersed slowly as they noted the practice for the day was done.

"Yes, Tiago, I don't know how you do it, with all the ale that's in you." Manuel shook his head as if in great disbelief. There was some truth in what he said though, although he was not feeling tired at all. He just wanted to go back to the market with the hope that somehow the woman who passed by his window that morning was back. "I have to go back to town. Thank you again for a wonderful workout."

"Anytime, *Capitán,* the pleasure is mine. I cannot get a decent practice from all these pieces of horse dung who call themselves soldiers!" Tiago waved his hand toward the soldiers who had begun to disperse and go back to their chores or to their card and dice games. "Not one of them could even handle a kitchen knife properly."

Some of the soldiers had lingered around and laughingly ignored Tiago's rants, but their demeanor showed their respect and appreciation in the exceptional display of swordsmanship that they had again witnessed. Tiago and the *Capitán* acknowledged them, calling some of their names out, and reminding them to behave when they visited the town and get drunk probably, which most of them would certainly do, as they usually did on Sundays.

Manuel was not a strict commander and openly let his soldiers go about with a carefree hand as long as they did their duties within fair and just bounds. He always practiced that chivalrous sense of justice instilled in him by his father and he lived by it and expected his soldiers to do so also. But there were always those who lost their heads after a few glasses of wine and who would invariably find themselves waking up in the holding cell in the fort or at the *calaboso* by the *municipio* the following morning.

Manuel bade Tiago good-bye and he went back to his quarters to change. He planned on going back to the plaza and catch what was left of the market day. Besides, he knew that his presence would calm down the soldiers a bit, lessening the potential of trouble between them and the Indios.

We have enough trouble as it is with the rebels, Manuel thought as he returned his practice sword in the armory.

He went out to the courtyard from the armory, walked around the place, chatting with the soldiers every now and then and checking that everything was in order, or at least a semblance of it. The Indio workers busied themselves cleaning up, sweeping the leaves that had fallen from the Acacia and Tamarind trees, giving him a wide berth as he passed by, answering timidly as he asked about their welfare and their families.

Satisfied that there was nothing that required his immediate attention, he walked toward the well at the opposite end of the fort. He drew a bucketful of water from the well, took off his shirt and washed his face and upper body, drying off using a towel that seemed clean enough hanging from the clothesline where the local help washed the soldiers' clothes.

He went back to his quarters bare-chested, not bothering to put back on his sweat-soaked shirt. The soldiers nodded their appreciation at his well toned body as he walked past them but Manuel was oblivious of their glances. His mind was occupied with the thought of the *Señorita*. Try as he did, he could not remember where he had seen her before never once thinking that he could have been mistaken and it was the first time that he had set eyes on her.

Manuel dressed up quickly and was on his way to the stables when he heard one of the guards yelling for Tiago to go up the wall and take a look at something or someone. He could not quite make out the excited words, so he wandered off to the wall where the commotion came from. It was the southwestern part of the fort facing the river.

He saw Tiago who was still in his training suit run up the stairs going to the top of the ramparts where the guards, with several soldiers who were not in uniform were standing around, pointing at something outside the fort below them. His curiosity aroused at what caught their attention, Manuel followed Tiago up the wall at a leisurely pace.

At the rampart on top of the wall, Manuel stopped and watched the strange spectacle below. His lips curled to a smile at almost the same moment as the soldiers and Tiago hooted and clapped gleefully in appreciation at what they were seeing. Then a sense of recognition flashed into *Don* Manuel's mind and his smile flattened into a scowl that bordered into a concerned frown. He walked slowly to where Tiago stood. The *Sargento* was so engrossed at watching the scene below that he did not notice Manuel until he spoke.

Tiago's smiling face also turned into a perplexed frown as he listened to *Don* Manuel.

Sargento Tiago stood there on the rampart for quite a while with a frown on his face long after *Don* Manuel went down and rode out of the fort and headed back to the town.

Chapter Seven

"Miguel! Miguel! Come down quick!" Pedro's frantic yelling woke Miguel up from a deep slumber. He felt a little bit of irritation since he had not slept that well for a long time, but there was a sense of urgency bordering on panic from Pedro's voice, so reluctantly he stirred up from his bed, but still with eyes closed.

Miguel gingerly opened his eyes, squinting with difficulty as the sharp glare of the sun coming through the open window hit him squarely in the face. It was already mid-morning and the summer heat was in full swing. He closed his eyes, bracing himself on the bed as he felt a bit of dizziness hit him, and he felt the dampness on his pillow probably from sweat. He hoped he did not puke in his sleep.

"Miguel!!!" He heard Pedro yell again, this time clearly coming from the back yard.

"What now?" Miguel grumbled as he slowly got up, squinting hard as he tried to open his eyes again. A sudden stab of pain hit him in the head and he winced as he shut his eyes again. He felt around and found his crumpled trousers lying on the floor by his bed, put them on and went through the kitchen to the *bangsal* facing the backyard, forcing his eyes open and fighting the pain that came from looking into the brightness of day. He saw Pedro gesticulating wildly and shouting incoherently by the well, holding an empty pail in one hand and pointing at the old Tamarind tree beyond the well with the other. Miguel peered but could not see anything other than the thick branches and leaves and the wide trunk of the tree.

"What?" he yelled back at Pedro. "What's the matter?"

Pedro ran closer to the house, still holding the empty pail, the rope attached to it dragging behind like a long tail.

"Your dog," he said. "Come down. Co-co-come, see," he stammered nervously, waving a trembling hand toward the tree. He finally noticed the pail he was carrying, dropped it, and was about to turn back toward the backyard without waiting for Miguel's answer when he noticed something on Miguel's face.

"Miguel, are you alright?" he cried. "Are you hurt?"

"What?" Miguel said, "What did you say? Hurt? Who? Me?" He felt around on his head and face and felt nothing other than the pain coming inside his head from another hang-over. Puzzled, he looked at Pedro and noticed the darkening splotch of blood on his forehead and neck. "You!" he exclaimed. "What happened to you? You're bleeding!"

Pedro gave him a puzzled look and felt around his body and found no trace of blood. He was beginning to think that his *compadre* was still too drunk and was seeing things, but his hands went up to his forehead and neck, mimicking Miguel who was also patting his neck and forehead. Both of them felt something slightly wet and sticky and looked down at their hands smeared with traces of drying blood.

Miguel turned around and went into the living room and looked at himself in the mirror hanging on the wall. He gasped as he saw the dark crimson that was smeared on his forehead and on his throat, just like what he saw on Pedro. He went into the bedroom, and was about to pull a towel draped by the headboard when he noticed a pool of drying blood on and by his pillow. Frantically he groped around his head and neck and exhaled a sigh of relief when he did not find nor feel any wound.

"What the hell is going on?" he growled.

He picked up the pillow and angrily threw it on the floor. He grabbed the towel and stormed out of the bedroom, through the living room and kitchen and out of the *bangsal* down to the well in the backyard where Pedro was now pulling up a pail of water.

Pedro set the pail down over the well's rim and started splashing water on his face and neck, rubbing wildly to get the drying blood off.

"Put the pail down on the ground, you id..." Miguel was about to yell at Pedro for dripping bloody water into the well when he suddenly stopped, his eyes riveted on the trunk of the Tamarind tree.

His breath caught on his throat, anger rising from his chest as he saw Guardia, his dog, dangling from a limb with a rope around its neck, its eyes glazed open and tongue grotesquely sticking out between grinning teeth. He knew from the stiffed swaying of the body that it was dead.

"*¡Hijo-de-puta!*" he yelled instead then turned around and ran back up the stairs, got a knife from the kitchen, and went back down to the tree. Without a word, he held the rope and cut it, letting the dead dog fall gently by his feet.

Pedro silently watched by the well, the blood-stained water dripping all over his face and chest.

"I'm sorry, *compadre*," Pedro said weakly. "I came down to wash and I saw it there, already dead."

Miguel did not say anything, his attention on the carcass by his feet.

"It's them, Miguel. They followed me here," he heard Pedro say.

"What are you saying?" Miguel glanced up at Pedro.

"They did this, the people from Abra." Pedro was breathing in shallow nervous bursts. "This is a warning to you and me. We're going to be next."

"What? You're not making sense, Pedro."

"Miguel, I know it's them. I know the signs. Look," he pointed at the tree trunk.

Miguel turned around and noticed for the first time the arrow that was stuck on the trunk. He gave Pedro a quizzical look.

"I don't understand," he said, trying to remain calm. The anger that he was feeling now diffused with a tinge of uncertain fear.

"The people I was talking about, Miguel, they are my people too. I heard the rumors. Some of them are not happy with what we did. It's not just the *Generala*."

"But why? What do your people care about us, or the Spaniards, or Diego?"

"In a way, Diego was one of us, a member of the tribe."

"Diego had no *Itneg* blood in him!" Miguel yelled. "He was pure Ilocano!"

"T-t-true, but Gabriela…" Pedro stammered.

"What? I don't understand what you're trying to say, *amigo*, you've lost me." Miguel shook his head.

"It's not about Diego, or the Spaniards, Miguel," Pedro said. "It's Gabriela. She is also one of them, of us, I should say. Like me, her mother is *Itneg*."

"So? What does that have to do with Dieg…?" Miguel started to say but he did not finish as his face slowly showed the delayed realization of what Pedro was trying to tell him. It came back to him now, the rumors and the warnings from the older folks when he was growing up about the clannishness of the *Itnegs*. You aggrieve one and you go against the whole tribe. An Ilocano married to a member of the tribe becomes one of the tribe. He looked at Pedro dejectedly.

"But she was not harmed."

"No, but we took her husband away. We killed him."

"And you? Why are they after you? You are one of them!"

Pedro took a deep breath and sighed slowly as he exhaled. "Because I broke the law of the *budong*. I broke their trust. I betrayed not only a friend but also a token member of the tribe."

Miguel did not say a word, but inwardly cursed himself. How did he get into this mess? He tried to calm down, forcing himself to breathe regularly as he felt his heartbeat raced up considerably. He looked at the arrow in the tree and the dead dog by his feet and exhaled a labored sigh. At least he was still alive. They could have killed him and Pedro where they slept. He wondered why they did not.

"But they did not kill us," he said. "They could have killed us easily and nobody would have known who did it."

"Yes, I know," Pedro said. "This is just a warning perhaps to let us know that they can get to us at any time."

Miguel did not say anything. His eyes nervously floated and scanned the banana grove and the fruit trees beyond, unsure of what to look for, seeing everything yet not seeing anything.

'The damn *Itnegs* can't do anything with me,' he thought after a while. 'They can't just come down in town and harm a decent Christian who also happened to have Spanish blood. They would not dare.'

But as his eyes focused back on his dog, the noose of the rope still taut around its neck, its mouth grinning hideously, and now he saw also that its throat was slit open, he felt nauseous and totally uncertain at the thought especially when it occurred to him that whoever they were, they were in his own bedroom.

They could have easily slit his throat as they did to his dog. Involuntarily, his hand went to his neck.

He looked at Pedro. The fear was apparent in his friend's eyes. He hoped his own eyes did not betray the same feeling that was slowly and surely gripping him.

"I think it's time to see the *Capitán, amigo*." His voice trembled nervously. He was certain that his eyes mirrored the fear that he saw in Pedro's.

"Maybe I'll go up to Isabela for a while to see how my family's doing," Pedro solemnly replied. "I heard the weather's nice there this time of year."

Chapter Eight

At the foot of Mount *Bullagaw*, Kulas and Akash stopped and sat down to rest under a huge *Lomboy* tree, leaning their spears within easy reach against its thick trunk. They have been walking at a good pace since before the false dawn. The sun was already halfway up in its morning rise and they could feel the heat despite the shade of the trees.

The leaves were still, with not even a whisper of a breeze to cause them to flutter. Even the birds seemed to have been lulled to a stupor for there was no sound, or perhaps they had flown farther away, scared of the presence of the two men.

Despite of the numerous times he had been down to the Ilocos, Akash could never get accustomed to its humid climate. He was sweating profusely and his *ba-ag* was sticking to his tired behind. He looked at his companion and noted that Kulas who had not been to the place seemed to be taking it well. He was walking along gracefully, as if he was just sauntering into the village after a dip in the river, and now as he sat down, showed no sign of discomfort. But then again, it seemed nothing ever bothered him. Or if something did, no one would ever know because his expression rarely changed. Akash had stopped wondering a long time ago how his friend did it, or what he was thinking for that matter.

And the man must have been running hard the day before yesterday when he caught up to him before he got to the town. Yet here he was, looking as fresh as if he just came from a swim in the river.

He snapped a couple of leafy branches from a small bush within his reach, arranged them on the grassy ground and lay down on his back, exhaling contentedly as his bare back settled down on the makeshift leafy mat. He squinted against the glare of the sunlight that came through the shade and closed his eyes.

"Where are you going?" he said as he felt Kulas stood up. If there was one thing Akash was certain about his friend, he knew that Kulas could barely keep still in one place for a spell.

"Food," Kulas said as he walked away without looking at his friend. He had noted some wild jicama vines nearby. The deeper green coloring on the leaves of some of them showed some promise of mature bulbs underneath.

He poked around the bushes and found a clump of the wild vines to his liking. He took out his dagger and tentatively scraped the soil around a thick vine, careful not to cut the tube when he got it exposed. It proved to be bigger than he expected. The soil was soft and loamy around these parts, suitable for all kinds of tubers and fruit trees and it took him no time to pull out the first one. He dug out a few more, and with a handful in hand, went back to where Akash was contentedly sleeping.

Sitting underneath the tree, his bare back comfortably resting against the gnarly trunk, Kulas looked at his sleeping friend with amusement. He had always wondered how Akash could sleep so easily and so fast at any place and any time of the day.

He put down the jicamas on the ground before him, pulled out a clump of grass by his side and wiped off the dirt from one of the bigger tubers. He nonchalantly peeled the skin off exposing the white flesh and took a bite a little too eagerly as his mouth started to water in anticipation of the taste of the succulent fruit. It did not disappoint. It was juicy and crisp at the same time and he munched noisily, savoring the fruit with relish. The crunching noise of his bite and his chewing made a big sound in the stillness of the forest.

Akash opened one eye, awakened by the noise, and squinted up at Kulas.

"Are you going to share, you bastard?" he said, raising a hand over his open eye to cover it from the glare of the bright sky. His other hand went to his stomach as it started to growl at the thought of food.

Kulas laughed. "I thought you were asleep."

"I was, but you were so noisy with your chomping a body couldn't get some quiet moment."

"No noise had ever bothered you before, 'times you want to sleep."

"Not when I'm hungry at the same time," Akash smiled as he slowly rose up to a sitting position.

Kulas threw him a couple of the tubers before he was fully up.

For a person who just woke up, Akash was fast. He deftly caught both tubers, one in each hand, and flashed a big grin at Kulas, but it quickly turned into an open-mouthed surprise as Kulas flicked a third one that hit him squarely on the chest.

Kulas snickered as he shook his head in mock disgust.

Deep down, Akash knew that his friend was hysterically laughing inside at his expense. He did not mind. They did this all the time. Only difference was that he laughed more openly. And a lot louder.

He picked the tuber that rolled off his chest, stood up and went down to sit by Kulas, peeling and biting as he did so.

"They're good," Akash said. "Glad you found some. I was getting hungry."

"So you slept?"

"Of course. I knew you're going to get food anyways."

"Of course you do." Kulas said. He was into his second jicama. The juicy fruit felt good going down.

"Hey, it's too hot to hunt for meat." Akash finished off his jicama and started peeling another. "Besides, fruit's a lot better when it's hot like this."

"Yeah, sure," Kulas said taking another bite.

They ate contentedly without talking for a while, the silence broken down only by their noisy chewing. After some time, Akash wiped his chin with the back of his hand, stretched them upward and arched his back, rolled his shoulders then relaxed. He wiped his hands off the grass by his side.

"We should have just killed them as I intended instead of the dog," he said.

"I was thinking about that," Kulas said after swallowing what he was chewing.

"Killing them or the dog?"

"The dog. That was a waste of good meat."

Akash looked at Kulas but as usual he was not sure if his friend was joking or not. Kulas looked back at him without any expression in his face. Then he took a bite and looked away, his eyes trailing a young eagle playing on a wind vortex high above the trees. It tried to go against the draft, flapping its wings furiously, then as if suddenly struck by a wise realization, settled and spread its wings serenely and glided with the current in a lazy, tightening, downward loop.

"No, seriously," Akash said, following Kulas's eyes but found the eagle uninteresting. He turned his attention back to Kulas. "Why did we not kill them? Nobody would have known it was us!"

Kulas did not say a word. Perhaps Akash was right. Perhaps they should have killed the bastards, but somehow it did not feel right at the time.

After leaving Dagyo, Kulas had caught up with Akash a few kilometers from the town but failed to talk his friend out into going back to the village with him.

"I have to see Awad," Akash had said, "to give word from Ama." But Kulas saw that there was something else in his friend's eyes. He had seen it before and he did not like it because he knew his friend was about to release the black dogs in his heart and throw all caution into the wind; and Akash had made up his mind and it was pointless to talk him out of it. Perhaps that was what Dagyo had seen also.

And they were right because Akash had been seething with rage since he got word of Diego's death. He had grown to like and respect Ilang's husband for Diego had always treated him with kindness and respect. He had vowed

77

to avenge Diego's death and he was on his way to fulfill that vow. He had waited for so long. Diego had been killed almost two months ago, or perhaps three, he had lost count of the days. He liked Kulas's company but this was something he wanted to do alone. Yet it seemed that Kulas had somehow divined his intent and he felt his friend was not going to leave him on his own.

"I'll go with you then," Kulas said but there was reluctance in his heart. He had no second thoughts about going through with whatever trouble Akash might get into. What bothered him was that he was not sure of what he would do if he saw Ilang in the town, in case she showed up to see her mother.

"No," Akash insisted. "This is something I have to do alone."

Kulas almost left gladly but they were so close to town that he resolutely buried his fear of meeting Ilang again. And there was just something in Akash's elusive eyes that he could not ignore and he knew he could not leave his friend to deal with his demons alone.

"I'm coming with you," he said. "I did not come all this way just to go back now. Besides I want to see the houses of the Ilocanos and how they live."

He turned toward the town before Akash could say another word. Akash wisely followed. He knew too well the futility of arguing with Kulas once he made up his mind, just like him.

They reached Awad's place without incident. Gabriela was not there and Kulas breathed a great sigh of relief, yet at the same time he felt a tinge of dismay. Gabriela had been gone for a while, Awad said. She was on the run; hunted constantly by the Guardia Civiles. It was very unlikely that she would show up in town any time soon.

Kulas left the siblings to talk in private and he walked around Awad's neighborhood for most of the day, taking in stride the curious stares of the Ilocanos, especially the children who openly gawked and followed him. He ignored them and went around warily taking in everything he could, putting especially the lay of the land to memory.

He found the narrow river and followed it into the town until he saw the walls of the fort. The river flowed close to the fort's southwestern wall, providing a natural barrier. Kulas reversed his hold on his spear which he was using as a staff, and had the tip pointed down now into the water as he walked by the riverbank getting closer toward the fort, seemingly looking for fish but taking in the fort and the guards on top of its walls at the same time. They would not be all guards, he thought, as he noticed most of the dozen or so soldiers were just standing around, curiously looking at the river and now their attention was on him.

He stopped and lingered on the riverbank when he was opposite the fort from its southern side and made a show of peering into the water as if he was intently looking for fish, his spear poised on the ready. He made some half-hearted stabbing gestures into the water aiming at nothing in particular. Then he noticed a clump of water lilies a few feet further ahead and he headed toward it. He had a better view of another side of the fort from this angle. He stopped, scanned the river and the fort beyond it, taking everything in, then a moving shadow flashed in the periphery of his vision. He reflexively thrust his spear and it pierced through the water lily leaf that caught his attention. He felt the faint vibration of the staff as the tip of the spear hit something. He quickly pulled it up and suppressed a big grin as he saw a big dalag flapping wildly at the spear's tip, futilely trying to break free.

Kulas heard a faint roar from across the river and looking up, he saw the soldiers hooting and clapping in appreciation, pointing at him and the fish that now hung limply from the spear. He raised the spear up in triumph for the benefit of the soldiers who were all looking down at the naked Itneg fishing with his spear below. Kulas laughed at the serendipity of it all, and made a desultory bow toward the soldiers. He waved his arm tentatively when he looked back up and then turned around toward the town.

Kulas felt a little annoyance at the attention he received for he did not wish to be too conspicuous when he decided to get closer to the fort. But like he said to Dagyo, they did stick up like a sore thumb in the lowlands. There was simply no going around that fact.

By the time he made his way back to Awad's house, he knew the best ways to get in, around, and out of the town. And most of all get into the fort if he had to.

Akash filled him in on what was going on with Awad and her daughter and finally revealed his intention of avenging Diego's death. Kulas wanted to talk Akash out of it but he saw the determination in his friend's eyes and so he reluctantly agreed for them to go see the man who killed Ilang's husband.

They left Awad in the afternoon telling her they were going back up to the village. They refused the food she insisted for them to bring, easing her worries by saying they were going to hunt along the way. They knew she needed the food more than they did.

Then they proceeded to the next town where the man lived. They waited by the woods outside of town until darkness fell, then as the noises in the town vanished in the middle of the night going into early morning, they moved in. Akash had been in and around the lowlands so many times that he knew where most people lived, especially this man whom he had wanted dead.

Kulas was sorry now they had to kill the dog. It started to growl and bark when they approached the house. Kulas did not know then but perhaps the men, for they found two, inside the house were too drunk to have had even noticed the dog's noise. But they had to do what had to be done. Akash shot it with an arrow before Kulas could whistle to calm the dog down. His friend seemed intent to kill anything that moved.

They went into the house without any trouble. Akash had his knife out and was about to do what he had planned all along. He could not contain his pleasure when he realized that the other man was the traitor Pedro Becbec. But Kulas held him back, shaking his head. Somehow he did not feel right killing sleeping men. And dead drunk too.

"Not this way," Kulas said, taking the knife out of Akash's hand. He led the seething Akash, who reluctantly followed without giving much of a resistance, out of the house.

Akash curiously watched as Kulas walked over to the dead dog and pulled the arrow out from the carcass then silently took out his short knife and slit the dog's throat, collecting the blood that oozed out into the coconut shell that served as food bowl for the dog. Kulas then set the bowl aside when the blood flowed into a trickle. Looking around, he saw the piece of rope that was obviously used at times to tie the dog to the post of the raised house. He made a noose and slipped it over the dog's head and dragged the carcass and strung it up the tamarind tree behind the house. As the dog dangled, he went back to where Akash stood rooted by the house, picked the arrow that he removed from the dog and stuck it into the tree trunk.

Akash watched without saying a word, wondering what his friend was up to. He watched as Kulas finally picked up the bowl of blood, signaled for Akash to stay where he was and stand guard, pointing at his own eyes with his extended middle and forefinger and went back up into the house. He came down after a moment with his hands soaked in blood.

"Did you kill them?" Akash whispered.

"No. Let us not start a war with the Ilocanos," Kulas said as they walked away from the house

They had not said much after that. Akash still bristled with anger every now and then for leaving the men alive as they walked in silence. He finally cold off as Kulas went on as if nothing happened. He could never understand his friend. There was no point in trying to explain him or whatever he did.

Yet he trusted him fully.

"I was thinking about that, too," Kulas finally said with a slight twitch in his mouth, his eyes still on the eagle. "I want them dead too, as much as you do, but I want them to suffer a little bit more."

80

Akash raised an eyebrow. "So you let them live? I don't understand."

"Yes, but think about this," Kulas said, his eyes still following the flight of the eagle which had abandoned the draft and was now gliding over a copse of trees, surveying the ground below for prey. 'Hunger winning over play,' he thought. He cast his eyes sideways at Akash leaving the young eagle to its hunting.

"They'll be constantly looking over their shoulders even when we're not there. No more peace for them, Akash. They'll be on edge all the time. They wouldn't know who are after them and when they strike. Believe me that is worse than dying. Besides, when the time comes, I want them to know that they are going to die. Last night, they were too drunk to care one way or the other."

Akash met his friend's eyes with mouth open trying to digest what he just heard. There was a tone in his friend's voice that told him Kulas was deadly serious. He nodded tentatively and took another bite, chewing pensively. He was not sure what his friend really meant nor did he totally agree with him, but he nodded his head. He trusted Kulas completely.

"Don't worry about it, Akash, you'll know when they will die," Kulas continued as if talking to himself, his eyes again searching for the young eagle. He could no longer see it. It had vanished from the sky.

He sighed, sensing the tightness in his body from sitting down. He stood up and stretched, rolling his neck and shoulders, relishing the popping sounds as the kinks loosened.

"Let's go," he said grabbing his spear that was leaning against the tree trunk. "We should be home by nightfall if we hurry."

"Aaargghhh!" Akash blurted, reluctantly rising up and scrambling after his friend who was already at least ten paces away. He could walk all day if needed but not at the pace that Kulas was holding.

They walked steadily for hours without resting, talking about everything that came to their mind, gabbing about nothing. Akash had finally settled down as they trudged along. Then as they caught sight of the village, Kulas stopped, turned back and waited for Akash to catch up as he was at least a good fifty paces behind.

"Go on home ahead," he said. "I am going up the mountain for a couple of days. Don't tell them I went down to the town with you, except for Dagyo."

"What?" Akash said catching his breath. "Why?"

"Nothing. They don't need to know I was with you and I just want to see something up there," Kulas said, pointing up toward the mountain top. "Maybe come down with meat or something. Just remember you were by yourself." He turned around and went up an unseen trail before Akash could respond.

Akash looked at his friend's back as he disappeared behind the trees. He knew better than to say anything or follow. Kulas came and went as he pleased and he was in his vanishing mood again.

He moved hastily toward the village, eager to get there, looking forward to a long, lazy dip in the river before dinner.

He started to jog then ran at a steady leisurely pace, surprised that he was breathing easily. He decided to leave the trail and took the shorter distance that went through a couple of small ditches gorged by the rains in previous monsoons. He took the first smaller ditch with an easy leap, flying over it smoothly like he used to do when he was a kid. Nothing to it, he thought, a wisp of a smile crossing his face as he resumed his steady gait. He was feeling good. He sprinted faster as he approached the second wider ditch, leaping with confidence, grinning proudly as he sailed easily over the more than ten foot gap.

He landed on the other side and found himself falling as his left foot hit and rolled against a coconut-sized stone hidden underneath the grass.

He hobbled to the village the rest of the way. There was no dip in the river when he got there past dinner time.

His foot had swollen to almost twice its size and the pain was bothering him too much even as he tried not to show it in his face.

His wife, Pol-looy took one look at his ankle, shook her head without saying a word and went to the kitchen. She came out later with a warmed piece of cloth and some foul smelling poultice that Akash did not dare to ask what it was made of. When Pol-looy was not talking it was best also to remain silent.

The poultice was cold and soothing as she applied it over the swollen ankle and the warmth of the cloth as she wrapped it around added a different sensation that somehow diminished the pain. Akash hoped it would diminish the swelling too because he could barely breathe from the smell.

But he kept his thoughts to himself. He knew better not to open his mouth. Pol-looy had not said a word the whole time, not even when she went back to the kitchen to look after dinner.

Chapter Nine

"Isn't there something familiar with that *Itneg*, Tiago?" *Capitán* Manuel had said as he watched Kulas casually walk away from the river holding the spear with the fish limply dangling from its tip.

"What do you mean, *Capitán*?" Tiago said, surprised when Manuel suddenly spoke by his side. He did not notice him come up the wall. He looked at the back of the *Itneg* getting smaller in the distance, his wrinkled face showing more lines as it turned into a deep frown.

"There was something familiar with him, Tiago. His walk, the way he moved and the way he handled that spear." The *Capitán* mused as if in deep thought. "We've seen him before."

Tiago looked at him then looked back at the *Itneg* who had vanished from their view.

"Pardon me, *Capitán*, but those savages all look the same to me," he said.

"You did not look closely, Tiago," Manuel said. "That man you call a savage is far from one. There's something regal in him."

'Heat must have finally gotten into him,' Tiago thought as he looked at his captain as if the man had gone crazy, but Manuel ignored him. His eyes were still riveted at the place where Kulas had disappeared.

"I have known and grown among the nobles back home, Tiago, and believe me that man is more noble than most of them," he said softly. Then he looked at the *Sargento*. "Yes, I am certain now, we've met him before, Tiago. You and I fought him in a mock battle. Remember, maybe three, four years back in Abra." He turned his back before Tiago could say anything. He need not remind the old man what the *Itneg* had done to both of them.

Tiago watched Manuel walk away, his mouth open, not saying the words he wanted to say, his eyes reflecting the delayed realization of what the captain had just said.

And it all came back to him, that day more like five years ago not three or four as the *Capitán* recalled. They had just been in the region for a couple of years and had not yet learned the dialect. Had it been that long? Time really did fly in this place.

He sat there nonchalantly on the side of the trail, his back resting snuggly against a boulder that went up a palm's width over his head. He would have been just one of the Ilocanos in the valley hunched before an early morning fire in the yard, warming himself up before heading out to the fields, except for the fact that he was wearing nothing but a band on his head and a ba-ag covering his loins. And he was sitting in the forest, surrounded by majestic trees that towered above the trail. Also beside him, propped against the boulder, was a mean looking spear, its metal tip pointed upwards, menacingly glinting in the sunlight that filtered through the trees. His face showed neither a look of surprise nor fear as the mounted soldiers drew up.

Don Manuel who was riding point hesitated briefly and cast a glance at Tiago who had slowly rode up beside him, ready to take orders or protect his captain if needed.   But there was not a hint of malice in the Itneg's demeanor. If at all he affected a disinterested mien, just casting a casual look at the approaching horsemen, like he saw them pass this way every day. He did not move as Don Manuel and his troop drew nearer, nor did he attempt to rise from his position. He sat there on his haunches, arms resting easily on his knees, his back pressed lightly against the boulder. Only his eyes moved as they darted furtively among the riders and their mounts, lingering finally on the face of Don Manuel, whom he regarded correctly as their leader not only due to his more regal uniform but mainly because of the way he carried his considerable form.

"Buenos dias," Don Manuel said stopping a few paces from the man, an Itneg no doubt, the dominant mountain tribe in Abra. The man did not respond, his expression not changing, showing neither comprehension nor disregard of Don Manuel's words. After a moment he nodded his head briefly, his eyes meeting Don Manuel's stare, yet he remained seated.

"Why, the impertinent pagan!" Don Manuel heard Tiago curse under his breath and felt him nudge his horse forward, no doubt his hand on his sword. He raised his hand without turning his head, his eyes holding the man's eyes, and he felt Tiago's horse stop.

"Relax, Tiago. Calma te. The man is not alone." Don Manuel had not seen any other man, but he felt there were more men in the shadows of the trees. No man would be so brave or so stupid to face a band of unknown horsemen alone, he figured.

Tiago and the rest of the troop looked uneasily around them but they saw no one or any sign of anybody else's presence.

"There's nobody else out there, Capitán," Tiago said.

"Tiago, listen," Don Manuel said.

"I hear nothing," Tiago replied.

"Exactly." Don Manuel looked around nodding his head.

Tiago frowned, but he remembered a day back in Santo Domingo, a long time ago when the Capitán was still a young soldier and the Capitán had said the same thing then, just before they were attacked by the Caribs.

"The birds, Tiago, and the small animals, the monkeys, they're not around. Something spooked them."

Tiago nodded in understanding. Perhaps the Capitán was right again, but it did not matter. Surrounded or not, he could easily kill the impertinent Itneg if he had to before anyone of his companions can do something with their primitive spears.

The man looked between Tiago and the Capitán, his eyes now showing a faint trace of amusement despite not understanding a word they said. He read signs well, be it on the ground or in the faces of men. No words were needed to show that the riders were puzzled with his presence and were surely debating whether he was alone or there were others among the trees. He understood their dilemma and seemed to take pleasure in it.

Don Manuel kneed his horse forward. His troop followed closely covering his back. He stopped a few feet from the man who still had not moved, still watching now with an amused look in his face.

"I am Don Manuel of the King's army of Spain. We're not looking for trouble. We're just passing through on our way to visit our garrison in Abra." With all the trees and the topography looking the same to him as soon as they left the scraggly plains of Nueva Segovia a day ago, Don Manuel was not certain whether they were already within the boundaries of the mountainous sitio of Vigan they called Abra.

The man looked up at Don Manuel, his eyes lighting up at the word 'Abra.' He finally stirred, rising up smoothly without using either the boulder or his spear for support. He nodded at Don Manuel, grabbed his spear with his right hand, turned around and headed up the trail. He raised his left hand and gestured forward without looking back, motioning for them to follow. It was more a command and not an invitation from the way he moved. Don Manuel was intrigued and decided to play along. Subconsciously he felt a tinge of admiration for the Itneg who moved with the confidence of someone who had seen the future and was not the least afraid of it.

"Let's follow but stay alert. Don't do anything without my command," he said as he nudged his horse forward after the Itneg. His troop warily followed in formation behind him. They had but gone a few paces when shadows silently emerged from behind the trees and the undergrowth like dark wraiths, until they formed, discernible, bare-chested men covered only in loincloths, holding either a spear or a bow with an arrow nocked on the string. They also had long and short knives strapped on their waists, their scabbards made of wood, and open on the outside that one can see the glinting metals they held. And slung across their backs were bamboo quivers stuffed with arrows, the fowl feathers bunched so closely that they looked like a bouquet of flowers instead of lethal messengers of death. The wraiths walked silently among the trees by the trail, flanking and keeping pace with the soldiers.

The Capitán was right as usual, Tiago thought, his right hand resting casually on the hilt of his sword. Surprisingly he was not nervous at all. He would take a bunch of these pagans with him before he went down, he promised himself, if it came down to a fight. He knew that all his men shared the same thought. He wondered though about their bows and arrows. He had fought with the Ilocanos and he never had to worry about bows and arrows. He was worried now for he was sure these Itnegs knew how to use the bow from the familiar way they held them like it was part of their body.

They marched silently for about an hour. Don Manuel entertained the thought of putting his sword between the bare shoulders of the warrior who fearlessly walked before him and let his men wreak havoc on the rest of the savages but his curiosity took the better of him and he held his martial instincts in check. He wanted to find out what the natives were up to, and perhaps, he could learn something that would be of use to his troops in the future.

Finally the Itneg in the lead slowed down as they approached an open space, where a lone tree stood by a slow flowing brook. An old man who was tending a fire over which spits of wild chicken and fishes were being roasted and grilled, rose up and faced them. From around the tree by the bank, two young boys came up carrying a string of freshly caught fish between them, and stood by the old man.

The smell of grilling meat hit Don Manuel's nose and he suddenly felt hungry. Breakfast seemed a long time ago although the sun had not reached the summit yet. So this is their camp, he thought, as he realized they were with a hunting party. Around the camp he saw several strips of venison drying on makeshift racks made out of bamboo sticks and tree branches. From underneath the tree, a majestic mahogany, a couple of deer carcasses were in the process of being cleaned and gutted.

The old man spoke in concise guttural sounds to the young Itneg who was the apparent leader of the hunters. He replied in like manner, waving his hand in the process. Then he beckoned to one of the boys, who moved forward with a big grin on his face.

"Buenos dias, Señores, welcome to our camp," the boy said.

"Muchas gracias," Don Manuel mumbled, too surprised to hear the boy spoke so fluently in Spanish.

"I'll be darned," Tiago exclaimed behind him, "a savage who speaks the King's language!"

"I spent some years down in the valley, Señor, and a good priest taught me the language," the boy said ignoring Tiago's remark. "My name is Sadang but the Padre, he named me Santiago when he baptized me."

"Bless the good Padre for his excellent taste in names!" Tiago exclaimed and the rest of the soldiers laughed. "I am named after the good Saint myself!"

The boy did not answer but bowed politely. Then he turned to the old man who had asked him a question and explained why the soldiers laughed at Tiago's remarks. The old man shrugged. He did not think it was funny.

Don Manuel got off his horse and introduced himself and Tiago, and waved to his troops to get down.

"Welcome to our camp, Señor. We are pleased to share our food with you," Sadang said, after a word from the old man. He then introduced the old man, Apo Dalalo, and the leader of the hunters, Kulas, who was the old man's son. The boy Santiago confirmed what Don Manuel suspected that they were a hunting party.

"You are a long way from Vigan, Señor," Sadang said after conferring at length with the old man and Kulas.

"True," Don Manuel answered but his eyes were on Kulas and the old man as they sat close to one another by the fire. "We had been out for three days now, on our way to our garrison in Bucay. It's just a routine visit to see how things are and bring in some supplies to the soldiers stationed there at the same time." He indicated the packhorses that were now grazing on the lush grass that grew near the banks of the brook. The rest of the troop had dismounted and were washing their arms and faces in the shallow water. Some of them held on to their horses as they let them drink their fill then let them graze in the clearing by the water below the camp.

"We are not looking for trouble and we hope we don't get into one," Don Manuel continued as Kulas and the old man talked softly between them after Sadang translated. "We plan to get to the fort shortly, stay there for a couple of days, give a chance for us and our horses to rest, then go back to Vigan. We'll try to get out of your way going back so we don't disrupt your hunting, and I apologize if we inadvertently did so today."

Sadang translated Don Manuel's words and Kulas waved his hand in dismissal, uttering a few words. Apo Dalalo nodded his head in agreement to whatever Kulas said.

"Neither do we seek trouble, Señor," Sadang said, translating what Kulas said. "And you did not disrupt anything. We have had enough hunting done in these parts and will pull out camp after today. Apo wishes you to share our food for lunch then you can go on your way if you wish. We don't want to detain you any longer."

"We thank you for your hospitality and please convey my gratitude to your elders." Don Manuel looked around to address his men and noted that the Itnegs were openly curious at the weaponry and uniforms of the soldiers, some with metal breastplates, touching them respectfully after asking permission from their owners through hand gestures. The soldiers cautiously let them, but with their hands close to the hilts of their swords. Most of the Itnegs though were gathered around the horses, laughing nervously among themselves when one or so of the horses shied away as the more daring of the natives ventured close enough and attempt to touch the magnificent beasts.

Don Manuel whispered to Tiago who stood up with a smile on his face. He bowed ceremoniously to Kulas and Apo Dalalo then went to a group of soldiers who were in the process of stripping their saddles to give their horses a good rub down. He talked to a couple of the soldiers who in turn nodded and smiled. They stopped from unsaddling their horses and re-cinched them and waited while Tiago went back to the fireside.

"Sadang, please tell your people not to be alarmed as two of my men, Manzano and Azada, will show you what they can do with their horses," Tiago said as he stood by Don Manuel. Sadang stood up and made the announcement which was greeted enthusiastically by the Itnegs.

After the uproar died down, Tiago yelled. "Now, muchachos, race to the edge of the forest then come back with your swords swinging but don't cut one another or we will leave you here!"

"Watch, hombre, and you may learn something," Azada said to Tiago as he stepped nimbly unto his mount, having taken off his armor a few moments beforehand.

"I doubt if the old perro would ever learn anything new," Manzano shouted back as he likewise mounted and sped off, leaving Azada scrambling to catch up.

"¡Puñeta!" Azada yelled amidst the laughter and heckling of his fellow soldiers. He spurred his horse after Manzano. The Itnegs watched in awe as the two raced wildly to the far end of the clearing. The horses were natural runners and they let go, eating the distance quickly and easily with flawless rhythm, jumping gracefully over the low bushes along the way. The riders turned around almost as one as they reached the tree line, and then they drew their swords, slashing at one another, without slowing down their horses as they rode back to the group. The sound of steel against steel and the drumming of hoof beats mingled resonantly with the boisterous yelling and clapping from both the natives and the soldiers, making the camp an impromptu site of a martial contest. The two combatants displayed such magnificent horsemanship and skill with their swords that the Itnegs looked at one another in awe as the two riders drew closer.

As they got near the bank of the brook, Azada and Manzano jumped simultaneously from their horses, landed on their feet with their swords still out and swinging to the delight of their audience. They fought on the ground, giving and taking measured attacks and parries and finally stopped in a draw with an appreciative clapping of the natives and teasing from the other soldiers who shouted their mocked criticisms all in good fun.

Don Manuel noted that neither Kulas nor the old man showed overt reaction to the exercise yet they watched attentively, their faces inscrutable, neither showing awe nor amusement. He was not certain if they were impressed or not.

"Perhaps you want to try to ride one of the horses," Don Manuel said as Kulas met his gaze. Sadang translated.

Kulas looked at Apo Dalalo who shrugged his shoulders. Kulas likewise shrugged in the same fashion, leaving little doubt in Don Manuel's mind that both men came from the same blood pool.

Kulas untied the rope that held his sheathed long knife and handed it to Sadang. Then slowly, he walked to where the horses were grazing, his eyes scanning the herd, finally focusing on a big unsaddled chestnut with his head down on the grass, its reins loosely trailing on the ground. The horse's head was away from Kulas and it was not aware of his presence until he was on top of it as he ran and jumped on its back when he was just a few feet away.

The soldiers were watching attentively as they noted his approach knowing that the big chestnut was a spirited one and ridden exclusively by Gomez, the horse wrangler, who was yelling for Kulas to stop while the soldiers by his side held him back, anticipating an entertaining and perhaps humbling experience for the daring Itneg.

Kulas grabbed the long mane of the horse with his left hand as soon as he landed on its back, then in one fluid motion he lay low and flat, almost sliding down its right flank as he reached down for the reins. The horse was just so stunned to react quickly enough until after Kulas had the reins in his hand, but true to its reputation, the chestnut reared and jumped, and twisted around as it landed in an effort to rid itself of its unknown rider. Kulas clamped his legs around the horse, anticipating its movement and miraculously stayed on top. He kneed it forward as it landed, and to everyone's surprise the horse lunged forward and settled to a swift run, instinctively responding to an authoritative handler. What no one knew was the fact that Kulas was a natural rider and could stay on top of anything with four hooves. In his youth he used to creep on wild deer and goats and ride them bareback until he got dislodged when they ran into the bushes. He always explained the cuts and bruises with a story of falling from trees while picking their fruit. He did not know if the old man ever believed him but he finally stopped asking when he came home bruised more often than not after going up the mountains. Then when he got older, he turned to wild horses that were plentiful in the valleys of Abra. But they preferred to walk up in the mountains so he never kept one. Besides, horses were useless in the places he loved to go.

Kulas let the horse go down the open stretch into the forest where it slowed down to a canter. He patted its neck, calming the horse down, as he turned it around and headed back toward the camp in a slow gait, enjoying a leisurely ride. He let the horse prance around as it reached the other horses which had gone back to grazing, as if they were not interested in the sudden activity of one of them running off with a strange rider. Kulas jumped off the horse nimbly as he led it to the water, let it drink, patting its neck lovingly as he led it back to where it was grazing. The soldiers whistled and clapped their appreciation as Kulas went back to the fireside.

"I see you have ridden before," Don Manuel said.

"Some," Kulas replied after waiting word from Sadang. "Nice horse."

"You know how to pick them," Don Manuel said admiringly.

"He surely does," Tiago added, grinning and shaking his head in disbelief at what he had seen.

Kulas did not say anything. He nodded to them, stood up and went to the water to wash and drink. The ride had made him thirsty.

The old man shouted an order and some of the hunters moved toward the deer carcass and pretty soon the smell of more grilled meat, seasoned with sweet smelling herbs, and grilled sweet potatoes filled the air. It was a sumptuous feast for the hungry soldiers, and both parties loosened up as the lunch stretched on for a good part of the day as the Spaniards took over the cooking for a while and treated their hosts with their own impromptu version of tapas in the forest. In the spirit of good will and bonhomie, Don Manuel ordered a small cask of wine to be opened from one of the pack-horses, and the mood became more festive and turned raucous as the soldiers engaged the natives in animated conversation by way of creative hand gestures. The poor Sadang ran all over the place as his services was very much in demand to resolve apparent miscommunications, but everyone was in a good mood that any misunderstanding was taken in good humor with both parties laughing about it once Sadang cleared it up. And the sun crept on silently across the sky above unnoticed as everyone had a good time.

Then by mid-afternoon, the natives started playfully wrestling with one another, but they did it with so much skill that the soldiers watched in fascination. But the matches became more intense and more competitive with the wrestlers going after one another with abandon, raising dusts where they grappled and fell, sometimes with a sickening thud yet they did not seem to get hurt.

The soldiers were certain a real fight would surely break out with the intensity the sport had turned into but they were surprised when every time a hard fought match ended, the combatants would grasp each other's arms, speak to one another and part amicably to take their seats and watch as another pair took their place. This went on for a while with the hunters so engrossed in their game that they paid no attention to the soldiers who were relegated to enthusiastic spectators.

Then as suddenly as it had begun, the wrestling stopped when there were no more volunteers. But then one of the more playful Itnegs, Bel-leng, motioned old Tiago to wrestle with him. Tiago laughed and raised his hand, shaking his head, indicating he had no desire to engage in a wrestling match, pointing to his knees and shaking them in jest, hobbling around in a pitiful imitation of a very old man, then perched himself on top of the log, exaggeratingly massaging his knees.

The Itnegs and some of the soldiers laughed gleefully, but some of the more raucous Spaniards started egging Tiago.

"C'mon, Sargento, show them how it's done in Barcelona!" Castillo yelled and the rest of the soldiers boisterously voiced their agreement.

"You do it then, bastardo!" Tiago yelled back. "And I am not from Barcelona. Barcelona has got nothing on my Compostela!" He eased down to the ground from the log and settled his back against it, stretching his legs in front of him, making a show of crossing his ankles. He was comfortable and he was not moving especially to participate in a sport where any of his old bones may be broken. He crossed his arms on his chest and smiled contentedly.

But Castillo and the rest of the soldiers would not be denied. They did not stop their boisterous egging.

"C'mon, Tiago. Show them you barroom tricks!" Manzano yelled.

"Yeah, Sargento, you can beat them Indios with one hand tied behind your back!" Bautista added.

"Just pull the loin cloth off and he will surrender!" Leandro, a Basque, shouted and followed with a bellowing laugh. The others laughed wholeheartedly, the Itnegs laughing with them despite having no idea what the white men were so crazily laughing about.

"Don't tell me you're scared, Viejo!" Castillo shouted loudly above the uproar.

"C'mon, Sargento!" the rest of the soldiers yelled in unison.

91

"Shut up, you ignorant bastardos, settle down!!" Tiago finally yelled in consternation. He slowly and reluctantly raised himself up from the ground, cursing himself for getting dragged into all the foolishness. He stretched his back with exaggerated effort like he was in pain. Might as well play the fool, he thought, smiling inwardly. He took off his helmet and unbuckled his sword and put them on the log.

The soldiers roared their approval, yelling, whistling and clapping their hands. The hunters joined in the ruckus, likewise yelling and stomping their feet, some of them patting Bel-leng on the back and giving him last minute instructions, anticipating a good wrestling match.

But Tiago raised his arms signaling for everyone to settle down. He scratched his head, looked around, and headed toward the brook. The soldiers roared their displeasure but Tiago ignored them. He may be old but he was no fool. He was not about to go wrestling with a sweating, buck-naked Indio. His Madre, God rest her soul, did not raise a stupid son.

He strolled to a patch by the water's edge where there was an abundant growth of straight inch-thick saplings. He pulled his dagger and cut two straight growths. He trimmed the leaves and small twigs off, measured and cut them equally to about a yard long. He put his dagger back in its sheath and went back toward the group holding the sticks in each hand. The soldiers nodded their heads and grunted, some of them loudly voicing their oohhs and aahhs, as they began to understand what Tiago was up to. Don Manuel smiled. Leave it to the old fox to come up with something where he could not be dirtied and bested.

Tiago stopped in front of Bel-leng, pointed to his sword on the log and to the long knife of one of the hunters, raised both sticks and handed one to the hunter who was now nodding his head and exhibiting a wide grin. There was no need for Sadang to interpret.

Of course, if the white man wanted to play with knives instead of wrestling, Bel-leng was more than willing to show his skills with the long knife. He accepted the stick, tested it by taking a few quick swings away from Tiago, nodded his head in appreciation and faced Tiago, teeth flashing in the sun in a still wider grin.

The hunters hooted and the soldiers clapped and whistled in approval. Tiago unflappably made a ceremonious bow. He raised his stick in a mock salute and started circling his opponent, making a show of it like he was hesitant to attack, uncertain of what to do next.

Bel-leng kept track of his circling opponent, his stick in a defensive stance, pivoting warily in place as he followed Tiago's movements. He wanted so badly to initiate the attack but he waited patiently for the white man to make the first move. He was certain he can move more quickly than the old man.

Tiago finally stopped and made tentative thrusts which Bel-leng parried easily. Bel-leng countered also but with such speed that Tiago had to retreat hurriedly to the delight of the hunters.

The old soldier smiled and shook his head at Bel-leng. Naughty boy, don't do that again. Bel-leng kept his grin. He was enjoying it. He was confident he could handle the old man with either one or two sticks. Aside from wrestling, the boys in the village grew up playing stick fighting, but they used two sticks, not one.

The two poked, slashed and parried tentatively for a while, neither one seemingly eager to best the other, simply contented in probing the range of the other's skill. There was an apparent difference in technique as Tiago used his stick like a foil while Bel-leng mostly slashed, using his like the one-side edged long knife that he used in actual combat.

With the seemingly polite give and take that they accorded one another, they seemed to be evenly matched that the oohs and aahs of the spectators became less frequent and loud. Then after a while, Tiago decided to raise the level up, satisfied that Bel-leng was skillful enough to defend himself honorably. He did not want to embarrass his opponent. Besides they were just using sticks anyway. A little bruise would not hurt the little Indio.

Tiago had been parrying and thrusting lackadaisically, lulling Bel-leng to do likewise. Then suddenly, after a seemingly lazy thrust which Bel-leng easily parried, Tiago quickly feinted to his left and with two swift flicks of his wrist tapped Bel-leng on both shoulders with the point of his stick to the delight of the soldiers who again loudly showed their approval.

Bel-leng stopped, stunned, aware that he would have been hurt badly if they were using real weapons. The hunters were astounded at the quickness of the hits that they were silent for a while then they erupted in gleeful shout in appreciation of the white man's skill. They clapped their hands and stomped their feet and danced in a frenzy raising dust in the small clearing. Some of them went around Bel-leng, flapping their hands and comically falling to the ground indicating that he had died. Bel-leng took it all in good humor, but he was no longer grinning. He merely shook his head and waved the hunters off the open space and motioned for Tiago to engage him again.

Tiago ceremoniously bowed his head and took a stance, saluting Bel-leng with his stick as he raised it and briefly touched it to his lips.

Their movements were quicker this time; their thrusts and slashes more forceful and resolute. They fought evenly for a while, with Bel-leng recovering and reacting quickly to Tiago's attack with such speed that the old soldier found himself shaking his head every once in a while. The Indio was indeed quick and his reactions fast like a cat.

Don Manuel who was watching with fascination now wondered how good a swordsman the Indio would be if properly trained in the art. Then he looked around at the other hunters wondering if all of them were as good and as quick and fast as the Indio that was now giving Tiago a fit as the old soldier could not seem to find his opponent with his stick. Don Manuel felt a warm glow grow in his chest, inwardly wishing that it was him and not Tiago who was engaged in the sparring, yet at the same time his feeling was tempered by a hint of caution. He involuntarily shrugged his shoulders as he forced himself to simply watch and enjoy the mock swordplay.

Bel-leng now dodged and weaved, parried and counter attacked with lightning speed, eager to redeem himself. His reflexes as well as his stamina were astounding as he seemed to run circles around the tiring old man. But with all his speed and determination, he could not touch Tiago with his stick. It seemed that the old soldier's stick had a mind of its own, placing itself in just the nick of time at the spot where Bel-leng wanted to hit, blocking his thrusts and slashes as effectively as an impregnable shield.

He tried some tricks and feints that were effective against the boys in the village but Tiago was able to evade them somehow.

Then a quick smile crossed his face as the old soldier seemed to falter and lose his balance. He moved in quickly for the kill, his lips opening to a wide grin at the prospect of victory.

Don Manuel shook his head and also grinned in amusement as he saw Tiago stagger and look like he was going to fall. 'Must you resort to that trick, Viejo?' he thought as he watched, bemused as Bel-leng rushed Tiago only to find the old soldier, with a quick pivot, had regained his balance and had the tip of his stick pushing gently against the Itneg's chest.

Bel-leng stopped in his tracks, with a bewildered look on his face, his grin completely gone. He looked at the stick on his chest, raised his eyes to Tiago then with a grin, lifted his arms in surrender.

The audience, soldiers and hunters alike, roared in approval. Don Manuel shook his head and clapped and turned his head toward the old man and his son.

He had noticed the old man intently watching Tiago during the swordplay but his face remained inscrutable and he barely uttered a word or sound. He was nodding his head from time to time yet his face remained impassive.

His son on the other hand was clapping his hands with a wide smile on his face. He must have felt that Don Manuel was looking at him for he suddenly stopped and turned his head to meet the Don's gaze, his smile abruptly gone. For a while their eyes locked, with neither one smiling.

Then Kulas nodded in response as Don Manuel smiled and gave him a brief nod in return, but the eyes that remained locked on the Don's were bereft of camaraderie. Suddenly the glow in the Don's chest flared back up and before he could control himself, he pointed at Kulas and swung his head and arm toward Tiago who was taking ceremonious bows at the center of the clearing. All eyes were on the old soldier with the exception of Don Manuel and Kulas who were looking at one another.

Kulas shook his head, pointed at Don Manuel and poked his own chest with his thumb then pointed to where Tiago stood. Sadang was not needed to clarify the silent discussion. The glow in the Don's chest burned into a slow fire. He nodded his head as he stood and slowly unbuckled his sword, his eyes still locked on Kulas as the latter likewise stood without saying a word.

The old man looked up at his son as he sensed him move and saw him looking at Don Manuel. He turned his head and a hint of amusement crossed his face as he witnessed the Don put down his sword on the ground. He spoke without moving from his seated position, his voice cutting clearly through the din.

The hunters suddenly fell silent momentarily then they roared again with glee, clapping their hands and raising their arms, waving them wildly over their heads. The soldiers looked in astonishment then also broke into a wild cheer as they saw Don Manuel move toward Tiago.

The old soldier grinned openly as he surrendered his stick to his Capitán.

Don Manuel took it without saying a word, examined it, took a couple of swings and nodded his head, contented with the response of the stick. He turned around to face Kulas and a frown crossed his face as he saw the Itneg walk toward the patch of saplings where Tiago got the sticks. He watched as Kulas chose and cut a stick of the same thickness as what Tiago and Bel-leng used but a little shorter in length. Kulas gave it a twirl, satisfied, and went back to where Don Manuel waited. The hunters and soldiers cheered in anticipation.

Kulas motioned to Bel-leng as he approached the center of the clearing. He held the short stick in his left hand. He extended his right hand toward Bel-leng, palm up, and Bel-leng placed his stick on it. Kulas grasped it, twirled it like he did with the short stick, then twirled them both simultaneously, up and down by his side and crossing his arms a couple of times without breaking the rhythm.

Don Manuel and Tiago watched curiously as they exchanged amused glances, shrugging their shoulders, although they were a little bit impressed by the coordination and fluidity of movement that the Itneg displayed. The soldiers clapped while the hunters hooted with relish.

Don Manuel said something to Tiago that was lost in the noise of the yelling audience and Tiago yelled back as he backed down to the fallen log and sat on it, his eyes glued to the combatants at the center of the clearing. He watched as Don Manuel and Kulas approached one another, touched sticks and moved back a couple of steps, sizing each other up. Tiago eased his butt to find a comfortable spot and stretched his tired legs, his eyes locked at the combatants, curious as to how the engagement would play out. He found the spot, commenced to settle down and stretch his legs when he suddenly stood up with disbelief in his eyes. The match had ended. He swore as he bent down and picked up the stick that landed by his feet and walked back toward the empty handed Don Manuel.

It was over in a flash. Don Manuel saw Kulas approach, sticks twirling wildly in both hands. He met the Itneg, thrusting quickly and surely, he thought, meaning to put the bout to a fast end, but before he knew what happened, he found his arm locked by the Itneg's sticks and with a sudden twist of the shorter stick, the movement so fast that his eyes could not follow, Kulas had pried the stick off his hand and Manuel saw it fly over his head to land where Tiago sat. He was stunned. He saw his soldiers look at one another, shaking their heads in disbelief while the hunters danced and hooted around wildly, but he could not hear anything. He instead was hearing loudly the answer to his question if the other Itnegs were as quick and as good as Bel-leng.

Then he saw Tiago approaching, offering him back the stick, but the flame in his chest had gone out, replaced by something else, hotter and fiercer and he fought it off. Now was not the time and place. He suddenly had no taste for further games. He shook his head at Tiago, turned toward Kulas and bowed, acknowledging defeat. Kulas in turn bowed his head with respect in his eyes for his opponent's gentlemanly behavior. His eyes courteously followed the Capitán as the latter walked back to his sword by the old man.

"My turn, Señor," Kulas heard Tiago say. He did not understand the words but he got the message as he turned and saw Tiago raise the stick in his hand. He shrugged his shoulders and waited, his hands on his sides, sticks held loosely, and Tiago moved forward and attacked quickly. Tiago was sure he had caught the Itneg by surprise but he hit nothing but air, then he felt rather than saw the Itneg's sticks tapping his sides, back and neck in quick succession and before he could show his surprise, his own stick was out of his hands flying wildly in the air. He had not seen anyone move so fast!

Later on that night at camp, away from the hunters, Tiago wondered loudly at Don Manuel how those Indios would do in real fight with real knives.

"Imagine if those sticks were knives, Viejo," Don Manuel said. "You did not miss that they all have a dagger and a long knife in their belts, did you? Trust me they know how to use them."

Tiago did not respond but he nodded his head in the dark. Despite the warm night he shivered slightly as he imagined the cold blade of a knife tapping his sides instead of a stick. He hoped they did not have to fight those Itnegs as he dozed off to a fitful sleep.

He dreamt that he was by himself in the middle of the forest and all around him were naked savages armed with long knives and sticks. He woke up wet with perspiration. The blackness of night was turning into grey when he finally was able to go back to sleep.

'You're wrong this time, Niño. It could not be the same man,' Tiago thought, as he watched Capitán Manuel walk the length of the courtyard below heading toward the stables. But deep inside, something nagged at Tiago, like a faint but persistent whisper that he was deluding himself into a state of denial.

"It could not be," he said stubbornly as he started toward the stairs that led to the grounds below, but in the back of his mind, he knew that the Capitán was right.

'The man has eyes like a hawk and the memory of an elephant,' Tiago finally conceded of the Capitán. Then aloud, he said, as his thoughts went back to the Itneg. 'I wonder what he's doing here in town.'

He felt a sudden chill on his back but at the same time also felt the surge of excited anticipation at the prospect of meeting the Itneg again and perhaps engage him in swordplay, friendly or not, it did not much matter to him one way or the other.

But he had a feeling that if they did meet, any swordplay would be far from friendly.

Chapter Ten

Don Manuel was still thinking of what he saw back at the fort as he rode the short distance back to town. He finally dismissed it as he got off his horse and left it at the small stable in his backyard. By the time he walked back into the marketplace, his mind was totally into the excited expectation of looking up and meeting the *Señorita* who passed by his window earlier that morning.

The crowd was thinning, and some of the stalls were already empty as the sellers who had cleared their wares early had gone home. And just like before, there was no trace or shadow of the *Señorita*.

Manuel finally gave up and went back to his place. His house help, Clara, stopped what she was doing in the kitchen and came out with a message that he was invited for dinner that evening at the Dela Cuestas.

"It was the *Señora* who came by herself, *Señor*, with Luisa, her housemaid, after they came from the market. She said she's not going to take no for an answer. She expects you to be there at *alas seiz en punto*, six o'clock sharp."

"You did not tell her that I will be out of town by tonight, Clara?"

"But, *Señor*, you just arrived. Surely you are not going back out again, are you?"

"No, Clara, I jest, but now I wish I were." He did not exactly like the company at the Dela Cuesta's party, but on the other hand, *Don* Jose kept a good selection of Spanish wine and cigars. And Luisa was an excellent cook.

"You are going to the dinner, of course, aren't you, *Señor*? The *Señora* would think that I did not give you the message if you don't." Clara was worried. She loved to go by the Dela Cuestas to gossip with Luisa every time she could.

"What message, Clara?" He asked seriously, trying not to laugh. He loved to tease Clara who always seemed so serious and proper about the way she ran the *Capitán*'s house, for as Manuel had long ago conceded, Clara did just that and he was grateful for it.

"*Señor!*" Clara's eyes grew wider. "This is no joking matter! You know how the *Señora* is!"

"Hah-hah, Clara. *Calma te.* Relax. I'll go. I'll just take a short *siesta* then will get ready afterwards. If you could just prepare my clothes, please, for later, whatever is clean enough."

"I already took them out, *Señor*. They are on the chair in your room."

"*Gracias*, Clara."

"You're welcome, *Señor*, and thank you," Clara smiled. She would still be of good standing with the *Señora* Dela Cuesta.

"This better be good, Clara," Manuel said.

Don Manuel sometimes wondered how he was able to survive socially for so long without a woman in his life. He was shaking his head in a futile effort to rid of it from thinking of the woman in the plaza as he walked to his room for his *siesta*.

He slept the sleep of a man with troubled thoughts, dreaming in episodes that did not seem to make any sense. In one instance he dreamt of being at home back at the Rancheria and walking alone in the forest when he got to a river where a beautiful siren with an ever-changing face blocked his path and would not let him cross unless he guessed her name.

Later on when he woke up he could not remember if he was able to cross the river. He could not remember either if he was able to give the correct name of the siren with a shifting visage.

He wondered if the woman with the *caimitos* had haunted him even in his dreams. He grudgingly walked out to the backyard and to the *baño* by the well. The tub inside the bathhouse was already filled with water. He took off his clothes and gratefully eased down into the tub, relishing the coldness of the water.

But even after taking a long leisurely bath, Manuel could not get rid of the thought of the woman. She stubbornly clung to his mind like a bad dream and he felt helpless. It was driving him mad.

"If this is what love is, spare me, *Dios mio*," he said as he went back up to the house to get ready to meet *Señora* Dela Cuesta's latest candidate.

Chapter Eleven

Apo Dalalo stirred at the crack of dawn. He cursed himself for staying in bed longer than he had planned the night before, conveniently ignoring the crowing of Kagaid's roosters a few hours ago. He should have been up when they started crowing at false dawn, and long gone by now with the boys. For today was the day that he promised to take Aklang and his other grandchild, Bagit, to go hunting and he had planned for them to get an early start.

But the nights had turned colder and last night was no different. And it was snug and warm under the blanket with the *ikamen*, the coconut woven mat, insulating his back from the cold seeping from the ground through the bamboo-slatted floor. Perhaps old age was catching up to him. He grimaced at the thought but he knew in his heart that it was the truth. He had been feeling aches and pains in his joints lately especially in the cold of the early morning.

He gathered his thin hand-woven blanket around his broad shoulders and grudgingly rose up, taking a quick look across the room to where Aklang still slept, curled snugly underneath his own blanket. *Apo* Dalalo stretched then walked slowly towards his grandson.

"Aklang, wake up," he said, shaking his grandchild's shoulders through the blanket. The boy merely turned over without opening his eyes, gathering his blanket tighter around him.

"Aklang!" the old man said again, louder this time, grabbing and pulling the blanket off the boy in one quick move. "Get up and get ready! We're going hunting today."

Aklang bolted up as if doused with cold water. He rubbed his eyes and focused them on the old man.

"Hunt?! Today, *Angkay*?" He asked with uncertainty in his voice, addressing the old man in his endearing title as patriarch of the family. "Now?"

"Yes, today. As soon as you're ready. Go and make coffee."

The boy got up hastily, almost running to the door when he suddenly stopped. He turned back and picked his blanket and folded it neatly. Then he rolled his mat and put them together, along with his pillow, in a corner of the room. He did the same with his grandfather's mat and pillow. He eyed the blanket that was still draped around the old man's shoulders, tempted to snatch it just like the way the old man did to his blanket, but he dared not reach for it.

He headed toward the door instead, stifling a smile as he thought of what the old man would have done if he had torn the blanket away from him. He might have changed his mind about the hunt, he thought, or worse gave him a good smack on the head. He was still grinning as he went down the bamboo ladder to the earthen fire pit underneath the hut.

He moved the rocks and the ashes away to uncover the hot coals that were left smoldering the night before and stoked them to life, feeding them with pine shavings until he had a fire going. He put in a couple of good sized firewood then he filled a clay pot with water from the big water jar that sat by the pit. He arranged the rocks around the fire and put the pot on top of the ring. When the water was boiling, he scooped a couple of handfuls of the roasted coffee nuts from the bamboo container hanging under the hut and stirred them into the pot. He added another handful for good measure as he remembered the old man liked his coffee strong.

"Get some sweet potatoes and roast them also," *Apo* Dalalo said from the top of the stairs. "We'll bring some for lunch in case we don't get any game by mid-day so roast some extra."

"We'll have wild chicken with them, *Angkay*," Aklang said with a wide grin on his face. "I know where to get them."

"Catching them may not be as easy as you think," *Apo* Dalalo cautioned.

"I've trapped them before, *Angkay*. We'll get one, I promise," Aklang said with certainty in his voice.

"We'll see," the old man replied, raising his eyes from looking down at Aklang as he glimpsed a shadow from across the yard. Aklang followed his gaze and frowned as he recognized his cousin Bagit walking briskly toward them, holding his bow in his left hand, a quiver full of arrows slung over a broad shoulder. Bagit was squat and chubby, and there was no mistaking his gait even in the dusk.

"Good morning," Bagit shouted as he made his way under the hut. A big grin plastered on his chubby face. "Are you ready?"

"Ready for what?" Aklang asked, not aware that his grandfather had invited Bagit to go hunting with them.

"He's coming with us." *Apo* Dalalo said from the top of the stairs before Bagit could reply.

"That's right, little man." Bagit winked at Aklang.

Aklang looked at the old man who simply looked back, his face inscrutable as always. He turned to Bagit with feigned disgust.

"Do you know how to use that?" He moved his head to indicate Bagit's bow. His hands were busy opening the sack of sweet potatoes. He would roast them as the coffee boiled.

"Watch and learn, little man," Bagit grinned. He loved to tease his younger cousin. "Is the coffee ready yet?"

"No, I just put it on," Aklang said shaking his head. "Didn't you eat breakfast at your house?"

"No. I know you're cooking so I decided to eat here and find out if you're any good in making breakfast. Perhaps there's something you're good at," Bagit reached out and ruffled Aklang's hair.

"Stop it or you're not getting anything!" Aklang said, pushing his older cousin's hand away.

"Lighten up. You'll have fun in the mountains. Stick with me and I'll show you some tricks. About time you learn something."

"*Apo* can show us his old tricks," Aklang replied.

It will be a long day of hunting with his cousin but Aklang now looked forward to it. He knew that he was better than Bagit with the bow. He had seen Bagit shoot and he was good but he knew he can outshoot his older cousin. Anytime and any day of the week, he thought. He had been secretly practicing by the banana patch close to the river ever since his grandfather gave him his first bow when he turned eight summers and that was ages ago it seemed. He was almost fifteen summers now.

He had grown much bigger and stronger since then. His shoulders were wide and his arms well muscled and powerful from drawing the bow countless of times. He remembered the nights he had gone home with the aches on his arms and fingers and shoulders almost unbearable that he could not sleep. But he never quit and he got a lot better with the bow. Better than any of the boys in the village, and most of the men too, he was sure of it. He could hit a small banana trunk consistently at more than two hundred paces. Sometimes without even taking aim, just drawing quickly, pointing and shooting. Once he had shot a small bird as it flew away from a tree that he was standing under, trying to figure out where a doe that he was stalking went. He felt rather than saw the bird fly and instinctively he looked up, his sight locking on the bird in a flash and let loose the arrow that was already nocked in his bow. All in one fluid motion as if he was doing it all the time. His arrow found the body of the small bird and it dropped a few feet from where he stood.

He felt bad afterwards for he remembered his grandfather's advise when he gave him the bow to use it only to hunt for food, and not to kill any game indiscriminately, big or small. He cooked the bird over an open fire and ate it in his effort to justify the deed, but the bird was so small that he didn't feel any better afterwards. He had shot at flying birds again in several more occasions after that but they were bigger, like wild ducks, herons and quails, which he brought down to the village to share. Yes, indeed, he can out shoot

Bagit anytime. And today he would show him a trick or two. It was good that Bagit was joining them in the hunt after all. He smiled inwardly at the thought, and he felt better as he proffered a sweet potato to his cousin.

"Here, cook your own breakfast," he said. "Make yourself useful for a change."

"Give me some more and let me do it so we don't eat burnt *kat'tila*," Bagit said, referring to the sweet potato in their dialect, reaching for a handful from the sack. "I don't think we could trust you with something as important as breakfast."

"Good, go ahead do it so I can go and get my gear ready." Aklang handed the whole sack to his cousin, rising gratefully and headed back up the ladder to get his bow and arrows. He took his time, selecting the best and straightest arrows from his stash, leaving behind his practice arrows. He put his selection in the quiver and counted them. Ten. That should be more than enough.

Bagit and *Apo* Dalalo were both nursing their steaming hot coffee in mugs made out of dried coconut shells when he finally went down to join them. They held the mugs with both hands, keeping their palms warm also in the process.

"What took you so long? You move like a girl." Bagit threw him a derisive look. "We're almost done. Hurry up!"

Aklang did not say a word. He took a mug from where they hung in a makeshift bamboo wall by the water jar and filled it with the steaming coffee, savoring the sweet aroma drifting to his nose. He made a face as he burned his tongue with his first sip. Bagit laughed. It took all of Aklang's self-restraint and a stern warning look from the old man for him not to pour his coffee over his cousin's head.

He felt better as he ate his sweet potato. Bagit had cooked it perfectly, he had to admit. His cousin usually took care of cooking when they went out to hunt in the foothills or fish by the river. If there was something Bagit could be relied on, it was cooking. He might be a pain on the side but he sure was good at cooking, he admitted grudgingly.

The boys bantered as they ate their breakfast, trying to outdo each other about what to do at the hunt and the number of wild game they were going to bring back. The old man wisely kept his silence, enjoying his coffee and the moment with his two grandsons, thinking back at the times when his own grandfather, the great *Apo* Lagam, perhaps the greatest warrior of their tribe, took him hunting as a boy.

They left the village as the morning sun crept over the mountain in the east.

'Ahh, Bangilo,' *Apo* Dalalo was surprised as the name of the place on the mountain where the sun was peering over suddenly came to his mind. He had been to the place so many times in his youth, had friends there, and he wondered why it came to mind now. He dismissed it, but the place stuck to his mind for a moment, for he remembered how he met a woman there who became the mother of his children. He sighed and he hurried the boys, noting that they were running late, but it was more in his effort to put the thought of his late wife, Mayang, away from his mind.

Apo Dalalo figured they would be at his old favorite hunting ground, which he gathered was favored by the boys also from their conversation at breakfast, by the time the sun was halfway to noon. Or so, he hoped, for he felt his old legs getting tight as they reached the foothills. He shook it off and after a while he felt better as he felt the early trace of perspiration from his brow.

He was feeling good and young again. I should go out more often, he thought, as he followed his two grandchildren at a respectable pace. He had not ventured out to the forest since *Ina* Mayang passed away about four summers back. He knew he could not catch up with the boys if they walked at their regular pace which was more of a fast trot. He had seen them walk and run in the village since they were little boys and he knew that they were fast and could go on forever it seemed at times.

The two boys seemed considerate enough though as they trudged up ahead, glancing back at their grandfather every once in a while to make sure that he was doing alright. The old man pretended not to notice, looking at the sides of the trail and the new growths and signs wondering how things had changed yet remained so familiar at the same time.

The trail had become narrower and steeper and the old man found himself breathing faster and harder. Yet he noticed the boys seemed as fresh as when they started this morning, still bantering with one another, stopping only when they noticed something moving along the way but *Apo* Dalalo cautioned them not to make too much noise as they got deeper into the forest. They were almost halfway up the mountain and there would be game soon, he hoped. He did not plan on going much farther than a half-day walk if he could help it. He was surely feeling his age.

He remembered when he could go on all day and all night if he had to as he did one time tracking a wild boar that had gored one of his hunting friends, Allak, who after that avoided hunting altogether, limiting himself to fishing the river. He let their two other companions, Banig and Banting, bring the wounded Allak down to the village and he followed the boar alone, vowing not to stop until he brought it down. It took him almost two days of relentless tracking and running through the forest, but he finally caught up with the boar by a spring at the other side of the mountain, close to Bangilo. And that was where he met Lum-kang, the feared warrior from that mountain tribe.

Lum-kang's arrow hit the boar that he was tracking just at about the same time as his own arrow hit it from the opposite side. So there they were, staring at each other from across the fallen boar, their arrows stuck as one in its heart, Lum-kang's arrow bent and broken under the weight of the boar. They took each other's measure for a long silent moment then each one decided he would be better off with the other man as a friend and not as enemy. They shared the boar but he brought back its head with the tusks intact to Allak after he told Lum-kang about its encounter with his friend. They had a good laugh as he narrated how Allak tried to run away from the boar when he lost his spear when the boar attacked. He and Lum-kang had become lifelong friends since then, meeting time and again in the forest to hunt together, until time and old age caught up with them. He had not heard from Lum-kang for a long time.

"My old friends have gone and joined their ancestors," the old man said softly. "And my enemies as well, I hope," he added shaking his head at the thought. He felt a whip of cold wind on his back as if the spirits of his ancestors had made known their presence. *Apo* Dalalo shivered and tried to shrug off the feeling, unruffled, for he had felt the same thing so many times before, way back from his youth, especially when he was alone in the sacred places of the mountains. He felt the shiver linger for a moment then it passed gradually. Perhaps it was just the cold morning breeze, he thought, but he looked around him furtively, his eyes seeking no one in particular among the shadows of the trees.

He noted some old marks along the trail, sorting new growth and changes from his memory when he traveled this trail regularly. He wondered again at the ability of the forest to grow everything back after a devastating lightning fire or heavy and windy, damaging downpour.

For a moment he wished that man had that same ability to recover but he knew that was not so. He was old and would surely soon join his ancestors. A sudden pang of loneliness hit him at the thought. He missed the friends he had grown old with who had gone ahead, realizing that Kagaid and Allak were the only ones left. And most of all he missed his wife, her beloved Mayang, who had passed on due to sickness almost three years ago. He remembered going into the forest for several days as soon as they buried her, not hunting, just getting lost in the shadows, looking for solace in the silence among the trees. He talked to her then, in the meadows, along the cool streams and the wild chicken and deer that got too curious, getting too close sometimes, almost coming nose to nose with the stranger resting underneath the trees who seemed to show no interest at them at all. He could have killed them if he wanted to but he did not have the heart to take another life at the time, man or animal. And that was the last time he had ventured away from the village. Like Allak, he had contented himself with fishing in the river since then.

Apo Dalalo slowed down as he realized he was alone. The boys had moved on beyond a turn in the mountain trail and had stopped their animated banter for he could not hear them. He wondered if his hearing had gone worst, among everything else that had seemed to be going worse lately. Like his sight and taste. Or maybe they spotted game, he thought, as he hurried silently up the trail.

Despite his age, he could still walk softly and relatively fast among the undergrowth, making barely a sound to note his passing. He was known in his youth, to have come so close to a grazing wild deer to touch it before it was aware of his presence, and that ability still showed as he seemed to glide silently, and vanish in the shadows of the trees. He turned the bend and he stopped, blending among the bushes, as he saw the boys crouching behind some thistles and high grass a few yards below him, as the trail dipped down toward a small ravine, a deep ditch really, carved through the years by flowing waters during the monsoons. Beyond it was a slight break in the forest, a small clearing where he now saw a six pointer buck and three does silently grazing on the grass and the surrounding foliage.

Apo Dalalo smiled. Perhaps he did not have to walk far today after all. He thanked the spirits silently. But his smile turned into a frown as he noted the boys bring out their arrows. Too far, he mouthed silently. He wanted to shake his head but he dared not move for he knew the sensitivity of the deer to sudden movements and unusual smells in its environment. Get closer, he thought, again thanking the spirits that the boys were downwind from the small herd. But as if in response to his thought, he saw the boys signal to one another as they moved farther apart, eyes focused on their prey, nocking their arrows but not attempting to get any nearer to their targets.

Move closer, again *Apo* Dalalo mouthed. Perhaps Aklang heard him for he saw the boy stop and edge closer but only to a slight rise on the ground. Bagit, sensing his cousin move, also stopped from getting ready to shoot. Both he and *Apo* Dalalo watched as Aklang drew three more arrows from his quiver and laid them silently in a row on top of the rise on the ground, his eyes never leaving the grazing deer.

Bagit gave his younger cousin a bewildered look, his eyes asking his unsaid question, 'What the hell are you doing?'

From his vantage point, *Apo* Dalalo saw Bagit's expression of disbelief and he was sure his face showed the same thing as he surmised what his younger grandson was planning to do. Surely Aklang did not intend to shoot all four arrows, did he? *Apo* Dalalo looked, mesmerized at the scene developing before him. Then a flicker of movement beyond the clearing caught his eyes. He looked up and saw a flash of flesh among the shadows at the other side of the clearing, but before he could focus on it, he sensed rather than saw Aklang rise to his knees, draw his bow and release the arrow in one swift motion. The arrow had barely passed from the bow when he snatched another one from the row on the mound, nocked and let loosed without aiming, and did the same thing successively with the other two remaining arrows. All four arrows shot in the blink of an eye, his grandfather swore later.

If he had not witnessed it, *Apo* Dalalo would not have believed it. But down below the trail on the clearing, he saw the four deer go down in quick succession. The buck jumped and staggered and fell a few feet from where it grazed. The three does fell quickly one after the other, all shot in the heart. It all happened so fast that not one of them had reacted quickly enough to get away.

Even Bagit was mesmerized, his jaw dropping in awe. His arrow remained stuck to his bow. He looked at Aklang and turned to the fallen deer with incredulity in his eyes, and back at his cousin again who was now rising nonchalantly from his crouched position as if he just finished eating another *kat'tila*, just like he did this morning at breakfast. Bagit looked again at the clearing, at the deer, each with an arrow sticking from its hide, and back at his cousin who now had a big grin on his face. Bagit looked up the trail, searching for *Apo* Dalalo, looking for affirmation of what he just saw, but he failed to see the old man, his jaw remained halfway down his neck, or so it seemed.

Apo Dalalo was sure his own face mirrored his older grandchild's expression, but he did not move from where he stood hidden among the trees, for again he caught movement in the shadows across the small clearing. He looked intently with his old eyes and thanked the gods that they were still good and clear for looking at a distance. Then he drew his bow from his shoulders, picked out three arrows, notched one on his bow, holding the other two with his left hand that also held the bow, and crouched lower moving silently down toward the clearing, avoiding the trail as he blended silently with the undergrowth. Despite himself, he smiled as he recalled Aklang getting ready with extra arrows.

He felt his heart beating faster than he would have liked. You're too old for this, he reminded himself, but at the same time he felt invigorated at the prospect of getting into trouble. For coming out from among the trees across the clearing, were hunters from the tribe at the other side of the mountain, this he was certain from their attire and weapons, and the distinctive markings on their arms, chests and legs. Bangilo, he thought, but he did not recognize the men. There had been peace between their tribes for a long time now but one never knew with these young, hot blooded hunters.

Chapter Twelve

"I hope they are friendly," *Apo* Dalalo prayed silently as he made his way closer to the clearing, confident that the hunters did not know of his presence. Their eyes were now locked at the two boys who had stopped for a moment from going down into the clearing when they saw the hunters approaching. Then to their credit, *Apo* Dalalo saw with pride, the two boys proceed down the slope slowly, each with bow and arrows on the ready. They stopped at the edge of the clearing.

There were three of them, all three strapping young men, each one a good ten or more summers older than the two boys. One of them was half a head taller than the other two, who seemed so alike in their demeanor that *Apo* Dalalo assumed they were twins or at least brothers, but one was slightly leaner than the stockier shortest one. The tallest had an assured way of carrying himself that somehow reminded the old man of someone he had known a long time ago. But he could not be certain who or what in the man exactly reminded him of at the moment. He crept closer to the clearing and stood, hidden behind an ancient pine, easing himself slowly around it, blending with the shade of its lower branches, his bow and arrows on the ready. He felt his arms and chest tighten and he tried to keep himself relaxed, breathing in and exhaling slowly, not making a sound.

"Are you boys alone?" the shortest hunter asked. The tall one did not say anything but his eyes kept moving along the trail and into the shadows.

"There are others behind us," Aklang answered before Bagit could respond. His older cousin looked at him, and then looked back at the stocky hunter.

"Yeah, there are others behind us," Bagit said, catching on to his credit. "There are four others," he added, his eyes drifting to the face of the tallest one, certain now that there were only the three in front of them.

Apo Dalalo suppressed a smile, his chest swelling with pride. But he did not see what Bagit saw from the eyes of the tall hunter. Bagit felt a shiver run down his spine as the cold expressionless eyes of the tall hunter looked back at him, boring at him like a limitless hole. Bagit fidgeted with his bow, averted his eyes back to his cousin and noting that Aklang had not moved a bit, his own gaze not wavering as he took in the three hunters at the same time. Bagit felt his admiration for his cousin growing at the moment. For the first time he noticed how Aklang had grown bigger at the right parts. His shoulders were wider and his arms were thicker. Wider and thicker than mine, he noticed. His legs and thighs were long and lean and well muscled too. My God, he thought, the boy had grown taller than me! He wondered how he had not even noticed it before.

The tall hunter looked at the boys, his face remaining expressionless, showing no indication whether he believed them or not. His dark eyes remained cold and fathomless.

"That was good shooting," he finally said looking at Aklang, his eyes softening a bit. *Apo* Dalalo noted a trace of admiration in his voice.

"Just lucky," Aklang said. His voice was even, his face and eyes as expressionless as the tall hunter. Funny, he thought, he didn't feel nervous at all. He was scared initially when he saw the hunters coming out of the woods, but the feeling passed and he now felt nothing but calmness. Almost a boring calmness that he half-expected for something to happen so he could do something. Do what? He did not know. But his body was anticipating something to happen and he felt it was ready to respond to whatever came. He did not know how he would respond but he was sure he would do something when needed. He was confident of it. Just like shooting at something that moved without thinking. He seemed relaxed but his muscles were taut and ready to explode.

"No luck involved from what I saw," the tall hunter replied. His gaze went to the fallen deer, stopping momentarily at each one, taking everything that needed to be noted with those brief glances.

Aklang shrugged in response. The stranger can think what he wanted. It did not matter. He had his kills and if it were up to him he was bringing them home one way or the other. But he knew they could not carry all four down to the village. Just one or two would be enough. He now felt bad for showing off and not thinking right. His thoughts went back to the little bird he shot a long time ago. It was a waste. He felt the same feeling of remorse now, but he suppressed it, his face not showing any trace of emotion. His eyes refocused on the tall one. He was their leader, no doubt about it. The other two would not do anything until the tallest said so. How he knew, he did not know, but of this he was certain. He felt it.

"You can ease up on your bows," the tall one said. His companions did not say a word. Even the stocky one who first spoke had remained silent now. They just stood there by his side, flanking the tall hunter, stolidly looking at the boys.

They glanced up once in a while at the trail beyond the bend. Their bodies seemed relaxed, yet *Apo* Dalalo sensed that they could spring into action at a moment's notice. *Apo* Dalalo knew men and he had seen such men before. And these men were such men. He was once like them, he thought. He hoped he still is if the conversation turned sour.

His eyes turned to Aklang who was standing tall in front of the hunters and his eyes grew wider for a bit as he realized that his grandson also carried himself in the same manner as these men. Looking at Aklang from behind, *Apo* Dalalo was seeing his oldest son, Ittok, Aklang's father, who himself was a noted hunter and warrior of the tribe, like his two other sons, Ayong, Bagit's father, and the youngest, Kulas who came late into their lives being almost ten summers younger than his older brother.

The boy has turned into a man, just like his father, *Apo* Dalalo thought with pride. Then his eyes went back to the tall one as he heard him say, "We're friendly. You would have been dead by now if we weren't." *Apo* Dalalo sensed a hint of bravado in his voice, yet there was a trace of humor too. His two companions grunted and smiled in affirmation, showing emotions for the first time.

"Yeah, you'd be dead," the stockier of the two said, nodding his head, grinning confidently.

"Yeah, dead. Good shot or not." The third one finally spoke, showing a gap toothed smile at Aklang. His two upper front teeth were missing. Aklang almost laughed but his expression did not change. He ventured a glance at his cousin and was surprised to see Bagit looking back at him to see what they should do. Aklang looked back blankly at the hunters but he did not let go of his firm hold of his bow and arrow. Bagit noticed and did likewise.

The tall hunter shook his head at the boys, his face showing annoyance but his eyes remained expressionless. Then he looked at the shadows behind the boys.

"You can come out, *Apo*," he raised his voice, his eyes idly drifting back to the boys. "We are not hunting trouble, just food for the folks back home." His two companions looked at one another, surprise showing on their faces, just like the two boys in front of them.

Behind the tree, *Apo* Dalalo was also momentarily surprised. Then he smiled and eased up on his arrow. I must be getting really old, he thought, or the man was extremely good. He decided on the latter for he was certain now of who the tall hunter reminded him of as he stepped out from behind the pine.

Bagit and Aklang turned and looked at him in disbelief, not aware that their grandfather had moved in so close to cover their backs. They looked back at the tall hunter with growing respect in their eyes, the string of their bows now slack, arrows gripped harmlessly by their left hands that held their bows.

"Young man, you remind me of my old friend Lum-kang," *Apo* Dalalo said as he stepped into the clearing, his eyes locking into the younger man's eyes.

111

"You must be *Apo* Dalalo," the hunter smiled for the first time, giving a bow toward the old man, showing his respects. "I am Biktol, *Apo*. I am *Ama* Lum-kang's youngest son." He stretched his right arm. *Apo* Dalalo reached for it and gripped at the younger man's forearm. Biktol did the same.

The young man had a good grip, just like his father *Apo* Dalalo recalled fondly.

"I have heard a lot about you, *Apo*, from my father, when we were growing up." There seemed to be joy now in his previously mirthless eyes, the two young boys noticed. "My father spoke highly of you. He still does."

"I am afraid your father may have exaggerated a lot in his stories," *Apo* Dalalo smiled. "He is a far greater man than me or will I ever dream to be, not that I have many more years ahead of me. I have heard of your mother's passing, may her spirit rest in peace with your ancestors. I regret that I could not make it to her burial. How's my old friend?"

"He's getting on in age, Apo, and can't walk far without a cane but he's well. We have heard also of your own difficulties a few years back with your wife, *Ina* Mayang. May she be at peace likewise with the ancestors."

"Well we sure are getting old. What can we do? And thank you, son. These boys," he swept his arm toward Bagit and Aklang, "are my *apos*, my grandchildren. They are cousins. The older one is Bagit, that boy who shot the deer is Aklang."

"Glad to meet you, boys," Biktol said addressing Bagit and Aklang. "These," he put his hands on the shoulders of his two companions, "are my friends. This ugly one is Ampit." He tapped the short, stocky hunter on the back as he glared up at him and the other one showed his missing teeth with glee which promptly vanished as he continued, "And this uglier one is Ambit. They're twins."

The boys nodded in acknowledgement. *Apo* Dalalo offered his arms which the twins took respectfully.

"From the stories I heard from my father, the boy shoots like his grandfather," Biktol said, looking at Aklang. He turned to Bagit. "Do you also shoot as well?"

"I taught him how to shoot," Bagit beamed, gesturing at Aklang who shook his head in disbelief but did not say anything.

"I could not still believe what I saw." Biktol shook his head, ignoring Bagit's bragging to Aklang's secret delight. "That was some shooting. Damn good shooting. Pardon me, *Apo*." He smiled at *Apo* Dalalo who simply shrugged.

The twins nodded their agreement.

"Pure luck," Aklang said again, finally finding his tongue.

"How old are you, twelve?" Biktol said ignoring Aklang's self deprecating comment.

"I am ff-fifteen," Aklang stammered, blushing. Bagit snickered.

"Almost fifteen." He glared at his older cousin.

"You're good for someone so young," Biktol said. "You're very good for anyone at any age for that matter," he said with emphasis.

Aklang shrugged. "Thank you, I guess," he whispered shyly. "There are better shooters in the village," he added.

"I doubt it," Biktol replied, shaking his head. "Nobody's that good, and I have seen the good ones."

"You haven't seen my father and my uncles shoot," Aklang replied hastily.

"Or I," Bagit added. *Apo* Dalalo did not say anything, amused with the banter.

"Perhaps," Biktol said. "But I doubt it. " His eyes locked on to Aklang's again, his head shaking slowly side to side. "Nobody's that good, boy. Nobody," he said again.

He turned to the old man. "My apologies, *Apo*, but I don't think anybody could have done any better, man or boy, in your village or mine." Again he smiled as he looked back at Aklang. "Who taught you how to shoot?"

"My grandfather," Aklang said without hesitation. "And my father," he added.

"I should have known. I apologize again, *Apo*, for asking."

"Stop apologizing, son," *Apo* Dalalo said. "I only taught him the basics. The rest he learned by himself. Truth is I never knew he was this good. Oh, I heard stories from the boys and some older men in the village, about how his arrows were placed in the birds and small game he brought down but I haven't seen him hunt big game until today." He nodded his head then shook it a couple of times showing his disbelief also. He looked at the fallen deer. There was no luck in it, he was sure. The boy could really shoot. He thought his youngest son, Kulas, who many considered the best hunter and warrior in the village was good, or his two older brothers, but no, the boy may be better than all of them. Perhaps a lot better for he could not remember any of his sons doing what Aklang just did at this age. Unless it was pure luck as the boy insisted. But *Apo* Dalalo saw what happened and he knew otherwise and his chest swelled with pride.

"We have been following this herd since yesterday afternoon," *Apo* Dalalo heard Biktol say, addressing Aklang. "We lost them last night in the dark and caught their trail again this morning after breaking camp over that ridge." He waved his arm towards where they came from. "We spotted them just at about the same time we saw you stalking them. We saw

113

everything. We can't lay claim on any of them, even if we want to. Your kills, they're all yours." He shook his head, his voice trailing. "Damn, good shooting," he said to no one in particular, still in awe.

"We don't need all of them," *Apo* Dalalo said. "You are welcome to half of them."

"That is very generous, *Apo*, but I think that would be up to the boy." He nodded at Aklang. "They're his kills."

"Like *Apo* said, we don't need all of them." Aklang said. "I just got carried away. I am sorry, *Angkay*." He turned to the old man. He looked back at Biktol, bowing his head slightly to show his respect and sincerity. "I apologize. I did not know that you were tracking them. Please pick two and we will get what remain."

"Don't apologize. Like I said nobody can lay claim to any game until they're killed." He smiled. "Thank you for your generosity, but I insist that you take your pick and we will get what you leave behind."

Aklang looked at *Apo* Dalalo who simply nodded.

"I would like to take the buck but it would be too big for us to carry. You can have it but I would like to keep the antlers if you don't mind. We'll get the smaller does."

"Are you sure?" Biktol asked. "We will be getting more meat than you do."

"Yes, I am sure, sir," Aklang replied. "We can't carry that big doe between the two of us." He nodded at Bagit who was for once tongue-tied. "We can manage with the two smaller ones. *Angkay* can carry the antlers, if you don't mind giving them up."

Biktol made a sign to his stockier friend in response. Ampit promptly turned toward the buck, pulling his knife that gleamed menacingly under the morning sun. He expertly cut the antlers in precise motions, then laying them aside, he made incisions with the tip of his knife on the base of each of the arrows and pulled them off the carcasses effortlessly. He picked the antlers and the arrows and wiped the blood off them on the grass and handed them ceremoniously to Aklang. He patted Aklang's shoulders as the boy accepted the horns and his arrows which he put back promptly in his quiver. He wanted to clean them up more thoroughly but he did not wish to offend the stocky silent warrior who was handy with a knife.

Then the stocky hunter, Ampit, plunged his bloody knife in the ground, sticking it in fully to the hilt and pulling it back effortlessly a number of times until the blade was rid of the trace of blood. He lifted the knife against the sky, examined both sides of the blade, and nodded with satisfaction as the knife glinted from the reflection of the sun. He flipped the knife up, watched it rotate as it fell, then he caught it deftly by its handle in mid-air.

He flipped it back up again over his head this time and caught it behind his back with the other hand, and without pausing, slid it back to its sheath. He smiled at the boys then looked sheepishly at the old man as if he expected a scolding. *Apo* Dalalo simply watched without expression. He had seen all the follies of youth. He had done his share. The boys on the other hand, smiled and nodded their heads in appreciation.

Biktol shook his head at Ampit's antics. Then he slapped the leaner one on the back. "He can do that too." The gap showed up again and this time the boys smiled but dared not laugh out loud.

"Perhaps, even better," Biktol added. Ambit's missing front teeth seemed to grow wider in approval.

Ampit merely laughed. He went back to the buck, now seemingly naked without its antlers. He squatted before it, grabbed its legs, hefted it, and had the whole carcass settled on his broad shoulders in one quick, fluid motion. He stood effortlessly, as if there was no buck on his shoulders. He turned toward the boys, and shifting his glance between the boys and *Apo* Dalalo said, "Thank you very much for your generosity and if you boys ever get in trouble, look me up." He smiled, turned and started up the trail.

His twin did the same with the other deer. He was deceptively strong for his lighter frame. "Yes, look us up if you ever need help," he echoed his brother and followed him up the trail.

"Same goes with me," Biktol said, again extending his arm toward the boys, who gripped at his forearm alternately, each awed at the sensation of seemingly gripping a hardened wood. He bowed his head toward *Apo* Dalalo. "Thank you again, *Apo* for your generosity."

"Don't mention it," *Apo* Dalalo said. "Give my regards to my old friend."

"I will, *Apo*. He'll be glad to hear that we met and you're well," Biktol said then he turned quickly and followed the twins.

They still had a mountain to cross.

Apo Dalalo waved after them. The boy sure moves like his father, he mused, as he took a final look at Biktol. The old man then took the antlers from Aklang and left the boys arguing as to who should carry which deer.

They would catch up with him, he thought as he took a leisurely pace back up the trail and down the bend heading to the village below. He had not used his bow but he felt good anyways. I should come up for a walk more often, he thought. But he decided against it as the day got hotter and then he thought of nothing else but the prospect of wallowing in the coldness of the river by the village. He loved to sit for hours in the shallow part of the river with the water up to his chin, enjoying the soothing caress of the water as it gently flowed around him.

He quickened his pace as he saw the river shimmering under the almost midday sun, way down below the mountain. *Apo* Dalalo smiled in anticipation, walking now with a little more spring in his steps. Behind him, the boys chattered spiritedly, still excited about the way the hunt turned out and their encounter with the hunters from Bangilo.

Chapter Thirteen

From high up on a ledge overlooking the clearing and the trail, a shadow stood up from the tall grass. Kulas squared his shoulders, feeling the tightness from staying hunched and immobile for so long on the ground go away, and watched as the hunters and his father and his nephews vanished from his sight. He slung his bow across his back, picked up the two spare arrows he had placed on the ground and put them back in his quiver along with the arrow he had previously nocked on his bow as he watched the scene unfold below. He walked back silently toward the shelter of the trees.

He had seen the hunters a couple of days ago, a few days after he parted ways with Akash, and he had followed them since, wondering why they were hunting so far away from their village. He knew they were hunting game from the way they were looking for signs, following the apparent trail caused by the buck and the does, the same herd he thought he had seen before. But the trail was leading too close towards his village. Usually tribes did not venture too far away from their own villages.

So Kulas followed them, keeping his distance yet always keeping sight of the three. That night he camped without a fire, chewing some jerky and wild fruit for dinner.

From his vantage point far back, he had crept forward, positioning himself on top of the ledge as he also saw his two nephews and his father approach the clearing. He was surprised at their presence, especially of his father, for he knew that he had not ventured into the forest to hunt for a long time since his mother died. He was not also aware of any talks of his nephews and their grandfather coming out to hunt. He was pleased that they did, but he was also worried at their unexpected encounter with the hunters from another tribe. He was ready to jump in and help if needed.

He had witnessed everything that happened below, and he shook his head in disbelief at what Aklang had done and sighed with relief as the two groups parted amicably. There was no need to let his presence known so he slid away without revealing himself.

He wondered now if he could have made the shots like his nephew did, with him shooting downwards from the top of the ledge, at men and not at deer. Perhaps, he shook his head again as his lips curled slightly to a trace of a smile as he recalled his nephew placing the three extra arrows on the ground before him, just the same way he did with two up on the ledge.

"Damn, the boy is good," he whispered, shaking his head in admiration as he replayed the scene in his mind. "Damn good."

Chapter Fourteen

It was mid-afternoon when *Apo* Dalalo and the boys finally got a glimpse of the village shimmering below the mountain. They had to make frequent stops for the boys to rest as they found out the deer on their shoulders seemed to get heavier with every step. Aklang was thankful that they only took two. Their grandfather would have had a hard time carrying one, he thought, but then again you never knew with the old man. He was still strong and no doubt could pull his own weight when it came to doing something that required strength.

There were little boys playing, climbing trees in the foothills as they made their descent. When the boys saw them coming carrying game, one of them immediately ran ahead to the village, shouting at the top of his lungs, announcing their arrival.

Apo Lakay Kagaid was in the backyard cleaning the fish he had just caught from the river when he heard the shouting from the little boy who had ran ahead to the village. The *Apo Lakay* put down the fish in the wood bowl and stood up slowly; grimacing as the pain in his knees that had been bothering him lately flared up suddenly. He frowned as he looked toward the sound, concern showing in his gnarly face. He strained his ears, trying to understand the excited and garbled words of the boy. As the village chief, *Apo* Kagaid was always concerned when he heard yelling especially in the middle of the afternoon when most people were out in the forest hunting or tending the little plots that they tilled, or perhaps fishing just like he did or taking a nap under the trees in their yards, seeking comfort from the heat of the day. Yelling usually meant trouble was afoot.

Apo Kagaid shrugged off the pain in his knees and walked hurriedly towards the noise, finally catching the boy's words as he got nearer. The boy stopped suddenly when he saw the old chief, ran closer and relayed his news. *Apo* Kagaid nodded and sighed with relief, shading his eyes as he strained to see Dalalo and his two grandsons come down the trail, the boys each carrying a deer. He dismissed the boy who promptly started his ruckus again as he ran toward the center of the village. *Apo* Kagaid sat down on a tree stump by the path and waited for *Apo* Dalalo and his grandsons who were followed by the boys who had abandoned whatever game they were playing in the foothills.

Apo Dalalo and the boys stopped by the old chief who had risen from where he was sitting as they got nearer. The two boys put down the carcasses on the ground with relief, wiping their brows and smiling broadly as *Apo* Kagaid examined the deer that were staring at him with glazed lifeless eyes.

"One shot," *Apo* Kagaid said admiringly as he put a finger on the hole where the arrow went in one of the deer. "You haven't lost your touch yet, my old friend." He nodded at *Apo* Dalalo.

"Ahh, old friend, I wish I could take the credit but I only watched. The boys did all the tracking and shooting." The old man decided to give credit for the successful hunt to both boys, not wanting to make Bagit feel left out.

Apo Kagaid looked and smiled at the boys, nodding his head in appreciation. Then he looked down at the carcasses again and turned his head to *Apo* Dalalo and the antlers that he was carrying, with a puzzled look on his face.

"Ahh, there was a big buck too where this came from," *Apo* Dalalo raised the antlers, "and a third doe but we only brought these two. We gave the other two to Lum-kang's boy and his friends." Briefly he relayed their encounter with the hunters from Bangilo, again leaving out how Aklang shot all four deer so as not to sound bragging.

"Lum-kang's boy? You met his boy of all people? I wonder how that old dog is doing." *Apo* Kagaid could not contain his surprise. Then he smiled at Aklang and Bagit without waiting for an answer from *Apo* Dalalo. "You boys did well. I can't believe you got four at one time."

"They didn't see us, *Angkay*. They were busy grazing so we were able to get close," Aklang said.

"Yes, *Apo*," Bagit added. "They were not even twenty five yards away."

"Twenty five yards? Did you mean twenty five feet?" *Apo* Kagaid was good with the bow himself but he rarely dared a shot beyond fifteen yards.

"Boy's right," *Apo* Dalalo said. "Twenty five yards at least. I thought they were too far myself. I wouldn't have believed it if I had not seen it."

"Really? So, each of you got two apiece?" *Apo* Kagaid addressed the two boys.

"No, *Apo*, he did all the shooting," Bagit pointed at Aklang.

Apo Kagaid's face now showed disbelief and consternation as if Bagit and *Apo* Dalalo were making him the recipient of a bad joke. He looked at Aklang who seemed uncomfortable with the conversation. The boy stared back at the old man, who was also his maternal grandfather, then lowered his gaze without saying anything.

Apo Kagaid turned to *Apo* Dalalo for confirmation. His old friend would not lie, he knew.

Apo Dalalo simply nodded. *Apo* Kagaid shook his head with disbelief and looked again at Aklang as if noticing the boy for the first time. Ittok's son had really grown to be a fine man, he thought. He smiled at Aklang then he turned around toward the village and on to the river where they would clean and butcher the deer. The hunters and the children followed. There would be meat for dinner in the village tonight.

By the time they reached the river, a group of men and women were already there with knives ready. Close by, a bonfire had been started where they would burn the furs off the deer. They would be cooked in different dishes, skin included.

As the deer were cleaned and butchered, the talk was on Aklang and his shooting. But the boy was nowhere to be found. He went up river with Bagit and their friends to swim and take the grime off the hunt. Aklang preferred not to be around the crowd. He was uncomfortable with all the attention he was getting.

"You should go out hunting more often," *Apo* Kagaid said to *Apo* Dalalo, blowing a twin stream of smoke through his nostrils. "It was good of you to go out with the boys today."

It was later that night and the two old men were sitting by the *balitang*, the all-purpose open-air bamboo platform that served as a sitting, sleeping and gathering place underneath the avocado tree between their huts, doing their after dinner ritual of smoking reed pipes. It was also the time when they discussed rumors and issues in the village and how to deal with them.

Apo Dalalo took his time to answer. He looked at his pipe in the dark, satisfied that the tobacco that he just lit was still glowing softly. He put the pipe in his mouth and inhaled deeply, the ember changing into a sharp flash of orange as he did so. Slowly, he blew the smoke through his mouth, fanning it out with a wave of his left hand as it lingered by his face, blown back by the soft breeze coming from the river.

"Yes, I think I should. I did not realize how much I missed hunting, although I did not even have the chance to use my bow." *Apo* Dalalo coughed as the smoke caught in his throat, his eyes smarting.

Apo Kagaid squinted at him. "Are you alright?"

"Yeah, I am," *Apo* Dalalo answered, clearing his throat. "This tobacco from the lowlands that Ittok brought back needed getting used to. It's not too bad though, is it?"

"Yeah. Not the same as the stuff that Allong grows by the river, but yes, it does have a pleasant aftertaste. A little mild though so I wonder why you are coughing."

"Something just caught in my throat. No worries at all."

"Sometimes I worry about you. You are growing old, my friend. You have to take care of yourself." *Apo* Kagaid said seriously, suppressing a sly smile in the dark. He loved to tease *Apo* Dalalo even when they were small boys.

"Hey, look who is talking. Remember you're a year older than me," *Apo* Dalalo retorted.

"Am I now?" *Apo* Kagaid said.

Apo Dalalo shook his head but did no answer. He knew that the best way to deal with *Apo* Kagaid's teasing was to ignore his comments or change the subject.

"You should have seen Aklang when he shot those deer," *Apo* Dalalo finally said. "I would not have believed he was capable of such shooting if I had not witnessed it."

"So tell me," *Apo* Kagaid said.

Apo Dalalo narrated the hunt again, in detail this time, not leaving anything, including their meeting with the hunters from Bangilo. *Apo* Kagaid did not interrupt him except for a few exclamations in the form of purely unintelligible grunts.

"I knew there was something special with that boy," *Apo* Kagaid said as *Apo* Dalalo finished his narration, his voice impressed and full of pride at the same time. After all, Aklang was also his grandson, him being the son of his youngest daughter, Kannoyan. "He took after his father and his uncles," he added diplomatically.

"Or maybe us," *Apo* Dalalo chuckled.

"Yeah, you're probably right." *Apo* Kagaid retorted, also giving out a short laugh that somehow ended up in a snort. *Apo* Dalalo refrained from laughing. He put his pipe in his mouth, inhaling the smoke deeply and slowly exhaled, watching the smoke curl away from his lips and nostrils with amusement.

Then for a spell, both men became silent, each one lost in his own thoughts, simply enjoying their smokes, contented with their world at the moment. They had known each other for so long that they felt secure and comfortable with the long stretches of silence between them.

"I heard from the valley," *Apo* Kagaid finally broke the silence.

Apo Dalalo did not reply. He waited patiently. The valley meant Awad, *Apo* Kagaid's oldest daughter who had gone down to live among the Christians when she was barely fourteen summers of age. That was a long time ago, *Apo* Dalalo thought as he remembered he was still a young man then, going into battle against the other mountain tribes. How long had it been? It was ages ago.

They barely discussed Awad now, but *Apo* Dalalo could not forget the girl who had married a Christian, had her own daughter, had in fact even brought her daughter back up in the village to live for a while, but then they went back down to the lowlands so the little girl could live as a Christian as was the wish of her Christian father and grandparents. *Apo* Dalalo found out

121

later that Awad wasn't even married properly. He remembered one of *Apo* Kagaid's sons, Akash the youngest, getting drunk one time, gathered a group of young warriors and planned to go down to the lowlands to avenge the perceived dishonor done to his sister. Fortunately *Apo* Kagaid got wind of the plan and talked them out of it.

That was surely a long time ago, *Apo* Dalalo thought now as he blew another smoke. This time he made sure to face away from the river and the breeze coming off from its direction and the smoke vanished silently into the night.

The last time *Apo* Dalalo heard of Awad and her daughter, the little girl had grown and had been married herself, widowed and had remarried again but still had no child of her own. He remembered they called Awad's girl Ilang here in the village but down in the valley she went by her Christian name, Maria Gabriela. As for Awad, she had been gone for a long time and never returned to the village even for a brief visit but *Apo* Kagaid talked of her as if she were just there and had never left ages ago. But *Apo* Dalalo tolerated his old friend when he talked of Awad and her girl for he knew how Kagaid loved his older daughter.

Apo Dalalo waited for his friend to continue, expecting the news of the arrival of a great grandchild. Above them, the avocado leaves rustled softly in the breeze. An owl hooted solemnly from the direction of the forest.

"Awad's daughter is widowed again. Her husband was killed, from what I understand, by his friends, over two moons ago," *Apo* Kagaid said slowly, shaking his head. "I can never understand the lowlanders. How can they kill a friend?"

"If they killed him, they were never his friends," *Apo* Dalalo said, taken a little bit aback with the news.

"Maybe, that could be so." *Apo* Kagaid nodded in the dark, the glow of his pipe bobbing up and down with the movement of his head. "They were his friends, according to Akash. Very close friends. They were with him from the beginning of his fight against the white men."

Apo Dalalo took out his pipe and studied its embers and said nothing. His mind was not on his tobacco though but on Akash and the stories he brought back now and then from the land of the Ilocanos. Akash, tall and lanky and a close friend of his youngest son Kulas had come and gone to the lowlands to see his sister and his niece so many times that he had affected the Ilocano way of dressing in trousers and shirts. Akash had gone down again a few weeks back. He must have come back, *Apo* Dalalo thought, although he did not remember seeing him by the river.

"Sometimes I wonder how a friend can turn into your worst enemy," *Apo* Kagaid continued, staring languidly into the darkening sky as if looking for an answer there.

Apo Dalalo lifted his eyes from looking at the pipe in his hand that was resting on his lap and watched his friend, his face toward the far-off sky. He followed Kagaid's gaze and noted the dark clouds gathering against the grey. I hope it will turn into rain tonight, he thought, but he refrained from voicing it, conscious of how his mind always wandered when the topic with his friend was that of Awad and her family.

"Like I said, they were never his friends. A true friend will stick by you no matter what and he won't kill you," he said instead, nodding in emphasis although *Apo* Kagaid was not looking.

But *Apo* Kagaid nodded his head in agreement in the dark, although he remained silent, deep in thought.

"I knew nothing good would come out of his fight with the white men. They are too well armed for their bolos and bamboo spears," *Apo* Dalalo added, sucking at his pipe, exhaling the smoke slowly and managing not to cough this time.

"Akash said they could fight, those Ilocanos, and they are brave. They are not scared to charge at the Spaniards with only their bolos and bamboo spears." *Apo* Kagaid turned to *Apo* Dalalo, his face wrinkling with an amused smile.

"But surely the Spaniards would cut them down with their *fusils*."

"Yes, their bolos and makeshift bamboo spears are no match against the soldiers' guns. But word is the rebels have *fusils* of their own, captured from dead soldiers, and they know how to use them too."

"Ah, I hope they do. It would be foolishness to fight against those soldiers with their guns and their protective armors which I heard some of them still use, with only bolos and bamboo spears." *Apo* Dalalo shook his head, placing back the pipe in his mouth and drew a deep breath through it, savoring the smoke that flooded his lungs and exhaling the smoke out leisurely.

"It would be but those Ilocanos are brave." *Apo* Kagaid did likewise, pursing his lips and the smoke came out in swirling circles. "They've been known to rush headlong at armed troops with no thought for their own safety."

"Bravery could kill you as fast as a poisoned arrow shot from behind a tree," *Apo* Dalalo said through the smoke.

"Yes, you and I have seen that so many times." *Apo* Kagaid shook his head sadly. "That's what they need, bows and arrows, Akash said, but they don't have them and they don't know how to use them even if they did."

A few months back, Akash had witnessed an ambush by the rebels of a platoon of soldiers. The rebels had the element of surprise and were at an advantage initially but they were eventually repelled back by the guns of the soldiers. Akash had to help them out with his arrows before they could make a safe retreat. It was the second time he had helped the rebels.

"No, I haven't seen any Ilocano with a bow and arrow yet," *Apo* Dalalo shook his head. "They have their bamboo spears but those couldn't go far."

"True. It would be a messy massacre if they keep fighting that way."

"War is messy. Always was. A massacre in a battle's ugly. It shouldn't happen."

Both old men had been in so many battles against hostile tribes and Ilocano interlopers where they had shown their bravery and skills. Both carried scars in their bodies as daily reminders of the callousness of battle. Again they fell silent for a spell.

"They ask for help," *Apo* Kagaid finally said, softly as if he did not want to say the words. "Awad told Akash that Ilang and the Ilocanos need help. Our help."

Apo Dalalo gave a start as he realized the implication of what his friend just said. He looked at *Apo* Kagaid but he remained silent, words eluding him at the moment. He puffed at his pipe, studying the glow of the embers as he inhaled and exhaled the smoke from the side of his mouth in short bursts without taking the pipe off. Then he took a long pull and held his breath for a moment, took the pipe off with his left hand, and cradled it on his lap. He exhaled the smoke slowly from his mouth making a soft hissing sound.

"It's not our fight," he finally said without looking at his friend, feeling regret as soon as the words came out, but he continued. He knew he was right. "We can't risk the lives of our boys for what the Ilocanos think and believe in."

"I thought the same thing," *Apo* Kagaid said with relief but his face was clouded with a shade of disappointment and regret. He wished his friend would have thought otherwise for he felt a sense of obligation to see that his grandchild was safe. Yet, his friend was right. "You're right, it's not our fight. I'll send the word back."

"Who's the messenger, Akash? I haven't seen him in the river."

"He's back but he broke his ankle. I'll have to send Sadang. He knows his way down there and he speaks both Ilocano and Spanish fluently," *Apo* Kagaid said. Sadang went to school down in the Ilocos and practically grew up in the place but he was back now with his own people.

"Does anyone else know?" *Apo* Dalalo said cautiously.

"Just my sons, Allong and Akash. I told them not to talk to anyone else about it."

"Let's keep it that way for now," *Apo* Dalalo said. "No need to give ideas to the young men." He knew the heady excitement the rumor of battle would put into a young man's mind. He had felt it many a time in his youth. In fact he still felt it, surprised now as he fought to suppress the faint stirring of lust for battle that again had woken up in his breast as they discussed the possibility of their involvement. He felt his heart quicken and he found himself puffing again at his pipe in close succession to calm down. Old fool, he thought, your fighting days are behind you.

"Yes, I agree. Let's keep it to ourselves. I'll tell Sadang that," *Apo* Kagaid said, nodding his head in the dark.

Apo Dalalo saw his friend nod against the darkening sky. He didn't say anything and waited for a while if *Apo* Kagaid had anything else in mind but the older man remained silent, buried deep in his thoughts.

"Yes, I'll talk to the boys," *Apo* Kagaid finally said as he slowly rose, a decision having reached. "Nobody else would know. It was good talking to you about this. Good night." He turned slowly, suddenly feeling tired and showing his old age at the same time, and headed toward his hut.

"Good night, old friend," *Apo* Dalalo murmured behind him, his friend's disappointment not lost to him. But he knew he was right not to get the village involved.

He stayed at the *balitang* for a long while. His pipe had turned cold and the mist had started to form when he finally stood up and slowly walked home. He paused for a moment when he reached the ladder going into his hut and looked up at the sky and at the stars glimmering in the distance wondering at the mysteries they held. Then he lowered his gaze to the darkness of the mountain now dappled with the softly rolling fog, beckoning like a seductive mistress of the night. He resisted its silent call reflecting on how something so dark and foreboding could also be so calm, beautiful and alluring at the same time.

Or was it the other way around? Who knew of the dangers that lurked under such beauty and calm?

Chapter Fifteen

The sun peeked to a clear sky with barely a trace of cloud over the mountains, just the low lying fogs that lurked beneath then drifted up to the crown of the forest. A soft breeze from the north brought a chill in the early morning and Allong shivered as he stepped out of the warmth of his hut. He shrugged the coldness off, shaking himself vigorously like a dog just out of the water. He took a deep breath, savoring the crisp morning air that went into his lungs, held it for a moment then he exhaled slowly. He did the exercise a few more times, holding his breath longer each time, then he headed toward his younger brother's hut. He had seen a small fire in Akash's backyard and he was sure he would find his brother there, warming himself up, perhaps with a freshly brewed mug of mountain coffee in his hands.

Akash was indeed sitting by the fire under the Tamarind tree but he was not drinking coffee. He was binding the iron head of a spear with a strip of wet leather. By his side was an earthen bowl half-filled with water, and in it soaked several strips of leather bindings. The fire flickered under a soft morning breeze and distorted shadows danced behind him on the tree trunk and beyond it, like silent mimics of an animated play.

The distant rustle of the banana leaves from the grove at the eastern side of the hut broke the serene silence of the morning, joined by the soft crackle of the firewood, punctuated every now and then by a persistent hiss as trapped sap got liberated by the heat only to perish in the fire. From beyond the banana grove, the *Ba-ay* River flowed lazily by the village in a soothing murmur as it sought its way to meet the Abra River a little bit further down to the east where they will eventually disgorge into the sea by the land of the Ilocanos. It was an idyllic tableau of peacefulness and serenity and Allong noted wryly the incongruity of the spear that his younger brother held in his hands, a vivid reminder of the constant dangers that lie beyond the safety of the village.

Allong slowly squatted by the fire opposite his brother without saying a word. He watched and waited patiently as Akash tied a finishing knot at about a palm's length from the base of the iron spear head. His breast swelled with pride at the ease and skill his younger brother displayed in his craft. Nobody in the village, or in the nearby villages for that matter, was better than Akash when it came to making spears.

Allong had the look of an old man although he had barely reached middle age. He was short and squat, very muscular in the shoulders and legs. His younger brother on the other hand was about a head taller and slightly built.

But Akash was deceptively strong and could last, it seemed forever, when it came to walking and running. But not at his present condition, Allong thought, for Akash's left ankle still looked swollen from twisting it as he jumped over a ditch coming back from the valley a few days ago.

"Kind of too early to be doing that," Allong finally said softly, picking up a piece of an almost burned out firewood and feeding the rest of it to the fire. He stretched his arms and spread his palms over the fire, pleasantly feeling the soothing heat on his cold hands.

Akash did not answer. He tilted his head as he raised the spear over the fire, inspecting his work more closely. Allong watched his brother and at the spear he held in his hand. He could not hide his admiration for the perfectly lined leather binding that wrapped the shaft firmly holding the spearhead. It would be close to impossible to move the steel head of the spear once the wet leather strip dried up and shrunk.

"'Can't sleep. Damned foot keeps me awake," Akash finally said, nodding at his ankle then looked at his older brother for the first time. He looked back down at the spearhead as he held it closer to the fire, twirling the shaft every now and then. He jerked it away from the fire as the unmistakable smell of over-heated leather permeated the air.

"Hah," Allong snickered. "You'll end up burning the whole thing. Better have it dried by the sun. It should be out and hot today." He looked up at the eastern sky, noting again the lack of clouds over the mountain.

"I may not be around to watch it; may be going back down to the valley today," Akash said.

"Not today, you won't," Allong said.

Akash looked up over the fire and met his brother's eyes questioningly. Allong used his head to gesture toward his brother's ankle.

"Can't walk with that."

"It's not too bad once I start moving."

"Sure, and you can't even sleep."

Akash didn't respond, his attention shifting back to the spearhead, arrested by its glint reflected by the fire.

"So what's the word?" he finally asked, looking up at his brother.

"No help. We don't fight. And Sadang is going down to give the word and perhaps bring Awad and Ilang back up," Allong pulled his hands away from the fire and rubbed his face, liking the feeling of the warmth transferred by his hands. "You can't walk the distance with that bum foot."

"It doesn't bother me much once I start walking," Akash said thinking Sadang of course would be the best person to go down to the lowlands. He had spent some years down there.

127

"So you say, and you can't even sleep on it," Allong reminded him again, shaking his head for emphasis.

Akash shrugged. His brother was right. The foot would bother him in the long trek to the lowlands, even if he used a crutch. He silently chastised himself again for failing to see the rock at the other side of the ditch when he leapt across.

"Who decided?" He caught his brother's eyes through the smoke.

"*Ama* and *Apo* Dalalo, as far as I know."

Akash did not respond. He knew that the village would follow whatever his *Ama* Kagaid and *Apo* Dalalo had decided.

"And Kulas?" he said.

"No. No word from him. He's still up there," Allong eyed the mountain top.

For a long while nobody spoke. The brothers knew Kulas came and went as he wanted. There was no use speculating when he would return. There was always the wooden drum if the village needed him.

"They won't come up," Akash finally said. "Awad and Ilang, they won't come up here. Sadang won't be able to convince them. I tried before and they wouldn't listen."

"I'm afraid so," Allong replied. "But we have to try. Maybe they'll change their minds now that Diego's gone."

"Maybe, but Ilang is leading the rebels now..." Akash's voice trailed, shaking his head and not finishing the sentence. There was no need. Allong understood.

"Maybe, Awad would come at least," Allong said.

Akash merely shook his head. He laid down the spear and stretched out a hand to get another pole from the bunch laid in a row by the base of the tree. Allong now noticed the woven basket filled with spearheads sitting slightly behind his brother, some were made out of stone, and some in iron. He expected for us to fight, he thought, as his brother selected a strip of soaking leather, letting the water drip back down to the earthen bowl as he held the wet strip over it. From where he sat, the leather strips in the bowl looked like small eels to Allong and reminded him of breakfast, but he remained seated, waiting for more questions from Akash. He knew his brother. Akash did not speak until he made up his mind. He was thinking while he kept his hands busy.

"Why?" Akash said suddenly that Allong was startled for a moment and was unsure of what his brother meant.

"Why what?" he said.

"Why are we not going to fight and help Ilang?"

"Not our fight. We don't get involved."

128

"And *Apo* Dalalo, what does he think?"

"Those were his own words, 'not our fight and we don't get involved'," Allong said. "*Ama* agrees with him."

Akash nodded. He knew *Apo* Dalalo and *Apo* Kagaid were not only the recognized leaders of the tribe but also the best of friends who think the same way most of the time. The tribe followed whatever they decided. He pulled the basket closer to the fire and picked up a stone spear head. He fitted it on the split end of the pole and started binding it with the strip of leather. His hands moved skillfully with precision, culled from constant repetition of the process which he had been doing since he was a little boy.

Allong took a stick and stirred the fire mindlessly, causing sparks to fly and the ashes danced like fairies over the flame, vanishing in a swirl of smoke that wafted in the air. He looked at his brother anticipating him to speak.

"Our blood runs in her veins." Akash raised his head and met his brother's gaze across the fire. "She's one of us."

"You don't agree with them," Allong said. It was not a question. Just a simple statement of what he assumed his brother felt. He felt his body warming up, and not from the fire. He felt the same way too.

Akash sighed. His brother knew him too well. He had always been like that since they were little. He always seemed to know what he was thinking. Yet he was the same way too. He had the knack of sensing what the other man was feeling and what he was about to do. And this talent had proven useful now and again, getting him out of trouble, especially when he was down in the valley among the Ilocanos. He wound the strip tightly around the shaft as soon as he was contented of the placement of the spearhead, and he watched disinterestedly as his hands moved in practiced easy flow around the shaft.

"And you as well," Akash finally said without looking at his brother. "You don't agree with their decision."

Allong did not answer. He nodded silently. There was no need for words. His brother knew. They may not agree with the old men but what they decided was the way it had to be. They were not going to get involved. Yet, still there was that reservation in their minds.

"Tell me again about Awad's daughter." He said changing the subject. As far as he was concerned, the topic of getting involved in the troubles of the Ilocanos with the Spaniards was closed. There was no need for further discussion on the issue.

"She's a fine woman, like her mother." Akash's hands did not pause from going around the shaft with the leather binding. "She doesn't say much but she has fire in her. Once I saw her break into a conversation between her

129

husband and his friends and she argued with them for a while and never backed down. I don't remember now what they were talking about but she stood her ground and the men listened. Funny thing, they took her as their equal." He smiled and shook his head fondly at the memory.

"Damn," he added, grinning at his brother. "She reminded me of you, stubborn as all get out."

"And now she leads them," Allong said, ignoring his brother's allusion to his stubbornness. It was true enough, he never wavered from his opinions or on anything he had set his mind up to do.

"Yes," Akash said, "You taught her well, those summers she was here when she was little."

"She spent more time with you."

"True." A trace of a smile flitted across Akash's face as he fondly recalled Ilang following him around for protection from the other kids who teased her a lot because she was fairer than most, calling her a Christian half-breed.

"She always did get into fights with the other kids," Allong said.

"Yeah, but that stopped after you showed her how to defend herself."

"She already knew a few tricks when I started teaching her. She said Awad taught her. And you too," Allong added.

"I wasn't always around to protect her so I had to teach her how to fight also."

"She fought better than most of the boys, especially with the sticks and the long knife; shot the arrow better too." Allong allowed himself the briefest of a smile.

"She still does." Akash's hands paused, a thumb pressing on the leather strip to hold it in place. "Good thing Kulas was around also to protect her or she would have been in fights all day. She never backed down."

"Yeah, Kulas always had a soft side for her." Allong nodded his head, and he raised his head from staring at the fire, looked at is brother, worried in a way for what Akash was going to say next. It occurred to him that the issue of the Ilocanos would not just go away.

Akash did not meet his gaze. "I wonder what he would do," he said softly as his hands started their fluid movement around the shaft again.

Allong barely heard him from across the fire, but he flinched inwardly. He remained silent, he understood what his brother meant, and he had a good suspicion of where Kulas would stand on the issue. And where Kulas stood, so too did most of the young warriors. He sighed. He was not looking forward to troubles with the white men.

"The Ilocanos," he said, finally accepting the fact that there was no skirting the topic, "do they have a chance?"

"They are brave and they can fight, but against those guns and artillery, they don't have much of a chance." Akash did not even pause before answering. Neither did his hands stop what they were doing.

"Don't they have guns?" Allong said.

"Some, stolen from the soldiers, but they don't have enough to go around. They don't even have bows and arrows." He shook his head in disgust as he remembered that time he witnessed the Ilocanos ambush a troop of soldiers on patrol a few months back when Diego was still alive.

Akash had arrived in the valley shortly before noon and after a quick lunch with Awad and her daughter, he went under the Caimito tree behind their house to rest. Underneath the tree was a balitang and he had it all to himself. He lay down in it carefully putting his bow and arrows within easy reach by his side and tried to take a quick nap.

He was drifting off pleasantly down the river back in the village in a trance-like dream when subconsciously he heard the hushed voices of men. He awoke with a start, momentarily confused with his surroundings. He heard the voices again coming from the house.

'Diego must have arrived with some of his men,' he thought. He looked at the sun and was surprised to see that it was almost way down to the west.

He got up slowly, gingerly stretching his arms and back to loosen the tightness in his muscles that had settled in while he slept. He picked up his bow and arrows and placed them closer to the trunk of the Caimito tree then he sat back down on the balitang, his head tilted toward the house, catching a word now and then but he could not make out what the discussion was about. He fought the urge to go inside.

Finally a form emerged from the back of the house, paused a bit by the door as others followed. The leader said something and waved his hand toward the trail at the back of the house and his men headed that way while he moved towards the Caimito tree where Akash sat.

Akash recognized Diego as he got closer.

"Good afternoon, Apo," Diego said while he was still a few feet away. He held a rifle in his left hand; a long bolo hung sheathed from his left hip. A dried squash shell hat sat on his head, held by a braided piece of thin abaca rope, knotted under his chin.

"Good afternoon to you, too," Akash stood up and clasped Diego's extended right hand in a firm handshake.

"Had a good rest?" Diego leaned the rifle against the tree trunk.

"Yes, slept longer than I thought. There's a good breeze out here."

"That's good," Diego tried to smile but it was obvious to Akash that something was bothering him.

"What's going on?" Akash nodded at the gun and looked toward the house.

"Ahh, that's what I need to talk to you about," Diego replied, "but please sit down."

Diego waited for Akash to sit then he himself sat down beside the older man.

"I have to go someplace and I want to ask you for a favor. Please stay here with Maria and your sister for a few days while I am away and wait until I come back."

Akash did not respond. He looked at the house while he waited for Diego to continue.

"There's danger," Diego continued. "I may be gone for a while and I may not be back. If I am not back in three days, please take Maria and Ina Awad away from here. Bring them back to the village."

"What kind of danger are they in?" As far as Akash was concerned, Diego could take care of himself. He only worried about the women.

"You must have heard of our troubles with the Spaniards. They want me dead. I am afraid they will take them if they cannot take me."

"Is Ilang involved in the fight too?"

"No, I would not let her, but she supports what I do."

Akash nodded. Just like her mother, he thought, loyal as a dog.

"Will you promise to take them?" Diego asked.

He met Diego's pleading eyes. "I'll take care of them," he said. "Go and may the gods keep you safe."

"Thank you, Apo. And you as well." Diego clasp his hand turned around and followed his men.

Awad and Ilang watched him from the window as he went out the backyard gate flashing a quick look at the house. The women silently waved their hands at his back.

Akash sat under the Caimito tree for a while long after Diego disappeared among the trees, then he slowly got up and went inside the house without knocking. He found Awad and Ilang talking to one another in the dining area by the kitchen. They sat by the table across from each other. A covered plate of rice cakes was between them but neither was eating. They briefly stopped talking as Akash entered.

"Uncle, come sit down and eat something." Ilang stood up, removing the cover on the rice cakes and pointing at the bench where she sat. "I'll get some coffee."

"Don't bother," Akash waved his hand in dismissal as he sat down. "I'm still full."

Ilang ignored him and got a clay mug drying upside down from a bamboo stick tied into the ledge that held the water jars by the kitchen window. She went to the clay stove and filled the mug with coffee from the pot sitting on the hot coals covered with ash and returned to the table. She placed the mug before Akash and sat down beside him, pulling the plate full of rice cakes closer to her uncle. "Eat some. They are good. Mother made them."

Akash nodded but he reached for the mug instead and wrapped his hands around it, liking the warmth that slowly emanated from the coffee mug. He raised the mug gently with both hands and took a tentative sip. The coffee was hot enough and good. A little milder and sweeter than the strong coffee back home but it was pleasant to the taste. He put the mug down and reached for a piece of rice cake. He bit the piece in half and chewed for a while, the two women looking at him in amusement. He swallowed the pasty cake then chased it down with another sip from the mug.

"Good," he said, pushing the plate to the middle of the table so the women can also get some of the rice cakes. "So, what's going on with Diego?" He looked at Ilang then moved his eyes to his sister.

"He's fighting the Spaniards, Uncle," Ilang lowered her head then she talked for a good part of an hour. Awad put in a word every now and then. Akash listened patiently.

"There's a troop of soldiers going on patrol and they're going to ambush them tonight. I am scared," Ilang finally said, shaking her head as she stared out the window.

"Ambush the soldiers with just the handful of men he had?"

"There are more of them out there, Akash," Awad said. "A lot more. The men you saw were just his trusted friends and advisers. They are the leaders of the rebels. They just dropped by for a short visit."

Akash put the rest of the rice cake in his mouth and took a long drink of coffee, almost draining the mug. He stood up and walked toward the window as he chewed, looking at the backyard and the trail beyond where Diego went with his men. He could track them down if needed, he thought, as he debated if he wanted to go after them, his curiosity now piqued. He strained his neck closer to the window to look at the position of the afternoon sun. It would be dark soon.

"I want you to stay here but there may be trouble," Awad said as Akash returned to the table. "Rest for a couple of days then it is best perhaps for you to go back to the village. Tell Ama I am fine and grateful for the venison and the pindang-igat that you brought." Her family in the village knew that the pindang, the dried salted eel, was her favorite breakfast food.

Akash looked at his sister, ignoring her words. "Are you and Ilang in danger?"

Awad looked at his brother's face but did not immediately answer. She lowered her gaze and found a spot on the table that seemed to have caught her attention. "We will be fine," she said finally, emitting a deep sigh."The soldiers have not bothered us."

"You and Ilang come with me to the village until this thing blows over. You will be safe there." Akash said, sensing his sister's discomfort on the subject.

"I can't leave Diego," Ilang said." My place is here with him."

"I will stay here also," Awad said. "I'll die with worry up in the village not knowing what's going on down here with Ilang."

"Then I will stay for a while, at least until Diego comes back," Akash sat back down on the bench.

"Don't get involved, Akash." Awad reached out and gently touched her brother's arm. She knew her brother could be emotional sometimes when family was involved. "Don't get the whole village involved in this fight."

Ilang bowed her head not daring to look into her mother's pleading face. She knew that if a member of the tribe got hurt, or God forbids, get killed, then all the warriors of the tribe and their allies in the Budong, the tribal coalition pact, would come down to the valley for retribution and justice, which usually ended with another life or more taken.

"I won't," she heard Akash answer. "I am only staying to see that both of you are safe until Diego returns."

"We will be alright. Don't worry about us."Awad patted Akash's arm affectionately. "We will be alright."

Akash did not answer. He took another piece of rice cake, and refilled his coffee from the pot. He ate slowly without saying anything, taking a sip now and then and thinking of what to do next. Then he made up his mind. He would follow Diego's group and see with his own eyes what they were up to. The women watched him silently, futilely guessing what was in his mind.

"I'll be sleeping outside under the tree. It's too hot for me here," he finally said as he put down his empty cup.

"I'll get you a blanket and a pillow after dinner," Awad said.

"No need for that. I'll be fine. I am already full so there's no need for dinner either." Akash said, looking out the window. Awad followed his gaze. In her heart she knew her brother will not be sleeping under the Caimito tonight.

"Stay here, Akash. Don't go out there." She knew her brothers. There was no talking them out when they made up their minds, just like their father, but she felt she had to say something. She was scared.

Akash looked at her. He could never hide anything from his sister, even when they were little kids. Somehow she always knew what he felt.

"Lock the doors," he said. "I'll be alright. But if I am not back by noon the day after tomorrow and the soldiers come, both of you run up to the village."

"Where are you going, Uncle?" Ilang asked.

Akash did not answer. He turned around and gathered his bow and arrows where he placed them by the door when he entered.

"I'll be back," he said as he went out the door.

"Be careful," he heard Awad say behind his back. He raised the arm that held his bow in acknowledgment without looking back.

The tracks were easy enough to follow. Akash recognized Diego's sandals print as he followed the footprints of his men. The tracks veered off the dusty trail some ways outside the town limits as it got closer to an area where the trees grew thicker. Akash kept his steady pace. There were plenty of signs as the group did not bother to hide their tracks. There was a wide swatch of depressed grass and broken branches as evidence of their passing.

The sun was going down fast in the west and the birds had started to flock to their roosting place for the night. Akash could hear their shrill twitter overhead among the dense foliage of the trees as they staked their roosting places. He studied the tracks and figured he should catch up with them before the sun fully went down. He quickened his pace.

He was coming up to a clearing when he saw them. He was surprised at their number. Awad and Ilang surely were not exaggerating when they said there were more of Diego's men. And he saw them now, sitting and standing in groups under the trees, ragged and determined men.

Diego was in their midst, obviously talking as he gestured wildly with his hands to emphasize a point. Akash was too far to hear what he was saying but he dared not go any closer. He did not want his presence known. He watched, keeping to the shadows. Diego's men were in rapt attention, taking in his every word.

Akash retreated further into the shadows, easing himself down slowly behind a huge pine tree. He rested his back against the trunk, facing the way he had come from, away from the group. He could hear them well enough if they moved. He had resolved to follow the group to find out what they were up to but he had no intention of getting involved. At least not yet, he smiled wryly. He, like most of the young men in his village, loved a good fight but he was not about ready to face the Spaniards with their fusils yet. He had seen their guns and had heard about the damage they can do but he had not actually witnessed one yet. Maybe he would find out tonight or the next day. He smiled at the prospect as he closed his eyes for a much needed rest but his ears were attuned to the sounds of the group beyond the clearing.

He felt rather than saw them when they finally moved out. There was a sudden stillness and Akash knew they were gone. He took a peek around the

135

trunk of the pine tree and saw nothing but shadows where the group had been. He wondered if he had dozed off. He quickly scrambled to his feet, adjusting the bow astride his shoulders as he stood up and entered the clearing at a run, careful not to make any unnecessary noise. He passed the clearing quickly and moved stealthily from trunk to trunk as he reached the trees. He looked at the signs and breathed a sigh of relief as he realized they were not that too far off. He went to a higher ground and finally saw them not too far ahead.

The group had slowed down on a promontory at the edge of the tree line. Akash could see the trace of a wide trail slightly below the promontory where Diego's group stopped. It curbed below it and disappeared around a bend a short way to the south. Beyond the trail was a berm covered with shrubs and grasses tall enough to hide men lying on the ground. Akash saw some of Diego's men move across the trail to the berm at the opposite side. If they were planning for an ambush, they had picked a good place, he thought. He looked up the sky noting that the sun had started its descent behind the mountains to the west. The day had gone colder and he exhaled softly through his mouth, enjoying the cold caress of a passing breeze. He figured there would be a few moments more of daylight before darkness took over.

He moved down from his observation point and headed toward the group. He stopped behind a huge tree a few yards from the men who were hidden among the bushes, leaned his back against the trunk and slowly slid down to his haunches, back pressed lightly on the trunk, ignoring the harsh bark scraping against his bare back. Then he closed his eyes and waited.

The day had gone colder as the sun went down. It was calm with nary a breeze rustling the tree leaves as they hung limply on the branches. Akash breathed slowly, in and out, until he felt his muscles loosened and more relaxed. All the walking and running he had done in the past couple of days seemed to be catching up to him. He eased himself lower, his back searching for a comfortable spot against the tree, found it, then stretched his legs in front of him without taking his back off from where it fit snuggly against the trunk, his bottom gratefully finding the grassy ground. He kept that position for a while, got more comfortable and dozed off. He was sure the group was not going anywhere soon, not from the way they had staked themselves on the area by the trail.

The sun had gone down and dusk had settled in when Akash heard the unmistakable sound of approaching horses, their shod hooves tinkling against stone every now and then. He opened his eyes and moved around the trunk. He could not see the soldiers yet except for the dust that they created up the trail, visible under the faint hue of the dusk, and now hearing the metallic sound of their steel scabbards and their horses' hooves.

Akash took a deep breath and rolled his shoulders to ease the tightness that had set in while he rested. Then lowering himself, he crawled closer to the trail, well below the place where Diego's group waited. The men were so engrossed at watching the trail that they would not have noticed if Akash was walking erect behind them. There was a thick growth of bushes further down the trail and Akash headed towards it, crouching and dashing through the last few yards. He squatted behind the bushes and watched Diego's men, just a few paces away, so unaware of his presence. If he were the enemy, he could have had killed two or three of them, he was sure of it, before they knew he was there. These Ilocanos would not last long in a battle, he thought.

Then he saw the soldiers, their lances and rifles glistening in the dusk. A small troop on recon patrol, but they were well armed and without a doubt always ready to fight.

Akash saw the Ilocanos move closer to the top of the berm, their few rifles and spears ready. The man closest to the soldiers, Diego, Akash now realized, raised his left arm, signaling for his men to hold and wait. The soldiers came up the trail below them, unaware of the impending ambush, their pace steady and unhurried. The lead soldiers passed Diego yet he held his hand up and the rebels waited patiently, immobile as the soldiers plodded on below. The lead horses were but a few paces away from where Akash was hidden when Diego dropped his hand and yelled, "Fire!"

The rebels responded eagerly, rising from the grass and yelling as they opened up with their rifles, and those armed with spears hurled their sharp pointed bamboo spears in abandon at the mass of soldiers who were totally caught by surprise. But they were a veteran group. They lost four in the initial volley, with more wounded but superficially, and they fought to control their mounts which were frightened and agitated by the sound of the rifles and the yelling of the rebels as well as the smell of blood. The horses whose riders fell at the initial volley ran off wildly up the trail, past the lead soldier who had stopped and started to shoot back, while the rest spurred their horses forward in unison, closing rank. They stopped and dismounted when they reached the lead soldier, forming a circle with their mounts, using them as shields.

But the spears flew thickly through the air and Akash watched as the soldiers and their horses fell one by one until there were just two left, bleeding but still standing. The rebels were now running down the hillside toward the fallen soldiers and the two survivors looked at one another and came up with an unspoken common decision. They remounted their horses

137

which were surprisingly unscathed and spurred away from the massacre. Spears flew after them as the rebels came down at a rush but the two had a pretty good start and their horses were as eager as them to get away from the crazed ambushers and they were ready to run. The spears dropped futilely behind them.

Akash watched in awe as the horses caught their stride and ran fluidly up the trail toward him. Then he caught Diego's booming voice coming loud and clear above the din, urging his riflemen to shoot at the fleeing soldiers.

"Don't let them get away! They'll go for reinforcement! Shoot them!" he yelled. A couple of shots came from above the trail but missed their targets as the soldiers sped on, past where Akash crouched behind a bush a few paces from the trail. Akash watched as Diego frantically waved his hands at his men urging them to go after the fleeing soldiers but the two survivors had a pretty good start. They were moving at a good clip past Akash now and were soon totally out of range from the rebels. More shots came from the rebels but the two fleeing soldiers never broke stride. Their horses ran with gusto, but suddenly each snorted and reared in surprise as their riders fell off with a couple of arrows sprouting from their backs. They stopped for a while then cantered toward the trees as their riders did not move from where they fell on the ground.

Down the trail, the rebels who were running after the fleeing soldiers likewise stopped when they saw them fall from their mounts. Then someone started yelling again and rushed forward and a half a dozen of the rebels followed. They stopped when they reached the fallen soldiers and looked at one another, bewildered as they saw the arrows sticking from the soldiers' backs. They knew no one from their group who had a bow, much less knew how to use one. They looked around but they saw no one.

Akash sat hidden behind the bushes then he silently eased back toward the trees. He slung his bow back on his shoulders when he reached the safety of a huge Narra tree, then headed back toward the town. There was no need to hang around. He had seen how the ambush went and he cursed himself for not having the control not to get involved. But he could not let the two soldiers get away and report what happened. Perhaps the rebels could cover their tracks but he knew that was wistful thinking. Whether they liked it or not, the Ilocanos were in a war which, he was afraid, they could not win. They were just lucky this time as they caught the soldiers by surprise and they had the numbers. But it would not always be so.

There was no light in the house when he got back to town that night. He slept in the balitang under the Caimito tree. Despite being tired he slept lightly, half expecting either the rebels or the Spanish soldiers to march into town at any moment, but the night passed peacefully. He was up at first light then went into the house as soon as he heard the women moving about in the kitchen. Awad looked at him questioningly without saying a word as he entered, and Akash knew he could not lie. His sister would know.

He told them about the ambush including his involvement. There was no need to lie for he knew that Diego would know where those arrows came from that killed the fleeing soldiers. Awad of course was understandably upset with his involvement and bid him to go back up to the village right away and made him promise not to come back to town. He consented and asked them again to go with him but the women were obstinate about their decision to stay. He left after breakfast but he did not keep his promise to stay away from the town. He went back down every now and then without letting Awad know of his presence, inconspicuously mingling with the Ilocanos and other Itnegs in the marketplace and staying out of sight of the Spanish authorities as necessary.

By then, just a few months from that eventful ambush, Diego and his unlikely band of rebels had grown dramatically in number especially when it was rumored that the British were sending help although he remembered that Ilang was suspicious about it.

"I don't trust the British, Diego," he had heard Ilang say one time. "They will be just like the Spaniards. They'll end up slaving us just the same."

"We need their help, my dear wife," Diego had replied. "We have to trust them. We have not much choice. Don't let your hatred of the Spaniards cloud your thinking about all the white people."

"No, it's not just that, husband. Those people did not come all the way here to hand you this land." But Diego dismissed Ilang's concern and clung to his hope for the help that never came. Yet they surprisingly won a decisive battle in Cabugao.

And shortly after that, they took over Vigan and Diego proclaimed the liberation of the Ilocos from the Spaniards, making himself the President of the Ilocos.

But it was short-lived, as was his life.

"We need to bring Awad back."

Akash looked up with a start as he heard Allong speak, breaking his thoughts.

"What?" he asked, shaking his head slightly as if clearing it of some cobwebs.

"Tsk-tsk-tsk!" Allong said, smirking. "For a while there you're out of it that I thought you were sleeping with your eyes open, but your fingers kept moving. What were you thinking about anyway?"

'No-nothing," Akash said. "Just remembering things about Awad and her daughter."

"We have to bring them here," Allong said, his eyes on his brother's inscrutable face.

"You know she wouldn't listen, not to Sadang, especially now that Diego's gone," Akash replied, meeting his brother's gaze over the fire. His eyes mirrored his resigned thoughts but there was a glint of stubbornness in them.

"I know. I'm afraid of that. You'll have to go and talk to her again. Give it a couple of days and go as soon as your ankle heals. Tell her *Ama* is not doing well and he asks for her. Tell her anything but get her back up here." Allong stood and turned around without waiting for his younger brother to respond. There was no point in asking Gabriela to give up her fight with the Spaniards, not now as she had all the right to avenge her husband's death, but Awad, maybe they can still get her out and away from the troubles.

Akash nodded after his brother. He knew it was useless to talk to Awad but he also knew that he had to go back down to the valley to make sure she is safe. He had a feeling his sister would not heed him. If so, maybe he could just turn around and kill that traitor who killed Tiago, despite what Kulas thought. Then his travel would not have been a waste. He smiled as he warmed up to the idea.

He tied a knot to finish the binding that he was doing and held the spearhead over the fire without inspecting his handiwork. He leaned the spear against the trunk after a while then he picked up another pole and groped for a loose spearhead in the basket. His hand fell on a stone head but he did not lift it up. The mood to make some more spears had suddenly left him.

His stomach growled, looking for breakfast, and that decided it for him. His hand in the basket came up empty and he put the pole back down. He stood up gingerly. He stretched and tensed his back, sighing with relief as his muscles loosened up, then he bent down and pulled the firewood away from the fire, grinding the burning ends in the ashes. He picked up the finished spears and the poles and went to his hut, walking slowly, favoring his left foot. He stowed the poles and spears underneath the raised floor of the hut. Then he went to the water jar, filled a coconut shell cup with water and went back toward the dying fire in the backyard, its embers glowing silently in the grey of the morning. They sizzled in protest as he doused the embers with the water from the cup. He spread the ashes around to make sure all the embers were gone. Satisfied, he went back to the hut, bringing with him the basket of spearheads.

His son Bagto was still fast asleep in his coconut frond woven mat on the floor. He fought the urge to wake him up and he tiptoed silently by the sleeping boy, making his way toward the kitchen where Pol-looy was busy preparing breakfast. He watched her silently from the doorway as she moved by the clay stove unaware of his presence. Her hair was pulled to a tight bun on the top of her head and her elegant neck arched gracefully as she bent down to blow at the fire using a hollow bamboo tube. She was still as beautiful as that first time he saw her in her village at the far side of the mountain, a couple of days trek away. He smiled, realizing how lucky he was for having a woman like her. He would surely miss her again when he went down to the valley. Sometimes he wondered why he even wanted to get away from her even just for a couple of days. He was a fool, he knew, but a brother must do what he can for a sibling. He limped soundlessly into the kitchen and wrapped his arms around her waist. She straightened up, startled for a moment. He held her tight and kissed her bare neck.

"I'll burn your breakfast," she protested halfheartedly as she tilted her back and pressed her cheek against his.

Chapter Sixteen

Maria Gabriela woke up with a slight headache. She could not sleep the night before despite being in a warm bed again for a change. Truth was she had not been sleeping well since Diego was brutally murdered. She had been on the run, and yes, sleep did not come easy to a pursued prey. She needed a safe place to rest and most important of all she needed help.

She had sought refuge here, where she knew she was safe, at the foot of the mountains, the Cordilleras as the Spaniards called the mountain range, although she never heard the highland people call it that. There was a small hut, one of several that were scattered about in the mountains that tribal hunters built and stayed when they went far from their villages in pursuit of game, and this one she had sought, relying from a long time memory buried from her youth to find it. She had found the place, thank God, at almost the point of exhaustion, with some of the battle-hardened men and several of the women beginning to doubt the soundness of their decision to go with her.

It was hard to comprehend but they followed her, this rag-tag group of men and their women who had devotedly followed Diego, vowing their allegiance to his widow and renewing their commitment to the cause. "For whatever it is," she hissed under her breath. She herself had begun to have doubts in the futility of it all. For the cause, whatever it was or whatever it had morphed into, she wasn't certain now. Was all this worth it, she asked herself as she sat up and looked at the tents of the sleeping band below her hut. It did not matter much to her now, one way or the other. When they killed Diego in cold blood, to her, it had turned personal. The cause and these men and women were just along for the ride.

She pitied them, these people who now followed her when Diego died. Murdered, she reminded herself again, fueling her hatred and resolution to go on. Some of them were sleeping in the open despite their thread-bare clothes, rags mostly, some underneath the trees, too tired to set up their own tents. Most of them have never ventured out this far before from their lowland homes, much more go up a mountain and into a dense forest with thoughts of hostile tribal headhunters lurking in the shadows playing with their imagination. For they were lowland farmers and fishermen who believed in a cause, or were forced to fight due to personal injustices done to them by the Spaniards and their local lapdogs. She herself had begun to doubt the judiciousness of their fight. But she must move on, she resolved, for there was no other option but to go on. If nothing else, the feeling of revenge still burned hot in her heart.

But she needed help, much more help than these men could provide for they were pitifully outnumbered and outgunned. And she knew where she could get help, she hoped. A good couple more day's trek up the mountain would take her to another place that had been buried deeply also in the memory of her youth.

She tried to remember with trepidation the path she would take. Could she find the place after all the years? She had to, she resolved, for there was no other place to go for refuge or for help. She knew that if she followed the river, they would eventually get there. Whether they would be welcomed was an entirely different matter. Or if they could even get the help they needed.

But she must try. There was no other choice.

She had a commitment to these men who had put their trust in her. They whispered among themselves when they approached the mountain and into the forest but they followed her, with her Uncle Nicolas by her side, Diego's old and long time friend, and Miguel Infiel and Esteban Flores, her delegated officers, and Diego's cousin, Sebastian, for they had nowhere else to go either. Just like her. Their families had been killed, and those who had survived were on the run themselves. They could not return to their towns for they were all marked men, and their women along with them. So they followed her, these men who had blindly followed Diego. She had become a leader by default. And the biggest joke of them all, she had heard that the Spaniards have been calling her *La Generala*.

She shook her head in disgust. She did not like the idea of being called *La Generala* for she did not know how to lead men. Much more murdering rebels, as the men and women were called by the Spaniards. No, she did not like the prospect at all, and the thought that she was leading them all behind a fruitless cause and to an eventual damnation at the cruel hands of the Spaniards was adding to her worries. Perhaps a dip in the nearby *Ba-ay* River, one of the two headways of the Abra River below, would help clear her mind and perchance get rid of her headache too.

She walked through the makeshift camp, making her way among the sleeping bodies who were so tired that no one stirred while she passed by. They would have been all dead, she thought, if the enemy chanced on them. But they were safe here for the time being. The Spaniards never ventured this far up in Abra and so far away from *Ciudad Fernandina*. So she let them sleep. They deserved it, but they should have posted a guard. They had to be vigilant all the time if they expected to live through this. She was about to kick the last man sleeping at the fringes of the camp when a voice stopped her.

"Good morning, Maria. You're up early. Shouldn't you be resting?"

Maria was startled by the sudden voice then sighed with relief. There was a guard who was awake after all. She should give her men more credit for after all most of them had been in the struggle much longer than she did.

"I couldn't sleep, Badong. I thought everyone was asleep."

"Not me, and the other three guards posted in the perimeter."

"Thanks, Badong." Maria nodded. Perhaps she really had underestimated these men. "I was planning on a quick swim before everyone wakes up."

"Do you want me to go with you?" There was no malice in his voice, just concern for her safety.

"No, there's no need. I'll be safe, thank you. Please make sure nobody comes that way until I return," she gestured. Somehow she felt her face blushing in the dark.

"I will, Maria. Be careful."

"Thank you," Maria Gabriela said without looking back.

She trudged through the wet morning grass, down the slope toward the river. There was just enough light to see where to put her feet between the stones by the riverbank. She did not want to step on them for they were still slick wet with dew. She could not risk a broken ankle.

She made her way toward a huge boulder that abutted a deep part of the river. She remembered the boys in the village using a boulder similar to this as a diving platform when she was little. She herself had taken her first dive there on that boulder by the river in the village amidst the protestations of her mother.

And she remembered her mother now as she took off her clothes under cover of the boulder, for it seemed that everything in the place was a reminder of her mother. She went through a lot, her dear mother, suffering too many things unjustly, mostly from the hands of the lowlanders, the so-called Christians, including the family that took her when she sought refuge in their midst to avoid tribal troubles in the mountains. The poor woman thought she had found a family when she had her, but even her own father, Anselmo, the family's older son, did not stand right by her.

Maria Gabriela shook her head as she clambered up naked to the top of the boulder, trying to shake the bad memories in the process, but they came, in droves, even as she plunged down into the cold river below with a perfect swan dive that would have made the boys in his mother's village gape in admiration.

And she was headed to that village now, with her lowlander, Christian men in tow, for help from the *Itnegs*, her mother's people. She smiled at the irony of it all as she came up for air.

"We don't need their help," Sebastian had said when she first brought out the idea.

"I don't want to ask for their help, Sebastian, but look at us. How many people do we have left? How much more can we fight in our present condition? Do you honestly believe that we can win against the soldados the way we are now?" she replied.

"She's right, Sebastian," her Tió Nicolas said. "We need help."

"But not from the Itnegs! How do you know that they'll help us anyway? They are not affected by the presence of the Spaniards!"

"Yes, you're right, I don't know if they will help, but where else can we go to get help?" Gabriela said.

Sebastian had not answered. He knew that it would be hard to get any more help from the Ilocanos. "Can they fight?" he asked instead.

"Remember the Itneg who helped us in that ambush a few months back?" Nicolas said. "He was Gabriela's uncle on her mother side. All the Itnegs can fight like him, I'm sure of that. Yes, they can fight."

Sebastian remembered the Itneg and he had no option but to concede, as did the rest of the rebel leaders. And that was that.

Her movements in the water were graceful and effortless like she was born to it. She swam with ease, her arms flashing in and out of the water in perfect rhythm, her legs strong and confident as she went down with the current, then back up again. She felt her headache vanishing as her body began to relax but her thoughts kept going back to her mother.

She was so deep in thought that she did not see the pair of eyes watching her from the shadows of the trees at the opposite bank. Not that she would have known for the man was invisible in the dark. He sat hunched, immobile like a stone, mesmerized at the sight he was seeing below.

He had heard of tales of mermaids from the old folks, stories that they brought from the lowlands. He thought he was seeing one come to life.

Yet somehow he felt that there was something familiar with the woman.

Chapter Seventeen

She was a beautiful mountain girl her mother, Gabriela was lost in her thoughts, as she trod water.

Regal in every respect, her mother carried herself well. She came down from the mountains for her tribe was at war with another mountain tribe. Land disputes, hunting ground disputes and other personal issues and injuries and injustices brought out, some real, some imagined – she could not be certain now, but trouble came. Alliances were made between and among the tribes, but still trouble came. The men welcomed it for they were born to battle, all mountain men, from any tribe. They would unite to fight a common enemy but if there was no common enemy then they would fight among themselves. No holds barred, all out fighting. And their viciousness, bravery and fighting skills were parts of legend, not just in the mountains but also in the lowlands as well where the Ilocanos lived. They thrived in war. They respected bravery and acts of courage for by these were their manhood measured.

But down in the lowlands they were called savages.

Trouble anyplace, even in the mountains, was not a good time for womenfolk. Especially if one came from a clan of feared warriors and head tribesmen for they were prime targets for tribal raiders as hostages for high ransom, or worse, as slaves. Priced slaves. For the greatest indignity of them all to a respected mountain clan was to have one member become an indented slave of an enemy tribe.

So she went to live among the lowlanders. Or more like forced to live among them, for she did not want to leave the mountains she loved. She would have had preferred to stay and fight for she could wield a bow and arrow or a knife as well as any man in the village. Well, almost any man, aside from her brothers and cousins for they were all fighting men, and she learned from them well. But her old man could not be swayed. So she went to live among the lowlanders. With a family who was supposed to be a friend of her father.

They welcomed her for they were good people and soon she felt at home. She saw and learned new things that fascinated her, things she never saw up in the mountains. She learned fast, soaking everything new like a sponge, for she was highly intelligent, like the majority of her people. And she adapted well to the life and customs of the lowlands. Like the womenfolk of her tribe, she did not shirk from doing chores around the house helping in any way she could. She wanted to please her father's friend, Don Ignacio, the head of the family, so she welcomed the tasks given her. And she was a tireless worker, until she was doing all the work around the house expected of a housemaid. But she did not mind for they were good people although at times, especially when she got homesick, she felt nothing but a housemaid. Yet she did not return to the village when her father sent one of her brothers to fetch her after the mountain troubles were over and there was peace among the tribes. For by then she fell in love with the older son of her father's friend, who had been giving her his extra attention, for she was beautiful. And they became lovers.

But beauty, whether of a person or something as pure as true love, was no match for honor, or more precisely, the perception of it from the lowlander. Her lover's mother, a woman with a narrow face and a narrower mind, did not approve of their union for she could not see beyond the fact that she was a mountain girl. To the old woman's warped mind, Awad was an Itneg, uncivilized and a savage although she could not have held a candle to Awad's beauty even in her primest prime. So she clung to her perverted notion that no son of her, a respected Castilian, could ever marry an uncivilized Itneg, not even one so beautiful and learned. And the domineering matriarch turned from a compassionate person to an unreasonable monster.

The young lovers hoped that the mother would change when the young mountain girl was with child, but it did not happen even when Maria Gabriela came along, who was a precocious, intelligent child from all accounts, and every inch as beautiful as her mother. The old woman wanted the little girl but did not change her mind about the marriage. There was no way the family name would be tarnished by a civilized union to an uncivilized Itneg. Not ever while she was alive. And that brought her father to drink, and started abusing her mother.

Gabriela had always wondered as she got older why her mother took the abuse without fighting back when she knew how to defend herself especially with the blade. For as Gabriela grew up, her mother secretly taught her the ways of the mountain folk, especially the art of fighting with the short and the long knives. Yet her mother took the abuses from both her weak lover and the narrow-minded mother silently. But everyone has a saturation point and one day, her mother had had enough and she took off to the mountains with the little girl.

But they came for her. They sent messengers to take her back for the little girl must not grow up to be another savage. Their Spanish blood, diluted and tarnished it may had been, still ran in the girl's veins and she must be raised not as a heathen but a proper Christian lady, to be married later on to a Spanish Don, and not to a tribal savage.

However they did not account on the resolve of a proud mountain girl. Her mother, bless her soul, resisted and kept her at the village sending the messengers back home time and again empty handed. But she had become a stranger in her own village, silently ostracized for returning with a child, and worse a child of a weak lowlander who worshipped a foreign God. And the little girl had her share of cruel jokes and teasing from the other kids in the village, boys and girls alike. They called her names, about her father, the color of her skin, her features. So she learned to fight back. But then she remembered with fondness the tall silent boy who had seemed to be always there to protect her when she got in trouble. She wondered how he was now. Married probably and raising a family. She smiled as she realized she felt a twinge of jealousy at the thought of him having a wife. It was foolish, she knew, but somehow the feeling persisted.

She and her mother returned to the lowlands eventually when her mother realized that perhaps her daughter was better off raised and educated by the so-called civilized Ilocanos. But her mother was never the same afterwards. Again she took the abuses silently, a broken-down woman, perhaps for her daughter's sake even after her father died. She gave up, she just gave up, Gabriela kept thinking, and vowed again to never, ever let herself suffer like her mother did.

And so her grandmother had her way. She had Maria sent to a rich, older Don when she was old enough. And with him, Gabriela found the comfort and love she craved from her family, especially from a father. Don Tomas was a lot older but he was kind and generous, and most importantly from her grandmother's perspective, he was rich. And so, as her grandmother had planned, she became a bride to Don Tomas. Gabriela did not care for his money, she cared for him in her own way for he loved her. But with her, she couldn't rightfully say if it was love. She suspected Don Tomas was aware of this, but she did care for him enough for he was a real gentle man. But she came too late in his life and she found herself a very young but very rich widow after just a few short years.

She had made peace with her grandmother. She had realized as she grew older that in her own perverse way, her father's mother wished for her to be well provided for and have a good life. Her only regret was that the old woman had died without acknowledging her mother as a worthy wife and partner for her son. For that, Gabriela had never forgiven her and neither had her mother.

She and Diego had discussed one time the blatantly unfair treatment of her mother from her grandmother. And Diego, ever the glib orator had some fancy words for it.

"It's the nature of the beast, Maria," Diego said.

"Nature of the beast?" Maria had asked, uncertain as to what Diego meant.

"Yes, your grandmother, that's her nature. Like the rest of those damn Spaniards, they think that they're far superior to us, especially to a mountain girl, an Itneg, like your mother."

"And yet they preached the equality of all men in the churches," Gabriela mused.

"Ironic, isn't it?" Diego said. "But that's the nature of the beast."

"Do you mean she couldn't have changed her attitude, their attitude towards us?" Gabriela asked.

"She could, they could, but it would be hard because it is against their nature," Diego replied. He paused for a bit then said, "Sometimes they need some help for them to change. That's why we fight. It is up to us to make them change, to help them open their eyes to the truth that they're no better than us because of the color of their skin. We are, as they preach, all equal in the eyes of God and men and we should be treated as such and given the respect we deserve. And if force was needed for them to realize that, then so be it. Sometimes violence is needed to affect a change. I wish it wouldn't be so but it seemed that is our destiny."

"And where would that put me? I have half of their blood," Gabriela said.

"That, my dear wife, puts you in a unique position to be the instrument for them to see that truth. It is your destiny."

Instrument, was that what she had become? Was it her destiny? Was she even ready? What if she failed? Would that be because of destiny also? No, she must not fail, Gabriela resolved. She must not fail, if only for Diego, destiny or not.

Destiny.

She wondered if it was also destiny that had brought her and Diego together.

Chapter Eighteen

She knew it the moment she saw him at her Tió Nicolas' house.

She was visiting there herself, in the far municipality of Tayum, nestled in the valley of Abra, the picturesque land of her mother. She needed to get away from Ilocos, away from the sea, for it reminded her too much of Tomas who loved to stroll by the beach in the evenings. And the mountains of Abra seemed the perfect place to forget. Perhaps a change of scenery would help ease the pain of his passing.

They had been married for three years, three good years, but so short for a marriage to end. It had been a couple of years since he passed away, but the sadness was still heavy in her heart, not only from Tomas' death but more so for the fact that she was barely in her twenties and already a widow. A very well off young widow for Tomas was a very rich man, true, but nonetheless still a very young widow. And a widow was not exactly a prime prospect for an honorable Spanish gentleman seeking to get settled when there abound in the Ilocos available single Señoritas for the taking.

Yet she knew the moment their eyes met at her Tió Nicolas' sala, that here was the man who would make her forget Tomas and erase the loneliness in her heart. How right she was, and yet, how wrong at the same time. Tomas faded into distant memory yet the loneliness remained constant in her heart.

He did not pay her singular attention for he barely looked at her direction when he walked in with two other gentlemen. Not that he looked into the general area where the women gathered at the opposite end of the room, where she was in their midst, offering drinks of lady's basi, a much weaker and sweetened version of the potent sugarcane wine that the Ilocanos produced and loved. Not that she initially noticed him either, but her interest was roused when the women guests around her stopped gossiping about everyone else who was not there, and started a lively whispering among themselves, with their eyes trained at the men who just arrived.

Gabriela pushed through the group of women and found herself at the front where she hesitated for a moment, assessing what caught the women's attention with a quick sweep of her eyes across the room. The new arrivals had stopped by his Uncle's side, talking and shaking his hand. From the whispers behind her, Gabriela learned that the man with the shiny dried squash hard hat tied behind his back was the rebel Don Diego. She looked at the man who was now grasping her Tió's right hand with both hands like a long lost kin and earnestly saying something while his two companions *flanked him, each one quietly surveying the room. He was not a very good looking man this Don Diego, Gabriela mused, nor was he particularly tall or macho as the Spaniards would say, but there was something in the way he carried himself that demanded attention. Her curiosity now fully aroused, Gabriela started across the room and she heard the women collectively gasp behind her.*

'Damn this stupid custom of men and women not mixing together in this so-called social gatherings until they sit down and eat,' she thought ignoring everyone's eyes as she stepped boldly into the space separating the men from the women.

Nicolas was intently listening to what Diego was saying but the flicker of movement from the middle of the room caught his eye and he briefly glanced in that direction, his eyes held, growing wide as he recognized the apparition that was his niece coming toward his general direction. Don Diego, sensing Nicolas' shift of attention stopped in mid-sentence and turned his head to look at the cause of his host's distraction, and he suddenly became aware that the usual party buzz was gone, replaced by silence which was interrupted now and then by the sound of the soft footfall of the most beautiful woman he had ever seen in the Ilocos. He watched, mesmerized as Gabriela walked towards him but as she drew closer, he noticed with a hint of disappointment that her eyes were focused on Nicolas and she was not even looking at him. He felt a little annoyance, jealousy perhaps, he thought later on, yet he shrugged it off as he wondered what important message the woman had, beautiful she may be, to dare intrude into the men's conversation.

Without looking neither to the left or right, Gabriela determinedly walked up to her uncle, but her legs were shaking like bamboos caught in a typhoon underneath her long skirt. But with all the self-composure she could muster, spoke sweetly, trying hard for her voice not to tremble.

"Tió, perhaps your friends want coffee, or maybe, if the gentlemen prefer, a cold glass of basi?" Her voice trailed down but thankfully without a quiver.

"Ah, pardon me, Don Diego, for not offering you anything to drink right away. I know you've traveled far tonight. Would you like coffee, or basi?" Nicolas smiled and put a patronizing hand on Diego's shoulder, extending the other with a sweeping gesture to include Diego's companions. "By the way, this is my niece, Gabriela." He stepped forward to take Gabriela's hand which was beginning to rise to meet her Tió's extended hand, but suddenly Diego's hand moved and caught it in mid-air, bowing at the same time, and before Gabriela could pull it away, his lips was gently brushing against it.

"It is my pleasure to meet you, Señorita. I am Diego at your service." Diego's lips lifted slightly up from the back of her hand, his brown eyes

151

intently staring up at her. "A glass of basi for me and my compadres will be fine."

Gabriela met his gaze and that was when she knew. She felt herself blushing and thanked God that the lamps in the room were far from where they stood. She felt her knees weakening and she instinctively leveraged herself against Diego's hand to keep her balance. Diego must have felt the tension in her hand for his grip on it tightened. Gabriela recovered her balance and tried to pull her hand away but Diego held it firmly yet gently, with a mischievous smile on his face. She gave him the look that she had used so many times to scare the boys in her mother's village when she was growing up, but he merely smiled. This was the wrong thing to do with Gabriela, for now she felt her nervousness gone and replaced with growing annoyance and anger. She took a deep breath and held her gaze at Diego, her eyes giving him a subtle warning.

"Please let go of my hand." Her voice was cold and even, her nervousness totally gone.

Diego saw the growing anger in her eyes and he reluctantly let go of her hand, but giving it a gentle squeeze as he did so, amused at the fire in the woman. Gabriela's expression did not change.

"Ah, I'm sorry, Señorita. Please forgive my brashness." His grin vanished and he bowed sincerely, yet his eyes stayed locked on Gabriela's eyes.

'Damn those brown eyes,' Gabriela thought, her face softening. "I'll get your coffee," she managed to say. "I mean your basi." She quickly added, regaining her composure.

"Yes, Señorita, a glass of basi would be fine, but not too much, just enough to wash the dust from the throat," Diego again smiled. "And basi for my compadres as well."

"Very well then although you'd be missing on a great coffee," she said.

Diego smiled. "Perhaps, but my compadres, pardon me, Sebastian and Miguel here," he nodded to his companions, "drink nothing but basi."

The two grinned in agreement.

Gabriela thought, 'I bet they do, and perhaps you too,' but she said instead, "As you wish," bowing slightly for after all she was still a lady. "I am glad to meet you too, gentlemen. I apologize for interrupting your conversation." Then she quickly turned around toward the kitchen before anyone could respond or see her amused smile.

"My niece is right. We have great coffee from a place beyond the river, grown in a little village called Canan. A good friend of mine, Demetrio and his son Tinoy, they have a plantation there. Best coffee I have ever tasted! Well, perhaps we can all have a taste of it after dinner. But of course, we have the best basi in these parts too!" Nicolas rubbed his palms together with relish as if he could not wait to hold a glass of the wine.

Diego did not respond for his full attention was still focused at the receding vision of Gabriela, fully unaware that his host was now looking at him with a bit of consternation. Sebastian wisely cleared his throat and the sound brought Diego back.

"Yes, yes, of course." He caught himself saying, wondering what Nicolas had just said. Sebastian and Miguel exchanged amused glances which did not escape Diego's eyes.

"Ah, Señor, I apologize," he said, "but where were we? I am sorry I got distracted but I must say your niece is an extraordinary and a very beautiful woman."

"That she is, Don Diego. But sometimes I worry for her. She is very strong-willed that she's scaring the gentlemen in the town away." Don Nicolas' face softened, his voice filled with genuine concern.

"They are just probably awed by her beauty, Don Nicolas."

"I don't know. Perhaps. I hope there would be a brave enough good man for her out there. The poor girl deserves some happiness. She had been through a lot for someone so young."

Diego gave Nicolas a puzzled look but before he could ask a question, the latter patronizingly wrapped his arm around his shoulder and herded him towards the balcony.

"Let's get some air, Diego, and continue our talk at the balcony where we would not be interrupted."

Diego reluctantly followed, throwing a glance back at the door where Gabriela went through hoping for her to emerge from it before he left the room. But Gabriela was sitting in the kitchen, elbows on the table, her face buried in her hands, as she tried to make sense of the gamut of emotions she was feeling from meeting Diego. The two housemaids wisely left her alone, busying themselves with the pots and dishes that cluttered the kitchen.

'There's something in his eyes that makes him so endearing yet at the same time he can be annoying,' she thought. Does she like him? Love him maybe? She did not know for she had not fallen in love before. Even with Tomas, she was sure of that. Perhaps it was due to the vast difference in their ages. She liked Tomas but she did not love him, and Tomas was also aware of that, but it did not matter to him for he cared for her so much. She cared for him enough as well for Tomas was a good man. But with Diego? She did not really know but she was sure that Diego liked her a lot. 'Poor man's so easy to read,' she finally smiled and rose up to get their basi. She would sort her feelings later on and let the evening run its course. But in her heart she knew that her fate was tied to this man.

Gabriela went back out with a tray of empty glasses and a pitcher of basi, found Sebastian and Miguel mingling with the other gentlemen guests and gave them each a glass and filled them to the brim with the wine much to their delight.

"Gracias, Señorita. Your Tió and Diego are at the balcony," Sebastian said to her questioning eyes. "You can leave the pitcher with us after you give them their share."

"Yes, that would be great if you did. Thank you," Miguel added with a grin.

"Of course, gentlemen." She gave them her best smile and the two grinned back like fools. Gabriela amusingly shook her head as she headed out to the balcony. 'Ah, men and they thought they were the superior gender,' she mused. 'The evening may yet turn out to be interesting after all.'

She found Diego and Nicolas in an animated conversation but they promptly stopped as they noticed her approaching. She briefly nodded and smiled at them and wisely placed two glasses on the little table by their side, filled them with basi, put the pitcher down on the table and left without saying anything.

"Señorita, where's the pitcher?" Miguel called after her as she passed them.

"I'll get another one just for you, Señor," she said, smiling.

"Bless your heart, Señorita!" Miguel said.

"Yes, bless your heart indeed," Sebastian added. Their glasses were already empty.

"Men, really. Pity," Gabriela said to herself as she walked back to the kitchen.

Gabriela and Diego did not have a chance to talk afterwards until the party was practically winding down for she made sure not to go near him although she was fully aware of his gaze following her every move. She busied herself mingling with the guests and helping her Tiá Juana and the housemaids in replenishing the table, bringing out food and drinks. For a couple of times though during dinner, Diego caught her surreptitiously looking at his direction, but she quickly averted her gaze, looking openly at some of the guests pretending to find out what they needed. But every time she looked back at Diego, he had this foolish grin on his face as if he knew what she was doing, much to her annoyance.

Then somehow, as the guests were leaving, she found Diego by her side, once again catching her hand before she could move it away, and kissing its back gently.

"Thank you for a most wonderful evening, Señorita. The food was superb as well as the basi, and the coffee was great as you promised, but none could compare to the pleasure I have for meeting you." He squeezed her hand again before letting it go, not daring this time to hold it much longer as he did earlier in the evening.

"You flatter me, Señor, but you are welcome." Before she knew it, Gabriela found herself briefly touching Diego's arm, but her face remained stolid, not betraying the fluttering of her heart.

"I'll be back, Señorita, and not for Don Nicolas," he whispered and before Gabriela could respond, he quickly turned and left to join his two companions who were waiting in the yard, already mounted on their horses, with Sebastian holding the reins of his horse. They could hardly sit upright on their horses for the prodigious amount of basi they had put away. There would not be any talking on the ride back to camp for the two would be asleep on their horses. . .

Diego went down the stairs, with a noticeable spring in his steps. He ran quickly and ignoring the stirrups, jumped with exaggerated flourish on the back of his horse hoping that Gabriela was still looking, but when he looked back up with a smug grin on his face, there was nobody there. His grin vanished in disappointment and thanked God that his two companions were too drunk to have noticed what he just did.

"¡Vamonos!" he said as he kneed his horse, snatching the reins from Sebastian.

From behind the curtains, Gabriela shook her head in amusement. "Men," she whispered to no one, "they'll forever be boys. What a pity."

"So what do you think of Don Diego?" Her Tiá Juana asked as they were putting away the leftovers that Tió Nicolas would surely bring to the sharecroppers in the morning. Nothing much went by her Tiá Juana although she was not the chismosa, the gossip that her sister, Tiá Remedios, surely was.

"I think he has foolish ideas, Tiá," she said evasively. "He can't win against the guardia civiles."

"I agree, but I am not talking about his ideas. What do you think of him as a man?"

"Short and not very good looking," she joked. She knew her Tiá Juana and she had a pretty good idea where their conversation was headed. They had been through this dance more than a couple of times than she wished to remember. Tiá Juana had been playing the matchmaker for her ever since Tomas passed away.

"Oh, hija, but he's a gentleman, is he not?" Tiá Juana ignored her teasing. "How do you feel about him?"

"That he is, Tiá." She conceded, getting serious this time. "If you mean, do I like him? I do, I think… I don't know," she said ruefully, "I just met him but there's something in him that-"

"Yes, he's got this charisma yet there's also something that makes him sort of aloof," Tiá Juana interjected, finishing what she wanted to say. "Like there's something that holds him back from being a regular sociable person, as if he doesn't want people to know him on a personal level."

"True, Tiá. He talks so much of abstract ideas, of books, of different ways of doing things, just like…"

"Si, just like your Tió Nicolas," Tiá Juana said as if reading Gabriela's thoughts.

"Yes, just like Tió Nicolas," Gabriela concurred, and she laughed, ignoring her Aunt's bewildered look at her sudden mirth. She went to the sink and washed her hands in the small basin, drying them with the basahan, the all purpose rag hanging on the wall. "No, Tiá, I don't think I like him much with his ideas, but," she faced Tiá Juana and looked in her eyes, "I think he's committed and driven, but yes, if you want to know, I'd be glad to see him again."

Tiá Juana held her gaze. "You love him, hija?" she asked after a while.

Gabriela lowered her face then looked out the window. "I don't know, Tiá, I just met him but I think he's special. Perhaps," she said softly, "but how-?"

"Oh, hija," Tiá Juana cut her off again, moved up to her and held her in a tight hug. "I know exactly what you feel. I felt the same way with your Tió Nicolas. I really did not like him at first but there was something in him that intrigued me so and I could not get him off my mind! But for the life of me, I still don't know what it is!" She squeezed her fondly.

"But, Tia," Gabriela tried to catch her breath, freeing herself gently from her Tiá's arms. "How could it be when I just met him?"

Tiá Juana smiled. "Hija, don't think too much when it comes to the matters of the heart. Just follow what it says. You'll feel it and you'll know. Just listen and follow. Nothing else is of any consequence."

Gabriela thought for a moment then she leaned down and kissed her Tiá Juana's cheeks. "I'll remember that, Tiá, thank you," she whispered. "Good night."

"Good night, hija. Go sleep. Rest. It had been a long day."

But sleep did not come easy for Gabriela. For a long time she lay in her bed, wide awake, thinking about what her Tiá Juana said, and of Don Diego, wondering if he would fulfill his promise to visit.

The roosters had started to crow when she finally dozed off to a fitful sleep.

156

Gabriela felt her tears welling as she remembered Diego. She tried to suppress them but she failed and they flowed down her cheeks. She stifled her sobs and dived under water when she knew she could no longer hold them off. She stayed submerged for a while as she cried freely; releasing the pain she had kept in her heart for so long, forgotten from the rigors of fighting and eluding the *guardia civiles*.

She felt better when she came up, gasping for air. She floated on her back for a while until she finally calmed down.

After a while, she swam back toward the boulder and gathered her clothes from its shadow. She rubbed herself dry with her extra *bidang*, her woven wrap-around skirt that also doubled as a shawl, and dressed. She ran her fingers over hair then rolled it into a bun over her head as she headed back to the camp.

Across the river, under cover of the trees, the shadow likewise moved, stood up and gazed at the receding back of the woman in the river, wondering if what he had seen was real or both his eyes and memory were playing tricks on him. Confused and bewildered, he moved slowly and paused for a long moment as he reached the relative safety of the deeper woods.

Chapter Nineteen

Diego was still in her mind as Gabriela approached the stirring camp, and she saw him now as if he was alive standing with a group of men by a fire. She stopped and shook her head and Diego vanished and in his place she saw his cousin Sebastian instead, talking with some of the men who were up and gathered around a fire like devoted worshippers to an ancient god, arms stretched toward it to avail themselves of its warmth. Beside him was her Tió Nicolas, her father's younger brother, a friend and avid supporter of the cause. She had led these men from Vigan to her Tió Nicolas' home in Abra where she had set up her temporary headquarters.

But the Spaniards did not let up their pursuit of her and her men and they did not have the numbers to meet them head-on so they continued their retreat and came up here deeper into the mountains to seek help from her mother's people. There was no choice if they wanted to continue the rebellion and at least have a fighting chance of winning. They need the help of her mother's people. Her own people, too, she reminded herself.

If she could get them to help.

If, it was a big if as far as she was concerned. Would the elders even consider it? She was not sure but she had to try. She was too well aware of the enmity between the *Itnegs* and the Ilocanos.

She wondered now if she had just been leading all these loyal men to their doom, following her blindly to share her miserable life. She steeled herself and walked into the camp, putting on a brave and unruffled face.

There were other small fires scattered around the camp, tended by the few women who were with them, looking after the pots sitting over the flames. The smell of brewing coffee and cooking rice mingled with the sweet scent of burning pine wood. There was another smell that reached Gabriela's nose that she did not immediately recognize until she saw several sticks of skewered fish grilling over another fire pit. She smiled in appreciation as she reminded herself that most of these men were fishermen and had been fishing the rivers and the seas since they were little boys. She was just thankful that they placed their traps away from where she was swimming.

Some of the men saw her and shouted morning greetings, telling her breakfast and coffee would be ready in a few minutes. She waved and answered back a few questions, wrapping herself up with her *bidang* as her still wet hair dripped and made her dress cling to her body, noticing that some of the men's eyes were straying to her breasts. She stared back at the men who dared look at her until they lowered their gaze and looked somewhere else. Men, she muttered under her breath as she made her way up to the hut.

"I'll be down in a moment after I dry my hair. If anyone needs to take a bath in the river, do it now. We move out right after breakfast," she said.

"You heard the woman, let's get a move on." She heard her Uncle Nicolas say in his usual calm voice. He did not need to yell his orders to the men. He had a quality in his voice that commanded respect. She loved her Tió Nicolas. Sometimes she wondered how two people who came out from the same womb could be so totally different as she again thought of her father.

She ignored the groans that came out from some of the men but she felt some of them moving away from the fire. They may complain but she knew they would be ready after they ate. And so would she, headache or not as she felt her headache coming back. We'll be at the village by dark tonight, she promised herself.

She headed to the corner of the hut where she kept her *balkot*, a woven piece of blanket that she used to wrap the little belongings she brought with her, and took out the comb her mother gave her when she was a little girl. It was carved out in one piece from a cow horn. She rubbed her hair vigorously with the bidang she used from the river and then slowly combed her long, black hair. When was the last time she washed it with burnt rice stalks and treated it with coconut oil? It had been so long that she could not remember. She gathered its end that fell just a little above her waist, bundled a handful and brought it up to her face, smelling at it dolefully. It smelled of fresh spring water, she smiled, and gathered the rest, making a tight bun on the back of her head, a *pinggol* as the old women called it.

"*Generala*?" The voice from outside the hut startled her. She frowned in annoyance. She hated it when they called her *Generala* for that was what the Spaniards and the Ilocanos had started to call her.

She walked out to the window and saw Nardo, the youngest of the group, all fourteen years of him.

"Yes, Nardo? And please don't call me *Generala* again, understand? How many times do I need to tell you that?" She rattled on before the boy could respond.

"So-sorry, *Manang*," Nardo stammered, addressing her as older sister in the vernacular. Maria knew the boy stuttered especially when he was nervous as he was now and she immediately felt sorry for her outburst.

"Oh, alright," she said in a softer voice, feeling guilty at unnecessarily getting annoyed. "*Apay, ania't masapulmo?* Why, what do you need?"

"*Awan, Manang*, nothing. I just want to tell you that breakfast is ready."

"I'll be down in a moment. Tell them to go ahead and eat. Thank you." She wasn't really hungry yet this early. She would just grab something and eat it on the march.

"Alright, *Manang*." Nardo bowed and turned back toward the men who had lined up and started gathering around the fire pits where the womenfolk had set up small stations to ration their breakfast. It was not much, but in addition to the usual rice, corn and dried fish dipped in tomatoes were the grilled *dalag* and catfish, fresh from the river.

"I guess there's no need to tell them," Nardo muttered as he fell in line, grabbing a piece of banana leaf to use for plate.

They were halfway through breakfast when Maria came out, all dressed up in a clean *bidang* and wrinkly *camison*, a plain woven but sturdy shirt common to the Ilocanas. On top of her head sat a *kattokong*, a hat made of dried squash gourd, hardened, cured and sun dried, then polished to a bright sheen. It was Diego's favorite hat and she wore it with pride and affection.

The men parted and made a place for her as she walked through them, throwing nervous glances at one another, and hurrying with their food as they noticed her bundle hanging by her back. She was ready to move. She grabbed a piece of banana leaf from a sheaf sitting on top of a makeshift table then went to get her breakfast. The men eased up a bit but immediately resumed their harried eating as they saw her wrap her food instead and place it inside a small food pouch she carried by her right hip, beside her wicked looking dagger. Hanging by her left hip was her long *kampilan*, its well sharpened blade glinting through its open sided wooden scabbard. It was her mother's and she treasured it as much as she treasured Diego's hat. Besides, it had gotten her safely through several scrapes with the soldados, both Castilian and locals for there were many of them who were conscripted by the Spaniards as *Guardia Civiles*, the dreaded Civil Guards.

Maria looked up at the sky through lush crowns of the trees covering the camp. Except for a few light feathery clouds, the sky was clear. She remembered the afternoon cloudbursts in these mountains even when the sun was shining but she saw no sign that it would do so today.

"Good day for a walk," she said casually, trying to make light of the long trek ahead. It would not be easy for they would be going up and over the mountain. It would take the whole day of constant walking. She figured they could afford an hour of rest for lunch then move on to get to the village by nightfall. "Let's break camp in fifteen minutes then let's get a move on."

There were a few mumblings but no one voiced any objections. The men who were still eating chewed a little faster.

160

"Would we get there by this afternoon?" Her *Tió* Nicolas asked. He had suggested to Maria to ask for help from her mother's people when their ranks were decimated after their last encounter with the Spaniards in the vicinity of Vigan.

"If we hurry, *Tió*, but it would most probably be closer to nightfall, if we don't get lost along the way. I hope I did not forget how to get there."

Her *Tió* shook his head. "Just lead, *hija*. We'll follow."

Maria smiled back. She truly loved this old man. He seemed to be the only decent folk from her father's family. She wondered again how her father could be so different from this caring, responsible, and kind gentleman.

She looked around the camp as tents were folded and pots stored and loaded to jute sacks and strapped on to backs of men and horses. It would be a long day for all of them but more so for the men assigned to carry the extra loads as there were not enough horses for all of them. She would have to remember to give them short but frequent rest breaks, she thought. She hated moving at night, especially in these mountains, but she did not want to waste another day just to camp. But she knew they must if they had to for it would be downright dangerous for them to approach the village at night. They were not expected and they might be mistaken for a hostile raiding party. Perhaps she could go ahead when they got closer to the village by nightfall and warn the folks in the village about her men. She hoped in her heart that they would still remember her.

"No turning back now," she mumbled, more to herself than to the old man.

Her *Tió* Nicolas simply nodded his head. He turned around and said in a loud voice, "Let's move!"

161

Chapter Twenty

At the other side of the river, Kulas moved deeper into the shadows of the trees, hunched behind a thicket where he silently watched the lowlanders awaken from their sleep and broke camp. He had been following their progress into the mountain for two days now, almost a week from the hunt when Aklang bagged the deer at the clearing. He had not gone back to the village all that time. He did not see any need and he had learned from another village hunter that he encountered in the mountains about Akash getting home with a sprained ankle that he got from jumping over a ditch. He had a good laugh by himself when he heard about that.

But now there was no mirth on his face as he wondered what the lowlanders were doing this far up from their place. They were armed, but they did not seem to be on a hunt, contented only with just setting traps in the river so far. They could not be a raiding party for they had women among them. If anything else, to him they seemed to be on the run.

He could have taken the guards out last night or the night before if he wanted to, but he held back for there was that woman who caught his attention and who appeared to hold a special place among them. She could not be their leader for no woman could lead a group of armed men. But the men seemed to respect her, giving her space when she walked among them, holding their heads low in deference as she spoke to them.

Kulas was drawn to the group when he came across their track, curious about their objective in coming to the mountains. Then he got more intrigued when he saw the woman. There was something in the way she moved and carried herself that seemed familiar. He had watched her in the dark as she undressed behind the huge boulder and took a dive from on top of it. And as she hit the water, he remembered laughing at a girl a long time ago who took that same jump, but unlike the woman who made a perfect dive, the girl landed on her belly with a huge flop. But that was on the first time she tried. The girl promptly went back up again and took a running perfect dive on that second try, just like the woman. And he had seen her do it over and over again, during the summer, by the river in the village, jumping off *Apo* Allak's raft instead of a rock.

"It couldn't be," Kulas whispered as he watched her swim, utterly dumbfounded not just by her beauty but of the thought that the woman could be that girl of his youth. "It can't be. It's not her."

He moved swiftly and silently into the shadows. There was a path he saw in his mind, away from the river, that would take him to the village before

162

noon. Time enough, he thought as he looked up at the sky and looked back at the camp.

"No, it couldn't be," he whispered again but with less and lesser conviction. And deep inside him grew a feeling of uncertainty that began to open his heart to a gamut of emotions if he were wrong.

And now the Ilocanos were on the move. And by the direction that they were taking, Kulas had a pretty good idea where they were headed and he knew then with certainty that he was wrong.

He did not have to go down to the lowlands to look for her after all.

Ilang had found her way back.

Chapter Twenty One

A couple of days prior, Akash had tightened the two-finger wide strip of soft leather around his ankle and secured it with a practiced knot where the edges tapered into elongated strings. He had gone through a whole mug of Pol-looy's stinking poultice and it did reduce the swelling a lot. He stood up and tried a few steps, satisfied that he did not feel much discomfort and the binding helped. His ankle was healing fast but not fast enough for him and he did not plan on aggravating it further with the long walk ahead of him. It had been three days since his talk with Allong under the *Salamagui* tree. He wanted to wait another day before going down to the town to talk with Awad, certain that Sadang who was probably on his way back, would fail to convince her to leave the town. And he was also getting antsy with staying around the village. He might as well go today. He will cut a sapling along the way and use it for a crutch. That should lessen the burden on the sore foot, he figured.

And he would just take his time.

He went up inside the hut and put a few pieces of food and clothing that the Ilocanos favored in the sack that he always carried when he went to the lowlands. He did not mind wearing the Ilocano garments when he entered the town. It lessened the curious looks that he always received, although that was less frequent now that his presence was becoming more familiar especially with Awad's neighbors.

Then he took his bow and a quiver full of arrows and slung them across his wide chest like bandoliers. There was no need to look them over if they were battle-ready because he took great care of them. And he had checked on them again the night before. He had done the same thing with his spear which he now held as a staff as he stepped out of the hut, tentatively favoring his injured foot. He felt pleased that it did not bother him as much.

He found Pol-looy washing clothes by the river, and his son, Bagto, swimming by himself, unmindful of anyone. Pol-looy saw the sack on Akash's shoulders and she understood. There was no need for explanations as she had expected the trip. Akash went to her and gave her a brief and quick embrace. Bagto stopped momentarily from swimming in the river and gave him a peremptory wave. He did not even bother to come out of the water.

Akash smiled and waved back. "Don't go too far out!" he shouted to Bagto but the boy had already swam underwater and waved again when he surfaced, grinning, showing no indication that he even heard his father.

Akash shook his head and walked away without looking back. Then he stopped as he passed *Apo* Allak's hut, his eyes caught by the sight of the two bamboo rafts tied separately to two of the hut's posts. His eyes lingered on the smaller raft which was almost half the size of the other. It was the raft that *Apo* Allak used to fish up and down the river. He made up his mind and headed towards the hut.

"*Apo*," he said as approached the short ladder leading up to the hut.

"*Apo*!" he said again, louder this time when he heard no response from *Apo* Allak. The old man was hard of hearing, he remembered, so he went up the ladder after shouting for the third time. He found *Apo* Allak sleeping on the floor, mouth open and snoring comfortably, an empty coconut shell faintly smelling of *tapuy* by his side.

He hated to wake up the old man so he went out of the room, down the ladder and walked back upriver to where his wife was wringing the water out of her wash, looking at him now with questioning eyes.

"Tell *Apo* Allak that I am borrowing his small raft!" he yelled as he got to shouting distance.

"What?" Pol-looy said, unfolding and shaking the blanket that she was wringing and laying it down on the stones to dry.

"The raft, the smaller one, I am borrowing it!" he said. "Tell *Apo* Allak when he wakes up. I'll bring it back in a couple of days!"

"Alright," she said. "Perhaps that would be best with your foot the way it is!"

But she did not have to tell Allak for he suddenly appeared at his window, yelling, "What are you all shouting about? What was that about my raft? Can someone around here get a good sleep without you all making all that noise?"

Akash shook his head, surprised that *Apo* Allak woke up and was able to get to the window as if he was never out from the *tapuy*.

"I'm going down to the valley to talk with Awad and bring her back, *Apo*," he said. "I'm borrowing the small raft. Don't worry I'll bring it back."

"Why? Can't you walk?" *Apo* Allak said, looking at Akash's feet. He heard that he twisted an ankle but he could not remember which one. As far as he could see, Akash was standing and walking alright although there was some binding on his left foot. That could be it unless Akash had decided to add a binding to his attire. One could never tell with these young folks when it came to adorning themselves.

"I could, *Apo*, but this still bothers me a bit," Akash said raising his bound left foot.

Apo Allak looked at the foot then raised his eyes to where Pol-looy was standing, looking at them.

"Alright," he said reluctantly, "but make sure you bring it back in one piece."

"Don't worry, *Apo*, I will," Akash said. "If not, I'll build you one."

"Yeah, sure you will," *Apo* Allak said then turned around and went back to his sleep.

Akash shrugged and looked back grinning at his wife who was shaking her head in amusement yet there was worry in her eyes. He waved again then headed toward *Apo* Allak's hut and picked up a paddle and a short pole hanging underneath it. He set them down on the raised platform on the raft along with his sack and spear. He untied the raft from the post, gingerly stepped on the platform and sat down, careful not to get his bound foot wet. He grabbed the short pole and guided the raft toward the middle of the river and straightened it as it glided down with the current. He looked back again at his wife and son and waved one more time.

Bagto had come out of the water and now stood by his mother's side on the riverbank, frantically waving back, Pol-looy's right arm lightly resting on his shoulder, her left hand daintily swaying by her head.

Akash let out a deep sigh and concentrated on steering the raft in a straight course as he reached the middle of the river. He nodded his head agreeably as he tried to get comfortable. This surely beat walking down to the valley although it would take him over half a day longer to get there if he had gone through land all the way.

That night, he tied the raft to a sapling by the riverbank, and slept on board after eating a small portion of the dried meat and some fresh fruits that he brought. He did not even bother going out to the bank to build a fire. The night air was warm enough and there was the pleasant breeze that hovered over the water. He tried counting stars and looked for the patterns that they made up in the dark sky and was soon lulled to a deep sleep by the soft murmur of the river and the gentle swaying of the raft.

He woke up at the first crack of dawn, faintly hearing the far away crowing of wild roosters in his sleep. He took his time, stopping now and then to take a quick wash, eat and fish when he found a good spot to cast a lure or use his spear. He caught sight of the scattered houses outside of the town late in the afternoon of the third day. He pulled the small raft out of the water as he neared the town proper, hiding it among a clump of bushes and small trees by the riverbank, far away from where the townspeople usually go to swim or wash clothes or bring their farm animals to bathe and cool down in the river. It would just be a relatively short walk to Ilang's house from there.

He took a quick dip in the river, noting with satisfaction that the swelling in his foot had gone down when he took off the leather wrapping, feeling no pain at all. He washed his hair and rubbed his body and arms with some sweet smelling leaves from the small shrubs that grew in abundance by the riverbank then let him be dried down by the warm breeze and the soft afternoon sun. Then he changed to the Ilocano garments and waited until the sun went down. He wanted to get into Ilang's house when it was dark. The fewer people knew of his presence the better.

He kept away from the lighted houses and the yard dogs that grudgingly slunk away when he blew a sharp but low whistle that was barely perceptible to the human ear, a trick that he learned from Kulas. He did not know why but it seemed to work all the time.

'Awad must have turned in early,' he thought as he approached Ilang's house, noting the lack of light either from a candle or a lamp. The dog that usually slept under the tree by the backyard seemed to be absent likewise. Perhaps it was in heat and prowling the neighborhood.

He knocked on the door as soon as he reached it, softly saying Awad's name. He knew his sister was a light sleeper and would be awake by the slightest sound, but there was no response or sound coming from inside the house. He knocked again, louder this time, speaking his name also, announcing his presence, thinking Awad was just being careful, not knowing who was at the door.

But still there was no response. He wondered if nobody was home. Had Awad gone out and joined her daughter and was likewise on the run?

He knocked again, more persistently this time. He was about to go into the backyard to let himself in through the back door when a lamp appeared through the neighbor's window and a face peered behind it, glowing eerily in the glow of the lamplight.

"Who's there?" a woman's voice cried out.

Akash recognized the voice of Awad's nosy neighbor whose name, he recalled, was Ana.

"It's me Akash, *Manang* Ana," he said loudly enough for her to hear amid the barking of her dog tied to a tree in her front yard. Akash was tempted to calm it down with his whistle, but he decided against it.

"Ah, Akash," Ana said, "It's good to see you. Have you heard then?"

"Heard what, *Manang* Ana?" Akash walked closer to the neighbor's house, ignoring the dog that was going crazy trying to get at him, stretching the rope tautly that held it to the tree.

"Hush, *Guardia*! Shut up!" Ana yelled at the dog. "Akash, wait, come over! I'm coming out."

The lamp and the face disappeared behind the closing window.

The dog ignored its owner and went on barking as Akash approached the neighbor's front door. Getting irritated, he pursed his lips and sharply blew his low whistle as the dog persistently barked and growled. The dog's ears suddenly perked up, its bark turned into a soft whimper then it slowly slunk away close to the tree trunk with its tail tucked between its legs. It lay on the ground as it reached the tree, eyeing Akash suspiciously as he waited for Ana to open the door.

The door opened and Ana in a night robe, beckoned from behind it, the lamp now sitting on a table. Standing by the table was Quintin, Ana's husband clad in his sleeping clothes as well.

"Come inside," Ana said in a low voice. Quintin nodded without saying anything.

Akash stepped in and Ana closed the door after surreptitiously looking outside noting that the other neighbors had not bothered looking out their windows to see what caused the commotion from *Guardia*. It was a good thing that the neighbors knew that the stupid dog barked at anything or anyone, she thought, sometime even at its own shadow.

"Sit down, Akash," Ana motioned to a chair by the table where the lamp stood.

"Thank you, but I'll stand up. I won't be long. I need to see and talk to Awad right away," Akash said.

"Well, it's about Awad," Ana said, her voice quivering slightly. Her husband remained where he stood, not saying anything, his face showing a hint of apprehension. Akash waited, a small worry slowly growing in his chest. He did not like the expression on the neighbors' faces.

"Awad, she's gone. They took her away." Ana's eyes moistened as she looked at Akash.

"Who took her away?" The worry growing in Akash's chest turned into a lump in his throat. He swallowed hard but the lump stayed there. He felt something else growing beside it, anger, which he vainly tried to suppress.

"The soldiers, the *Guardia Civil*," Ana whispered. "They came two days ago, a day after Sadang showed up. They were also looking for him but he was gone by then."

"But why?" Akash said. "She is not a rebel. She never joined in the fight against the soldiers!"

"Akash, she's *La Generala*'s mother," Ana said as if that explained it all.

"They must have thought that Sadang brought word from Gabriela," Quintin spoke gravely from where he stood. Ana nodded this time as if in agreement to what her husband said although she always found something disagreeable to whatever he said and did.

"Yes, that must be it because I heard them asking her about Sadang so many times before they took her away," Ana said.

Akash took a deep breath, his mind racing in so many directions, filled with questions that he did not have answers to.

"Where?" he finally said. "Where did they take her?"

"Most probably to the fort," Quintin said somberly.

"Yes, they must have brought her to the fort and are holding her there," Ana added.

"Tha-thank you," Akash said. "I'll go see her."

The couple looked at one another with concern in their eyes.

"Not tonight, they won't let you in once it gets dark," Quintin said. "Besides, nobody walks the streets at night nowadays. Go in the morning." He did not voice out his thought that the *Guardia Civil* may not even let Akash into the fort even at daylight. Or worse, that Awad may not be there at all.

"Yes," Ana said. "I have a spare key to their house. Let me go get it."

She turned around towards their bedroom then stopped suddenly.

"Have you eaten yet?" she said.

"Yes, yes, thank you," Akash lied. He did not wish to stay longer. He wanted to be alone to gather his thoughts and plan what to do for tonight or tomorrow. Awad's absence had changed everything. He hoped in his heart that his sister was alright.

"Alright then," Ana said and proceeded to the bedroom. She came out shortly with a key in a string loop which she handed to Akash.

"Here you go," she said. "I assume you can stay as long as you want. Please don't hesitate to let us know if you need anything."

"Yes, yes," Quintin said. "We have food if you don't mind what we eat," he added uncertainly.

"You're very kind," Akash replied. "Thank you very much. I'll be fine. Besides, I don't intend to stay long. I'll give you the key before I leave." He turned around and went out the door.

"Good night," he said as he stepped outside. "I'm sorry for the bother."

"Hush, it's no bother at all," Ana waved a hand.

"I hope everything's alright," Quintin said. "Good night."

"Me too," Akash murmured as Ana slowly closed the door behind him.

Guardia looked at him cautiously without a whimper this time as he walked towards the Silangs' house.

That night he slept fitfully as a child going on a trip the following day, anxiously anticipating a tomorrow filled with possibilities, but in his case, all of them were uncertain.

Chapter Twenty Two

Don Manuel stood back and looked critically at his reflection, his eyes going up and down the full length of the life-size mirror. He allowed himself a little self-satisfied smile as he approved of what he saw. Standing before him was the visage of a gentleman dressed in full regalia of an officer of His Majesty's army. Tall and regal, muscles toned and skin glowing and tanned from the tropical heat, he appeared a perfect specimen of a man in his prime. Then something caught his eyes and he leaned closer to the mirror. He canted his head and his eyes focused on the slivers of white hair that had seemed to appear suddenly on his temple. He touched it furtively and was relieved when he saw that it was just a reflection of the mirror. But just to be sure he tried to pull it out and his fingers came up with a dark piece of hair. He sighed with relief and shook his head as his errant sense of vanity hit him.

In the scheme of things, a full head of white hair would not matter, but 'I'm too young for that,' he reasoned silently.

Young? Perhaps. But he surely seemed to be losing his mind. And the thought of the woman in the plaza and the feeling that he had seen her before yet could not remember where and when was surely not helping to refute that prospect. He shrugged and turned around one more time, eyes not leaving the reflection of the man in the mirror. Satisfied, he grabbed his Captain's cap from the top of the credenza, put it on with a brief final glance at the mirror and went out of the room.

Clara smiled approvingly as he passed her on his way out.

"Have a great time, *Señor*," she said. "You look charming as usual."

"Charming?" Manuel said without pausing from his walk.

"Yes, and dashing too," Clara quipped. "*Señora* Dela Cuesta will be pleased, and I hope her niece would be too."

"Niece?" Manuel stopped and slowly turned around and looked at Clara. "What niece? *Señora* Dela Cuesta doesn't have a niece!"

"Oh, yes, she does, *Señor*. She's visiting from Abra."

"Abra? The Dela Cuestas have relatives in Abra?"

"Apparently, *Señor*. That's what I heard. I don't know if it's true," Clara said with a twinkle in her eyes, trying to suppress a naughty smile.

Manuel caught the mischievous smile and it dawned on him that *Señora* Dela Cuesta was probably trying to play matchmaker again.

"Ah, Clara, I hope you're not into this conspiracy," he said.

"Conspiracy? What conspiracy, *Señor*?" Clara tried to sound puzzled but her eyes belied her.

"*Tsk, tsk*, not you, too," Manuel shook his head. "It's not going to work. I'll find someone somehow in my own time." He turned around and walked away. He might as well go. He was already dressed up as it was anyway.

"I heard she's very pretty, *Señor*!" Clara said at his back.

"Yeah, yeah," Manuel said, waving a hand. "I heard that before." Certainly, *Señora* Dela Cuesta's perception of beauty differed a lot from his own.

"But seriously, you look dashing, *Señor*. The *Señora's* niece would be all over you, or maybe even the *Señora* herself, God forbid, so please try to act the gentleman and forget about whatever *Don* Tiago told you about treating women," Clara yelled after him with a mischievous grin as he walked to the rear of the house.

"Whatever happens, it's your fault, Clara," he said without turning his head. "You should have walked out the back door when you saw the *Señora* and Luisa coming!"

"You'd thank me later, *Señor*. Like I said, the *Señora's* niece is nowhere like the *Señora*. She's gorgeous and very beautiful, Luisa said so."

"I heard that before, Clara," Manuel said as he went out the back door to the stable. "And tell Luisa she needs a new pair of *anteojos*!"

He heard Clara laughing behind his back.

Felix, the stable boy, had already saddled his horse and it stood waiting, hitched to a rail by the stable. Manuel mounted and pointed the horse to the direction of the Dela Cuesta's house.

"Here we go again, *castaño*," he said to the horse, feeling like he was *Don Quixote* on another fool's errand.

The horse snickered in reply and flicked its tail to ward off a pesky fly.

"I wish I could do that to a thought, *castaño,* just flick a finger and get rid of it," Manuel said as the woman with the *caimitos* came back to mind. "Or perhaps not," he said as he noticed the horse kept flicking its tail. The fly proved to be as pesky as the thought of the woman.

As he rode, his mind wandered then eventually led to the prospect of *Señora* Dela Cuesta's niece turning out to be beautiful. But what's beautiful and what is not, he wondered. Then a distant memory suddenly hit him like a lightning out of the blue.

Early dawn, a river, and out of it, a woman, a very beautiful siren of a woman, he thought then, of that he was certain despite the distance and the grey of dawn.

And now he remembered. No, he knew with utmost certainty where he had seen the woman with the *caimitos* under his window.

Chapter Twenty Three

The day after meeting Tiago the first time, Gabriela woke up at the break of dawn, as was her habit. She felt strangely refreshed despite the lack of sleep the previous night. She quickly and quietly dressed, went to the kitchen and brewed coffee. The house maids were still asleep but she did not have the heart to wake them up. The poor girls also had a long night.

She poured herself a cup of coffee when it was ready, then pulled the firewood out from the fire, pushing the burning ends into the ashes. She gathered the embers, covered them with ash and placed the pot of coffee on top to keep it warm for the rest of the household. She left the house through the bangsal, the all-purpose area behind the house that served as prep area for cooking, bathing, as well as for laundry and washing dishes.

She went out to the small pathway behind his Tió's house, to the narrow trail going west towards the river. It would be about a half-hour's walk, and she moved briskly, wishing to get there before the sun was fully up. She passed huts that were already astir with their early rising occupants preparing to set out to their fields. She hoped there was nobody yet at the river. She wanted to swim alone.

She loved it when she was by herself, alone in the water, with nobody around to bother her. It seemed that she was the only person alive in the world. The village was her own, the fields and the hills, everything in them just for herself. Even the river, yes, the mighty Abra River, in all its grandeur with its fishes and its gold nuggets that were rumored to freely roll down the Ba-ay river from its source high up in the Cordilleras until it emptied into the great Abra river especially when the floods came. She sighed in anticipation as she shrugged off a cold wind. She had heard stories of spirits of the night that passed by like a cold breeze but she did not believe in ghosts and spirits. She hurried, her bakya, her wooden clogs, making a racket in the stillness of the morning as they clanged against the stones especially when she got nearer to the river. She uttered a curse as she slipped off a wet rock in the dark, almost falling, and wishing that she should have ridden one of her Tió's horses instead, as she usually did, but she wanted to be alone today, with not even a horse for company.

She undressed quickly by the big flat topped boulder that served as wash bench for the women in the village when they came to do their laundry, carefully placing her clothes and bakya on its top. Slowly, she eased down into the cold water, shivering slightly. She immersed herself to her chin, feeling her body get warmer as it adjusted to the coldness of the water. She waded down toward the deeper part of the river, then taking a deep breath she went beneath the surface and stayed as long as she could underwater, her arms and legs moving easily. She was in the middle of the river when she came up for air. She trod water, scanning the riverbank and the dark shadows beyond. Except for herself and the softly flowing water, nothing moved. Even the breeze had died down.

She always felt at ease and contented in the river as if it was her home. She swam flawlessly, without much effort, her pale golden body gliding through the water like a nymph. She swam upriver, then she floated on her back, riding the gentle current downstream, then she swam back up again as she realized she was getting too far from her clothes. She was breathing heavily as she got abreast of the big boulder; the river's flow was deceptively stronger than she thought. She trod water again for a while, until her breathing got back to normal.

Then amid the rippling of the water and the far off drone of the shallow rapids downriver, she heard the unmistakable sound of metal against stone, then the steady rhythm of horses' hooves. Instinctively she ducked underwater and swam toward the boulder that held her clothes, hugging the underside of the huge boulder where it leaned over the water as soon as she reached it, cautious and scared to get out of the water. The sound of the horses got louder and she dared not look over the boulder, nor tried to reach for her clothes on its top. She hoped nobody would notice them in the grey of the dawn.

But her curiosity got the better of her so she slowly moved, lying flat on her stomach in the shallow water, her hand holding on to the base of the boulder, and peered around it. From out of the fog, a dozen or so Spanish horsemen appeared, looking drawn out and tired from the way they sat stolidly on their mounts, heads bowed as if asleep, like eerie apparitions in the pale light. The horses walked languidly on their own, their shod hooves making slow rhythmic cadences over the stones as they passed by barely a hundred paces away. Gabriela held her breath hoping the horses were too tired to smell her presence. She nervously watched, her eyes barely above the water line, and breathed a sigh of relief as the cavalcade of the dreaded Guardia Civil rode on with not one of them bothering to cast a look toward her direction. Before long they vanished in the mist, like ghostly apparitions, with only the echo of their walking horses marking their passing.

Gabriela waited until there was just a faint sound from the horsemen when she finally ventured to move and got out of the water. She grabbed her woven towel and quickly dried herself with it, looking around nervously as she hurriedly dressed, thankful that she was alone as she noted the faint light of morning coming from the east. She put on her wooden clogs and headed back to the town, giving a parting glance at where the soldiers vanished. It may have been her imagination but she thought she saw the faint silhouette of a horseman on top of the rise far off through the mist like a ghostly statue. She averted her eyes and walked quickly toward home.

Don Manuel sighed, lowered his spyglass and put it away in his saddlebag. He had stopped on the rise, took out the glass and watched as Gabriela stepped out of the water.

He held his breath as he watched the lovely India dry herself and put on her clothes. A mestiza, he thought, mesmerized at the beauty of the woman through his spyglass. He fought the urge to ride back, contenting himself with watching from a safe distance.

He had noticed the big boulder for it looked like the shadow of a man sitting in the dark, and he saw the clothes on top of it as his troop went by, but he was too tired to stop. He did not see anyone moving in the water so he had assumed that the clothes were inadvertently left behind by the town lavanderas, the laundrywomen. However he could not shake the feeling that someone was out there. He let his troop go ahead as he stopped on top of the rise, took out his spyglass and scanned the river by the boulder for a final look. He got rewarded with the sight of a beautiful siren stepping out of the water.

He felt a stirring in his loins that he had not felt for a long time as he watched the lovely vision dry herself and put on her clothes. He wanted to go back to make sure she was real, but his horse was tired, and he was tired, and it was still a long way to Villa Fernandina, which they fondly call Vigan.

Besides, the troop was up ahead, and they had stopped to wait for him, sitting immobile on their horses like mysterious ghosts in the vanishing fog of the early morning.

"Perhaps some other time, Señorita, perhaps some other time," he murmured longingly as he turned his horse and nudged it gently to join his troop. The horse trotted in response, eager to be with the other horses.

Capitán Manuel reined the horse up to a walk. There was no hurry.

They would be in Villa Fernandina soon enough.

"It's not possible, perhaps I'm mistaken," Don Manuel whispered, feeling a sense of doubt now at the accuracy of his memory as he nudged his horse that had slowed down, perhaps sensing that its rider was in a deep thought. "This lady is much younger." Or so he thought.

Yet there was that something in the way the lady underneath his window walked and moved that reminded him so much of the woman in the river.

He looked back toward the plaza as if he could see down the overhang where the woman had vanished, subconsciously wishing for her to walk back so he could see her more clearly, and erase all his doubts.

"It's not possible," he murmured again, shaking his head, his tendency toward practical reasoning taking over. "It's not possible. There's no way. She could not be the same girl. It just is not possible."

But deep inside there was that persistent hope tugging at his heart that his memory was right.

No, it's impossible, he reasoned. It was too long ago. He could be wrong.

"I better get a move on otherwise I will be too late," he mumbled finally, giving the horse a not too gentle knee, urging it to run faster and leave the thought of any woman behind. The horse responded to a trot but the thought that the girl from the river and the lady in the plaza were one and the same stubbornly rode with Manuel.

Chapter Twenty Four

Kulas heard the distinct throbbing sound of the wooden drums shortly before noon. He got up to a promontory and looked down in the distance where the village was located. He could see no smoke rising from the village and he breathed a sigh of relief, wondering what caused the beating of the drums that called for an emergency gathering of the people. He moved higher up the mountain to a clearing where he had a better view and saw some of the outlying huts and the river shimmering in the distance. But as far as he could ascertain there was not much activity in the village, no alarming sign of a smoke, nothing, except for the persistent sound of the drums.

He looked at the distance, his eyes gauging and instantly mapping the shortest way of his descent to the village. He should be there shortly, he figured. He started to jog, not following the trail, cutting through the trees and holding on to the path that only existed in his mind. He would cross the main trail going into the village in about an hour if he maintained his pace.

Less than an hour later, he hit the main trail and he followed it abandoning the shadows of the trees. He quickened his pace, the intermittent beating of the drums prompting him on. He found himself running to their rhythm.

The beating of the drums stopped shortly when a boy watching the trail saw Kulas coming down in it and promptly ran and reported what he saw. Kulas slowed down to a walk as he approached the village. There was no need to hurry. He did not see any activity that would cause for immediate concern.

But it seemed that everyone was in the middle of the village, fronting *Apo* Kagaid's house, as Kulas walked in and he hurried toward the gathering. Sadang was talking animatedly with everyone intently listening to his every word, but all eyes turned toward Kulas when he squatted beside Allong. Sadang paused from his talk, as Kulas acknowledged the elders with a courteous nod. Allong nudged him on the shoulder and pointed to an open spot behind the elders. Kulas looked at Allong and without a word both of them stood up and went to sit behind the elders. As they settled down, *Apo* Kagaid nodded at Sadang who resumed his talk.

"I went down to the valley about a week ago to see *Ina* Awad but *Ina* Ilang wasn't there," Sadang said. "I stayed around town hoping she would show up somehow but she did not. *Ina* Awad had no idea where she was. I heard later that she and her troops were fighting the soldiers north of Vigan,

176

trying to enter the city, but they were repulsed and beaten badly. Last time I heard they were being pursued by the soldiers and they were headed toward Abra. I heard further, coming back, that this time, the Spaniards will not stop until every one of the rebels is captured or killed. The young *Capitán*, the one they call *El Niño* is leading the hunt himself." Sadang spoke mostly looking at Kulas as if he was repeating what he had already relayed to the rest of the village folks. "They said she had more than three thousand people fighting with her after her husband died, but after that last encounter with the soldiers, she only now has a thousand or so. And *Ina* Awad, *Ina* Awad did not want to come up here with me, so I left her there in town. And, yes, she asks again for our help, as she said, 'for her daughter's sake.' And she asked me to tell everyone," Sadang's voice trailed softly as he paused for breath.

Kulas nodded somberly then a faint smile crossed his face. Sadang, whose eyes were still on him frowned in puzzlement, raised a questioning eyebrow. Kulas saw the younger man's puzzled look and stood up. All eyes turned to him.

"She has a lot less, five to six or seven hundred men maybe, perhaps less and they are in pretty bad shape. They can't win a fight with the soldiers in their condition. And they will be here by nightfall, perhaps earlier if they don't get lost," he said calmly, certain now that it was Ilang and her remaining soldiers that he saw heading toward the village. He should have recognized her, but how could he have known that she would grow up to be such a beautiful woman?

"I have been following them for the past two days," he continued. "I did not know that it was Ilang and her troops so I did not approach them. I wasn't sure if they were friendly. I came to warn you of their coming. I am sure now that it is Ilang and her group."

"Why are they coming here?" A voice from the crowd asked.

"They're on the run and they need help," *Apo* Kagaid answered. He looked at Kulas who held his gaze, unsure of what was to come next. "Our help," *Apo* Kagaid continued, his eyes staying on Kulas. "Awad sent word through Akash asking for help several days ago. Sadang went down to tell her we could not help, but it seems like Ilang doesn't have any place else to go, and obviously now she desperately needs help so that's probably why she's on her way here."

"Why? Why can't we help?" Kulas asked puzzled, his eyes boring on *Apo* Kagaid's eyes like hot coal. Ilang was the old man's grandchild after all.

"Dalalo and I have discussed it and we have decided not to get involved. The trouble between the Ilocanos and the Spaniards is not our concern. We should stay out of it."

177

"But she is your blood," Kulas said. "Our blood runs in her veins. She's one of us!"

A murmur of agreement came from the young men behind him. Sadang also nodded his approval as he slowly took his seat among the younger men.

"I am aware of that," *Apo* Kagaid stood up, leaning on *Apo* Dalalo's shoulder who was seated by him, for support. "Dalalo and I cannot in good conscience allow our warriors to die for a cause that we have no concern with, nor affect us in any way."

Kulas looked at his father. *Apo* Dalalo met his gaze and nodded his confirmation to what *Apo* Kagaid stated. Kulas scanned the faces around him. Some were nodding their heads, mostly the elder villagers, but most of the young men were shaking theirs, meeting his gaze, showing him where they stood on the matter.

'Be calm,' he cautioned himself silently. He himself was not sure of what to do. Part of him wanted to help and fight, but reason also had him siding with the older men's decision.

"So, *Apo*, what should we do when they get here?" he asked calmly, addressing *Apo* Kagaid.

"Nothing," *Apo* Kagaid replied. "We do nothing."

"Very well," Kulas said understanding that the elders have reached a decision and that was that. He started to sit back down before anybody could say anything, but then he suddenly stopped as something occurred to him.

"Akash?" he said. "Where is he?"

Most of the gathered warriors looked around and at one another as if realizing for the first time themselves that Akash was missing, then Allong spoke.

"He went down to the village to try to get Awad back up here," he said. "We had a feeling she would not listen to Sadang so he went, despite his bad foot. I haven't heard back from him."

A dark shadow moved across Kulas' face and he barely heard the hub-bub as everyone seemed to speak at the same time. He stood up, turned around and headed toward the river. Akash, alone down in the valley, and Ilang was about to show up in the village after all these years!

He needed a good swim real bad to sort out and clear up his thoughts.

Kulas took his time in the water, floating lazily downstream then swimming back leisurely up-current, his strokes even and effortless. He felt relaxed after a while, enjoying the coldness of the stream. He remembered with disgust that he had not bathed for over a week.

178

He swam across to the other side, floating a little further down river in the process. He did not fight the flow, going with it until his feet touched bottom. The sand and polished stones felt good on his feet.

He ducked under water, grabbed a handful of sand and rubbed them on his teeth, careful not to swallow the grit. He dipped his mouth into the water, filled it, and rinsed the sand out, gurgling and spitting a few times until he could no longer feel a grain left inside. Then he hunched down and removed his *ba-ag*, rinsing the cloth vigorously under water. He eased closer to the bank and reached out for a handful of the sweet smelling leaves of a young eucalyptus plant. He crushed the leaves in his hands and rubbed his head and body with the crumpled leaves. He grabbed another handful and did the same to his *ba-ag*, careful not to put too much stain on it, not that it mattered since the once white cloth had faded into a dirty brown. He rinsed the *ba-ag* a few times then he sidled closer to the bank and draped it on some bushes to dry.

He eased back into the water and swam again into the middle of the river, treading water until his legs felt a little tightness. He lay on his back, and relaxed as he floated downstream, moving his arms now and then to steer him closer to the bank where his *ba-ag* hung drying in the warm air.

His *ba-ag* was almost dry when he finally got out of the water. He held it up on one hand above the water as he swam back across the river towards the village. He got out of the water where there were several tall cogon grasses and bushes growing by the bank and put on his damp *ba-ag* under their cover. He found a good-sized stone with a flat surface and he sat down on it. It felt warm and good through the damp cloth and he sat on if for a long time, looking at the flowing water and not exactly seeing anything.

His mind was racing around in so many directions belying the calmness of his face and posture.

Ilang was coming. What would he say? What is he going to do? What would she think of him? Would she even remember him? What was she going to say? What is the tribe going to do? Would they help her cause? Would they help the Ilocanos? Should they? Would he? He tried not to think about it but he knew how he felt about that last one. And he was not sure if that was the right thing to do.

And there was Akash. Why had he not returned yet? Was he safe? Was Awad safe? He was confident that Akash could take care of himself, but what can one man do if faced by many?

Reluctantly, he stood up and looked around pensively, grateful that his *ba-ag* had dried. As his eyes went up the trail coming down from the mountain, he saw the band of Ilocanos walking consciously toward the village and his people getting out of their huts to meet them.

179

'Might as well face it,' Kulas thought dejectedly, as he spotted Ilang. 'It's about time.'

Somehow he felt like a man going into a hanging as he walked toward the village.

And he was the victim.

Chapter Twenty Five

The yard of the Dela Cuestas was full of carriages and horses as *Don* Manuel dismounted and handed his horse to the stable boy.

"Don't bother taking the saddle off," he said as he handed the reins to the boy. *Don* Manuel did not expect to stay long. He just wanted to make an appearance.

"*Si, Señor,*" the boy replied, curtsying a little, his head bowed then turned and led the horse away toward the nearby hitching post.

Manuel looked up at the house, now brimming with guests in flashy display of colors and jewelries. He heard laughter and the tinkling of glasses as he went through the front doors. A house help that was not Luisa, was there to greet and show him the way, but as if on cue, *Señora* Dela Cuesta appeared and rushed to meet the *Capitán*.

"Ahh, *Capitán*! You're finally here! I was afraid you were not going to show up yet again!"

"It never crossed my mind, *Señora*!" Manuel lied. "And *yet again*? Have I ever declined your summons?"

"Don't let me remind you, *Capitán*!" *Señora* Dela Cuesta said mischievously as he grabbed Manuel's arm and led him inside the house. "I want to introduce you to someone. She's my niece so be nice."

'Here we go,' Manuel thought and tried to brace himself from another round of fruitless matchmaking attempt.

"Look who we have here!" *Señora* Dela Cuesta announced to the room as they entered the living room. The party murmurs stopped for a moment, but it promptly resumed as the *Capitán* briefly nodded an acknowledgement directed to no one which was met by courteous nods and friendly waves that neither he nor *Señora* Dela Cuesta noticed and acknowledged.

Señora Dela Cuesta led the *Capitán* across the room, toward the kitchen where a lady holding a tray was coming through the doorway. The *Capitán* stopped in his tracks, pulling *Señora* Dela Cuesta back from her momentum as she was clinging to his left arm and she tottered briefly.

Señora Dela Cuesta's smile left her face momentarily as she tried to regain her balance, and looked up questioningly at the *Capitán*, curious why he had stopped. The smile on her face came back slowly as she noticed the *Capitán*'s attention was totally focused on the lady coming out through the doorway, his mouth slightly open as if he was caught in surprise.

"Come," *Señora* Dela Cuesta nudged the *Capitán*. "Let me introduce you to my niece."

Manuel barely heard her and he let himself be led willingly across the room like an obedient pet dog, consciously aware that their path was towards the lady in the doorway who was holding the tray, and somehow he felt his heart tremble nervously in excited anticipation. As they drew closer, the beating of his heart grew faster and louder for Manuel was absolutely certain now that it was the same woman who passed by his window that morning.

And he was also most certain as he grasped the woman's hand, after *Señora* Dela Cuesta had graciously taken the tray from her and made the introductions and found himself raising it to his lips, that she could not be the same woman in the river a long time ago. This one was a lot younger and much more beautiful, he thought, although he only had a faint and distant view and a far more distant memory of the visage of the woman in the river. He realized he had put a face on the woman in the river and somehow he was looking at her at the moment in *Señora* Dela Cuesta's niece.

And yet, yes, as the woman before him gracefully took back her hand and discreetly moved away a few decent steps, the *Capitán* noticed that there was something in the way she moved that absolutely reminded him of the woman in the river.

Manuel was confused and bewildered, and he let go of the woman's hand without even remembering her name. He tried valiantly to smile as he looked at the woman's face. She's beautiful, he thought, as he felt his breath being taken away.

"*Encanta, Señor,*" he heard the woman say.

"No, *Señorita*, the pleasure is mine," Manuel managed to gallantly murmur thinking he did not even catch her name.

Señora Dela Cuesta's face beamed with a big satisfied smile as she noted the smitten look in the *Capitán*'s eyes. Somehow she could smell victory, finally. God knows she had been trying to have the *Capitán* get married for a long time! "I'll leave you two to get acquainted," she said batting her eyelashes. "Isabella, *hija*, give the *Capitán* a drink. Looks like he needs one," she winked impishly as she handed back the tray to her niece.

Isabella! What a beautiful name, after the good Queen herself, Manuel thought.

Isabella merely smiled her dainty smile as she curtsied at the *Capitán* and lifted the tray to him. *Don* Manuel grabbed a tall glass without looking at what it contained and raised it to a short salute toward the lady and put the glass to his lips. He covered his mouth quickly as he coughed, the sudden sting of the alcohol burning his throat. He usually sipped his drinks. He felt his face burning in embarrassment and he forced a smile.

The lady's eyes twinkled with mirth yet she did not laugh. Classy, Manuel thought.

"Are you alright, *Señor*?" she said with concern in her voice.

Manuel tried to speak but his voice came out as a squeak.

"I'll get you some water," Isabella said and she turned around quickly to hide from the *Capitán* a big and amused silent laughter that she could no longer hold inside.

Don Manuel looked at her receding back as she walked away and thought that he saw a slight tremor from her shoulders and his blush deepened.

But despite his embarrassment, for the first time in his life, *Capitán* Manuel was convinced he was in love.

Chapter Twenty Six

It was long past midnight when Akash was finally able to sleep, yet he found himself awake at first light. He had found the jar of coffee that Awad kept in a makeshift cabinet pantry the night before when he was scrounging for food, and he brewed a potful now. He wanted the coffee to be strong enough to keep him awake for the rest of the day if needed. He did not know what the day would bring, but whatever it will be, he wanted to be prepared. Alone in a strange place, he had cut down his choices to two: fight or flight, and he had no intention of leaving without knowing what became of Awad.

As the coffee was brewing, he found some dried fish in a basket hanging by the fireplace, away from the reach of a curious and hungry cat, he thought, although he had not seen any cat or dog around the place. He was about to cook the dried fish over the fire where he was brewing coffee but he caught sight of a jar of pork lard and he decided to fry the dried fish instead. He likewise fried last night's leftover rice using the same pan and the excess oil from the fish fry. There were some tomatoes also in an earthen bowl and he cut some, adding a dab of *bagoong*, the fermented salted fish sauce that was a mainstay in Ilocano dishes. He ate with relish, ignoring the various scenarios of what he would do and expect in his search for Awad that were flashing in his mind. After he was full, he drank some coffee. It was strong and black just like the way he wanted. He only allowed himself to really think of what he was going to do after he had his second mug of coffee.

Quintin and Ana said the soldiers took Awad away and had probably brought her to the fort, so obviously that's where he would go first, he decided. But what if the soldiers would not let him in? And if they did, what would he do if Awad was not there? What if the soldiers would deny that they even took her? Or his worst fear of all, what if she were harmed or even killed? What would he do then? There were lots of questions running through his mind that he began to feel annoyed and irritated.

'Calm down,' he reminded himself. 'Deal with it whatever comes.' As his old man always said, it was a wasted effort to worry over things you have no control over. He took a deep breath and felt a little better after a while, but as he stretched up under the flickering light of the lamp as it was still dark out, he wished that Kulas was down there in the town with him. Somehow he had the feeling that there would be trouble before the day was over. And he would be in the thick of it.

"So be it," he murmured softly. He stood up and gathered the empty dishes and mug, and holding the lamp, went down to the well in the backyard. He washed the dishes in a clay basin then he hauled some more water from the well and took a quick wash. There was a small bar of laundry soap left on top of a stone by the well but he did not use it because he did not like its smell. He stripped off some young leaves from a nearby guava tree instead and used them to rub the dirt off his body. The water was cold and he felt better when he was done. He went back up into the house, stowed the dishes, pots and mug away then went to change into his Ilocano garments.

When he was done changing, he looked longingly at his spear, bow and arrows and the pair of knives, one long and one short, the latter, a *daga* as his Ilocano friends called the dagger, and decided that It would not be a good idea to go out to the fort openly armed so he reluctantly left them where they lay in a corner of the room. He slowly went out of the room but stopped a little past the door. He turned around and picked up the dagger and strapped it around the small of his back, un-tucking the unwieldy Ilocano shirt to cover it. Somehow, despite the Ilocano garb that he had on, covering his neck down to his ankles, he felt naked without a weapon. The dagger was small and not easily detected, he figured, but it would come handy in a fight. He did not wish to get into one knowing that he was alone, but he could not shake the feeling of trouble coming up ahead as he walked out the door.

Guardia started to growl as he passed by Ana's house but slunk away and went back to its spot under the tree when Akash hissed at it. The house was still closed and dark. 'They must still be sleeping,' Akash thought feeling a tinge of remorse for waking them up the night before. But inside the house, Ana nudged Quintin who was snoring beside her.

"He's leaving," she said. She had been awake for sometime but she did not find the inclination to get up so early and prepare for breakfast. There were no more children to feed anyway. There was just Quintin and her. Their children were older and gone, raising their own families.

"W-who? What?" Quintin sputtered, grasping for breath and rubbing his eyes in the dark.

"Akash," Ana said. "I think he just left."

"But it is still dark out," Quintin looked around adjusting his eyes in the dark. He saw the faint grey of dawn through the cracks of the bamboo walls of the house. "They won't let him in the fort this early."

"Maybe he's not going to the fort. Maybe he's going back up to the mountains."

"I hope so for his sake," Quintin murmured then promptly went back to sleep.

Outside, Akash looked up and down the deserted main road and went across it where there were more trees to provide a shade although the sun was still a good hour away. Except for a few houses that emitted the soft glow of lamplights, the town was still pretty much in a slumber. He walked towards where he knew the fort was located. It would take perhaps the good part of an hour to reach it at a steady leisurely walk and he took his time, taking the opportunity to run again the options he had in his mind. Besides, he wanted it to be at full light when he reached the fort. His appearance at full daylight would surely appear to be less confrontational or belligerent, he hoped.

Akash neither met nor saw anyone and he was glad but he kept to the darker side of the road. He did not wish to be openly seen by the townspeople consciously aware of the fact that he had no idea who would be sympathetic to Awad and Ilang. Again he wished that Kulas was there with him. He should have let him know that he was coming down to town. It was a foolish notion, he thought, for Kulas was not even in the village when he left and he had no idea that Awad was missing.

The sun was up and shining brightly on a clear morning and held the promise of a sweltering day when Akash finally caught sight of the fort. He walked towards the river that ran by the west side of the fort and sat down under the shade of a berry tree, a *Lomboy* that was thick with the purple fruit. While he caught his breath and rested, he kept his eyes on the fort. He saw the guard covering the western side of the fort making his rounds, mechanically walking up and down the length of the wall, stopping now and then at the guardhouses that connected the ramparts to exchange a word or two with the other guards manning the adjacent walls. He could not see them, but Akash knew they were there.

After a while, he stood up and went by the river. He stooped down and dipped his hands into the water, splashing his face and neck, liking its cooling effect. Feeling refreshed, he stood up and let the water trickle down his face and neck, damping the cotton shirt he wore. He did not bother to wipe the water off. With the way the day was shaping up, he would be dry by the time he got to the front gate of the fort.

There were two guards lounging in front of the gates when Akash approached. They stopped their soft conversation and appraised Akash up and down as he slowly walked towards them, his hands open and hanging loosely by his side. One of them held up his hand signaling him to stop when he was ten paces away.

"*Buenos Dias*," the guard said. "Who are you and what do you want?" His companion, an older soldier, did not say anything but Akash noticed that his hand was lightly resting on top of the handle of his sword.

"*Buenos dias, Señor*," Akash replied bowing his head courteously as he had seen the Ilocanos do when addressing the Spaniards. "My name is Akash. I am looking for a woman, Awad, who I believe is being held here."

The soldiers looked at one another. Then the other soldier who was older and still had his hand casually resting on the hilt of his sword spoke. He was obviously the more senior of the two.

"Awad?" he said. "*Perdon, Señor*, but there's no Awad here among the women who are helping us out in the fort." He looked at Akash with unblinking and curious eyes.

Akash held his gaze, showing no emotion. "Awad, *Señor*, is my sister and the mother of the one you call *La Generala*. I heard that your soldiers took her away a few days ago. Her daughter may be a rebel but my sister has nothing to do with it."

The older soldier's eyes momentarily showed a hint of surprise at the man's apparent impertinence but his stern expression did not change.

"Ahh, *Señor*," he said, a slight smile breaking his stolid face. "You must have heard wrong. I would surely have known if anyone of my soldiers had done such a dastardly deed. And as I said, we have no woman here at the fort as a prisoner or as a guest, except of course, as I said before, for the few helps who work in the kitchen and clean around. I am sorry but your sister is not here."

Akash felt a lump on his throat that fell down slowly and settled at the bottom of his stomach. He fought to quell the growing fear for Awad and the anger that was slowly rising inside him. He took a deep breath and held the old soldier's gaze.

"All the neighbors had seen soldiers take her away, *Señor*," he said slowly and very deliberately holding the soldier's stare. "Surely they did not lie and all of them could not have been mistaken."

The old soldier's eyes darkly flickered for a moment, showing for the first time a hint of irritation. He had not encountered nor seen an Indio as bold and impertinent as this one fearlessly standing before him. Even the old rebel Diego had not shown such composure. He examined the Indio more closely, curious now. He tried to remember the faces of all the known males in the town, suspected rebels or otherwise and he could not place the man. But somehow he felt a sense of familiarity with the *hombre*.

187

"Have you seen this man before, Bersalona?" he softly asked the guard who had not spoken since he stopped Akash.

"No, *Sargento*," Bersalona answered softly back. "But you know, I heard that *La Generala*'s mother was an *Itneg*."

"Ahhh," the old soldier said, as if a light had turned on inside his head. Of course, he thought. Only an ignorant *Itneg* from Abra would act this way, undaunted and unafraid. He looked at the Indio and imagined him in a *ba-ag* that was favored by the native mountain people of Abra. A flash of a smile crossed his lips as a faint ray of recognition dawned on him. He was one of the hunters, he thought, a few years ago, in Abra.

The *Sargento* had always practiced the habit of looking around and noting everything and everyone around him in a strange place and he remembered now one of the hunters who had remained in the sidelines while he and the *Capitán* engaged a couple of them in a mock swordplay. He blushed momentarily as he remembered the outcome of his and the *Capitán*'s duel with one of them. This one, he thought, was one of a group of three or four who had not shown much of a reaction during the mock fights. Neither had they participated in the merry-making, preferring to stay and watch cautiously in the background as if waiting for trouble.

Then the *Sargento*'s face clouded as he remembered the appearance of the other *Itneg* who beat him and the *Capitán* in the mock duel a few days ago, here at the fort also, although the other one was fishing by the river. What's going on? Was it mere coincidence? The *Sargento* was a pragmatic man. He did not believe in coincidences.

"Ahh, *Señor*," he said softly, trying to sound as friendly as he could. "Now I remember you, although you may not remember me. A long time ago in Abra, you were in a hunt. I still remember and appreciate your hospitality."

Akash was taken aback at the change in the old soldier's tone and attitude. Then as he looked at the soldier closely, he remembered now the old soldier who had tricked Bel-leng and bested him by pretending to fall. He should have known, he thought, but then again all these white folks looked the same.

"Come," the *Sargento* beckoned to him as if inviting an old friend. "Come, come inside and let me repay your hospitality with the meager provisions we have in the place. And let me show you around also so you can see with your own eyes that contrary to what you may have heard, your sister is not here, nor was she ever here."

Akash hesitated for a moment then walked toward the *Sargento* who had turned around as the guard held the gate door open. The *Sargento* stopped and waited for Akash a few steps beyond the gate.

"I trust you're alone," he said as his eyes lingered for a moment to the guard who caught the look and nodded briefly in acknowledgement. He would surely keep his eyes open for any other visitor, *Itneg* or not.

"Yes, *Señor*, I am alone," Akash said as he heard the gate close behind him. He walked toward the *Sargento* and together they proceeded inside the fort.

The *Sargento* brought Akash first to the officers mess hall where they had a short repast of rice cakes and coffee, and where the *Sargento* asked a few questions about Abra and the people in the village in an almost too friendly manner, which Akash answered as briefly and truthfully as he could. The *Sargento* believed that a man sharing your food rarely lied and he was determined to find out if there was reason to believe that somehow the *Itnegs* were getting involved in the troubles with the *rebeldes*. The *Itneg's* straightforward enough answers appeased the *Sargento's* suspicions a bit.

'Yes, the old man is well. Yes, Kulas was in good health as well, and no, he did not know where he is at the moment, except somewhere hunting in the mountains. No, they were not in trouble nor were they looking for one, either with the Ilocanos or with the other tribes.'

Then the *Sargento* took him on a tour of the fort as he promised. The orderliness and arms and provisions of the fort were impressive to Akash and he said so to the *Sargento* who smiled proudly. The *Sargento*, doubts banished from his mind, was in a friendly mood all throughout as if he had nothing to fear or hide. Akash also loosened up after a while as they walked through the halls and to the calaboose where the prisoners were kept, mostly some dejected looking Ilocanos. Despite the friendly tour, Akash maintained his vigilance to any sign that Awad was ever brought there. But as the *Sargento* had said at the gate, Awad was not there and Akash did not see nor noticed anything that indicated her presence, nor was there any sign that she was even there at any time, just like the *Sargento* claimed.

He finally thanked the *Sargento* and left with a heavy feeling in his heart. And underneath it, a little ember of fear and anger began to grow.

From the top of the wall, the *Sargento* looked down at the receding form of the *Itneg*, eyes squinting in deep thought under furrowed concerned brows.

The *Itneg* had not seen anything, but did he believe what he saw? Did he believe that they had nothing to do with the disappearance of his sister? He turned around and yelled at the first soldier he saw.

"Albano! Tell Cortez to come see me in my office! *¡Ahora mismo! ¡Andale!!*"

"*Si, Sargento!*" Albano said, snapping a quick salute and hurried away.

Moments later, Cortez showed up, still tucking his shirt as he approached *Sargento* Tiago who was quietly sitting on his desk, staring at the wall, obviously in deep thought.

"*¿Que'tal, Sargento? ¿Que pasa?*" Cortez said.

The *Sargento* looked at him with a start then glared at the soldier as he gathered his thoughts. He stood up and walked around the desk and stopped a foot away from Cortez who instinctively took a step back.

"The woman," he hissed softly as if he did not want anyone else to hear. "I don't want to know where she is, but could anybody find her?"

"No, *Sargento*," Cortez said confidently. "There's no way anyone would find her, not even the wild dogs if there are any around these parts."

"I hope you're right, *hombre*," the *Sargento* said somberly. "I hope you're right, and pray that you're right or I'll have your sorry arse. We don't need trouble from those *Itnegs* also. We already have our hands full with the damn Ilocanos."

"I assure you, *Sargento*, no one would find her. Not even Miguel and his friends could find their way back to the place." Cortez tried to hold *Don* Tiago's stare but he found himself looking at the blank wall where the *Sargento* was previously staring at as if he was inspecting the quality of the masonry. He had never seen the *Sargento* this agitated, drunk or sober. He tried to control his growing nervousness.

"Don't tell me about Miguel and his stupid friends! They put this on us!"

"It was an accident, *Sargento*, I swear!" Cortez looked at the *Sargento* with pleading eyes. "It was an accident. It happened so fast that it was over before Alfonso or I could do anything."

Don Tiago sighed. He did not want to go through the whole thing all over again. Cortez and Alfonso had told him the same thing and they never wavered from their accounts. The woman tried to escape and one of Miguel's friends killed her by accident. Silently he wished they had not used Miguel and his fools of friends.

"Cortez, I won't say it again, but make sure Miguel or any of his friends would not talk," he said softly.

"You can be certain of that, *Sargento*. I'll see to it myself," Cortez answered and waited for a bit before slowly backing out of the room when the *Sargento* did not respond and went back slowly around his desk. Cortez had a knowing grin on his face as he walked out the door.

Don Tiago sat down heavily in his chair like an old, arthritic man. He was feeling his age.

He again stared at the empty wall, as if he was unaware that Cortez had left or the man had even been in there just a moment ago.

Finally he shook his head and buried his face in his palms, rubbing it vigorously for a moment. 'How could a brilliant idea go so wrong?' he moaned. 'Or perhaps, it was a fool of an idea in the first place? Why had he ever known and listened to that *perro* Miguel or that *loco* Cortez?'

He shook his head one more time, pulled open the bottom drawer of his desk and pulled out a half-empty bottle.

"*Que sera, sera,*" he said softly as he pulled the cork off the bottle and raised it to his *lips*.

He was never partial to using a glass when he drank alone.

Chapter Twenty Seven

"You are not married yet?" Ilang asked, her brows furrowing in incredulity. They were walking around the village after a lengthy welcome for her troop. She was going to meet with the elders, headed by her *Angkay Kagaid*, later on after dinner. Her rebels were down by the river putting up camp. She had decided for them to stay in the village for at least three days, or longer if needed, to rest and for those wounded and sick to recover and recuperate.

And for the warriors of the tribe to get prepared for battle, she hoped, after she asked for their help.

She still had ambivalent feelings about asking for their help and dragging them into the Ilocanos' cause, but she felt she had no other options except to give up and surrender. But she was too stubborn to do that. And besides, doing so would be tantamount to giving up on Diego. She would rather die before she did that. But for now, she tried to keep the thought out of her mind as she walked and talked with Kulas, feeling an odd yet familiar sense of security and fondness as she did so. She tried to ignore the feeling, letting her eyes wander around the village in a futile effort to suppress it.

"No," Kulas said softly, lowering his eyes, fearful that they may betray the emotions he was likewise feeling inside. "No, somehow I never had the chance," he said more loudly as he furtively looked back at Ilang who thankfully had her eyes roving around the village trying perhaps to recognize faces and sights culled from childhood memory. "Time just went by and there was just no one around to marry," he added again softly, surprised at what he just said and hoping that Ilang was not paying attention.

But he was wrong. Ilang was listening to his every word. She quickly stopped and faced him.

"Why, Kulas, no one to marry? Really?" Ilang exclaimed. "Look around us," she gestured to the villagers, especially to a group of young women who were amusedly looking at them, some of them pointing to the woman who was once their playmate. "There are so many beautiful women around here! How about Ammanay? Or, what was the name of her cousin who always followed you around? She must be all grown up now and is no doubt a beautiful woman!"

Despite herself, Ilang found herself smiling as she noted the discomfort on Kulas's face as he looked around the village in apparent embarrassment.

Kulas sighed and tried to compose himself, yet he felt his face and neck still warming up. How did he get into this predicament? He tried to grin but his lips failed him. He gently touched Ilang's elbow and nudged her forward to continue their walk, steering her to the path going towards the river, away from the curious looks of the villagers.

"Ammanay surely is a beautiful woman, and so is her cousin, Bug-gan, but they're both married now and have children of their own," Kulas said.

"Well, it's your fault if you let them go," Ilang teased.

"I was just not interested in either one of them," Kulas smiled. "Or anyone else in the village for that matter," he added before he realized what he just said.

Ilang abruptly stopped and held Kulas's arm, stopping him, and forced him to face her.

"What? What are you saying? No one in the village is good enough?"

"No, no, no," Kulas said hastily, getting confused as he sensed Ilang seemed to be getting angry. At what, he had no idea. He was sure he would never understand women! "That's not what I meant. Sure there are lots of beautiful women in the village but there was just no one that I want badly enough to be my wife. It would not be fair to just marry someone for marriage's sake."

He looked at Ilang's eyes and he felt a sense of relief as he saw that her face softened at his explanation although he himself did not totally understand what he had just said. It did not matter as long as Ilang seemed to be appeased.

Ilang let go of Kulas' arm and resumed walking towards the river. Kulas had unknowingly hurt her feelings for what he said was exactly what happened with her and Tomas although she cared for him later on. She did marry Tomas for marriage's sake. She walked deep in thought and Kulas dutifully followed.

"And what was it exactly are you looking for that you can't find in the women from the village?" Ilang asked as Kulas reached her side, recovering from her slighted feelings for she knew that Kulas could not have known the reasons for her marriage to Tomas.

"I don't know. I really don't know," Kulas said slowly. 'I was waiting for you to come back,' he wanted to say but for all his bravery in a fight, he could not bring himself to say it aloud.

"You have a big problem, Kulas," Ilang said with amusement in her voice. "You'll never get married if you don't know what you're looking for in a woman."

"Yeah, I know," Kulas said. He was getting comfortable as they walked and talked easily now, the old cozy feeling of long ago slowly returning and he felt a warm glow in his chest. He was feeling better, all nervousness and apprehension of their meeting finally slowly vanishing away.

But the feeling did not last long as he heard Ilang say suddenly.

"Were you ever in love?" Ilang blurted. She covered her mouth in mild surprise as she had no intention of asking the question. She was not thinking and it just came out of the blue.

Kulas was also taken aback by the question. He had been asking himself the same question but it was totally unexpected coming from Ilang.

"L-l-lo-love? I-i-in love? Ever?" he stammered feeling foolish as he spoke each word.

"Yes," Ilang said emphatically, more determined this time. "Yes, in love. Were you ever, with anyone, or with even more than one?"

Kulas did not answer. He paused from walking and opened his mouth but nothing came out. He resumed his walk to gather his thoughts but he did not know how to answer. Ilang likewise paused then walked hurriedly to catch up with Kulas, waiting anxiously for an answer.

"Well?" she said as she fell beside Kulas, matching his steps.

"Yes, I think so," Kulas finally said. "Yes, I have been in love but I did not know it then," he added truthfully.

Ilang cast him a questioning sideways glance that Kulas caught as he was looking at her as he spoke. "You think so?"

Kulas looked forward and did not answer and subconsciously walked faster as if he was trying to walk away from the question. Ilang also quickened her pace, keeping by his side.

"Who?" she said. "Who is the lucky girl? Or should I say unlucky? Is she from another village?"

Kulas kept his silence but he slowed down then stopped, turning toward Ilang and this time holding her arms in both hands. He looked at Ilang's eyes without saying a word. He wanted to say her name so much but he could not get himself to say anything, so he just looked longingly at Ilang.

Ilang looked back at him then comprehension slowly crept into her eyes. She felt her heart beating rapidly and the warmth of a blush rising from her breast spreading quickly to her face. She had no idea that Kulas regarded her as anything other than a childhood friend. She had been fond of him when they were young, feeling secure in his company but that was it. Sure, she had thought of him at times especially when she was lonely as she was growing up in the Ilocos but she had never thought of Kulas in a romantic way. Yet as she met his gaze, she was not too sure. For a moment she felt her composure slowly slipping away and being replaced with a puzzling feeling of uncertainty that was somehow giving her a warm glow inside that

194

she had not felt for a long time. It felt strange and she fought inwardly to get rid of it, but she could not.

"Ohh," she finally uttered softly, surrendering to the feeling. She looked up at Kulas, whose face seemed to exude unequivocal calmness, strength and security, yet at the same time also of tenderness. "And now?" she asked softly. She held his gentle gaze and for the first time she was looking at him from a different light. Kulas had grown and matured to such a striking man. She realized that he was much better looking and surely seemed much stronger than either of the men she had married, strong yet tender at the same time. She felt her heart melting but she steeled herself, fighting the feeling. It was not right, she thought. Nothing good would come out of it. Not now. The timing was just not right.

"Now? Now, I'm sure. I have waited for you, Ilang. You're the one that I want. The only one. There was never anyone else." She heard Kulas say so softly that she barely heard his words. She felt a rush in her breast that she could not explain. It was something she had not felt before in either of her previous relationships with men and she felt a sense of uncertainty, of somehow being lost, like a rudderless boat out of control. She lowered her eyes lest they betray her confusion.

Kulas took a deep breath, Ilang's confusion not lost to him. He let go of Ilang's arms and took his eyes off her, letting them roam around the village, to the forest beyond, then to the river and to the Ilocanos pitching their tents by its banks, downstream from where they stood. He wished he could take back his words but at the same time he felt like a big burden was lifted off his shoulders and somehow he was glad. Whether Ilang had the same feelings for him or not was suddenly of no consequence.

"Are you angry?" he finally said as he turned back to Ilang.

"Angry?" Ilang looked up at him, her face showing more confusion from his question. "Angry? No, no. Why would I be angry?"

"I don't know. You did not say a word. I am sorry for what I said. I have no right."

Ilang raised a hand, calmly resting it on Kulas's arm.

"No, no, please don't apologize," she said, raising her eyes to look at him. "I was just surprised. I did not know."

Kulas held her gaze. "And?" he said.

"And what?" Ilang asked, knowing that in her heart that Kulas was about to ask the same question she had asked a moment before.

"And now, now that you know?" Kulas said.

Ilang lowered her gaze and did not respond. She truthfully did not know how she felt and she found herself telling the truth.

"Now?" she said, looking back up at Kulas. "I-I don't know, Kulas. This is all so sudden."

Kulas did not answer keeping her eyes on Ilang, feeling more remorseful now that he had not held back his tongue.

"I'm sorry," Ilang said. "I have not expected this, especially from you," she gestured helplessly, pushing a palm up toward Kulas as he tried to open his mouth to let her talk. "I am flattered and I am glad that you care for me enough to want me, but I can't deal with love or romance right now, not at this time in my life. I have just lost another husband a few months ago. You have always been kind to me and I'm eternally grateful, and please know that you always have a special place in my heart, but I can't, right now, I don't think I can deal with it."

"I'm sorry, Ilang," Kulas murmured again. "I am sorry I said what I said. I had no right."

"No," Ilang said. "No, you have every right and I am glad you brought it up. I just wish, I wish I had known before, before all this," she gestured toward the Ilocano camp that now showed a few tents standing up and strands of smoke curling upwards from scattered campfires. "I am sorry but I don't know what to do, with them, with you. I am honestly confused."

Kulas did not say anything. He looked at Ilang who seemed so helpless, so different now from the woman who had confidently led a rag-tag army of men toward the village that he wanted so badly to hold her close in his arms but he did not move from where he stood. It would not have been proper. He had no right, he thought, although all his being shouted for him to take her and comfort her in his arms. Strange, he thought, as he had always wanted to do the same damn thing when they were little.

Then as if another force had entered his body, he found one arm reaching out to Ilang, holding a seemingly fragile shoulder and drawing her protectively close to him. Ilang found herself relenting, unable to resist and she took a step toward Kulas. She buried her face in the shallow of his neck then it seemed as if a dam broke and she cried, her shoulders shaking uncontrollably despite the strong, comforting arm of Kulas that held her tightly.

They stood there for a long moment, with her crying on his shoulders, and he, one arm around hers and the other helplessly dangling by his side, not knowing what to do, totally oblivious and unconcerned of what went around them.

Then Ilang finally regained her composure. She drew herself out from Kulas's embrace and wiped off the tears from her face. "I am sorry," she said trying to put up a brave face and a smile that failed. "I'm sorry," she said again, extending an arm toward Kulas to wipe off her tear marks that she noticed running down his neck.

Kulas flinched involuntarily as he felt her hand on his neck but then he raised a hand and caught hers and held it there by his chest. Ilang did not pull her hand away, surrendering it to the firm yet tender hold of Kulas' hand, feeling the sandy roughness of his calloused palm against the softness of hers.

"Don't be sorry," he said tenderly. "I understand. I wish I had done what I promised a long time ago."

Ilang's eyes grew wide, showing a bit of surprise.

"What promise?" She said.

"To come after you," Kulas said before he could control himself. He found suddenly that he could no longer hold back from her what he felt and what he wanted to say. It was a revelation that here was finally a woman that he could speak with freely without feeling any sense of trepidation.

"I was here the day you left," he said, letting go of Ilang's hand. "I did not know that you were leaving until Akash came up the mountain and told me. I ran down as fast as I can, and I saw the raft pushing out from there," he gestured towards *Apo* Allak's hut by the river. "I was up there," he pointed at the trail going up the mountain. "And I shouted your name, but it was too far, but I thought you heard me anyway because I saw you raise your head and wave."

"I heard a voice but I did not know it was you," Ilang interrupted, her eyes lighting up in remembrance. "I looked around but I did not see you. I also went by your house to say goodbye but you were not there either," she added shyly.

Kulas looked at her with a glint of gladness in his eyes. "But, I was up..." he began, waving an arm and looking up the trail, and suddenly stopped as he realized that from this distance, a half-naked body would be hard to spot against the brown trunks of trees and dried bushes beyond the trail.

"I was there," he continued anyway as if confessing to a crime. "Then I ran down as fast I could towards the river, but by the time I got here, you were way down there." His arm gestured limply downriver. "I went into the river and called your name again when I came up by the middle, but you never looked back."

Ilang sighed. "I could not," she said. "I was crying. I did not want to go."

But Kulas continued as if he was never interrupted. "And I swam across to the other side, and stayed there for a long time then I promised I would come after you."

Ilang held her breath, a mix of emotions rampantly running inside her as she remembered the day, and now listening to Kulas as he poured out his

197

feelings, they all came back again yet somehow in a good way. She felt a sense of calmness that she had not felt for a long time, and most of all there was that comforting feeling of security, as if she was home.

She looked up at Kulas tenderly and she heard herself say, "But you did not come." It was merely a statement but somehow Kulas felt like there was some hint of accusatory hue in it.

"No," Kulas whispered as he lowered his eyes dejectedly. "No, I did not. I was scared."

"Scared? Scared of what?"

"That you did not want to see me. That you had forgotten about this place, me, the village, the mountain, the river, the trees. That you have another life entirely different from all this and it was better, and you were happy." Kulas gestured helplessly.

"And, above all else, I wanted you to be happy," he added softly.

"Oh, Kulas," Ilang said as she flung herself into Kulas' arms, not caring if anyone was watching. "You always did look out for me. Thank you!" She held on tightly and felt a warm glow from the reassuring pressure of strong arms circling her shoulders. She wanted to say she loved the man, but she could not bring herself to say the words. She knew that if she did her world would be totally turned upside down yet again and there would be no turning back.

She was not ready for it. Not now. Not yet.

But somehow Kulas knew. He held on to the woman he loved knowing that this moment would not last. Yet he felt no remorse or rancor.

He finally eased Ilang out of his embrace and held her at arm's length and looked lovingly in her eyes but he saw there not the soft helpless eyes of the little girl he once knew and fell in love with but the angry and defiant fire of an aggrieved woman bent on avenging a dead husband.

And there was no space or time for love or romance.

He recoiled inwardly but his eyes and expression remained calm.

Fate had drawn its lines.

So be it.

Chapter Twenty Eight

Akash was a naturally calm and calculating man. His brother Allong knew this and so did the other men and women in the village. But Akash did not consciously know. He simply acted that way. But what the people in the village did not know and which Akash also simply did without dwelling on it was that he could be unreasonably impulsive when he was troubled. It was not a common occurrence for he was a naturally calm and calculating man and not troubled easily by most of anything, but now he was troubled.

His sister was missing, and it troubled him greatly, and he was getting mad.

How could a person vanish in such a small town without anyone knowing where she went?

It was just not possible. Someone knew but no one was talking. And it gnawed on him. He was getting angry at the whole town and getting angrier every moment as he sipped the umpteenth cup of coffee he had that day inside Awad's house. It was almost late afternoon. He had gone around town after his fruitless visit to the fort, asking anyone he knew and even total strangers if they had any idea where Awad was or who took her if she was abducted. He had no reasons to doubt Ana and Quintin but he wanted to look at all the other possibilities. And he came up with nothing.

His sister had simply vanished. And it troubled him a lot. And he was seething inside.

He finished his coffee, rinsed the mug and stowed it away. He went inside the room and took off his Ilocano shirt, leaving the loose, woolen pants on. He felt better without any shirt. He lay down on the bed in the dark. He had not bothered to open any windows when he got back and he did not open the bedroom window now. Let the neighbors think that there was no one inside.

He needed to rest and think of what to do yet no thoughts and ideas came as he drifted on and off into a fitful sleep. It was a few hours later when he got up, feeling as miserable and tired as before he went to bed. The only thing that changed, it seemed, was that the room was a lot darker.

He grudgingly stood up and went to the window, pushing it a bit to look outside. The sun had gone down and some houses in the neighborhood showed a hint of lit lamps inside. He closed the window and he turned toward the door as his stomach growled, reminding him that he had not eaten anything solid since breakfast. He went to the kitchen and scrounged around, finding some dried *tapas* and tomatoes. He coaxed a small fire from the coals buried in the ashes in the clay stove and warmed the *tapas* over it without thoroughly cooking them, and cut some tomatoes. He found some left-over rice and dumped the cut tomatoes and dried tapas over it, eating the concoction with his hands.

As he ate, the old questions about Awad came back, yet he found no answers as before. And the feeling of anger came back, more intense than ever. By the time he pushed aside his empty plate, he was beside himself with rage.

He washed his hands and plate, wiping them off with a dry rag. He poured the left-over water from the clay basin over the smoldering coals, watching the smoke rise up as the coals fizzled in a watery hiss. Then he went back into the bedroom, pulled off his trousers, rolled them and his shirt into his cloth pouch and slung it across his shoulder. He went out of the room, picking up his bow and quiver full of arrows and his spear that were leaning by the door as he walked by them. He glimpsed at his reflection in the mirror of the *aparador* as he passed by it, seeing a man naked except for a *ba-ag*, fully armed and ready for war, with a grim look on his face.

Silently he went out of the house, locking the door behind him as he stepped out. He went to Ana's house, glaring at the dog that remained silent, watching him with suspicious and wary eyes, yet it did not move from where it stood under the tree. He knocked at the door and handed the key to Quintin who had opened it. He heard Ana bustling about in the kitchen.

"I am going," he said quickly before Ana had a chance to come to the door, refusing Quintin's invitation to go inside. "Thank you for everything."

"I am sorry about Awad. I am sorry we could not be of help," Quintin said in his somber way. Akash knew that he meant every word of it. Despite his seemingly surly disposition, Quintin was a decent man.

Akash simply nodded his acknowledgement, not knowing what to say. He extended his hand in the way of the Ilocanos and Quintin firmly gripped it and they shook hands briefly. Then without saying a word, Akash turned away and walked briskly toward the road where he shortly vanished in the dark.

The last glimpse that Quintin saw of the *Itneg* was the glint of the tip of his spear against the moonlight.

"*Vaya con Dios*," Quintin whispered as he gently closed the door. For once, Ana who had come out from the kitchen and stood by Quintin was speechless, lost in her own thoughts.

Akash paused for a moment under the shade of the huge Acacia tree across the street from Awad's house. He squatted in the shadows close to the tree's enormous trunk, his form lost in the darkness of the evening. For what seemed a long while he did not move, listening and watching if anyone would move and follow him. He was not sure if anyone was watching Awad's house and who would be curious enough to find out what he would do. But no one appeared, and the dogs in the neighborhood remained silent.

He finally stood up and made his way through a broken fence, across the yard of someone's house, to the open field beyond. Thankfully the house did not have a dog and he passed unmolested. He crossed the field quickly, hating every moment that he was out in the open, and he breathed a sigh of relief as he entered the sparse woods beyond it. He slowed down as he walked through the woods, thankful that there was not much of undergrowth beneath the trees, mostly soft pliant grass. And there was the moonlight so he had no trouble picking a path, not that he needed one.

He knew where he was going, at least its general direction. He looked up at the moon when he reached a little clearing and nodded with satisfaction.

He should be at the place close enough to the preferred time that he wanted to be there.

Chapter Twenty Nine

"Sit down," *Apo* Kagaid said to his granddaughter, indicating the wooden bench in the backyard.

They had just finished dinner. The dishes were cleared and the rest of Ilang's Ilocano friends who had joined *Apo* Kagaid, *Apo* Dalalo, Allong, Kulas, Ittok, Ayong and their families and several other villagers, had gone back to their camp by the river.

Ilang sat down without saying a word. The subject of asking for help was never brought up during dinner, but somehow she had the feeling that the whole village knew about it. She looked at the faces of the men and women around her, and she found herself thinking that she was a stranger to them. And yet, strangely enough, the thought that they were her mother's people and therefore hers also entered her mind and it brought a little assurance.

But she could not shake the feeling that she was a total stranger and very much alone. Even her Uncle Nicolas had left and went into the camp. There was just her and the villagers despite the reassuring look that Kulas gave her. They are my people too, she tried to convince herself as she waited for her grandfather to speak up.

"Know that we love you, *apok*, my grandchild, as much as we love Awad, your mother," *Apo* Kagaid said, sucking deeply at his reed pipe. The tip of the pipe glowed brightly in the dark like a hot ember. Slowly he exhaled the tobacco smoke as if with great reluctance. "And we're deeply sorry to hear about Diego," he said as an afterthought, and then he paused again for a while, taking another draw at his pipe.

"Thank you, *Angkay*," Ilang said softly, bowing her head.

"I know you must be in deep pain. I know you must be angry, very angry and perhaps in great wish to get back at your husband's killers," *Apo* Kagaid continued. "I understand if you feel that way. The whole village understands, but where would this fighting end? After you killed your husband's killers? After you or your friends are killed? When would this trouble end?"

Gabriela was lost for words and she remained silent. She looked around at the faces that were intently looking at her from the edges of the light coming from the small bonfire that *Ama* Allong had built. Everyone was looking at her intently, with sympathy in their eyes but likewise curious also to know what she felt and thought.

"I-I-I don't know, *Angkay*, I really don't know," she stammered in all honesty. It was the truth. Only God knew how or when or where all this was

202

going to end, she thought. For a moment she did not care anymore as she watched the worried faces of her relatives. Perhaps it was all a useless, fool's cause, this thing that Diego started. There was no way they could win against the Spaniards. Perhaps it was time to drop it and let it go, let all the rest of the survivors go back to their fields and fishing boats and get on with their lives.

But the face of Diego, twisted in pain as she cradled him, dying in her arms, flashed through her mind and she knew she could not let go. The moment Diego died in her arms, the struggle had become personal for her. There was no giving up. She was going to continue the struggle and if she died in the process, then so be it. There was nothing else to do. To abandon the fight now would be abandoning Diego's' memory and dreams also. And that she could not do. Besides, there rankled deep in her breast the desire to avenge his death.

She scanned again the faces around her until her eyes settled on Kulas. Their eyes locked together and for a moment her resolve wavered as she remembered their tender moment that afternoon. But a voice in the back of her mind reminded her that she was chasing a foolish dream. Kulas was a dear man but a romantic relationship with him was not going to work. There was no way she could live up here in the mountains. And she knew, Kulas could not, and surely would not live anywhere else.

She lowered her eyes, and looked at her grandfather as *Apo* Kagaid cleared his throat, a smoke trailing from his mouth as he did so.

Apo Kagaid shook his head slowly as he lovingly met his *apo*'s gaze.

"Perhaps it's best for you to stop fighting," he said in all sincerity. "Let the Ilocanos go back down to their homes and you stay here. You will be safe here. We will bring your mother back up here. She will come back and stay if you are here."

Ilang likewise started shaking her head even before the old man was finished talking.

"No, *Angkay*, I could not," she said emphatically, avoiding looking up at Kulas who, she knew as if she can feel his eyes, was looking at her. "I appreciate and thank you for your offer, but I could not give up the fight. Those people," she gestured toward the camp by the river, "they are relying on me to lead them. I could not let them down. Besides they can no longer go back. They will be killed by the soldiers if they showed up in their towns. And most of them no longer have anyone to go back home to." Her voice trailed to a tremor that she could barely stifle, her emotions taking the better of her.

"We may die in the fight, many of us, perhaps even all of us will perish, but we will continue the fight," Ilang continued, her voice stronger now showing her full resolve. She looked at her grandfather and she saw the old man's disappointment in his face. She sighed, feeling a little remorse and a lot of guilt. Perhaps it was not a good idea to have come up here, she thought, but she was desperate. There was just no way for them to continue the fight without help. Not at their present condition. "I know you mean well, but I am so sorry I could not follow your suggestion. And I sincerely apologize for our intrusion here."

Apo Kagaid raised a hand. "Don't, *Apok*, don't apologize," he said soothingly. "You are one of us and you will always be welcomed here. We are glad, I am glad," he averred, "I am extremely glad that you are here. You and your friends can stay here and rest as long as you wish. There's no intrusion."

"Thank you, *Angkay*," Ilang said as the old man paused and took a deep drag on his pipe.

"You're welcome, and as I said you are always welcome here and don't you ever forget that," the old man said as he slowly exhaled, the grey smoke swirling out of his mouth and nostrils. "Now, I know why you're here."

"You do?" Ilang was surprised. Had someone from her group talked about their intent? It could not be since she specifically told everyone that the plea for help would be coming from her alone and she had been around her grandfather since their arrival. She would have known if anyone had talked with him and broached their purpose of coming up here.

"Yes, as obviously your mother must have already relayed to you our answer to her request," the old man said.

"Wait, *Angkay*," Ilang interrupted, "what request? I haven't talked with my mother for a while now."

"Ahh," *Apo* Kagaid stopped from raising the pipe to his lips. He slowly lowered his hand, resting it on his lap. "Ahh, so you do not know then."

"Know what, *Angkay*?"

"Awad sent word about two weeks ago that you needed help. She wanted us to join you in your fight against the Spaniards," *Apo* Kagaid said.

"But, *Angkay*, I did not ask her to do that," Ilang said, her brows furrowing as she thought of her mother's reason for her actions. Had she known of their dire predicament somehow?

"Ahh, I wonder what prompted her to do that," *Apo* Kagaid said pensively. "So you don't need help then? You are just here to hide from the Spaniards, to rest and get provisions perhaps?"

"About that, *Angkay*," Ilang said softly, taking her time to frame her words properly. She had envisioned and practiced what she wanted to say but now that the moment had come, she was not too sure of how to go about it. "Yes, we're here to hide from the soldiers, and to rest and give time

204

for our wounded fighters to recuperate, and to gather provisions as well because God knows we're short of everything." She paused and took a deep breath and looked at her grandfather with pleading eyes. "And yes, like *Ina* Awad said, we also need help in our fight. I don't know how she knew, but yes, we do, very badly. That in all honesty is the main reason why we came up here, to ask for your help."

Apo Kagaid solemnly looked back at his granddaughter with kindness and sympathy in his eyes. He wanted to reach out and hold her but he remained where he sat. It was with a heavy heart when he spoke the words which he knew were not what Ilang expected to hear. He looked around at the faces of the villagers gathered around them and he knew he had no choice even if it hurt his granddaughter.

"Awad would have known that you needed help even if you had not told her," he began. He could not bear to tell his granddaughter his adverse answer without trying his best to soften it somehow. "She is special that way. She has had always shown the gift of somehow knowing of things to come since she was a little girl, so I am not surprised now why she had sent word for help without your knowledge. And our elders have discussed it at length," he gestured at the faces silently looking from the edges of the firelight, "and we had sent word back to Awad a few days ago..." he paused as if he was unable to go on.

"We sent Sadang down there to relay the message," the old man continued after a moment, looking around again at the faces as if searching for Sadang who was not there. He turned his face back to Ilang. "We told her, and I am telling you now with great sadness in my heart that we could not help in your fight. I am sorry but I could not in good conscience let our young men die for a cause that does not concern us."

The old man broke his gaze from his granddaughter as he saw the apparent dismay in her eyes. He looked down at his pipe and noted that it had turned grey. He raised the pipe to his lips and gave it a fruitless suck. He kept it in his lips anyway as he looked over it at Ilang who thankfully had her eyes averted, seemingly studying her hands that were playing with each other on her lap.

He waited, as did everyone else, for Ilang's answer but she did not say a word for a long time. There was silence, interrupted only now and then by the crackling of the fire. The shadows danced behind them in the backyard. Somewhere up in the mountain a wild dog howled in the night.

Then Ilang raised her face and looked at the old man.

"I am sorry to hear that, *Angkay*, but I understand. I know that the decision did not come easy for you and for everyone," her voice trembled as she spoke but she held her face up. "I apologize, I am truly sorry that we

205

even came up here to impose on you. I am so so-sorry..." And her voice broke as she felt total helplessness enveloping her whole being.

In the shadows, Kulas turned away and silently walked toward the river. He sat by the riverbank away from the Ilocano camp and stared at the stars for a long time. Then he closed his eyes, Ilang's sad face stubbornly stuck in his mind.

He must have fallen asleep for the bright star was low and close to the horizon when he looked back up at the sky that was giving way to the grey of dawn. He stayed where he was and waited wide awake, unable to go back to sleep, for the morning.

The Ilocano camp was stirring when Kulas finally moved. The smell of brewing coffee and dried fish and meat grilling in open fires reached him after a while. He reluctantly got up, stretched stiffly, trying to loosen his muscles then slowly made his way to the river. He waded in until the water came up to his knees. It felt warm and soothing against the coolness of the morning air. He took a deep breath and took a dive keeping underwater as he let his momentum propel him forward, then he started kicking vigorously, his arms locked together forward in a sharp triangle. He was in the middle of the river when he finally surfaced.

Downriver he noted the smoke swirling up from the campfires of the Ilocanos as they cooked their breakfast. Somewhere from the village, the crowing of the roosters reached him intermittently as they welcomed the new day.

He wondered what it would bring and his heart was not too hopeful as he remembered Ilang's sad face the night before.

For a moment he wondered where she was at the moment. He did not know if she slept at her grandfather's hut or was down there at the Ilocanos' camp.

He fought the urge to swim down to the camp and he stayed where he was. He swam in laps, going back and forth across the river until his arms and legs felt heavy and he was breathing hard. He finally got out of the water feeling refreshed from the vigorous swim, and let the morning air dry him up. He looked up east toward the sun peeking above the mountain ridge and imagined himself sitting underneath the shade of one of the majestic twin pines.

Somehow he began to feel better but it did not last. His stomach growled and reminded him of breakfast.

Chapter Thirty

Akash sat on his haunches in the dark, underneath the old *Salamagui* tree where Kulas had hanged the dog, intently watching the house. There was no light and no movement inside yet he stayed stock-still at where he sat. He waited patiently, staring at the house and scanning the neighborhood once in a while. But there was no movement. And he thanked the spirits that Miguel had not replaced his dead dog, not that it would have mattered.

He had little doubt that somehow Miguel knew about the disappearance of Awad. There was just something in the eyes of Quintin and Ana, and from the evasive answers of the people he talked to the day before, that gave him a strange feeling that Diego's killer was also involved somehow in his sister's disappearance.

If not, he was going to kill him anyway before he went back up to the village, regardless of what Kulas thought. After what he did to Diego, Miguel deserved to die. He was not particularly close to Diego but he was fond of the man and he was family. Besides, Diego was a pretty decent man even for an Ilocano.

He looked up at the stars and figured it must be a couple of hours after midnight. Perfect, he thought as he slowly stood up, flexing his arms and legs to rid his muscles of the knots he was beginning to feel after sitting motionless for so long. He strapped his bow across his shoulders and cautiously moved toward the house.

The flimsy lock which was a sort of a contraption made out of wood and rope provided no hindrance to his entry into the house. He stopped briefly inside, stepping by the wall behind the door and stood silently, letting his eyes adjust to the darkness. There were two doors leading off the living room. He listened but nobody stirred except for the faint sound of somebody snoring. He took a deep breath and exhaled slowly through his mouth then he moved again.

In the darkness and silence of the house, the labored snoring of someone sleeping in the bedroom closer to the front door became louder. That was what he expected and his somber face flitted briefly with a satisfied smile.

He took out his dagger and he walked silently towards the noise, his bare feet gliding with nary a whisper on the smooth bamboo floor. The bedroom door was open and he could see the form of the sleeping man in the bed as he paused again by the doorway. The body did not move as he tiptoed closer to the bed.

He stood over the sleeping body and looked at it for a long time in the dark. Then slowly he lowered his right arm that was holding the dagger and pointed its tip at the base of the throat of the sleeping man, at the same time covering the man's nose and mouth with his left hand.

The man's eyes opened wide in a big surprise, all sleep forgotten as he began to struggle and gasp for air but Akash held him down firmly, the knife point going in a fraction deeper, breaking skin and serving as a warning for the man to stop resisting. A faint trace of blood trickled off from the tip of the dagger.

"Don't move," Akash hissed, "or you are a dead man."

The man stopped struggling.

"Don't make any noise when I take off my hand," Akash continued. "If you do, I'll kill you, you understand?"

The man blinked and tried to move his head so he can talk, but Akash did not loosen his grip until he felt the man struggling to breathe. He lifted his hand and the man gagged as he rapidly gasped for air.

"Wha-what do you want?" His eyes were wide and watery as he spoke, his voice trembled with fright. Akash realized that the man was not the one they called Miguel. But he was in Miguel's house, there was no doubt about that, so this man had to be a relative, or a friend. Either case, he had to know something.

"I'm going to ask you a question and I want an honest answer," Akash said, putting an added pressure on the dagger that he now held steadily under the man's chin.

The man gasped in pain as blood trickled down anew on the side of his neck, seeping into a portion of the pillow and coloring the bed covers. It was hot and the man was not using a blanket at all. He tried to nod but the tip of the dagger kept him from doing so and he blinked with frightened eyes instead.

"Where is Awad?" Akash asked as coldly as he could. He was fighting hard not to show his contempt to the man who was obviously cowering in fear. These Ilocanos are only brave when they are in a pack, he thought. "Gabriela's mother, where is she?"

The man opened his mouth but no sound came. He blinked again and swallowed hard, his Adam's apple bobbing just below the dagger poised on his throat.

"What? Where is she? Where did you bring her?" Akash hissed, irritation now apparent in his voice and the man felt a little more pressure from the dagger.

"I-I-I don't know," the man managed to say, cringing.

Before he could finish saying the last word, he felt the dagger lifted off his neck but in a flash a searing pain caused him to impulsively reach up to his right ear. He felt the dampness of the blood that trickled through his fingers and he howled in pain and panic as he realized a part of his ear was missing.

"One more time," Akash said in a cold voice that was now bereft of any emotion. "Where is Awad?" The tip of the dagger went back to the man's throat.

"She, she is," the man started to say then Akash sensed that his attention had shifted to the door. Reacting in pure instinct, Akash dropped to one knee as he turned and flipped his dagger with all his might to the dark figure that was coming through the door. The figure stopped in its tracks, uttered a surprised gasp then toppled down to the floor. The *kampilan* that he was holding clattered on the bamboo floor making a rattling sound like a kid made from raking a piece of stick against a fence as he walked by.

Akash quickly smashed a clenched fist against the breast of the man in the bed as he tried to take advantage of the distraction and attempted to get up. The man grunted and fell back in the bed with a moan, a hand still clamped tightly to his damaged ear.

Akash rose slowly then went to the figure by the door. He turned the body over and felt for a pulse. He felt nothing. He pulled the dagger off the man's chest and peered out the door to the living room. It was empty. He flicked his wrist a couple of times, shaking the blood off the dagger, droplets streaking across the living room floor. He swore silently for missing the other man who was obviously sleeping silently in the other room of the house. Was there anyone else? He had no time to check, he decided, so he hurried back to the man cowering in the bed.

Akash grabbed the man's hair, forcibly raising his head up and poised back the dagger on the man's throat.

"No more games," he said. "Talk!"

"I-I only went along, I swear," the man said sensing the desperation in the *Itneg*'s voice. "Me and him, Dado, there," he pointed to the form by the door. "W-w-we did not kill her," he stammered.

"Calm down," Akash said, not sure if he caught what the man had just said. He let go of the man's head but kept the dagger on his throat. "Start from the beginning."

There was a Spanish soldier, the man said, who gave him and Dado and Miguel soldier's uniforms and promised to pay them to bring Awad to him. They went to Awad's house and asked her to go with them to the fort to answer some questions about her daughter. Awad went with them peacefully but she became agitated when she noted that they were going away from the town and the opposite direction from the fort.

She started to argue, claiming that she knew nothing about Gabriela's activities or plans and much less so of her daughter's whereabouts. She pleaded with them to let her go back to her house, but they were paid to deliver her to the Spanish soldier who was waiting with another soldier at a hut in a remote farm close to *sitio* Paing and that was what they did.

They left the woman with the Spaniards alone in the hut, the man swore, and they could hear them interrogating her about *La Generala*, while they waited in the yard. Yes, they could hear that the Spaniards were hitting the woman also as she denied any knowledge of her daughter's location and plans. Then they did not hear anything and when one of the Spaniards called them back up, the woman was all bloodied and not moving on the floor.

They buried her under a tree behind the hut.

"The Spaniards, what are their names?" Akash asked. Surprisingly his voice was calm and he did not feel any anger at all. He had a feeling that something bad had happened to Awad and now that he knew he seemed to be not affected at all and it bothered him.

"I don't know, honestly," the man said softly. "The man in charge never talked to us. He only talked with Miguel."

"Mi-guel," Akash said emphasizing every syllable as if committing the name to memory, "where is he?"

"I don't know," the man said hastily. "He went with the soldiers and he has not returned yet. I honestly don't know where he is," he added before Akash could react to what he said. "He told us to come here and wait for him so we can get our money."

Akash did not answer. There was a cold blank look in his eyes that the man could not see yet somehow sensed and he squirmed nervously.

"Please, I am telling the truth," he said.

"What's your name?" Akash finally said as if he was in a conversation with a friend.

"Timoteo, my name is Timoteo," the man said softly.

"Timoteo, you should not have gotten yourself involved with the woman. She was my sister," Akash said in a seemingly apologetic yet disembodied whisper that brought chills down the man's spine.

"I know. I'm sorry for what happened," Timoteo's voice trembled. "I would not have agreed if I knew that the woman was going to get killed. That's the truth. I swear that's the truth. Please..." His voice trailed to a whisper as he felt the growing pressure of the dagger against his skin and before he could even blink, it went through his throat. He gasped and emitted a soft gurgling sound as blood frothed out of his half-parted lips.

210

Silently, Akash pulled out the dagger, wiped it off the pillow by the man's head and turned around. He stepped over the prone body by the door and headed out of the house. There was nothing else he could learn from these two.

Somewhere a dog howled in a plaintive cry into the night.

At the darkened *garreta*, Miguel woke up and stirred from the bench where he had fallen asleep. He quickly grabbed his head as the world spun around him. He fell back down and was asleep again almost as soon as his head touched the wooden bench. He had no idea his drunkenness had saved him that night.

He would not wake up until the sun was almost halfway through the morning sky and by then Akash was well into the trees halfway up Mount *Bullagaw* on his way back to the village.

Akash should have been much farther away by that time but he was walking slowly, not because of the lingering pain from his ankle that had somehow returned, but from a heavy feeling of fury growing in his chest.

And finally, covering his heart too like a dark shroud was a dense and cold feeling of sadness.

Of all his siblings, Awad was the closest to his heart.

Chapter Thirty One

The first time that Miguel felt something was wrong when he entered his house was the silence that greeted him. Neither Dado nor Timoteo was up and about. Knowing them, they would not have gone away without getting their money first. Not those greedy *bastardos*, he thought. But somehow it was not like them to be sleeping still at this hour. It was almost the middle of the day.

Then he saw the faint trail of droplets of blood on the floor and his eyes followed them going toward his bedroom and suddenly his hang-over and dulled sense from his night of drinking vanished. With his heart beating wildly now in his chest, he ran towards the bedroom and stopped abruptly by the door, his hand covering his mouth as he felt the bitter taste of vomit racing up his throat. He quickly turned around and ran to a window in the living room that was still closed, roughly pushed it open, leaned out and let go of the late breakfast he had at the *garreta*. For a long time he stayed there until he was just heaving rancid air that left a bitter aftertaste in the back of his mouth.

Then, breathing heavily, he let go of the window, and he slid down to the floor, legs splayed before him. His mind was racing with so many questions. Who killed them? Did they get into a fight between themselves and somehow killed one another? What must he do now? He gathered himself the best he could and he slowly got back up to his feet. He went to the kitchen, grabbed a coconut mug and dipped it in the water jar, raised it to his mouth and gurgled loudly. He went out to the *bangsal* and spat the water out in a wild stream to the ground below. His eyes roamed his backyard and his neighbors' houses and yards, not certain of what he was looking for, and not finding anything amiss, went back hesitantly into the house.

He took a deep breath and returned to the bedroom, much calmer now, and he studied the corpses, Timoteo in the bed and Dado on the floor by the door. He noted the wounds and his brows wrinkled in puzzlement as he could not find a knife close to the bodies or anywhere inside the room.

"Someone else had done them in," he said softly, and he felt the return of panic in his chest as he thought of the possible suspects. Who? The soldiers? The *rebeldes*? Or robbers maybe who had found no money and killed them instead? But it could not be. The people knew he had no money. Unless word had gotten out about the reward money he was getting from the Spaniards.

But as he thought of possible motives, it seemed that nothing made sense and it was driving him mad. Then a crazy thought came to him that now, at least, he did not have to explain to the two that somehow he did not know what happened to their money that he received from the Spaniards. He truthfully could not remember if he spent all of them in drinks or lost them somehow in the game of cards he played with the people he drank with last night. Perhaps both, only God knew, but it did not matter anymore. The money was gone and so were his friends.

He stood up slowly from kneeling by the body of Dado that was sprawled on the floor. He looked down at it one more time and then at the body of Timoteo that was staring at him blindly from the bed and decided that he needed to report the crime to the constables. He stepped over Dado's body and moved toward the front door but stopped suddenly in the middle of the living room when a faint smell of sour vomit reached his nose. He wrinkled his nose and his face contorted in disgust as he realized the smell was coming from his shirt. He took it off as he turned around and walked back into the bedroom. He took a clean shirt from the *aparador*, put it on and went back out, dumping his vomit smelling shirt at the foot of the bed. The smell would at least neutralize the smell of death, he thought cynically.

It occurred to him that he would have to leave the place as he stepped out into the daylight. There was no way he could live in this same house after what happened. And in this town for that matter, he thought. Somehow he had the feeling that the killer or killers were after him and not his friends.

He decided to go to the fort instead of reporting the deaths to the constables at the *municipio*. He was certain now that the soldiers had nothing to do with what happened inside his house. There was no reason for them to kill Dado and Timoteo and yet let him live.

213

Chapter Thirty Two

"Awad is not coming back," Akash said.

"Why?" Allong asked before his brother could continue.

"She's not coming back, ever," Akash said again as if Allong had not interrupted him. "She's dead, Allong. They killed her."

Allong, stunned by the news felt his body sag as if all strength had drained out from him. He found a bench and sat down. Finally he looked up at Akash who had not moved from where he stood and noted for the first time the faraway look in his brother's eyes. Akash was looking at him yet his eyes seemed hollow and not seeing anything, even him, as if he was not there.

Allong stood up and grabbed Akash's shoulders and shook him slightly. "What happened?" he said.

"They killed her, Allong. The soldiers did," Akash said.

"Let's go to *Ama*. He needs to hear this." Allong turned Akash around and led him out to the direction of their father's hut.

"Sound the drums," *Ama* Kagaid said as soon as the brothers told him the news of Awad's death. "We'll meet at the center of the village." The old man wanted his sons gone for he felt the tears coming out of his eyes. He turned around before either of his sons could move and with shoulders bent lower than they usually were, he went into the inner room of the hut. His frail shoulders convulsed as soon as he entered the room. He did not move until he heard the persistent beating of the drums.

The old man was composed, all emotions drained off his face and bearing, when he walked into the gathering crowd in the middle of the village. The gathered villagers opened up before him as he made his way into the front. He nodded at his friend, *Ama* Dalalo, who had stood up as soon as he saw him approaching. They patted each other's arms in a sympathetic gesture and together they sat down and faced the crowd.

Apo Kagaid scanned the faces around him noting that almost everyone he wanted to see was present. He was about to speak when he noticed the form of Ilang hurrying up the trail from the river, a few of the Ilocanos trudging behind her. He raised a hand instead to signal the crowd to settle down and the murmurings slowly subsided. He stood up and beckoned for Ilang to sit by him as she came up to the gathered crowd. Ilang hesitantly approached her grandfather and took his extended hand as they sat back down together side by side on the wooden bench reserved for the elders. Her companions stayed well back behind the gathering.

Ilang looked around at the faces in the crowd, some squatting on the ground, most of them standing up. She noticed her uncle Akash but he did not look at her, his eyed focused some place above the heads of the crowd. Then her eyes settled on Kulas. She gave him a lingering look, silently asking for explanation for the gathering but his eyes remained impassive. He just nodded briefly and then he turned his attention to *Apo* Kagaid who had started to speak.

"Akash had just arrived from the lowlands with news that I wanted all of you to hear." Despite his grieving feelings, the voice of *Apo* Kagaid was loud and clear. The soft whispers from the perimeter of the crowd subsided and there was silence as everyone waited for *Apo* Kagaid to continue. Ilang felt the old man's grip tighten in her hand and she realized he had not let go of her hand when they sat. She looked at the old man and met his eyes as he turned to look at her. She saw the sadness in her grandfather's eyes even before he spoke again.

"Awad is dead," *Apo* Kagaid said as if talking to Ilang alone. He lowered his face as he felt his granddaughter dropped her face on his shoulder, her own shoulders shaking as she cried. The old man and his granddaughter held each other in a tight embrace unaware of the drone of whispers growing louder around them as the word of Awad's death was passed around. Then the clamor subsided as the loud voice of Akash cut through the hub-bub.

"The neighbors saw soldiers take her away a couple of days before I got there. I went looking for her at the fort and around town but I did not find her. Yesterday I finally found two people who told me that Awad was dead. They knew because they were there and they buried her. They're now dead too. I killed them."

There was hatred and a tinge of anguish too in Akash's voice. He stood erect and defiant and Kulas knew then that with or without the elders' decision not to get involved, there was no holding his friend back from going down to the town and exact more vengeance for his sister's death. He felt a flutter in his breast and he knew that he could not let his friend go back down to the town alone. Akash did not have to ask for his help same way as he did not need his permission to join him.

As if reading his mind, Kulas saw Akash looking at him. Their eyes locked together and Kulas gave his friend an assuring nod, then he turned around before anyone else spoke. The silent meeting of their eyes was not lost to the other young warriors who were watching Kulas for his reaction. They likewise nodded somberly as they saw Kulas nod and their eyes followed his retreating figure walking toward the river.

"This changes things," Kulas barely heard *Apo* Dalalo start to say as he walked away. His old man had taken over the gathering and *Apo* Kagaid would just sit and listen. He would go with whatever *Apo* Dalalo decided to do.

And Kulas did not bother to stay and listen. He knew what would follow. He was going to get ready, but first he needed a good soak in the river.

Akash watched his friend leave the gathering but he stayed where he was. He did not need to listen any further either. He knew what he wanted to do and somehow he felt better knowing in his heart that his friend would be there with him watching his back. That's what real friends are for, he thought. You did not have to ask for them to help and cover your back.

Chapter Thirty Three

"So convince me, Miguel, that you did not kill Timoteo and Dado so that you did not have to give their share of the money." Miguel stared in amazement as *Sargento* Tiago spoke, looking at him with half-closed eyes like a crocodile eyeing its prey.

"Y-y-you could not be ser-serious, *Sargento!*" Miguel stuttered.

"But I am, Miguel," Tiago said with lidded eyes. "So tell me again exactly what happened."

"I already told you, *Sargento*," Miguel's tone was pleading. He and *Don* Tiago had already talked a few hours before, then the Sargento left him for a few minutes and now he was back and he could not believe they were talking about the same thing all over again. "I got home and there they were inside the bedroom, dead. Timoteo was in the bed and Dado was lying by the door. There's a stab wound on Timoteo's throat while Dado was stabbed on the chest."

"And you did not see a knife or a dagger perhaps?"

"No, *Sargento*, none, nothing. I have searched the house and I did not find anything."

"How convenient," *Don* Tiago smiled as he fully opened his eyes and looked up at Miguel who was standing in front of his desk.

"That's the truth, *Sargento*," Miguel said meeting the *Sargento*'s gaze.

"And you have witnesses that you were not home all night?"

"Well, yes, *Sargento*, at least until Inso, Carding, Berto and Inggo left me when I fell asleep at the *garreta*."

"And what time would that be?"

"I-I-I don't know, *Sargento*."

"Like I said, Miguel, how convenient," *Don* Tiago said shaking his head patronizingly. "You don't know?"

"It's the truth, *Sargento*. You can ask Inso, or Carding and the rest of them."

"That I will, *Señor*, that I will," *Don* Tiago said. "In the meantime be our guest and stay around the fort and don't leave until I tell you so. Let us wait until Cortez and his companions come back. There's a vacant holding cell out there," he gestured towards the door, "I know it's a cell but it's quite comfortable. Catriz here," he indicated the soldier who was holding guard by the door, "will take care of all your needs. Just let him know if you need anything." He took a piece of parchment and arranged it on his desk and pretended to study it, indicating that the discussion was over for the moment.

Miguel took the hint and turned around as the guard moved to guide him out of the room. But before he went through the door, Miguel paused and turned. "Am I a prisoner here, *Sargento*?" he asked.

Don Tiago looked up with an exaggerated expression of surprise in his face. "Why, *Señor* Miguel, of course not; whatever gave you such an idea?"

Miguel did not answer but he was bristling inside. He simply nodded and resumed walking as he felt the hand of Catriz nudge him forward. It took all of his self-control not to slap the guard's hand away, his annoyance now very apparent.

The man's story at least did not waver from the first time they spoke, *Don* Tiago thought. Maybe he was telling the truth. Or maybe he was lying as usual and just came in to divert any suspicions of the killings from him. *Don* Tiago smiled and shook his head in amusement. But it was only for a brief moment as he contemplated on the recent turn of events and what he should do next. He hissed an expletive directed to no one in particular although at the moment he was thinking of Cortez and what he had brought him into. The *hombre* had a brilliant and cunning mind but now he was feeling a little sense of regret for listening to the soldier's scheme.

He had sent Cortez and a couple of soldiers to Miguel's house to look things over after Miguel came in to report the killings at his house.

"*This may have turned out for the best,*" Cortez had said when they were alone after listening to Miguel.

"*What do you mean?*" Tiago asked.

"*We could get rid of the bodies and we only have this drunken fool to worry about,*" Cortez said, gesturing with his head toward the outside of the room where Miguel was waiting. "*And we could keep him locked up in here and out of the picture, permanently, if needed,*" he added, grinning, "*and nobody would know the truth, least of all the Capitán.*"

Tiago did not answer but started to cotton to the idea, although with a little reservation. Nothing had come out good so far with their plan. The *Capitán* had no idea of what he and Cortez had done and he wanted to keep it that way. He surely did not want the *Capitán* to know that so far three people had died as a result of their plan to abduct *La Generala*'s mother to find out where her daughter was, or as Cortez had said keep her as hostage to force the rebel woman to surrender.

"*Vaya,*" he said to Cortez. "*Go, take a couple of soldiers you can trust and make sure they don't talk and do what you have to do.*"

"*Of course,*" Cortez said still grinning as he left.

Miguel could not believe what was happening as he sat in a daze on the cot inside the cell. The guard had graciously left the cell door unlocked and it was ajar now, but still he was sitting inside a jail cell! After all he had done for them, the Spaniards, his own people albeit half only, was still treating him like trash. No, worse than trash. They were treating him as if he was a common criminal! Well, there was the death of Diego but he did it for them. He should have been rewarded with honor, but this was what he got instead? Miguel bitterly seethed inside that he could almost taste the bile going up his throat.

Then a sense of hopelessness swept through him again. He lowered his elbows until they rested on his knees and buried his face in his palms. He stayed in that position for a while as he dwelled on his predicament, fighting the tears of anger and sadness that flowed out of his chest. The *Sargento* may not have said so explicitly but he was a suspect for the death of Dado and Timoteo. He was certain of this. He raised his head and took a deep breath. He scooted on the cot until his back rested against the wall. He let out a sigh and he tried to compose himself. This surely was not the result he expected when he came to the fort. He was seeking for refuge and not to be treated as a suspect and a criminal.

He looked at the open door of the cell and beyond it to the guard, Catriz, who was engrossed in something and was paying him no mind. He could try to walk out of here and not come back, he thought. But where would he go? He could not go back to his house and live there, not with the memory of the dead bodies. And surely whoever did the killing would come back for him. He was convinced that the killings were planned and he was also the intended victim.

But by whom and why? He thought of Pedro and the *Itnegs*. Was Pedro right perhaps?

As he dwelled on it he realized that there was a list of possible suspects who would have reason enough to want him dead. He did not exactly lead a saintly life. Then it came to him that even the Spaniards, especially the *Sargento* would have a reason to keep him silent. They were just supposed to take the mother of *La Generala*, question her about her daughter's whereabouts, and if necessary hold her hostage to force Gabriela to lay down her arms. He was told she would be forgiven if she surrendered and could go back to her former life. After all she was of Spanish blood, and a wealthy one at that. It seemed a reasonable enough plan and he went for it. And well, there was the money too, of course.

But Gabriela's mother was not supposed to die. Cortez said she fought and if he knew the *Itnegs*, they can fight, man or woman. But a veteran soldier, make that two soldiers, could not handle a woman without killing her? Miguel had a hard time accepting that. Regardless, the fact was that the woman died, and it was not his fault, but he was in the middle of it. Then it hit him like a bolt of lightning and he straightened up and edged away from the wall.

They're going to blame me for the killing of *La Generala*'s mother too, he thought as he stood up. He looked at Catriz who glanced at him as he got up from the cot. Their eyes met momentarily and Miguel decided then that he had to get out of there. He would think of where to go once he was out.

"I have to go to the outhouse," he said to Catriz as he went through the cell door.

"Let me go with you," Catriz said.

"I know where it is, Catriz," Miguel said as pleasantly as he could. "I've been here before."

"But the *Sargento* said to keep an eye on you."

"I'm not a prisoner here, am I?" Miguel said sounding annoyed. He knew Catriz was just following orders but these guards were simpleminded peons who folded in front of authority.

"Of course not, Miguel," Catriz said. "You heard the *Sargento*, you're a guest here, and I was ordered to make sure you get whatever you wanted."

"Then don't worry about looking after me, Catriz. All I want for now is to go to the outhouse. Alone."

"I can't do that, Miguel. I can't let you out of my sight. *Sargento*'s orders."

Miguel sighed. "OK, then, lead the way," he said and followed Catriz outside.

The row of outhouses was at the far end of the fort, close to the southern wall, and beyond it was the river that curved past the western wall also. There was a back gate close to where the western and southern walls met. Miguel took this all in and decided there was no way he could get out and outrun Catriz and his gun. He went grudgingly into the first outhouse and stayed there for a while trying to come up with a plan. Catriz was patiently pacing outside when he finally came out.

"It stinks in there," he said casually to Catriz.

"It's an outhouse, Miguel, it's supposed to," Catriz said, smirking.

"Yeah, I know, but it's real bad. Smell got into my clothes too. Whew!" Miguel said in exaggeration as he sniffed at his clothes.

Catriz laughed.

"I think I need some fresh air and take a swim in the river, get rid of this smell," Miguel said casually as he turned and walked toward the back gate before Catriz could say or do anything. "You can come if you want," he glanced back at Catriz who was clearly taken by surprise. "Or you can watch me from the top of the wall or by the gate, it's up to you."

"I'll come with you," Catriz said after thinking a moment.

"C'mon, Catriz!" Miguel spread his arms in mock exasperation. "Can't I have any privacy? Besides where would I go from here? It's an open field out there!" This was not exactly true because a short distance downriver where it bended there was a copse of trees and beyond that some cover for someone familiar with the place. And Miguel knew the place well. He would take his chances and he hoped Catriz would ease down and fall for his act. "But if it makes you feel better, hey by all means, come with me and we'll swim together," Miguel said with a wink.

Despite his predicament, Miguel almost laughed at Catriz's reaction. The guard had instinctively taken a step back with a chagrined look in his face. Miguel was aware that the guards talked behind Catriz's back and one of the gossips that got back to him about the reason why he was not married yet was that he preferred men. He did not know if it was true and it never occurred to him until now that he could use that stupid rumor to his advantage hoping there was a bit of truth to it.

Miguel suppressed a relieved smile when Catriz paused as if in deep thought.

"Look," he said, to rattle Catriz and keep him from dwelling on the issue too much. "I don't want to get you in trouble. Like I keep saying, if it makes you feel better, you can go ask for the *Sargento*'s permission."

"He's not here," Catriz said. "He rode out to town."

"Alright then, c'mon, let's go. This smell is killing me!" Miguel turned around as if he had made up his mind and was going with or without Catriz and walked briskly toward the back gate of the fort.

Catriz ran after him.

"Miguel, wait!" he said, grabbing Miguel's arm. "I'll be by the gate. Stay where I can see you!"

"Whatever you say, Catriz," Miguel said then walked away without looking back. He breathed a sigh of relief halfway to the river when he realized that Catriz had not changed his mind. And for the first time that day a trace of a smile crossed his lips.

He bided his time studying the river when he got to its bank like he was deciding where to get into the river. He saw a bush growing close to the water that was visible from the gate and he walked towards it. He took off his white woolen shirt and draped it over the bush like a wash set out to dry. Then he untied the rope that held up his woven trousers, pulled them down along with his underpants, and rolled them together into a ball. Buck naked, he deliberately turned around and waved at Catriz who instinctively turned his face away. Miguel kicked his rolled pants and underpants into the water and dived in after them, grasping and holding them underwater. He tucked them between his legs and surfaced, making a show of enjoying the water. He waved at Catriz who was once again looking at his direction. Catriz ignored him.

The river was shallow where he was, but he crouched down until the water was up to his chin. He moved his arms as if he was treading water and started walking toward a clump of willowy reeds. He knew that these were hollow, and when he was a young boy, he and his friends had bet a few coins on who could swim the farthest underwater using the hollow reed as a breathing device. The best among them was Immong. He never could beat Immong but he was close to beating him once. He looked down the bend of the river and knew he could get there fast enough before Catriz could notice that he was gone.

He picked the stoutest reed that first caught his eye, pulled it off its roots quickly and snapped its top off. He did the same to its roots ending up with almost a yard long of hollow tube. He went underwater one more time and swam to the middle of the river, keeping his rolled pants and the reed out of sight under the surface. He came up, raised a hand at Catriz who seemed to have started a conversation with someone inside the fort. He was alternately keeping an eye inside the fort and at Miguel in the river.

Miguel kept on doing laps, like he was making it a routine, but slowly he was veering into a position behind the bush where he placed his shirt.

At the gate, Catriz was getting bored as he watched Miguel swam back and forth. He craned his neck at times when Miguel was hidden by his shirt draped on the bush, but the man always appeared when he got into the middle of the river. After a few more moments of this, human nature took over and Catriz simply concentrated on the most visible thing: Miguel's shirt on the bush every time his attention reverted back to the river from his conversation with Bautista inside the walls.

By the time Catriz finally noticed that Miguel had not surfaced for a while, his ward was almost three hundred yards away from where he came up across the river, way below its bend that was not visible from the gate, its view blocked by the copse of trees along the riverbank.

Miguel was shoeless, shirtless and his pants were dripping wet but he was out of the fort.

Chapter Thirty Four

"You flatter me, *Capitán*," Isabella said for the umpteenth time as she passed the platter of *Lengua Afritada* to *Don* Manuel.

Manuel smiled and scooped a decent portion of the dish which he found out later to be cow's tongue, but it did not matter then because he found the dish delectable. He in turn held the platter as Isabella took some and he passed it on down the table, giving the lady to his right a gentlemanly nod as he urged her to try the dish. He recognized the wife of the *Vice Alcalde* but for the life of him he could not remember her name. Fortunately the lady did not talk much as she daintily spooned a small portion of the dish.

"It's the truth, *Señorita*," Manuel turned his attention back to *Señora* Dela Cuesta's niece. This had been the third dinner in a week that he had attended at the Dela Cuesta's household to the delight of the *Señora*. His house help Clara surely was not complaining for not cooking every night and neither was he, and yes, he did thank her for meeting Isabella. He was beginning to enjoy himself socially and was eagerly looking forward to the evenings spent with Isabella. He was barely interested with the topics of the conversations, like it was at the moment, but somehow he had managed to give Isabella a compliment. For what, he had no idea, but there it was slipping unbidden from his lips. He blushed a little thinking of what old man Tiago would think if he heard him.

"So *Don* Manuel," Isabella said, suddenly sounding somber. "What is the latest word on this *La Generala* that the townspeople are talking about?" Her voice was low but it seemed that it echoed around the table for everyone seemed to pause momentarily.

"It's not a subject that I would like to discuss at a dinner table, *Señorita*, but since you asked, I honestly don't have anything on the so-called *La Generala*. As far as I am concerned, if I don't hear anything about her, it would be great news!" Manuel said flippantly. From out of the corner of his eye he saw *Padre* Joaquin put down the piece of potato that he was about to put in his mouth. The *Padre*, *Don* Manuel had noticed, seemed to be too concerned with the fate of Gabriela. Well, he should not be surprised. After all the late Diego was the good *Padre's* ward. Manuel gave the good *Padre* his best smile but he received no reaction.

Padre Joaquin looked down at his plate and raised the fork with the potato back up to his mouth and chewed as if in a deep thought.

"C'mon now, *Capitán*," Isabella said leaning toward the *Capitán* conspiratorially. "I heard that her mother is missing."

Manuel stopped from chewing. He had not been to the fort lately and this certainly was news to him.

"Come again?" he said.

"I heard that *La Generala*'s mother is missing. There's no one living there now at their house. She's gone and no one knows where she went."

"I did not know that, *Señorita*. Could it be perhaps that she went for a vacation? Or went back up to Abra, to her people maybe?" *Don* Manuel said, but there was no conviction in his voice. Somehow some warning bells started ringing inside his head. For what, he did not know, but they were there. He had heard them before when something big was going to happen and he was hearing them now.

"Or maybe she had joined up with her daughter," *Don* Jose Dela Cuesta said from the head of the table. For an old man the *Don* had a pretty good ear.

"Perhaps, perhaps," *Don* Manuel agreed but the ringing that only he could hear persisted. He reminded himself to make it a point to go to the fort tomorrow and see what Tiago knew. If there was anyone who would know what was going on in the town it would be the old goat. He held down the growing irritation in his chest on the fact that Tiago or anyone in the fort had not apprised him of the situation if they knew of *La Generala*'s mother's absence from the town.

"Oh, let us not talk about the *rebeldes*," *Señora* Dela Cuesta finally piped in. She liked social innuendos but not politics or anything that required her to think. She was seated beside the *Alcalde* who was busy chewing on a piece of chicken leg and was nodding in agreement. The *Alcalde* did not care about the rebeldes either as long as they were not bothering him.

"Yes, yes," the lady to his right, the *Vice Alcalde*'s wife, said and Manuel courteously nodded. He still could not remember her name.

Padre Joaquin remained silent which was highly unusual for him.

"I am sorry I brought it up," Isabella said defiantly looking around the table. "I was just wondering because it troubles me that someone would just vanish. I heard there were a couple of men too that somehow disappeared without a word to their families and they do not know what happened to them. Well, perhaps they could have probably joined the *rebeldes* also." She paused, picking up a piece of bread, put butter on it and was about to put it in her mouth but changed her mind. She put down the piece of bread on her plate and looked up musingly.

"But then there's *Don* Miguel," she said as if talking to herself. "He too could not be found and his house burned down the other day. If what I heard were true, I would not think that he purposely burned his house and went up and joined the rebels again. I mean, the *Generala* would surely kill him, wouldn't you think?" She turned to the *Capitán* who was beginning to wish the dinner was over but it had yet a long way to go. The information coming down from Isabella was just too much and was hitting him like stinging hailstones out in the plains back home during a late summer outburst.

Everyone's eyes were at Isabella now and it was not for her impertinence but for pure curiosity. The majority of the people around the table were appointed public officials but they could not care less about what the Indios did or did not do as long as they had their ports, tapas and siestas. But Isabella had their attention now. They knew about Miguel and what he did to Diego. And now he was missing? And his house burned down? And two other men were missing aside from *La Generala*'s mother? This was too much to ignore.

"That was his house that went up in smoke in Santa?" *Don* Manuel asked. He had heard about a house burning down from Clara but he did not remember her saying it was Miguel's. And now he was missing too? And two other men were missing aside from *La Generala's* mother? Suddenly the *Capitán* felt he was losing his appetite. He pushed his plate away, still half-full, hoping no one would notice.

Isabella saw the gesture but she did not say a word.

"Yeah, yeah, I heard about the fire too, but I had no idea it was Miguel's," *Don* Adriano, the *Vice Alcalde* said. "And he's missing?"

"I hope the poor soul did not die in the fire," the *Alcalde* said, putting down the bare bone of the chicken leg. "Pardon me, but I heard the man loves to drink and he smoked too."

"That's an awful thing to say, Alejandro," the *Alcalde's* wife said in mock horror. "That would be a terrible way to go, charred in a fire like that!"

"Nobody got burned, *Señora* Carmen," *Don* Jose said. "At least I have not heard that they found anyone in the ashes, for surely the neighbors must have looked when they could not find Miguel."

"That is true, *Don* Jose," the Judge whose name was Rodolfo Atmosfera, said. He had been listening patiently to the banter. He knew about Miguel's house burning down in the night and he knew too that some neighbors claim that they saw some people around the neighborhood the evening when it happened but no one knew for certain who they were and what they were doing because it was dark and nobody dared to go out and investigate. And the house burned down just a little after midnight. It was all very convenient and suspicious indeed but the constables had nothing to go on. And there were no witnesses. Or at least anyone brave enough to come out anyways.

And he told them so.

"You knew about this and did not bother to tell us, Rodolfo?" *Alcalde* Alejandro said.

"I thought you all knew," Rodolfo said defensively and no one quibbled because as town officials they should have known even if Santa was just a *sitio* of Vigan. "And besides, like the *Capitán* said, this topic is not good around a dinner table."

Judge Rodolfo picked up his glass of wine and drained it wishing he had not opened his mouth and left these bastards blissfully wallowing in their ignorance. He was just here for the food and the drink and the nagging of his wife who insisted it was good for his social standing and so far had not said a word. Sometimes he wondered why she even bothered to attend. As for himself, he could not care less for the crowd's company. 'But it is good for your career,' the wife had kept on saying and he just went along to shut her up. He caught the eyes of one of the maids and he smiled when she approached with a bottle of wine to refill his empty glass.

For a moment no one spoke as if everyone was engrossed in their own thoughts. The objection to the topic was totally gone yet no one seemed to dare to add anything sensing the *Capitán*'s lack of enthusiasm in pursuing the subject. Even *Padre* Joaquin remained uncharacteristically silent.

"What are you going to do, *Capitán*?" Isabella finally broke the silence.

Don Manuel did not answer right away. For a brief moment he wished the woman would keep silent but he loved hearing her voice. He picked up his napkin, wiped his mouth and looked around the table finally resting his eyes on Isabella.

"For now, nothing *Señorita*, except drink a good cup of hot coffee if you have one," he said with a smile.

"Ahh, of course, *Capitán*," Isabella said. "But you have not finished your food yet!" She pointed at *Don* Manuel's half-empty plate.

"I'm still working on it," *Don* Manuel said still in his cheery voice. "I would need a good coffee to push it down though after the conversation that we just had."

"I think we are still having that conversation, *Capitán*," *Padre* Joaquin finally opened his mouth. He was curious now of what the *Capitán*'s plans were. "What are you going to do?"

Don Manuel sighed and looked at the *Padre*.

"Honestly, *Padre*," he said, all the levity gone from his voice. "I don't really know. I'll have to talk with the constables, the *Guardia Civiles*, and find out what they know. I'll go from there."

Padre Joaquin nodded in agreement as did most of the diners. Only Isabella kept her head fixed and unmoving as she stared at her plate.

"I'll get the coffee," *Señora* Dela Cuesta finally said breaking the silence and *Don* Manuel exhaled a sigh of relief which was not lost to both ladies on his flanks.

But being ladies of manners that they were, they kept their heads bowed to their plates as both of their faces broke into knowing smiles.

But of course, *Señora* Dela Cuesta noticed them before she turned around toward the kitchen. She held her tongue for once. Let the young ladies have their fun, she thought, even at the young officer's expense. She did not see any harm in that. In fact she did a lot of that too when she was younger.

Actually, she still did.

Chapter Thirty Five

"And when were you going to tell me?" Manuel said.

He and Tiago were sitting side by side on the bench in the shade of the Acacia by the stables. The fort was silent for it was the time for *siesta*.

It was the day after the dinner at the Dela Cuestas. Manuel had wanted to get to the fort early but decided to walk around the town instead that morning; talking to people he knew who might have knowledge about Miguel, or Awad or the two missing men. But he did not learn much. People were reluctant to talk or they simply had no idea. He should have known better that the locals tended to be reticent with him but he was a careful man and he wanted to cover everything, leaving no stone unturned in his quest for the truth.

So he went to the fort as soon as he was finished with his noontime meal. And he found Tiago whistling for the breeze to come under the Acacia. As usual this time of the year, the place was hot and humid.

And the old soldier told him about the *Itneg* coming into the fort looking for his sister, found nothing and left.

"Do you have any information about the woman? Rumor said that soldiers took her," Manuel had asked.

"I have no idea, *Niño*. Maybe the neighbors were mistaken. All the men were here; nobody left the fort. I would have known if anyone did," Tiago was adamant about this. "Maybe they were rebels dressed up as soldiers?"

Manuel did not answer. It was possible, so they could get to town safely and get the mother out to a secure place, but why go through all that trouble, he had voiced out. The woman was free to move around.

"So nobody would bother them, *Niño*. Who'd dare stop a bunch of uniformed *Guardia Civiles*? I heard she did not want to leave town so she probably needed some convincing, and a group of them comes down as soldiers. Nobody bothers them of course and then she vanishes, joins her daughter, and we get the blame for her disappearance! More Indios and perhaps even the *Itnegs* get mad and maybe join the *rebeldes*." For an off-the cuff explanation, the old soldier was very pleased with himself as he saw Manuel pause and think.

Tiago surely had a point but deep inside, Manuel was not convinced. There was just something in the whole situation that was suspect yet he could not exactly put a finger on it.

"And how about the two men from Santa who are missing? And Miguel as well, with his house burning down? Something strange is going on around here, Tiago, and it is stranger still that no one seems to know what's going on, and I of all people am the most ignorant of all!" *Don* Manuel said in exasperation.

"You were busy, *Niño*, take it easy on yourself," Tiago said placatingly. "You deserve the break. And I must say it's about time you did something for yourself." He turned sideways to the *Capitán* and gave him a teasing grin.

"What do you mean, *Viejo*?" Manuel said although he fully well knew where the conversation was going. Nothing escaped the old goat.

"I heard the *muchacha* is very pretty," Tiago said smiling. "Don't let her go away. Don't worry about things. I'll take care of them."

The *Capitán* sighed, shaking his head with exaggeration.

"Ahh, that's what I'm so scared about," he said.

"Hah! What? You don't believe I could?" Tiago exclaimed. "Why, let me tell you, I could run these islands better than that half-wit Governor-General Anda we have in Manila if I was running things!"

"*I were*," *Don* Manuel said before he could control himself.

"'*I were*' what?" Tiago asked.

"Never mind," *Don* Manuel said. Then his face and tone turned more serious.

"I'm really concerned, Tiago," he said gravely. "No one has come out in the open but people are worried about these disappearances, especially *La Generala*'s mother, the burning of Miguel's house, and on top of all that, *La Generala* and her troops are still roaming out there. We need to do something."

"What did the constables in town say?" Tiago asked.

"Nothing. They know less than I know and I practically know nothing."

"I'm not surprised knowing those ignorant bastards, but don't be too hard on yourself, *Niño*. Things have a way of taking care of themselves. We'll be alright."

"I hope you're right, *Viejo*, I hope you're right," Manuel said softly as he stood up. The day was not turning up to be what he wanted. "Send some men out. Have them ask around, talk to people. Hell, round up the usual suspects and bring them here if you have to. Pay them, beat them up, I don't care but let's get to the bottom of this. Someone out there must know something. It's a small town."

Tiago nodded without saying a word. He looked up at the *Capitán* who was looking down at him with no humor now in his eyes. He had not seen the *Capitán* this grave looking since they were running away from the Indians ages ago. He must be really worried and it worried him a bit too but he kept his face expressionless as best as he could.

"I want to know, Tiago, whatever goes in this town. If somebody breathes, I want to know. If someone sneezes, I want to know. And right away. Don't wait for me to show up here at the fort. Come and tell me or send somebody up." The *Capitán* turned around before Tiago could say anything, but the old man remained silent. For the first time in their long association, Tiago was speechless.

Furls of worry creased Tiago's brow as soon as the *Capitán* was out of sight. Somehow, despite his display of ignorance, Tiago felt that the *Capitán* knew more, much more than he let on. He was now really worried. And with it was a heavy sense of guilt that rode him like a burr. The least he had ever wanted to do was break the *Capitán*'s trust and he felt he had done just that. It was something he would have to live with. But the *Capitán* need not know. He must not, by all means, know the truth.

He stood up and went to look for Cortez, hoping the *Capitán* would not get to the man before he did.

Fortunately Cortez was still pretty much deep in his *siesta* and the *Capitán* had not bothered to look into the barracks. Not that he had any reason to, for he did not suspect anyone of his soldiers of any wrongdoing, although he was not entirely discarding that possibility. He was relying on the belief that if Tiago knew, he would tell him.

Tiago grabbed Cortez's shoulders and shook him up; ignoring the latter's open mouth and the foul breath that braced him in the face as he leaned down.

"Wake up, Cortez, wake up!" Tiago said in a loud enough voice, in a vain effort not to wake the other sleeping soldiers.

"Pipe down, *Sargento*, and let us sleep," someone mumbled.

"Just get back to your dreams, *hombre*, or you'll be having nightmares the rest of your miserable life," Tiago said and nobody dared say anything more. He nudged Cortez's shoulder once more. Cortez stirred and opened an eye.

"Wha'?" he said then opened both eyes as he realized it was Tiago who woke him up. "What now, *Sargento*?" Cortez sat up on the bed as Tiago stood erect.

"Dress up and come with me. I have something for you to do," Tiago did not elaborate as some of the soldiers who were wakened up were now looking at them with interest. "By the stables," Tiago said as he turned away.

Cortez stayed where he was for a moment, wondering what Tiago wanted. Had something come up? Was Miguel back or have been found, maybe? Dead? Surely the *Sargento* would not mind if that happened. He, Cortez, would not be grieving either. Reluctantly, he finally rose from the bed, grabbed a pair of trousers, put them on and followed Tiago.

"Go back to sleep, you mangy *perros*," he growled at the soldiers who were staring up at him as he passed by their beds.

Nobody said anything. Nobody dared ever to challenge Cortez. He was known to be the meanest *hombre* in the fort. Besides, everyone thought he was a little messed up in the head although no one dared to say it to his face, except perhaps Tiago when he was drunk.

"We have a problem," Tiago said.

"What? Who? Miguel?" Cortez said. "That man was a problem since he was born."

"Worse."

"What could be worse than that dastardly traitor? The woman?"

"Yeah, well she's certainly part of the problem too," Tiago said. Once in a while, Cortez showed incisive insight on things that sometimes Tiago wondered if his crazy acts were just that, an act. "It's the *Capitán*. He wants to know what's going on and I have the feeling he has some suspicions that somehow we are involved."

"Well, we are, aren't we?" Cortez said, grinning. "Why don't we just tell him what we did?"

"No!" Tiago said quickly. All doubts about Cortez's sanity likewise quickly vanishing from his mind. "No, I don't want him to know that we had anything to do with the woman, or Miguel and his friends. Ever! You understand that?"

"Alright, but why not?"

"Why not? You fool! Why not?" Tiago almost yelled but he controlled his voice. "We did not tell him that we were going to take the woman, and then she got killed in the process! And you were there and you could not stop it?"

Cortez was taken aback by Tiago's sudden outburst that the grin left his face and he was speechless.

"He did not want any harm done to that woman, and I honestly don't know why," Tiago added in a now reflective tone. "It was some noble code that he has about not troubling and faulting the mother for the sins of the son or in this case, the daughter. Or perhaps he knew that the woman was related to the *Itnegs* and for reasons that I cannot see, he somehow has great respect for those mountain people. A sense of affinity perhaps since he came from the mountain regions in Spain himself. Who knows? But yeah, I agree with him, that woman should not have been killed. Perhaps you would never understand that."

Cortez inhaled deeply thinking back to that day. He was questioning the woman in a very professional, and to him, even in a gentlemanly manner while old Alfonso watched from a few feet away. Why, he even did not put her in shackles nor bound her hands! And he had not even started threatening her or roughing her up a bit to encourage her to talk although he was about to do so since the woman was not cooperating. Then she suddenly made a move, kicking and hitting him so fast and so furiously that he almost went down on his back. Even Alfonso was of no help. He had not expected her to put up a fight and then to fight so well. The woman was a tigress. And then it happened so fast that before he was aware of it he had drawn his dagger and plunged it into the woman's heart. He could not have stopped her with his bare hands. And of course he had to blame one of Miguel's friends. He did not want anyone to know that he was almost bested by a woman and that he had to use a knife to take her down. And Alfonso would not dare talk. Of all the soldiers in the fort, Alfonso was the least anyone worried bout. The man had no spine.

Then as if a gift from heaven, the lackeys that Miguel recruited got killed. The less people knew what happened that day with *La Generala's* mother the better. They did not know who killed them, maybe Miguel did but it did not matter. Cortez did not care and was not worried, and could not understand why the *Sargento* cared or even worried either. But to avoid further questions and unnecessary inquiries that may lead the disappearance of the woman to them, they got rid of the bodies and just out of spite, Cortez burned Miguel's house down, although he told the *Sargento* that it was the best way to clean up the bloody house.

Besides, the heaps of ashes buried the shallow graves underneath the house pretty well.

Cortez wished now that Miguel was in the house when he burned it instead of in the fort then where they thought they had him under control yet the fool somehow escaped. And Miguel knew everything they did except where the bodies of his friends were, or maybe he thought they were ashes now also. Whatever, the man was a problem and the gears in Cortez's mind began their motions that only he could understand.

"So we'll find Miguel," he said.

"Yes, find him and make sure he does not talk," Tiago said. He looked at Cortez and for a moment he felt a sense of pity, not for the man but for himself, for allowing himself to ally with such a man and leave his fate in his hands. Yet as he thought about it, if anybody could undertake the task of finding and silencing someone, no one he knew was more capable than Cortez.

"Should I bring a couple of the men?" Cortez said.

"No, do it on your own and don't say anything about this to anyone," Tiago said. But then he had a thought. "Maybe Catriz, yes, bring Catriz along. He had been itching to get his hands on Miguel."

"After the thrashing you'd given him for losing Miguel, I think he should be," Cortez said, a smile was back in his face.

Tiago nodded, pleased with the idea of giving Catriz a chance to redeem himself.

Cortez waited a moment, then when Tiago remained silent, he said, "If you don't have anything else, I'll go change and Catriz and I will be off then."

Tiago waved a hand in dismissal without lifting his head.

"*Buena suerte*," he mumbled as Cortez left, and he meant it.

Along the road going east towards the *barrio* of *Raois*, just before the bridge at the edge of the town proper, across the slaughterhouse on the right side was a row of wooden framed box houses, attached together forming one big structure. In them were small businesses and stores that were owned and ran by the Chinese.

In the middle of the structure was a rather large store that sold various sweets, rice cakes, preserved foods, fresh produce, dry beans and seeds, and Chinese medicinal herbs out front. But in the back, connected by a short dark corridor that had hardwood doors at both ends, was an elongated room that ran parallel to the storefront. It was partitioned into several cubicles, each one separated only by thick blanket sheets that served as flimsy walls for privacy. The quasi-doors were covered by a loose-hanging piece of cloth also made from the same material, although they were colored differently. Each partition was large enough for one cot, or a bunk bed, or in a couple of rooms, just plain woven coconut fronds floor mat called the *ikamen* by the Ilocanos, and at the moment, each cubicle was occupied.

As one passed through the second door at the back into the room, one would be met by a hazy smoke that smelled of something like a mixture of burnt incense and flower of indeterminate origin, peculiarly, and some say, dizzyingly pleasant. The smoke came from the pipes that each of the occupants in the partitioned cubicles held.

And in the cubicle farthest to the front door was the subject of the discussion between *Sargento* Tiago and Cortez. He was lying in a stupor on a filthy cot with half-open eyes. In one hand was a pipe with dying embers where a thin wisp of smoke curled up emitting a hint of that peculiarly floral smell into the confined space. The smell at least diffused the stench in the place from the sweat and unkempt disposition of its glaze-eyed temporary resident.

Just outside of the cubicle, two men in long robes, with hairs braided into long pig-tails, were talking animatedly in their native tongues. If only Miguel could hear and understand their language, he would know that they were talking about him.

"That stupid, filthy dog has been here for almost a week!" one of them, significantly younger than the other, said. "And he has no money. How much longer are we going to keep him?"

"I know, but be patient," the older man said, patting the other one on the arm. "He was a good customer for a long time. Besides, he had done us some favors in the past. Let him stay a few more days."

The younger man shook his head, his pig-tail of a hair dancing around his back. "Yeah, well, I know, Uncle, but we can't keep him here forever. He can't pay. I heard his house burned down and the *Guardia Civil* is looking for him. He's in trouble and we may get dragged into it."

"Don't worry about it. Nobody knows that he's here."

"Someone will find out and that someone will talk."

The older man paused, thinking.

"Then make sure no one knows he's here," he said.

"Of course, Uncle, but like I said we can't keep him here forever." He pushed the piece of cloth that was covering the door and peeked inside the cubicle. "Look at him he's totally out of this world. He'd been like that since the day he came in, shirtless, shoeless and God knows what else less! Money for sure!" He let go of the blanket which settled down and obscured the sight of Miguel's semi-conscious body in the cot.

"Remember he was a good friend to us for a long time. He kept the troublesome people away. And he could cause us some trouble..." the old man's voice trailed.

The younger man sighed. He knew he could not change his uncle's mind. Sometimes he wondered what the *mestizo* had on his uncle that he could not kick the man out.

"But, Uncle," he said. "He had been using and asking for more of the stuff, and I don't think he'll be able to pay although he kept mumbling about getting some more money from the Spaniards. As far as I know, the Spaniards may be paying money to find him. I heard people, especially the soldiers were asking about him."

"Ahh, rumors, simply rumors, don't listen to them. How much have you been giving him?"

"Enough to keep him from bothering me," the younger man answered.

"Mix local tobacco in it. Put dried papaya leaves. He would not know the difference," the old man said, smiling.

"Tobacco costs money, too. As far as I'm concerned they're worth more than that piece of garbage in there." He inclined his head towards the cubicle. "Besides, he's already into the white stuff."

234

"Ohh? Is that so," the old man said, not a question, just a statement as if he just received a message of mild interest. He leaned in and peered into the room. Miguel was snoring contentedly although his eyes remained half open.

"Put sugar cubes, or flour, or salt, even. Same thing, he wouldn't know the difference," he said as if handing down a sentence.

"That's a good idea," said the younger man with a little smile on his face as he walked beside his Uncle out of the room into the dark, short corridor that led to the storefront where his brother and Aunt and cousins were attending to regular customers. "But I have a better one."

"What?" The old man raised an eyebrow without looking at his nephew. The young man did not usually have any opinion much more express an idea.

"Why don't I just kill him and feed him to the pigs outside?"

"Let's not stoop down to his level," the old man said without breaking a stride.

Chapter Thirty Six

"I can't stand this waiting," Akash said. "You and I, let's go down to the valley tonight."

"We can't. We'll have to wait for the others. We'll go when everyone's ready," Kulas said.

Akash had followed Kulas to the river after the gathering broke up. The elders had decided to let the young warriors and any able bodied men to join the Ilocanos in the fight against the Spaniards. With the death of Awad, they now had a common enemy. They will leave at the earliest in ten days, *Ama* Dalalo and *Ama* Kagaid had declared.

"Ten days? That's too long!" Akash had said. "We could be ready in two days, Ama!"

"We need that time for the married men to settle their affairs at home or in the fields and hunting grounds and whatever else they're working on. Besides, we need that time for the other tribes to get here," Apo Kagaid said patiently.

"What other tribes?" Akash asked.

"Ket 'tay kakalon ah, our allies from Paganao, Bangilo, Bacooc, Cayapa, Libtek and the others. We have to let them know we're going to war. They may be offended if they found out and we did not send word," Apo Kagaid said. Ama Dalalo nodded silently in agreement by his side.

Gabriela felt elated for a brief moment despite the heaviness in her heart for her mother's death. Her hope of avenging Diego successfully, and now also her mother, was given back with a fresh life by the talk of more tribes joining in the fight. But she could not ignore the nagging feeling of guilt that was growing inside her. It meant more people were going to die and she did not want that. But on the other hand, with the death of her mother, did she really have a choice? She steeled her resolve by letting the hatred in her heart grow and overpower her sorrow and sense of guilt.

"I am going to Bangilo and have word with Ama Biktol," Aklang stepped forward. "He had promised to come if we get in trouble."

Apo Dalalo nodded again, remembering the hunt with his grandchildren. 'Yes, that boy and his two companions would surely come,' he thought.

"I'll go with him," Bagit said. "They know me too."

Apo Dalalo looked at his two grandchildren with a little trepidation but he set it aside as he saw the determination in their eyes. Then he remembered the way they comported themselves in the hunt and he simply nodded without saying a word. The boys could surely take care of themselves. They were no longer boys. They were men, yet he worried of the days ahead with all the talk of battle.

"Very well, you two can go to Bangilo and we'll send the word out then to the rest of the tribes. We'll give it at least two weeks or three if necessary for them to get here then we'll go down to the valley. The Spaniards are not going anywhere," Apo Kagaid finally said when Dalalo remained silent.

"Yes, two, three weeks, that should be enough. Let the Spanish think they have settled into a peaceful existence," Apo Dalalo said. The way he figured, it would actually be closer to a month before everyone would be ready and they showed up in the land of the Ilocanos, what with the usual ceremonies in preparation for battle when all of the tribes gathered together. Besides, with their expected large number, it would take at least an additional two to four days or a week maybe to get down to the valley.

So now Kulas and Akash sat brooding by the river, casting a glance now and then at the camp of the Ilocanos.

"I know, Kulas, but I cannot wait. I want to avenge Awad now," Akash said forcefully.

"I understand," Kulas said softly. "But what can the two of us do?"

"A lot, my friend, a lot," Akash said with renewed fire in his eyes. "We would be more mobile than with a whole band behind us. We'll hit them fast, we'll use our bows so we don't have to get near them, then we vanish, and hit them again. We'll get them running around like a headless chicken, keep them busy looking for us, keep them away from the fort and that way prevent them from preparing for the attack when all the tribes are ready!" The words came out of his mouth like he had not thought of them at the spur of the moment.

Kulas did not answer but he was warming up to the idea of keeping the soldiers busy. Hit them and run. Hit them again and run again. That should keep them mad and busy enough that they would not be ready when the joint forces of the tribes and the Ilocanos would finally show up. He nodded pensively. He must agree that his friend had a point, but what would the elders, especially their fathers Dalalo and Kagaid, think?

"We'll have to talk with *Ama* and yours," Kulas finally said. "They have to know."

"But what if they don't agree?" Akash said. "I'm telling you now I'm going ahead with or without you and regardless of what they say."

Kulas looked at his friend. He had forgotten how stubborn Akash could be once he made up his mind. He put a hand on Akash's shoulder.

"Hey, don't worry, I'm going with you," he said.

Chapter Thirty Seven

"We've looked around, *Sargento*," Cortez said, "The man had vanished. He's nowhere to be found. We went to Santa, to Paing, and all the way down to Narvacan, to all his usual haunts, and we could not find him. No one had seen him, and if anyone did, no one is saying anything."

"That's impossible," Tiago said. "No one could just vanish without a trace!"

"That's what people say about Miguel's friends too," Cortez said flippantly.

Tiago glared at him. "We know where they are, Cortez," he hissed.

"Oh yeah, we buried them. I still think it would have been better if we let them roast when we burned Miguel's house down," Cortez said smiling at his joke, but he stopped when he noticed Tiago was not smiling. He remembered Tiago saying that the bones would not fully burn and it was good that he had the sense to bury the bodies although he was not actually fond of the burning of Miguel's house.

"Are you sure you have looked at every place?" Tiago ignored what Cortez had said which was not lost to the latter and he likewise turned serious.

"Yes, yes, *Sargento*. Me and Catriz, and all the others you had sent out to canvass the *sitios*. We have practically turned the whole place upside down and there's no trace of that animal! Maybe he had gone to Manila," Cortez said.

"Maybe he did, but I don't think so. Someone would have seen him take to the road. It's a long way to Manila," Tiago said. Then as if an inspiration hit him, he exclaimed. "Boats! Boats! Did you ask around the villages by the sea? Talked with the fishermen and see if anyone had given him a ride? Or any boat missing?"

"We-ellll," Cortez started, "no, we really had not gotten around to the *sitios* along the coast," he admitted reluctantly. "Let me ask the other fellows." He turned around and left hurriedly before Tiago could detain him any longer.

"Go back with Catriz and tell everyone to scour the *sitios* by the sea *pronto*!" Tiago yelled at his back.

Cortez ignored him and went looking for Catriz. He did not have to go far. He saw Catriz by the back gate chatting with Bautista. He remembered hearing that the two came from the same village in Cordoba.

"Get ready, we're going out," Cortez said to Catriz.

"They found him?" Catriz said sensing from Cortez's face that the only reason he was looking for him would be something to do with Miguel.

"No, they haven't found him. We're going to the *barrios* by the sea. The *Sargento* thinks he may have gone someplace in a boat."

"Don't even bother," Bautista said. "We have already done that. We went up and down the coast for three days, from Cabugao down to Santa Maria and Santiago. No one saw him and no boat was reported missing. We even beat up a couple of village chiefs, just to make them remember how to talk and encourage others to come forward but nobody knew anything. Trust me, Miguel never got there. Go tell *Don* Tiago."

"Ahh, *hijo de...*" Cortez started to say but he controlled himself and sighed instead. It was a good thing what Bautista said. It meant he and Catriz did not have to go out. He was not about ready to go on a long horse ride in this heat anyway.

"*Gracias*, Bautista," he said and went back to report to Tiago. He found the *Sargento* still sitting in the same place, blankly staring at nothing in particular. He seemed to be in a deep thought that Cortez momentarily hesitated before he purposely cleared his throat as he approached to make his presence known. Startled, Tiago turned towards Cortez with a bit of irritation and surprise in his face.

"Is there something else, Cortez? What's the matter? You can't find Catriz?" *Don* Tiago asked, not even attempting to hide his growing annoyance.

"No, *nada*, nothing, *Sargento*," Cortez said. "I found Catriz talking with Bautista and Bautista just informed me that they already scoured the *barrios* by the coast and found nothing. He said Miguel never got close to the sea."

"Is that so," Tiago said pensively.

"Yes, I'm afraid it is, *Sargento*," Cortez said. "So what do we do now?"

"Well then we're back to square one, I guess," Tiago said, sighing loudly. "Damn that *bastardo*! He's got to be around town somewhere, *hombre*. He left the fort without a shirt and his house burned down so someone would have provided him with clothes! Somebody out there knows something, Cortez. Find him and we'll find Miguel."

"Well then, *Señor*, we're going back to town and look around again."

"I guess so, unless you have a better plan?"

"No, no plans at the moment, *Sargento*."

"Well, go back to town then and take Catriz with you again. Comb the houses. He's got to be around there someplace. Are you sure you talked with everyone? Looked into all the places where he could hide?" *Don* Tiago

239

said, thinking of all the likely hiding places in town where Miguel could have sought refuge. He could not remember any special place in particular.

"Yes, yes we did, *Sargento*," Cortez said.

"Searched everyplace, too?"

"Yes, I believe we did."

"Believe you did? C'mon, *hombre*, it's either you did or you did not!"

"Yes, we did, I'm sure. It's a small town, *Sargento*, we searched everywhere but the *bastardo's* vanished. Maybe he's left town for good."

Tiago did not speak for a moment then his eyes lit up as he remembered something.

"How about the Chinese place?" he asked.

"The Chinese place by the slaughterhouse?" Cortez said.

"Yes, did you go there? Did you look in the back rooms? I heard that they run illegal gambling in one of them backrooms. A man like Miguel may be known there."

"Well we actually went there but we did not look into the backrooms. We could not communicate with the damn Chinese. We ask something and they come up with all this Chinese gibberish. Why don't they learn to speak either Ilocano or Spanish?"

"They do speak Ilocano, Cortez, I am sure of it. How could they sell their wares if they do not speak the language?"

"Ahh, I see," Cortez said, his face clouding for a moment then transformed into an excited rage. "The bastards! They played us for fools! They pretended not to understand Ilocano then? I think I need to go back there and see if I could persuade them to speak a language I can understand."

Tiago knew that it did not take much to drive Cortez mad and he was witnessing it yet again. In his old village in Compostela, Cortez would have been into a fight most of the time, if not most likely be dead the first time he got into one. It was a good thing the man was from Madrid, a city where most people were as crazy as he was and thus had more tolerance to his sudden mood swings.

"Calm down, *hombre*," Tiago said. "Go back there but you won't get anywhere if you get rough with those people. They can take abuse and suffer silently if it was to their advantage, but I heard they can fight too. Find out what they know about Miguel first, where he went, and when we find him then you can go back and speak to them in any language you want."

"Just leave it to me, *Sargento*. I'll take care of it. Is there anything else?"

"No. Don't go alone, take Catriz with you," Tiago said. "And go when it's a little darker so they won't see you coming, or anybody else for that matter."

Cortez nodded, turned around and walked away still bristling with rage.

"Yeah, bring Catriz to at least watch your back, *cabrón*," *Sargento* Tiago softly said to Cortez's back, but more to himself, as if in a prayer. Somehow he had the feeling that the man was not going to heed his word about not getting rough with the Chinese. He hoped Cortez at least listened well enough to get to the place when it was dark, not for the element of surprise but to cover whatever acts of cruelty he might decide to commit. Not that any sort of decision was needed. Wanton cruelty seemed inherent to the man.

And the only language he knew when he got mad was spoken not with his tongue but by his heavy hands and whatever they held at the time.

At the Chinese place, Miguel was just leaving through the back door dressed in borrowed Chinese robes and not on his own volition. A conical woven coconut frond hat that was a little large was draped over his head covering most of his face. Two sturdy looking Chinese youths had his arms over their shoulders, walking him between them as if they were a couple of concerned friends bringing a drunken companion home. But they were headed opposite the direction to the houses. They were headed towards the river.

The two young Chinamen had taken a while to convince their uncle that Miguel had to be out after the group of Spanish soldiers went around the neighborhood asking for the man. They had pretended not to understand and just kept shaking their heads, speaking all the time in Mandarin, warning one another not to say a word in either Ilocano or Castilian. Frustrated with the apparent impossibility of communicating with the Chinese who were spewing gibberish, the Spaniards finally went away and did not even bother to go any further than peering into the storefronts, wrinkling their noses at the peculiar smells of alien herbs and Chinese cooking.

But the young Chinamen were concerned, and with good reason, that the Spaniards would return because they took notice of the leader of the soldiers who seemed hesitant to leave, casting a suspicious look at the closed door of the hallway going into the back room. The back room was emptied out of the usual customers when the soldiers were noticed in the neighborhood, except for Miguel who was still in a self-induced stupor. The young Chinese had to content themselves into stuffing the unconscious man into a small room where dirty laundry were kept and covered him as best they could with dirty robes and blankets hoping he would not make any noise if he woke up.

It took a lot of convincing from the nephews to finally make their uncle agree to get Miguel out of the place. There was a hut by a field just a short distance across the river and that was where they had agreed to put Miguel.

There was no need to ask the man for his opinion because he was still totally out, floating in space where no one could reach him or perhaps mired down in a place only he could imagine. The young men did not care one way or the other. They just wanted Miguel out and if it were up to them, they would have rather left Miguel in the *banca,* the wooden tub of a boat they used to ferry him across the river and let him float all the way down to the sea, perhaps to China.

But being obedient nephews as they were, they took Miguel across the river, half-dragged and half-carried him through the fields and set him up in the little hut as comfortably as they could manage. As instructed, they left the man some food and a jar full of water and some used clothing for him to change. Then they left him on his own, if he ever woke up. As far as they knew, the hut had been abandoned for a long time and aside from trespassing boys every now and then, it was mostly left alone.

And as far as the young men were concerned, their order was done and they had nothing more to do with the man. They left with clean consciences, although they really never bothered to contemplate on the issue of the morality of their actions. There was garbage in the house that had the potential of causing them trouble and they finally got rid of it. That was more or less the extent of their moral consciousness. They left the hut with smug smiles on their faces.

There was no need to say goodbye because Miguel was still flying somewhere up there.

Upriver, at least a good three hour walk from the confluence of the big Abra River and the smaller river that the young Chinamen had just re-crossed, Akash and Kulas were resting by the western bank. It was just the third time in the day that they took a break since they left the village at early dawn the day before yesterday. Kulas looked up at the afternoon sun and thought that they should be by the edge of the town of Vigan right after sunset, give or take a few hours depending on how Akash's foot would hold up. His friend was not complaining but he was still favoring his injured foot. The first *barrio* that they would get into was *Raois* and from there it would just be a half-hour walk into town.

Kulas looked up once again and decided they had time for a quick swim. Without saying a word, he stood up, loosened and took off the strip of leather that held his sheathed long knife and dagger, and dropped them off beside Akash who was spread out sleeping in the sand. He ran into the water and dived in creating a huge splash that awakened Akash.

"What the..?!!" Akash said as he hastily sat up, looking around with a bewildered look on his face when he did not see Kulas who was underwater.

Akash groaned in exasperation when he saw the head of his friend appear mid-river.

"C'mon and clean up your sorry ass!" Kulas beckoned when he saw his friend sitting up.

"Oh, shut up!" Akash said and went back to sleep.

After a few laps going up and down the river, Kulas finally came out of the water, breathing heavily but feeling fully refreshed. He put on his knives, picked up his bow and quiver full of arrows, slung them across his shoulders, picked up his spear then prodded Akash awake with it.

"Let's go," he said to Akash as soon as his friend opened his eyes. He moved before Akash had even started to rise up.

Akash shook his head both to wake himself up and in an expression of disbelief at his friend as he looked at his back still dripping with water. Kulas had not even bothered to wipe himself off dry, not that he had anything to use for he went into the water in his *ba-ag* and headband. And he wore nothing else.

"Unbelievable," Akash murmured as he stood up. He walked the short distance to the river and dropped down to his knees and washed his face and upper body. Then he stood up, gathered his weapons and hurried after his friend.

He was of course also dripping wet but he felt refreshed and well rested after the short nap. He looked up at the afternoon sun and nodded his head. They should be in Vigan by sundown.

There was no need to hurry.

Chapter Thirty Eight

Cortez and Catriz loitered by *Apo* Andang's *carinderia,* late in the afternoon where they decided to go for a bowl each of the steaming *sinanglao.* They quite loved the soup, savoring with gusto the tangy, sour and hot concoction of mixed beef innards, ignoring the lobs of fat swimming in the broth. The Chinamen's place was just a couple of blocks away from the *carinderia* and they were in no hurry at all. It was not quite dark enough yet. They had plenty of time to waste.

The other customers were at first apprehensive when the two soldiers showed up, but they finally settled down when the two just sat down on a table by themselves, ordered their food and did not bother anyone else.

"Give us a bowl each of that *sinanglao,* a plate of *chorizos* and a bowl of rice," Cortez said to Gorio as he approached them courteously.

"*Si, Señor,* anything else?" Gorio said.

"Anything else you want?" Cortez asked Catriz.

"A glass of *basi* each to go with the soup," Catriz grinned.

"Yeah, two glasses of *basi* then also," Cortez said. "Make sure the glasses are clean!"

"*Si, Señor.*" Gorio bowed and left and shortly got back later with a tray of the drinks while their food was being prepared.

"Say," Cortez casually said while Gorio set down the glasses. "You haven't seen Miguel around here lately, have you?"

"No, no, *Señor,* he hasn't been here for a while. Some people have been asking about him but no one seems to know where he went," Gorio said.

"Alright," Cortez said dismissively like he had just gotten an answer about the weather. There was no need to cause additional attention to themselves or cause any trouble with the locals. "Just let us know when he shows up, will you? We just want to talk with him."

"Of course, *Señor,*" Gorio said as he went to get their food.

It was a couple of bowls of sinanglao and four more glasses of *basi* each later when Cortez and Catriz finally stood up. The oil lamps had come out and most of the late diners and drinkers had already gone home except for a couple of old farmers arguing which town had the best tobacco in the region.

The lamps and candles in most of the huts around the slaughterhouse were gone; windows and doors were closed and shuttered. Out by the Chinese place, a few lamps and candles still flickered. A couple of the stores were still open.

Cortez and Catriz left without paying to the consternation of Gorio and *Apo* Andang, although they had expected it. They watched in silent anger as the two soldiers walked away, each one swaying a bit as they headed into the night toward the Chinese place.

By the dark shadows of the slaughterhouse, Akash and Kulas watched the two soldiers get up and leave. They arrived at the place, skirting the *barrios* of Raois, Rugsuanan and others along the way, and as they crossed the river, took shelter in the shadows of the empty slaughterhouse as they observed the locals eating at the *carinderias* just a few meters away.

They had noticed the two soldiers as they settled down to rest, and their presence immediately caught their attention. They planned to wreak some havoc in the land and keep the soldiers busy so they might as well start now, with the soldiers.

"What are we going to do?" Akash asked as the soldiers walked away.

"Why, follow them of course and see where they're going," Kulas said smiling in the dark.

"Just follow them?" Akash said, not sure if his friend was serious or not.

"Yeah, for now, see what they're up to. Why what do you have in mind?" Kulas said with a straight face as Akash leaned closer to look at him. Faint shadows from the faraway lamps of *Apo* Andang's *carinderia* played on their faces.

Akash did not answer as he sensed his friend was in a light mood. Nothing seemed to faze the man.

"Let's go," he said and moved silently after the soldiers without waiting for Kulas to say anything further. Kulas followed his friend out of the shadows of the slaughterhouse.

They were seasoned hunters who could track and move silently in the dark. And they did now, gliding like ghosts, neither making a sound as they moved from tree to tree, or a fence and shrubbery, always keeping to the deeper shadows. Fortunately there were no stray dogs but they were not worried. They could keep the dogs silent with the low whistle that both were adept in making. It had yet to fail either one of them.

It was not difficult to follow the soldiers as they took their time walking towards the Chinamen's place. They had to walk slowly because it was obvious now to the two trackers that the soldiers were drunk, one apparently more so than the other because he kept stumbling and the other had to hold him up once in a while to steady him. They realized that the white men would probably not even know that there were people walking behind them at the condition they were in. Besides, they were too secure in their thinking that no one would dare to cause them any harm, but still, Akash and Kulas kept to the shadows.

A moment later, they watched across the street as the Spaniards stepped up the walkway and into the first open store at the end of the structure. A Chinaman followed by his wife came up to meet them, bowing to his waist ceremoniously. But as soon as he raised his head, the soldier who was less drunk gave him a vicious slap to the side of his face that sent him sprawling unto the floor.

The sound of the slap reached Akash and Kulas like a distant thunderclap, followed later by the high pitched wailing of the Chinaman's wife as she went rushing to her husband's prone body on the floor. She held him down as he tried feebly to stand up, covering him with her frail body while all the time imploring the big soldier to let them be in a strange sing-song language that neither Kulas nor Akash understood. They looked at one another, their eyes locked in a silent conversation then both shrugged agreeing without saying a word that they were not going to get involved for the moment. They watched silently as the scene across the street unfolded before them.

The big soldier turned and spoke to his companion then he grabbed the hair of the woman and led her deeper into the store where they vanished from the view of Akash and Kulas. The other soldier held his rifle, pointed unsteadily to the head of the Chinaman who sat cringing on the floor holding the side of his face.

A moment later both the big soldier and the woman came back into view, the big soldier still had his hand on the tiny woman's hair, still dragging her like a child. He pushed her down harshly towards her husband and she fell on top of him as the Chinaman desperately tried to catch her fall. Both man and wife ended in a heap on the floor as they watched the two white men march to the next door.

The scene was repeated again and again with a slight variation as the two soldiers went down the line of doors. The big man almost always slapped anyone who showed up even before any word was spoken as they went from room to room obviously looking for someone. Sometimes sounds of merchandise breaking, especially glasses and ceramics, were heard as cabinets and furnitures were toppled over. In a couple of occasions though, the two soldiers were just content in going in and out without doing any further damage when a whole family, specially with toddlers, promptly lined up as the two soldiers entered, making no attempt to stop or even say anything while their house was searched.

Akash and Kulas watched as the soldiers finally emerged from the last door empty handed. The door was promptly and gratefully closed behind them as soon as they came out. They stood there in the elevated walkway for a moment, hunched in a hushed conversation, their eyes going up the length of the frame house again.

All the stores were now closed and dark with the exception of the biggest store in the middle where the two young Chinese who had escorted Miguel out earlier in the day were busy cleaning up the overturned merchandise. Broken glasses and ceramics were mixed with various herbs and roots on the floor and both were heard cursing in Mandarin. Three young girls and an old man and a woman were also busy sorting out produce and dried merchandise, putting them back up in baskets and framed stands.

At the sound of the sing-song voices, the two soldiers seemed to have woken up from their silent conversation and headed back up to the middle of the building and stopped at the door of the lighted storefront. The sing-song voices suddenly ceased at the soldiers' reappearance.

Akash and Kulas nudged at each other as they watched with interest.

"What are they going to do now?" Akash whispered. He did not hear Kulas answer but he sensed his friend move. He turned his head and his eyes grew bigger as he realized Kulas had taken off his bow and was now fitting an arrow into it. He looked up at his friend's face but Kulas was not looking back at him. His eyes were focused on the scene across the street.

Akash likewise took off his bow and nocked an arrow as he also watched the scene unfolding in the store. He saw the big soldier beckoning for one of the young Chinamen to come out. The young man put down the long-handled broom that he was holding and slowly approached the big man, stopping just beyond the man's reach. The young man instinctively cringed as the big man gestured inside again, this time beckoning to one of the young girls. The summoned girl walked briskly with head down and stopped by the young man's side but the big soldier stepped forward and grabbed her by the hair, pulling the girl to his side. He pulled out his dagger and pointed it to the girl's throat. The young Chinaman froze in fear and did not move. The rest of his family did not move either.

A thin trickle of blood oozed out of the girl's neck as the point of the dagger broke skin. The girl whimpered in pain but she could not move as Cortez tightened his grip on her hair. Catriz had again leveled his rifle, swaying, as it alternately got pointed between the young Chinaman by the door and the rest of the family that were frozen in fear inside the store.

"You, *bastardo*," Cortez said to the young Chinaman in halting Ilocano. "Kneel down or I'll kill this young lady."

Without thinking, the young man slowly dropped to his knees.

Cortez grinned, shaking his head.

"You stupid, lying bastard," he said, letting go of the girl. He quickly stepped forward and delivered a vicious kick to the young Chinaman's face who could not do anything fearing for the little girl's life. The young man

247

somersaulted backwards by the force of the blow and he lay crumpled on the floor, totally unconscious. "So you understand Ilocano after all!"

Then he pointed at the others inside the store and still speaking in Ilocano, yelled at them.

"Don't you ever lie to me again, you bastards! Who among you does not understand or speak Ilocano?"

No one dared to speak.

"I am not saying it again," Cortez said. "Who can't understand Ilocano?"

"We all understand the dialect, *Señor*," the old man said, "and all of us speak it too."

"And you all pretended not to understand any word I was saying the first time I came here, you bastards!" Cortez yelled. He flipped the dagger to his other hand and drew out his sword. The old woman cried in a piercing shriek of fear as Cortez advanced toward the old man. The soldier was a few feet into the middle of the store when he suddenly stiffened up, his face contorted in rage and in pain as an arrow sprouted from his back. He took a couple more halting steps before he finally collapsed and fell face down a few feet before the stunned Chinese patriarch.

Catriz took a while to realize what was happening, then he quickly sobered up as he saw the arrow on Cortez's back as the man fell to the floor. He turned around quickly and pulled the trigger as soon as he had the rifle pointed in the dark. The flash of the rifle shot had barely vanished when the arrow from Akash's bow lodged on the soldier's throat. Catriz dropped his rifle and put both of his hands around the arrow shaft but his arms seemed to lose all their strength, and they lay around the shaft feebly. Then he was falling and a feeling of helplessness and buoyancy enveloped him as his feet seemed to have melted and he was slowly falling down. He tried vainly to stay erect but his feet had vanished. He fell on top of his rifle with a gurgling sound coming from his throat as blood frothed from his mouth and trickled out also from the shaft of the arrow, dropping like teardrops to the floor.

The Chinese looked at one another in horror, not comprehending what had just happened before their eyes. They hurriedly huddled together and sat frozen in fear around the prostrate body of the young Chinese who was still unconscious, their worried eyes flitting between the bodies of the two soldiers and the darkness beyond the door. Their eyes grew wider as Akash appeared from the shadows, stepped inside and closed the door behind him. Outside, Kulas stayed well into the shadows, looking down the street to see if anyone was brave and nosy enough to find out what was going on, but nobody did. Not even the other doors in the framed structure budged open.

"I'm not going to hurt you," Akash said in Ilocano to the huddled family as they looked up to him. "But we need to get rid of the bodies." He bent down at Cortez's body and pulled out the arrow. He gathered the soldier's loose shirt and tried to put a part of it over the wound to staunch the blood that had begun to flow out and pool on the floor when the arrow was removed. The man was a bleeder and a large splotch of blood stained the floor where he fell. He did the same to Catriz, wiping the arrows off on Catriz's shirt before putting them inside his quiver.

"Get some water," he said to no one in particular, but the other young Chinaman stood up and went into the back room. He came back with a jugful of water, handing it to Akash with a puzzled expression on his face. He was not afraid anymore of the *Itneg*, his fear replaced with hesitant gratitude.

Akash took the jug and without ceremony and saying anything dumped half of its content on the unconscious young man. The others shrieked in surprise and quickly stood up as the young man sputtered awake and sat up gingerly holding his swollen face.

"Stand up," Akash commanded. "We need your help to move these bodies out. You," he pointed to the old woman and the whimpering young girls who were gathered around their mother. "You clean up as soon as we get the bodies out of here. Wash the blood off, all of it."

The woman and the girls looked at Akash, all of them wild-eyed in fear but they nodded.

Akash turned to the men, eyeing the previously unconscious young man more closely if he was up to the task.

"Are you ready?" he asked.

The three stared back at him blankly.

"Don't just stand there! Move!" Akash barked.

The three men quickly moved as if a fire was lit under their feet. Even the hurt young man dropped the hand that was caressing his swollen face, ignoring the throbbing pain, and approached the dead body of the big man who inflicted his pain. Rage appeared on his face as he got near the body and he gave Cortez's head a vicious kick. The dead head lolled for a moment at the impact.

Both the older and the other young Chinese quickly grabbed the angry young man and held him until he calmed down. Akash ignored them and stood back a bit to let the young man blow steam. Finally he signaled the two young men to grab Cortez's legs and motioned the older man to grab one of the dead man's arms. He took hold of the other one.

"Is there a way out there?" he said, gesturing with his head at the door going to the back room.

"Yes," the old man answered. "The back door opens to the backyard and on to the river."

249

"Good," Akash said then he caught the eyes of one of the girls. "You! Hold the door open for us. C'mon," he said in a softer voice as the girl hesitated.

The old man spoke to her in Mandarin and she moved quickly.

They carried Cortez out to the backyard then went back in and moved Catriz also.

"Alright," Akash whispered as they stood over the dead bodies in the dark. "We're going to dump them into the river. That's quite a ways off so let's try to make it easier."

Not one of the Chinese said a word. They were contented on having the man who saved them from the Spaniards take over.

"Do you have poles or boards lying around here?" Akash asked.

"Yes, we have a bunch of bamboo poles drying at the side of the house," one of the young men answered. The one with the swollen face grunted his confirmation.

"Find a couple about the same lengths and bring them here. We'll use them to carry these bodies to the river. Go! Hurry! We don't have all night!" Akash said.

The two young men quickly moved into the dark and came back shortly with two poles apiece.

"Easier with four poles," the unhurt young man said. "You and Uncle take one end and Ming and I here will get the other end. We can lay both of them across the poles and get it done in one go."

"No," Akash said. "This one's too big and heavy." He touched Cortez's cold body with a foot. "We'll move them one at a time. Let's go."

"Y'all talk too much." Kulas said suddenly from behind them and the three Chinese simultaneously jumped in fear. He had come around the house unnoticed except by Akash as the two young men were getting the poles. "Old man, you can go back in and help the women. I'll help these girls."

The young Chinamen looked at one another in the dark, their faces showing a hint of anger at the slight but they remained silent as it seemed that the other *Itneg* was also included and yet was taking it in stride.

The Chinese patriarch likewise did not say anything and he obediently started for the door but paused and turned back to face Akash and Kulas who were standing together.

"Wh-who are you? Both of you, and why are you doing this?" he asked, his senses finally coming back and taking the better of him after the whirlwind events of the night.

"You don't need to know, old man," Kulas said, his voice grave now, devoid of any hint of frivolity. "Now, do you want our help to get rid of these bodies or would you rather want the Spaniards come around and find them here?"

"But we did not kill them. You killed them," the old man protested.

"You're right, but will they believe you? Because tomorrow, trust me, nobody will see us."

The old man sighed and silently turned and opened the back door.

"Let's do it," Akash said as the door closed behind the old Chinese.

They laid the poles parallel to one another on the ground and lifted the big body of Cortez crosswise over them. Then holding two poles each at either ends, they lifted the body up and made a procession in the dark toward the river where they unceremoniously dumped Cortez into the water, pushing it with their poles towards the middle where it was deeper, until it got carried away by the current.

Then they went back for Catriz and they took a quicker time with him as he was a lot lighter of a load than Cortez.

"Push him toward the middle," Kulas whispered to the young men as Catriz slid off the poles. The two grabbed a pole apiece and together, they pushed the body of Catriz into the current. When they looked back up at the bank to where Akash and Kulas were standing, they found themselves alone.

The two *Itnegs* had silently vanished into the night as if they were never there.

At the store, the old woman and the three young girls boiled some water, added laundry soap and vinegar and used the concoction to scrub the blood stains off the wooden floor while the old man went back to setting up the overturned displays. The two young men arrived shortly and helped the old man pick up and re-arrange the merchandise, sweeping the floor, and throwing away the herbs and grains that were ruined by the fragments of mixed broken glasses and ceramics, anger and bitterness etched in their faces while they furiously worked. There was however a sense of satisfaction in their hearts with the knowledge that the perpetrators had paid for their dastardly deeds with their lives.

After a moment, the old man spoke. The others stopped and listened attentively then they bowed their heads in agreement and respect and resumed what they were doing while the old man opened the front door and stepped out. Moments later, he was heard discreetly knocking at the neighboring door to the right, softly saying who he was. The neighbor opened the door and listened respectfully as the old man talked. When the old man was finished, the neighbor nodded his head and respectfully retreated back into his house. The old man went down the row of doors then did the same at the opposite side, repeating what he said to everyone. He was their leader and when he spoke, everyone listened as they did now.

251

After he had spoken with the last storeowner, the old man went back to his own place, satisfied that now everyone had the same story to tell to anyone who may be coming around asking questions.

Back at the store, the woman and the young girls wiped the floor off with dry rags when they thought under the dim light of the oil lamp that they could no longer see any visible trace of blood. Then as the wet floor dried up in the hot night air, they helped in putting the place back up in order.

The old man gathered all the rags that they used to clean up the bloodstains, bundled them together then put them in the big clay stove. He poured some lamp oil on the bundle and lit it. He watched for a moment as the bundle burned, slowly at first then as he added more oil and the dampness gradually evaporated, at a steady rate. Satisfied, he went back into the store and surveyed the progress of the clean-up giving a close attention to the drying wet spots on the floor where the soldiers had lain.

It was way past midnight when they were finally done.

Early the following morning, the old man arose and checked the floor again that was almost dry. There were tell-tale signs of scrubbing and stains where the big man had lain and his blood pooled. It would dry off eventually in time, he hoped. He went into a cabinet, pulled out a rolled rug and unfurled it over the slightly damp spot. Then he went to a display bin, emptied its merchandise contents and half-dragged and half-pulled the bin over and on top of the rug. He arranged it for a bit to make it look like it was part of the whole store display, then satisfied with the way it looked, he put back the merchandise in it. He moved some of the other bins around a bit, just to make it appear that they had re-arranged the whole store. He stepped back and surveyed his work, gave an approving nod and walked toward the backroom.

The smell of brewing coffee met his nose as he passed through the second door of the short hallway. His wife preferred tea, but he liked his coffee in the morning. 'There's nothing like fresh coffee to keep you started in the day', he thought, 'especially after a night like last night.' His wife placed a steaming mug of coffee before him as he sat down at the head of the table.

A few hours later, the old man and the two young men opened up the store like nothing had happened the night before, the womenfolk staying in the backroom as a precaution, ready to bolt out the backdoor if any unanticipated trouble happened. A handful of local customers, Ilocanos and *mestizos*, came in and browsed and picked up some items. A few complimented them on the new set-up, and the young Chinese bowed and smiled back courteously in an apparent show of gratitude.

By mid-morning, a group of soldiers came, led by an officer who was obviously older than the rest. He asked them questions, almost exactly the same questions that the old man had anticipated, about Miguel, the *Itneg* woman, Miguel's missing friends, and most especially about the two soldiers who were apparently missing and were supposed to have been in the area the night before.

The old officer and his soldiers went up and down the row of stores and they heard the same answer over and over again from the overtly courteous, bowing and seemingly submissive people, their smiling faces hiding the contempt and anger that burned behind their eyes.

"No, we have never seen the woman, nor Miguel and his friends, not for a long time now. And no, the soldiers never came here. They never showed up. This is a place where rich and noble people like you don't visit, *Señor*." They smiled and they bowed their heads while silently invoking the spirit of their ancestors to strike these foul smelling ogres down.

Tiago and his soldiers went around the town and finally returned to the fort late in the afternoon, frustrated, tired and angry. And not anywhere closer to finding out where Miguel was or whatever happened to Cortez and Catriz. He hated the prospect of meeting and reporting to the *Capitán* later on in the evening.

However as Tiago finally decided to settle down for his late siesta, it occurred to him that if Cortez and all the missing persons including Miguel had somehow died, then he, Tiago, and Alfonso who wouldn't talk, would be the only ones left living who knew what exactly happened to *La Generala*'s mother. The thought gave him a sense of security and calm. He trusted Alfonso. The man knew which side of his bread was buttered. He would never talk.

He had nothing to worry about with the *Capitán* then.

He smiled, took off his shirt, and lay in his bunk. In a few moments he was sleeping the deep sleep of a tired yet untroubled man.

Chapter Thirty Nine

It was around noon when Aklang and Bagit walked into the village of Bangilo almost two days after they left their own village.

They had spotted a little spring just a little below the mountaintop after they crossed it, and surprised at finding one so high up in the mountain, they decided to stop and made camp there for the night. They drank and filled their water gourds in the cold spring, then Bagit set up some bird traps a little farther off the camp. A few hours later, as the sun was about to go down, they were feasting on a couple of wild quails grilled over their open campfire and some wild yams and taro roots that Aklang had dug up by the spring.

That night, they slept by the dying fire, with their spears, bows and arrows and long knives within their easy reach. Aside from the bit of a chill as the fire died down, the night passed uneventfully.

After a harried breakfast of the leftover meat and roots from the night before, they had started off early. It was easier going down the mountain, and half-way down, they spotted the village of Bangilo far off below. Thin fingers of smoke from probably open air cooking fires swirled up over the treetops like wraiths beckoning at them against the blue green hues of the foliage and the sky. Eagerly the cousins walked with renewed vigor and haste, eager to get to the village and meet with Biktol and his friends again. Each one silently hoping that their friends from Bangilo would be willing to join them in their fight to avenge *Ina* Awad. They had talked about it along the way, and both had decided they were joining the rebels not to fight for their cause, whatever it was, but for the death of their aunt.

Curious children had spotted them first and now the two walked into the middle of the village with a group of open-mouthed boys and giggling little girls surrounding them. In the yards and by the huts, the older villagers looked at them with a mixed tinge of curiosity and amusement. Then as they approached a group of men sitting under a huge Narra tree in the middle of the village, one of the men stood up with a big grin on his face and met them. As he drew closer, Aklang noted the man's missing front teeth and realized it was one of the twins. 'Ambit,' he thought, 'or was it Ampit?'

He had no time to answer his own question as the man excitedly pointed at him, looking back at the group of men and yelling, "That's him! That's the boy we were telling you about!" He turned around and hurried towards the approaching young boys. The group of village kids parted before him.

"Welcome! Welcome, boys! Welcome to Bangilo!" Ambit said grabbing the shoulders of the boys and led them toward the group of men who were now standing up. The crowd of children, their interest gone, scattered away and went back to their games.

Ampit, the stocky hunter was also there and he walked up and nodded at the boys with a big, pleased grin on his face. Bagit and Aklang looked around for Biktol but they did not see him. Aklang felt a fleeting sense of disappointment. If there was anyone he wanted to talk to about getting help, it would be Biktol. He was the one who promised and pledged help in case of troubles.

But Aklang's concerned face brightened up when a shadow emerged from the door of the nearby hut and Biktol walked out, his attention caught by the noise coming from the yard. Biktol's frowning face broke into an amused grin as he recognized the two boys.

"Well, well, look who's finally showed up!" Biktol said gleefully walking forward and gripping each boy's arm in his own. "Come, come, sit down and rest." He turned around and led them underneath the tree. A couple of the young men who had sat back down stood up to give them space on the makeshift bench that went around the tree trunk. Bagit sat down but Aklang remained standing.

"It's a long way from home," Biktol said eyeing Aklang's bow and spear. "You're not out hunting I suppose."

"No, no, we're not, *Apo*," Aklang said courteously. "We have word from our *Ama* Dalalo and *Apo* Kagaid."

"Ahh," Biktol exclaimed, understanding apparent on his face. "You must talk with my *Ama* and the elders. But first, rest a little then we'll eat. You're just in time for the noon meal. I just went in for a bit," he indicated the hut with a wave of his hand, "to check on the cooking. The wife's cooking, she's a good cook," he winked. "Come, sit down."

"Hey, hey," Ambit said excitedly chiming in, trying to get the boys' attention, especially Aklang who remained standing. "These good for nothing drunks think that we were lying when we told them about the deer you shot! This, this is the boy we were telling you about!" he proudly said again to the rest of the men.

"So let's see then how good he is," one of them quipped.

"Yeah, yeah," a couple of them chimed in while most simply nodded their heads, their curiosity obviously piqued. They looked at Aklang and although the boy appeared tall and fit for his age, he seemed a bit young, even too young to be so skillful with a bow and arrow as Ambit, Ampit and Biktol claimed.

255

Aklang looked around the group. He felt his face slowly burning with embarrassment at the attention he was getting. He shook his head and tried to smile managing a weak flutter from his lips.

Biktol noticed the young man's discomfort and raised a hand. "Let him be, people!" he yelled in a mock anger. "Let him be and let him rest. He's as good as I said and there's no need for him to prove it to you. Come, come sit down," he tapped again at the spot beside him on the bench.

Aklang gratefully walked over and carefully removed the bow and the quiver off his shoulders. He sat down and placed the arrow and the quiver side by side between his legs. He placed his spear beside Bagit's spear that was leaning against the tree trunk. As he settled down, he noted several of the men eyeing his bow as if they were taking its measure. He tried to ignore their inquisitive looks and concentrated on looking around the village. He was surprised to see how similar Bangilo was to his own village. Except for the strange faces, he might as well have been at home.

"How was your travel?" Aklang heard Biktol say to Bagit.

"It was alright, *Apo*," Bagit said. "It was quite a distance but it was no trouble at all."

"Good, good," Biktol said. "It must be important, the reason why you came all the way up here."

"Yes, yes, *Apo*, we came for help," Bagit blurted out.

Biktol immediately raised a hand, stopping Bagit before he could speak any more. He had a feeling the message borne by the boys was of utmost importance but this was not the proper time and the audience to bring it up. "We'll talk about that in due time with the elders," he said wisely. "Don't worry about it for now. We'll get to it."

"Alright. I'm sorry, *Apo*," Bagit said apologetically. Aklang did not say anything. He was thinking of the proper time and manner to bring up their request for help, yet somehow he had the feeling that *Ama* Biktol already knew the purpose of their visit but certainly not the reason behind it.

Thankfully the men around them gradually lost their interest in him and Bagit and soon the talk turned to the weather, then to recent hunting and fishing trips, and on to women, and who was seeing whom in the village. The boys listened respectfully and smiled and laughed with the men when they laughed usually at the expense of someone in the group. It was all in good fun and soon the boys felt at home.

After a while, a lovely woman showed up at the doorway of Biktol's hut and yelled for Biktol to come in and eat.

The laughter abruptly stopped as Biktol reluctantly stood up.

"Come, let's go eat. Don't worry we have enough food," he said as he noted Bagit and Aklang looking at each other suspecting that their silent conversation was about the two of them showing up unexpectedly for the meal and there may not be enough for everyone. "My wife usually cooks for the rest of these bastards because their wives can't cook so they hang around here during meal time!"

The rest of the men laughed but no one took offense because it was the truth. They did not have time to argue and talk much further because then the woman reappeared with wooden bowls.

"We might as well eat here since it looked liked the rest of you lazy monkeys were kicked out by your wives again, so I guess I have to feed you, again!" She said emphatically accenting the last word then stopped as she noticed Aklang and Bagit for the first time. Her face softened with a smile that took the breath away from the two dumbstruck boys. They had never seen someone as beautiful as *Ama* Biktol's wife, except perhaps for *Ina* Ilang. "So, who are these boys that you filthy men are trying to corrupt?"

"Oh, oh, Indra," Biktol said. "These are the boys I told you about who gave us the big buck and the doe a while back. They are *Apo* Dalalo's grandchildren, Aklang and Bagit. Boys, this is my lovely wife, Indra."

"It's an honor to meet you, *Ina*," both boys said almost simultaneously as they stood up.

"Lovely and she can cook too," one of the men said before Indra could say anything to the boys.

"Shut up or you're not eating," Indra said instead to the man that was met with hearty laughter. Then she turned her attention back to Aklang and Bagit. "Well, it's nice to meet you, boys. Welcome to Bangilo. Now, you come with me and eat inside and let these animals eat out here. You!" she pointed to one of the younger men. "Come and bring out the food. We're taking some off, and you can take the rest of the pots out here. If you're not coming, you're not eating. I'm not carrying those pots out for you, understand?

"And you better come inside and eat with us and the boys then," she said to Biktol and turned around before anyone could say anything.

"You heard the boss," Biktol said sheepishly. "Come, we can't keep her waiting."

After the hearty meal where Indra and Biktol mostly did the talking, the boys and their host went back under the tree, fully sated since Indra kept refilling their wooden bowls. She was indeed a great cook and the boys did not mind her giving them more food and they finished everything up with relish.

Most of the men had stayed to eat although three or four went home but now they were back again. The men had just returned from a successful hunt a couple of days ago and they were just enjoying their well-deserved free time, and they used it now to shoot the breeze.

The reappearance of the boys had renewed Ambit's interest in showing Aklang's prowess with the bow. And the conversation naturally gravitated to the best known shooters in the mountains. Names of long gone legendary hunters, some of them Aklang and Bagit had heard of before, others totally unknown, were mentioned and they listened with interest, smiling now and then when a story seemed so preposterous to be true.

"I heard from my *Ama* a long time ago that once he saw *Ama* Lum-kang shoot a wild duck down, one arrow, right on the duck's breast, while in flight!" one of the men said still in awe at the story.

'I did that to a quail in flight, and a thrush, too,' Aklang thought but he kept his thoughts to himself, remembering that *Ama* Lum-kang was Biktol's revered father.

But then Biktol deadpanned, "I'm better than him with a bow," and the village men laughed. Aklang and Bagit looked at each other, wondering why everyone laughed at what Biktol said.

Ampit caught the cousins' bewildered looks and while the laughter was dying down, said, "He barely uses the bow. He prefers the spear and the long knife," nodding at Biktol who pretended to ignore him.

The cousins smiled at one another, slowly getting accustomed to the ways of the Bangilo men who seemed very friendly and easy-going enough. They wondered where their renowned fierceness and brutality in battle came from as they looked at the men's laughing and smiling faces, making fun at one another and taking each other's insults in stride. How could these men inspire so much fear and awe from warriors of the other tribes in the mountains?

Then suddenly the calmness of the early afternoon was shattered by the loud cries of children followed by the persistent barking of dogs. The group of men lolling about under the tree stood up as one, their attention directed to the sound of the barking and crying that was mixed now with warning shouts from older voices, headed towards them.

The source of the noise came into view as a group of young children came up the pathway, running hysterically, emerging from behind a group of huts at the south end of the village. And right behind them was a dog barking and growling furiously with froths of saliva drifting from its mouth. Behind it, likewise running furiously were men with spears and long poles, some with ropes attached to their ends.

"Mad dog! Rabid dog!! Stay away!!" The men were yelling.

The group of running children was now about fifty paces away from the big tree by the center of the village where Biktol and his friends were

258

rushing to meet them but the dog was quickly gaining on the last straggling child, a girl of about six or seven who was crying hysterically and running with all her might. Then to the horror of the men and women watching from the safety of their huts, and the men who were rushing to help the children, the girl tripped and fell down, sprawling on the dusty ground.

The mad dog was just about ten paces behind, running at full momentum and as the girl fell to the ground, it covered half of the distance in a few quick leaps then it launched itself into the air. The rushing men stopped in their tracks in horror, mouths open as they waited in fear for the dog to pounce on the helpless girl.

But then a strange thing happened. The dog let out a pained whimper and dropped a few feet from the girl like it had hit head-on an invisible wall. It shuddered for a moment as if in extreme cold then it lay still, and from its mouth was an arrow shaft still quivering in the air like the wicked flicking tongue of a serpent. The arrow went through the dog's open mouth and its tip protruded out at the base of the skull like a shiny yet bloody piece of amulet sent to protect the innocent.

The crowd of watching villagers and the men from both the front and the back of the running children drew out a collective sigh of relief then a babble of excited cries erupted as they realized what happened. They looked at each other with disbelief in their eyes wondering where the arrow came from, some of them looking up into the heavens.

Biktol turned around and looked behind the men around him and watched with a smile on his face as Aklang put his bow back down to where it was previously leaning against the tree trunk. The rest of the men, realizing that the arrow came from their general direction, likewise turned around, now all of them shaking their head as they saw Aklang, unaware that they were looking at him, calmly trying to keep his bow from falling to the ground, unaffected by all the excitement. His attention was all focused on correcting the balance that was not quite right from where the bow stood on its tip, as the other end that touched the shiny trunk polished by hundreds of leaning backs kept sliding off. Exasperated, Aklang finally picked the bow up and was in the act of putting it over his head when he stopped, noticing for the first time that all eyes seemed to be focused on him. He shrugged his shoulders, his eyes innocently asking the silent question, 'What are you all looking at?'

"I told you so!!" Aklang heard Ambit say in a voice that seemed so loud that everyone in the village could have heard.

Biktol who was the first to turn around reached Aklang and gave the youngster a friendly tap on the shoulder.

"Boy, you are really good!" Biktol said, his face beaming with pride. Then Ambit, Ampit and the rest of their friends were all around them, talking at once and slapping Aklang's shoulders in admiration and awe.

Aklang could not think of anything to say so he remained silent, pleased but blushing and unable to smile from the embarrassment that was growing in him from all the attention that he was getting.

Then the crowd parted as a woman holding the hand of the still sobbing girl who fell to the ground approached. The woman and the girl stopped before Aklang.

"Thank you. Thank you very much," the woman said extending a hand.

"It's nothing, Ina, it's nothing, but you're welcome," Aklang said, clasping her hand in both of his.

"You're not from here," the woman said as she studied Aklang's face. The girl had stopped sobbing by her side and was looking up, open-mouthed, at Aklang.

"No, Ina, we're just visiting," Aklang said and he told her the name of his village.

"My father's sister was married to a man from your village," the woman said. "His name is Dalalo, Ama Dalalo."

Aklang and Bagit looked at one another and smiled. This was their first visit to Bangilo and to their recollection the woman had never been to their village either because they had never seen before.

"Ama Dalalo?" Bagit cried excitedly. "And Ina Mayang?"

"They are our grandparents!" Aklang said to the woman whose surprised expression at the boys' reaction to the name was now replaced with a big smile. She pulled Aklang to her and gave the boy a big embrace. Surprised, Aklang found himself hugging and patting the woman's back.

"My, my, my, my! Oh my! You saved your cousin! You saved your cousin!" the woman kept on repeating as she cried with joy.

Finally she let go, to Aklang's relief, aware now that a big crowd had gathered around them and everyone seemed to be talking at the same time.

"Yeah. Visiting. Ina Mayang's grandchildren. Their cousin. Their Aunt. Amazing. Arrow. Great archer. Hunter." The words echoed incoherently around him and Aklang was barely aware that Biktol was addressing the crowd. Then the crowd fell silent and a space opened up as it parted and an old man, walking slowly with a cane, came forward.

Biktol hurried forward and helped the old man, holding his arm respectfully and walked him to the bench then waited patiently by as the man eased down to sit.

260

"My *Ama* Lum-kang," Biktol said as he motioned for Aklang and Bagit to step forward before the old man. "These boys are *Apo* Dalalo's grandchildren, *Ama*."

"Ahhh, my old friend Dalalo," *Apo* Lum-kang said peering up at Aklang and Bagit. "Both of you do look like him, especially you," he pointed at Bagit who responded with a huge smile.

"You," the old man continued, pointing at Aklang. "You look like the youngest son Kulas, the last time I've seen him. My God, that was ages ago! He must be a grown up man now with children of his own! Are you his son?"

"No, *Apo*, I am his nephew, son of Ittok. *Ama* Kulas is not married yet." Aklang said respectfully.

"Not married? Ahh, it will come. Marriage comes when it comes," the old man said dismissively. "Except maybe for this guy," he pointed at Ambit who scratched his head in consternation as the rest of the group roared with laughter breaking the tension of the moment. Then as if remembering something, *Ama* Lum-kang added, "So who shot the dog?"

"I did, *Apo*," Aklang said softly, feeling his face blush again.

Apo Lum-kang nodded, looking more closely at Aklang, and nodding appreciatively.

"Yes," he finally said. "You must be Dalalo's grandson. Your grandfather was the best archer I have ever seen." He paused as if gathering his thoughts. "Until today," he finally added softly. "What you did is the stuff of legends."

"That's what *Angkay* says about you too, *Apo*, that you're the best archer he'd ever seen," Aklang said hastily, blushing again at being praised. "As for what I did, it was just a lucky shot. I don't think I could do that ever again."

Apo Lum-kang laughed and waved a hand as if dismissing Aklang's words then stopped as he bent down coughing, the waving hand ended up covering his mouth. Biktol gently patted his father's back.

"I'm alright," the old man said. Biktol stood back. "That's what he would say, your grandfather. He was such a gentleman, and very humble but don't you believe him. He was better than I am."

Aklang realized that the old man was just being humble himself like his grandfather and smiled at the similarity in character of the two old men.

"You're just like him, *Apo*," he said. "I bet you're both equally good."

"That we'll never find out," *Apo* Lum-kang said as if in deep thought. "And I'm awfully glad that we never got to find out." He sighed but not with regret. "So how's my old friend?"

"He's well, *Apo*. He sends his greetings."

Apo Lum-kang was silent for a moment.

"We're probably the only two left of our friends," he sighed.

261

"*Ama* Kagaid sends his greetings too, *Apo*," Bagit said.

"Ahh, Kagaid! Yes, of course! That man would be around forever. He never got sick!" The old man shook his head in wonder. "How are his sons, Allong and what was the other boy's name again?"

"Akash, *Apo*," Aklang said. "They're well."

"Good, good, that's good," *Ama* Lum-kang kept on nodding his head. The rest of the village people hanged around listening to the conversation, murmuring among themselves once in a while to repeat what were being said, adding bits and pieces now and then.

"How about that girl of his, the one who married a Christian, how's she?" *Apo* Lum-kang said as if he just remembered.

"Ahh," Aklang said, "about her, *Apo*, about *Ina* Awad, that's the reason why we're here."

Apo Lum-kang looked up at Aklang with concerned face, his brows raised in a silent question.

"Well, she's dead, *Apo*," Aklang said bowing his head. He had decided that he might as well get the message out then and there. It seemed that everyone in the village was present anyway. "The Spaniards had killed her." And he found himself telling the story of Awad and her daughter Ilang and her inherited fight against the Spaniards, and their flight to the mountains and finally, the request for help. Biktol did not interrupt the boy. His father was the chief of the village and if there was anyone who needed to know anything that concerned the village, especially an appeal for help, it would be him, *Ama* Lum-kang.

For a long time it seemed, no one spoke after Aklang was finished talking.

Finally, *Apo* Lum-kang slowly stood up with Biktol extending a hand to support his father.

"Give us a day to talk this over," the old man said to Aklang and Bagit. Then he looked around at the faces of the villagers, "Tonight, I want all the elders to come to my hut and we will talk. This is a matter that we all need to discuss." Then he turned to Biktol. "I want you there, too."

Biktol nodded. They watched as the old man started to walk away, the crowd opening a path again before him. Some turned around to follow his receding back.

"You must stay with us tonight," their Aunt said. "Or as long as you want. Come."

The boys did not argue. They gathered their weapons and after bidding Biktol and Indra who had also been drawn out by all the commotion, good-bye and thanking them again for their hospitality, they left with their newfound relatives.

262

Aklang for his part was relieved to get away from the adoring scrutiny of the crowd. He never did like to be the center of attention.

"I'll come for you in the morning," Biktol said as they walked away.

True to his word, Biktol showed up early the following morning. He found Aklang, Bagit and Igo, their uncle, drinking coffee before a small fire in the backyard. There was the usual chill in the morning and Biktol felt better as he sat down beside them by the fire. A little boy appeared from the house with a warm mug of steaming coffee and handed it to Biktol who thanked him and gave him a playful slap on the butt that the boy easily avoided and he ran away laughing.

After a short banter about the previous day and how well they slept last night, and the cold mountain mornings that seemed colder in Bangilo, Biktol turned serious.

"We met with the elders last night and we have made a decision. We will come," he said gravely. "We will come with a hundred of our warriors. We're getting volunteers today and tomorrow then we will be there at your village in two or three days later."

Aklang and Biktol both smiled.

"Thank you!" Bagit blurted out. "We thank you!"

"Yes, thank you! We're glad you're joining us, *Ama*," Aklang said respectfully.

"Count me and my brother in, Biktol," Igo said. "After all, we're avenging our kinfolk."

Biktol nodded. "Yes, yes, of course." Then he turned his attention to the boys. "We're sorry we could not send more."

"No, no, *Ama*," Aklang quickly said. "If what I heard from my elders is anywhere near the truth, a hundred of you are more than enough. Thank you." He had often heard to the point of irritation in their village that a Bangilo warrior was equal to five men in battle. He had doubts about that but they did seem well built and capable enough. Then he mentally estimated the troop *Ina* Ilang had and figured a hundred was almost a fifth of their number. One hundred warriors were certainly generous indeed.

"Well, that's settled then," Biktol said smiling finally. He loved the excitement of battle and he was looking forward to going down to the land of the Ilocanos. "Will you be staying here for a couple more days then go down with us?

The cousins looked at one another and came to a silent agreement.

"No, *Apo*," Bagit said. "We'd best go back today and give the good word as soon as we could. Maybe we will leave around noontime. The folks may be worried that we might have gotten lost on our way here."

"Or leave a little earlier before noon perhaps," Aklang added.

"Very well then," Biktol said. "I'd like for you to stay longer but I think it is best that you go back soon so your parents will not worry so much. And tell them we'll be right behind you, and again tell *Ama* Dalalo and *Ama* Kagaid we're sorry for the small number we can afford to send."

"I'll have your *Ina* Me-ey prepare some food for your journey," Igo said. He turned his face toward the hut and yelled, "Aloyyyy!!!"

The little boy came back, running.

"Tell your *Ina* to fix some food for your cousins to bring for their trip back home. They're leaving before noon!" Igo said.

Aloy gave his cousins a brief look that showed his disappointment for them leaving so soon.

"We'll be back, little cousin," Aklang winked and smiled.

Aloy's face broke into a grin then he turned around and ran back to the hut.

Chapter Forty

"I don't like this, Tiago, I don't like this a bit at all," *Don* Manuel said. "How could people simply vanish in such a small town and nobody knows anything?"

"It puzzles me too, *Capitán*," Tiago said meekly, "especially Cortez and Catriz. Some say they have deserted but I don't think so, not Cortez, or even Catriz for that matter. Besides, where would they go? Manila is too far away."

Don Manuel did not say anything. He and Tiago were by the stables in the fort. He just rode in and his horse was standing by one of the hitch rails, still saddled and sidestepping every once in a while trying to rid itself of pesky flies, its tail flicking constantly in irritation. He stared at his horse pensively for a moment, deciding on whether he was going to unsaddle it or just leave it on as he may be riding out soon anyway. He sighed and turned to Tiago.

"What do you suggest we do?"

"We have scoured the town, even the villages by the coast, and found nothing," Tiago said dolefully. "I'd like to send two or three patrols back out, spread them around farther, maybe rouse people up, rough them up if needed and see what comes out. Somebody out there knows something and I intend to find out. I think it's time to take the gloves off, *Capitán* and talk with them in our language."

Don Manuel looked down at his *Sargento* and saw the fire in Tiago's eyes. He was not sure if it was caused by the thought of someone getting hurt or killed.

"Let the patrols out but refrain from unnecessary violence, Tiago," he finally said. "We don't want to drive more of them to join the rebellion."

"Si, *Capitán*," Tiago said trying to predetermine what was necessary and unnecessary violence and deciding that there was no difference between them. He was simply going to do what had to be done.

The *Capitán* looked back at his horse. There was no need to unsaddle. It seemed he would just have to ride back and go to the Dela Cuestas instead. He'd rather see Isabella than stay in the fort for the rest of the day.

He was about to tell Tiago that he was riding back out to town when they heard a commotion coming from the front gate. Both of them walked briskly around the corner of the stables and through the parade ground to the courtyard by the gate where they met one of the guards, Cortazar, hurrying towards them and behind him was a *mestizo* that both recognized as the

265

teniente del barrio, the village chief of *Camangga-an. Don* Manuel searched his brain for the man's name but somehow it eluded him.

"Recognized the man, Tiago?" He said. "What's his name?"

"Macario, *Señor*. He's the *Teniente* of *barrio Camangga-an.*"

"*Capitán! Capitán!* The *caballero* here needs to see you!" Cortazar said as soon as he executed a harried salute.

"*Buenos Dias, Señores,*" *Don* Macario said. "I am afraid I have to be the bearer of bad news."

"*Buenos Dias, Señor* Macario. Go on." *Don* Manuel said. "What is it?"

Señor Macario beamed that the *Capitán* knew his name, but then he remembered the reason for his visit and his face turned grave.

"We found two dead bodies, *Señor*, by the river that flows through our *barrio.*"

"Who? The missing friends of *Señor* Vicos?" Manuel asked.

"I am afraid not, *Señor*," Macario said. "*Soldados, Señor*. Your soldiers. They are in uniform. One of them is that big soldier, *Señor* Cortez, I believe. I have seen the other one before but I don't know his name. His uniform was torn off from getting dragged in the river."

"Catriz," Tiago hissed under his breath. "Must be Catriz," he said more loudly for the others' benefit. "They went out together two nights ago looking for Miguel."

The *Capitán* looked at Tiago, then to *Don* Macario and Cortazar with no expression apparent on his face. "How? How did they die?"

"We're not really certain, *Señor*. The bodies are bloated but they seem to have puncture wounds, perhaps a knife, or a sword or maybe a spear?" Macario said.

Don Manuel sighed as he pondered what he just heard then he spoke gravely.

"We're bringing them in. Tiago, assemble a four-man detail, bring the flatbed carriage and we'll go as soon as you're ready. I'm coming with you. Ride with us back, *Señor* Macario, and I thank you for letting us know right away."

"*De nada, Señor.* I am sorry to be the bearer of such news," *Don* Macario said.

Don Manuel waved a hand in dismissal then looked at the guard. "Thank you, Cortazar. You can go back to your post."

Cortazar saluted smartly and turned toward the front gate. Tiago likewise walked away to get his men.

"Come, come, *Señor* Macario. Let's get out of this heat and have something cold to drink. The lemonade that our cook here makes is exceptional," *Don* Manuel beckoned to the village chief then turned around towards the mess hall. *Don* Macario gratefully followed. The ride from Camangga-an was hot and dusty. He hoped one of the guards had sense and kind enough to give his horse that he left by the gate some water.

Tiago meanwhile was troubled. Who among the timid Indios could have been brave and able enough to kill both Cortez and Catriz? He knew Cortez was a skilled soldier and a veteran of many battles. It would not be easy to kill him even if he was ambushed and taken by surprise.

Tiago thought of the possible suspects and as much as he wracked his brains, he could not come up with anyone, except perhaps a whole group of rebels, but he would have known if they were even in the vicinity of the town. And as far as he was aware of, there had been no reported sightings of them for the last month or so.

Then he remembered Awad's own brother asking for her and visiting the fort. He seemed docile enough but Tiago knew that one could never tell with the *Itnegs*. They were friendly but fearless and God only knew what they could be capable of when goaded to fight.

And then there was the other *Itneg* who had showed up by the river, the one who had beaten him and the *Capitán* soundly and so easily in their mock duels. Could he have had anything to do with Cortez and Catriz's death? Tiago did not know how good a fighter Awad's brother was but that other *Itneg*, Tiago was sure, could have bested either Cortez or Catriz easily. Or even both at the same time.

But why, what would his motive be? Have the *Itnegs* somehow found out about Awad's death? But how could they? How was it possible?

And Tiago shook his head in frustration. He had no answers. Just like how the *Capitán* felt, Tiago did not like it a bit, not a bit at all.

His head still swirling with unanswered questions, Tiago went to the barracks and roused up three six-man teams. The soldiers grumbled under their breaths, sore at being pulled from their siestas, but they were fired up and their faces turned to grim anger and determination when Tiago told them about Cortez and Catriz. Most of them hated Cortez's guts but he was still one of them. And Catriz was a likeable man.

Tiago sent them out in three different directions to look for Miguel and find out anything they could about the killers of Cortez and Catriz. Watching their grim faces as they left the fort, Tiago had no doubts that they would be coming back with answers, forced or not, and he pitied the unfortunate Indios who would cross their paths.

He would lead the fourth squad himself as soon they brought the bodies back to the fort.

He picked four more soldiers and ordered them to bring out the flat-bed carriage. They set out for *Camangga-an* with *Señor* Macario and the *Capitán* in the lead.

Chapter Forty One

"Settle down," Kulas said, "why don't you sleep?"

Akash paused from walking toward the window for probably the tenth time that morning. He looked at his friend who was squatting calmly on the floor, ignoring a chair that was right beside him.

After leaving the Chinese place, Kulas had wanted them to go through Paing and on to the foot of Mount *Bullagaw* where they could lay low for a while as they waited for Ilang's rebels and the helping *Itneg* tribes to make their move. But Akash, whose foot was still not fully recovered, suggested that they go to Awad's place instead. After thinking it over, it seemed a good idea because nobody would suspect them to be there as long as they kept out of sight.

They staked the house a bit to make sure it was not being watched then they went in without any trouble. Akash had kept one window unlatched when he returned the key to the neighbor, Ana, just in case he needed a place to sleep as he had intended to get back to town to continue the search for Awad, without having to bother the neighbors. He had not expected that Awad was dead, killed for that matter, and for him to ever get into the house, but it had worked out somehow. Although key or no key, or even if all the windows were latched, they could have had entered anyways. The latches were flimsy and easy to get to and they would have had the windows opened in no time at all. Akash never did understand why the Ilocanos locked their houses anyway. Did they not trust their neighbors?

They had chanced a fire that night, confident that the smoke coming out of the house would not be noticed in the dark. They cooked enough rice and dried fish and jerky that they found in the makeshift pantry that would tide them through the day, deciding not to risk cooking during the daytime for the smoke that may betray their presence. Akash hoped neither Ana nor Quintin would have reason to check on the house, but if it came to it, he would have to deal with them and hoped they would not say anything to anyone. It was a lot to hope for and expect of Ana who he heard could not keep her tongue still, but they would just have to chance it.

It was not easy for two active hunters who were used to open spaces to stay indoors in an extended period of time and the confinement was getting to Akash. However, Kulas seemed to be taking it in stride.

Akash looked at Kulas and wondered yet again how his friend could be so calm and composed as if he was sitting by a cold spring in the forest instead of a crummy, darkened strange room.

"I already slept," he said.

"So sleep again," Kulas smiled. "We'll be up all night."

They had expected this situation when they decided to stay in the house. Keep inside during the daytime and venture out only during the night. They had been up and out last night, same as the night before, hunting for soldiers, the *guardia civiles*, but they had not encountered anyone. Akash had wanted to go by the fort but Kulas talked him out of it. It would be foolishness for them to do so. If there were no night patrols tonight, perhaps they would venture going out during daylight although Kulas was not keen to the idea. Akash though was ready for an all out war. Kulas had never seen his friend act this way. He wondered if this was his way of mourning his sister. Or was he just fueled by sheer anger and the need for revenge?

Kulas stood up and walked into the kitchen. He went by the clay stove, picked up a piece of firewood and poked around the ashes looking for the sweet potatoes that he had covered in hot ash the night before. He was not exactly hungry but munching on something would keep him busy for a while and would certainly make the time seem to pass by a little faster. Or so he hoped.

"Want a sweet potato?" he asked Akash who had followed him into the kitchen.

"'Might as well have one," Akash replied. "Let me see if there's a *tagapulot* someplace," he added as he scrounged around the kitchen looking for the sweet dried molasses that the Ilocanos kept to sweeten everything from coffee to rice cakes and grilled roots like sweet potatoes and yams. He found a piece, shaped like the shell of a small turtle, in a basket that was hanging from the rafters. He went to the table, sat down and cut the dried molasses in half. Kulas joined him at the table, juggling two hot sweet potatoes in his big hands. They ate in silence for a while, alternately biting on their potatoes and the dried *tagapulot*.

"Not bad," Kulas finally said as he finished off the last of the sweet molasses.

Akash did not say anything but he nodded. He was actually feeling better after the snack. In fact he was feeling sleepy and he said so.

"Good idea," Kulas smiled, and he stretched down himself on the long bench that he was sitting on. Akash can go sleep in one of the beds if he wanted. This was good enough for him.

Akash sighed, looked at his friend and went through the living room and into the bedroom that he usually used when he was visiting. He felt a little sadness as he passed by Awad's room, but he ignored it and murmured a promise to his dead sister.

"They'll pay for this, my sister. I'll send as much of them to you in the afterworld, I promise."

In the kitchen, try as he might, Kulas could not sleep. His mind was racing in so many directions. Ilang and her fight against the Spaniards. Was it for her avowed cause to liberate the Ilocanos against the white invaders or was it more personal, simply just to avenge her husband's and now her own mother's deaths? Was she a true patriot to the Ilocanos or just a woman bent on vengeance? And how about him, was he gladly joining into the fray to avenge *Ina* Awad or to help Ilang in her cause regardless of what exactly it may be? Perhaps, it were all one and the same, Ilang's patriotism and her search for vengeance, and him helping out to exact that vengeance, for Awad or for Ilang's husband.

And people had to die in the process. That was the simple truth that nagged at him. It had always been so, since before the time of their forefathers. A death was avenged by another death. But should it always be so? Must people die to satisfy that thirst for vengeance? Was it exacting justice to do so? Sometimes he wondered, and he wondered now, and it was keeping him from falling asleep.

And he and Akash were already part of the killing and it surprised him how easy it was. A bow was pulled, launching an arrow that whispered in the air and somebody died. Actually two died the night before from their arrows and the count would surely grow. The killing had just begun. No, actually it had begun long before the death of the two soldiers. And more will die. That was another sad truth.

Yet despite all the questions that he had no answers to, he somehow did not feel any sort of remorse. The soldiers that he and Akash had killed may not have had anything to do with Awad's death but he did not feel sorry for them. They were the enemy and this was war.

That was his truth and Akash's truth for the moment and he felt no remorse yet somehow sleep eluded him.

He sprawled on the bench with eyes wide open, looking at the ceiling for a long time, having given up on having a quick nap or a decent shuteye. From within the house, he could hear Akash snoring and he tried to ignore the sound but it kept boring into his consciousness until he could not stand it any longer. He got up, picked his bow and arrow up then cautiously went into the backyard. There was enough foliage there from the various fruit trees that dotted the yard and he hoped the nosy neighbor Ana would not see him. Not that it mattered anyway, because after tonight, they would be out of here whether Akash wanted to or not. The damn place was too close to the fort and there was no easy way to escape without fighting your way out every step of the way especially if the backyard was covered.

He sat on the *balitang* under the *Caimito* tree, resting his back against its big trunk, thankful that he was hidden from the probing eyes of the neighbors. There was a cool breeze blowing softly and it relaxed him a bit. He closed his eyes, consciously banishing all thoughts away and pretty soon his breathing became regular and he was asleep sitting up with his bow clutched in his arms.

Chapter Forty Two

Lorenzo Ajel de Barrozo had no dreams of becoming a soldier. He was enjoying a trade as an apprentice to a cartographer at a small print shop across the Cathedral in Madrid when fate intervened in the form of a *Señorita* who turned out to be a *Señora*, and an ensuing brawl with the aggrieved *Señor* and his friends sent Lorenzo Ajel seeking the refuge of His Majesty's army. He had been a soldier since and that was almost ten years ago.

Despite the occasional lapse of judgment especially where women were concerned, Lorenzo Ajel had a good mind in his head. And he was thinking now as he led his six-man team out of the fort.

Lorenzo Ajel de Barrozo did not like Cortez much but Catriz was a decent enough human being who was actually regarded with fondness by everyone. He was gregarious and an easy man to talk to even when the weather was so foul and humid that everyone tended to be irritable and cantankerous just for the hell of it. As he thought more about it, he actually liked the man. But even if he did not, Cortez and Catriz were still his brothers in arms.

As for Miguel, Lorenzo did not care much for the man. He knew what the man did to Diego and despite his weakness for women, Lorenzo Ajel regarded himself an honorable man who did not condone treachery. So as far as Lorenzo was concerned, he was going to find the killers of Catriz and Cortez first. But in his heart, he hoped Miguel had a hand on the killings so he had a better reason to look for the man. And then he would not be asking him questions either.

And now as he led his team out of the fort, he decided to go first to the last known place where Cortez and Catriz were last seen alive according to the information that he received from the *Sargento*. One of the teams headed north towards Cabugao, while the other headed south. Lorenzo and his team headed towards the town and on to the slaughterhouse.

Apo Andang and her help, Gorio, as well as the customers eating around the sparse tables of the *carinderia* were not surprised to see the soldiers headed by Lorenzo when they showed up at the slaughterhouse, for by then everyone in town and the neighboring *barrios* and *sitios* knew about the deaths of the two Spanish soldiers. The locals watched in apprehension as the soldiers approached the *carinderia* when they did not see anyone at the closed slaughterhouse. From the look in the Spanish soldiers' faces, the locals knew that their appearance was far from a friendly visit and they were not looking for food.

Lorenzo Ajel dismounted and beckoned at Gorio who was going from table to table delivering food orders and collecting empty dishes. Gorio put down the empty dishes that he was holding at a vacant table and approached the soldier meekly, twisting and wringing the damp rag that he used for cleaning the tables in his nervous hands.

"*Buenos Dias, Señor*, how can I help you?" Gorio asked bowing his head respectfully.

"*Buenos Dias*," Lorenzo said cupping Gorio's chin with his left hand, forcing the young man's face up and looked him in the eyes. "There were two soldiers who came here two nights ago, where did they go afterwards?"

"I-I-I don't know, *Señor*," Gorio said nervously.

Lorenzo Ajel dropped his left hand but his right came up so swiftly that his open palm had connected with Gorio's face with a sickening slapping sound before anyone realized what was happening. Gorio, caught by surprise, staggered briefly to catch his balance but his legs gave way and he went sprawling to the ground. He sat up slowly, dazed and confused, but somehow he had held on to the rag and he now instinctively put it against his throbbing left cheek. He felt something coming out of his nose and without thinking, wiped it off with the rag. He looked at the rag, now colored with blood, and felt his eyes welling with tears. He slowly shook his head and looked up at Lorenzo with tears now flowing freely from his eyes.

"It's the truth, *Señor*, I don't know where they went after they left here," he sobbed.

Lorenzo Ajel reached down and grasped the boy's hair to raise him up. Gorio pushed himself up with his hands, terrified, but he stood up and defiantly looked at the soldier.

"I swear, *Señor*, I speak the truth," Gorio said. "I don't know where they went."

"He speaks the truth, *Señor*," *Apo* Andang's voice softly said from behind the counter.

Lorenzo Ajel de Barrozo looked at the old woman. He saw fear in the eyes of the *Ina* Andang yet she defiantly and bravely held his gaze. The old woman was telling the truth. And Lorenzo Ajel saw something else and his face softened. He thought he saw in the old woman's face the visage of his own grandmother. He let go of Gorio's hair. The boy hastily moved away.

Lorenzo Ajel slowly walked toward the counter of the *carinderia*. He stopped in front of the old woman, putting his hands, palms spread down on the counter.

"*Señora*, you must already know that the two soldiers are dead, murdered for that matter," Lorenzo Ajel softly said. "There's a killer or killers out there, and as you already may have suspected, we are looking for them.

274

The soldiers were last seen here alive. I am sorry to bother you but we need answers."

The old woman nodded but did not speak.

"Now, they ate here, right?"

Again the old woman nodded silently.

"What time did they leave?"

"We were closing, *Señor*, when they left so it was around nine o'clock," *Apo* Andang said.

"Very well," Lorenzo Ajel said. "Then which direction did they take?"

Apo Andang hesitantly pointed to the road heading east. "That way, *Señor*," she said. "They went that way. It was dark, *Señor*, and I do not know if they went straight ahead or changed direction later on when they disappeared in the dark. It's the truth, *Señor*."

Lorenzo Ajel nodded. He held his gaze at the old woman's eyes and saw the fear had gone out and what was left was the truth and with it a silent plea for compassion.

"*Gracias, Señora*," Lorenzo Ajel mumbled and was about to turn around when he remembered something. "They may have vanished from your sight, *Señora*, but have you heard anything afterwards?"

"Heard, *Señor*?" *Apo* Andang said.

"Yes, *Señora*, any sound, anything that would have been unusual in the night, especially coming from that direction," Lorenzo Ajel pointed to the direction that the old woman had previously indicated and noted the Chinese establishment down the road, and beyond it, he remembered now was the river that ran through the *barrio* of *Camangga-an*.

Apo Andang was silent for a moment as if she was trying to remember, but in reality she was fighting inwardly with herself. She had heard the shouting for the sounds traveled clearly during the night. And then there was the unmistakable sound of a rifle shot. She knew the shouting and yelling were from the Chinese place, would she dare bring the soldiers to their doors? She looked at the soldier's face and settled her gaze on his eyes. Where there was anger and fury before, the eyes of the soldier were kind and compassionate now, intent only in seeking the truth and not in inflicting any harm.

Apo Andang hesitated only briefly, then she said, "There were yelling and shouting shortly after, *Señor*, by the Chinese place. Then there was the sound of rifle shot. Afterwards there was nothing else, so help me God." The old woman lowered her face in anguish as if she had just betrayed her own son. She involuntarily stepped back as she felt the soldier's hand touched her shoulder but she settled down and raised her head as she felt the touch was gentle and the accompanying soft squeeze was of gratitude.

Her eyes spoke a silent plea for compassion for her, for her people and the Chinese as she returned the soldier's gaze, but the eyes that looked back at her had gone blank as the soldier simply nodded without any expression and turned away.

Without saying a word, Lorenzo Ajel mounted his horse and led his troop down the road toward the Chinese place.

There was a broken down fence made out of bamboo poles at the side of the structure and they hitched their horses there. The first two doors that they came up to were closed so without much of a ceremony they kicked them down. Behind the first door they found an ancient Chinese woman cowering in fear babbling incoherently. Lorenzo Ajel tried to talk to her in Ilocano and Spanish but the old woman just prattled on in incomprehensible chatter. Ricardo wanted to slap some sense into her but Lorenzo would not have any of it. He just could not let any injury done to such a frail old woman, besides, he had decided after they looked around the house that she could not have had anything to do with either Cortez or Catriz.

The second door opened to a store that seemed to sell bulk grains. There were big bins filled with milled rice, corn, peanuts, and various dried beans that lined one wall. In a room at the back they found a family of four, a middle aged Chinaman, his wife and two young children, an eight year old boy and a girl who was probably five years old. The family had obviously seen the soldiers coming down the road and hurriedly closed shop hoping that they would pass them by.

Lorenzo Ajel herded them to the front of the store. The man had been kow-towing incessantly since the soldiers found them in the back room and he was bowing now yet again. The wife was whimpering in fear, but bravely trying to placate the two young children who were nervously sobbing.

Lorenzo grabbed the Chinaman by the scruff of his neck and literally put his face up to the man's face.

"No Chinese gibberish, you understand?" he said in the Ilocano dialect in a low threatening voice. "I know you people speak Ilocano as well as I do."

The Chinese nodded nervously, "Wen, Apo." Yes, sir. He looked at the soldier's eyes that had gone blank, devoid of any emotion and the Chinese knew he had to tell nothing but the truth or he was a dead man. Perhaps even if he told the truth, he was already a dead man, but maybe, just maybe, the soldier would let his family live.

"The soldados who came here, and don't tell me they did not come, what happened to them?" Lorenzo Ajel said in a calm voice as if he was giving an advice instead of asking a question. He let go of the Chinaman as he did so.

276

"They came here looking for *Señor* Miguel but he was not here and they went to the store next door, *Señor*," the man pointed to the wall indicating the middle of the building. "And that's the last I've seen them."

Lorenzo Ajel made a sudden move and he had the Chinaman's pig-tail in his left hand, and in his right his dagger appeared as if from nowhere. For a big man, Lorenzo was quick, very quick. The Chinaman quivered fearfully as his wife shrieked in terror.

"Then what happened?" Lorenzo Ajel now had the point of the dagger under the chin of the Chinaman whose eyes had grown unnaturally big in sheer terror.

"I heard a commotion, *Señor*, then the sound of a gun, then nothing. That's all I heard. I was too scared to go out and look. That's the truth, *Señor*. I did not see anything." His Adam's apple bobbed up and down as he nervously talked and he tried to swallow but his mouth had gone dry. He could not lower his head not only because of the dagger against his chin but his pig-tail was also held firmly up by the soldier's left hand.

Lorenzo Ajel lowered his dagger hand down and the Chinaman's eyes showed a bit of relief but in a flash they went back to an expression of sheer surprise as he felt the knife cutting through his pig-tail. With a quick slash, so fast that no one was able to react until it was done and the severed pig-tail was dangling from Lorenzo's fist, the Chinaman's sign of male superiority was gone. The man cried in terror while his wife breathed a sigh of relief in not seeing any blood and her husband was still alive, regardless of his shattered perceived masculine dignity.

Lorenzo Ajel dropped the man's hair on the floor, gestured with his head to the other soldiers to go next door, and without a word walked out of the room. The family rushed together in a big embrace, everyone sobbing with relief that nobody was terribly hurt.

When Lorenzo Ajel walked into the next store he saw three Chinese men standing by the counter with their hands raised over their heads. Before them were three of his soldiers calmly holding their rifles, pointed casually at the chest of the man before him.

Lorenzo Ajel surveyed the store. It was obviously bigger than the other ones, bigger space, more merchandise, and more variety of products, produce and dry goods. He wondered for a moment that perhaps these Chinese owned the whole place and the rests were simply tenants. He caught himself and tried to concentrate on the Chinamen and banish the thoughts of commerce from his mind but it was something ingrained in him that he ended up giving the place another once over before he took a step toward his men. Then as he was in the middle of the room something caught his eye. He paused and his eyes roamed the whole store once again then back to a merchandise stand close to where he stood that had caught his attention.

Lorenzo Ajel grew up as a tradesman and was around stores and businesses a lot before he ran off and joined His Majesty's army and he always had that sense of the proper order in displaying merchandise. There was just something in the merchandise stand beside him that was somehow off yet he could not pinpoint what it was. He turned around slowly, taking in the whole room while his soldiers gave him quizzical looks and the Chinese nervously eyed one another. Lorenzo Ajel completed his survey of the room and his eyes went back to the stand and then looked down at the rug where the stand stood. That was what caught his attention. It was the only merchandise stand in the whole place that stood on a rug.

Lorenzo Ajel quickly took a couple of steps and kicked the stand toppling it over, the merchandise it contained flying and breaking all over the room. He bent down and yanked the rug. The three Chinamen looked at one another, trembling with fear. The old man was beginning to perspire. He always perspired when he got nervous.

The three soldiers had their attention on Lorenzo now, holding the rug in his hand and they followed his gaze that was focused on the scuffed and stained floor. With the soldiers' attention diverted off them, the two young Chinese bolted out the door going to the backroom. They were through the second door when the soldiers reacted and started shooting. All they hit were the walls and the swinging interior door.

Ricardo and two of the soldiers raced down the small hallway and on through the backroom where they passed the curtained cubicles inside of which the dope addled customers were stirring, wakened up from their stupor by the shooting. Ricardo stopped, surprised at what he was seeing, the two Chinese momentarily pushed from his mind. The other two soldiers likewise paused but Ricardo yelled at them.

"Go and get those two! I'll take care of these *bastardos*!"

The other two ran out the open back door where beyond they saw the backs of the two young Chinese running side by side. Behind the pig sty at the back of the house, unseen by the soldiers, the old Chinese woman and the young girls cowered in fear. They had run out when the soldiers were at the first store.

The pursuing soldiers stopped, aimed and fired their rifles at the fleeing young men, but the distance was too great for their poor marksmanship and they missed their targets terribly but they thought they hit one when one of the pursued tripped and fell down. His brother stopped a short distance away, then seeing the soldiers had also stopped and were in the process of re-loading their single shot rifles, he ran back to his brother.

"Ming!" he yelled kneeling down by his brother's fallen body, his face contorted with grief. "Ming!"

Ming, who had his wind knocked off him by his hard fall, stirred and began to rise to his brother's relief, said frantically, "I'm alright! I tripped and fell! Run, Ding Hap, run!"

Ding Hap stood up and reached down for his brother's stretched hand and pulled him up. They were about to start running when both noticed one of the soldiers running back to the house in a hurry but with great difficulty for just a little bit below one shoulder, the shaft of an arrow protruded like a growth of sapling. Behind the running soldier and where they stood a moment ago re-loading their rifles, one of the soldiers lay, also with an arrow in his prone motionless body.

The brothers, bewildered, looked around them and saw no one. Then a sharp whistle startled them. From a corner of the house, one of the *Itnegs* who had killed the soldiers a couple of days ago stood, signaling at them to run toward the river then he vanished from sight. The brothers looked at one another and ran as fast as they could without looking back.

Kulas had slept for a while under the *Caimito* tree behind Ilang's house, but somehow something was tugging at his consciousness and he woke up with a start unsure of what was bothering him. Was it Ilang? Somehow he felt a tinge of guilt for leaving her up in the mountains when they had just reunited after such a long time. He thought it over and decided that was not it. It was something else and he had no idea. He wanted to go back up to the house but he did not want to wake Akash up.

He stood up and walked to the woods behind the house, careful to avoid anyone of the neighbors. He found the trail towards the river and followed it and took a quick dip in the cold water. Refreshed he walked down its farther bank away from the town, going south realizing later on that he was close to the location where they had dumped the two soldiers a couple of days ago. Curious, he moved closer but he saw nothing. The bodies may have floated down unimpeded then. Looking across the river, he saw the Chinese house and before he knew it, he was crossing the river, swimming for a bit where it was deeper. He heard the cries from the second store as soon as he got out of the water. He ran, dripping wet, and crouched behind the pig sty where he startled the Chinese woman and her young children. He hushed them down, signed for them to keep silent then he ran to the corner of the house.

Then a short while later the two young Chinese came barging out of the house followed shortly by the two soldiers. When the soldiers stopped and started shooting, Kulas took out his bow.

Inside the store, Lorenzo Ajel had his sword out and pointed at the neck of the old Chinaman who was nervously talking, when Ricardo barged in from the back room.

"Lorenzo, *Itnegs* behind the house! Alfredo is down and Antonio is hurt, in the back room!" Ricardo yelled.

The Chinaman stopped talking. Lorenzo Ajel looked at Ricardo. "What *Itnegs*?"

"Out there in the back," Ricardo said. "Alfredo and Antonio were running after the two Chinese who ran away but they were ambushed by the *Itnegs*! Antonio was able to get away but he is hurt! He's in the back room."

"Have you seen them, the *Itnegs*?"

"No," Ricardo said shaking his head, "but it's got to be *Itnegs*, they're the only ones who use bow and arrows."

"Don't move!" Lorenzo Ajel said to the Chinaman who dutifully sat down on the floor. "Watch him," he said to the rest of his squad and he followed Ricardo to the back room, pausing in surprise as he emerged from the interior door at the peculiar floral smell that hit him and the curtained cubicles and at the men sitting on the floor looking back at him with glazed and unseeing eyes.

"Opium." Lorenzo Ajel heard Ricardo say but he could not get his eyes off the men. Then Antonio grunted in pain where he sat on the floor by the back door, legs sprawled apart, back hunched where the shaft of an arrow was sticking out.

"*Ajudame*," Antonio from Catalonia said, grimacing in pain.

"Help him," Lorenzo Ajel said to Ricardo as he peered outside the back door. He saw the body of Alfredo a few yards away. He looked beyond the body to the open field dotted with bushes and shrubs and to the river farther down and saw no one. The two young Chinese were gone and so did the *Itnegs*, if the shooter or shooters were really *Itnegs*. 'They must be *Itnegs*,' Lorenzo thought. The Ilocanos did not use bows and arrows. He had yet to see or hear about them using bows with accuracy.

Lorenzo Ajel stepped out into the backyard and walked to where Alfredo lay. The *hombre* was dead, shot with a well aimed arrow through the heart. "*Itnegs*, no doubt," Lorenzo said under his breath. He looked around him and saw no one. With a heavy heart he walked back to the house.

"Pick him up and put him on his horse. Tie him up so he won't fall down," Lorenzo Ajel said to Ricardo, gesturing at Antonio who was writhing in pain but otherwise fully alert. "I'm going back for Alfredo. He's dead. We're heading back to the fort."

Once more he went out the back door and walked to Alfredo. He grunted as he picked up and hefted the lifeless body over his broad shoulders. Then slowly he stood up and went around the house to the front yard where the horses were tethered. He was looking down as he turned the corner and he noticed barefooted prints on the dusty ground, parts of which were still drying up.

"*Itnegs*," Lorenzo Ajel hissed again in anger this time, "they must have come from the river." Then a moment later on as two of the soldiers were tying down Alfredo's body on his horse, he thought, 'Why? Why are they even in town and killing soldiers?'

Lorenzo Ajel had no answers. He did not know that Gabriela's mother was *Itneg* and she was dead. He took the reins of Alfredo's horse and led it beside his own tethered horse. He tied the dead man's reins to the horn of his saddle. Off to the side, Ricardo, holding in his hand the reins of Antonio's horse, had already saddled up. Antonio sat swaying on top of his horse, his hands clasped on the saddle horn, trying to stay awake and hang on, his face grimacing in pain. The rest of the soldiers had likewise mounted after they had secured Alfredo to his horse.

"Go, I'll follow," Lorenzo said to the other soldiers, then without further saying a word walked back to house. He entered the first store through the broken down door, then emerged a short while later guiding the old withered Chinese woman out. He led her to the fence and then he stopped and pointed to the road beyond. Without a whimper the old woman walked away and on towards the road.

Then Lorenzo Ajel turned around and walked back once more into the store. He came out shortly holding a couple of oil lamps. He unscrewed the lamps and splashed the walls with oil and poured the rest on the floors as he walked casually along the length of the wooden structure. When he stepped down to the ground, he took a match from his pocket, struck it against a post and tossed the lit match over his shoulders. The match landed on a patch of oil on the wooden floor.

Lorenzo Ajel de Barrozo, the once upon a long time ago a printer's apprentice who had not dreamt of ever becoming a soldier, stepped up on his horse and rode away while behind him the Chinese place went up in flames.

Over across the river, Kulas and the two young Chinese watched the smoke as the place burned. They saw people scrambling out of the burning building. The two young men hoped their Uncle was one of those who were able to get out. They sighed with relief as they spotted their Aunt towing their young cousins along and running safely away from the blaze.

"I keep saving your miserable lives," Kulas finally said to them in *Ilocano*. "What are you going to do now?"

The two Chinese looked at one another and began arguing in their language while Kulas watched with amusement. After a moment of listening to fascinating but incomprehensible sounds, Kulas finally had enough and started to walk away. He had gone a few yards off when one of the young men, Ding Hap, called after him.

"We want to come with you! You fight the soldiers, we want to fight too!" he said in *Ilocano*.

"We cannot go back to town. They will kill us," Ming added.

Kulas stopped and turned around.

"Can you fight?" he said.

"Yes, yes we can fight!" the brothers answered in unison.

"How about your uncle, maybe he is still alive. And his wife, and your cousins?"

"They can stay or go back to China, or down to Binondo," Ming said.

"Please let us come with you," Ding Hap said.

Kulas thought for a moment. He did not know of the places they mentioned, China or Binondo, or if they were near or far and he did not care one way or the other.

"Alright," he finally said. "But get out of my way."

He turned and the two young men followed uncertainly.

Chapter Forty Three

The *Capitán* was still at the fort when Lorenzo Ajel and his squad rode back in with the body of Alfredo and the wounded Antonio. He stood calmly as the soldiers approached but his burning eyes belied his outward composure. Beside him, Tiago stood grim-faced trying hard to control the rage growing inside him and he felt himself losing. Without saying a word to the *Capitán*, Tiago dashed to meet the approaching horsemen and he got there just in time to catch Antonio, as the soldier, with the arrow still sticking out from him like a marker and weakened by loss of blood, fell off his horse, barely conscious. Tiago grasped the man around the chest and slowly eased him down to the ground. By then a group of soldiers had gathered around them.

"Bring him to the infirmary, *andale*!" Tiago yelled to the soldiers. Two of them came forward and picked up Antonio, supporting him between them, and they headed toward the infirmary.

Another soldier took the reins of the horse that carried the dead Alfredo and led it off to the stables. Alfredo would have to share the flatbed carriage with Cortez and Catriz for the moment until their official burial was arranged, perhaps tomorrow. The soldier shook his head in disbelief. It had been a long time since they had buried more than two of their rank at one time.

"*Esto es malo*," the soldier said to himself as he positioned the horse by the carriage and gently pulled the dead body down to rest beside Cortez and Catriz. "This is bad." He covered his nose and breathed through his mouth as he whiffed the putrid smell from the rotting bodies of Cortez and Catriz. Both were covered with layers of lime and wrapped in a cocoon of heavy canvas blankets but the rotten smell still came through. 'We should have buried them as soon as we got them,' the soldier thought but remembered that *Padre* Joaquin was out visiting parishes without any assigned priests up north and would not be back until tomorrow. Poor souls had to have a proper Christian burial.

Inside his office, the *Capitán* stolidly sat behind his desk as he listened to Lorenzo Ajel and Ricardo recount what happened at the Chinese place. The two soldiers stood side by side in front of the *Capitán*'s desk. There was just one chair aside from the chair that the *Capitán* was sitting on and Tiago was straddling it. He had turned it around, and his arms were draped over the back of the chair and his sheathed sword was sticking behind him like a tail.

"Are you sure they were *Itnegs*?" *Don* Manuel asked after Lorenzo Ajel stopped talking.

Lorenzo Ajel looked at Ricardo. "You shot at one of them, didn't you?"

"N-n-no, no, I did not. I did not see anyone." Ricardo stammered. "When I looked out after Antonio ran into the house, there was no one there. There was no one to shoot at."

"Nobody actually saw them then?" Tiago asked incredulously.

Both of the soldiers shook their heads.

"How about Antonio, did he see the shooter?" *Don* Manuel asked.

"No, *Capitán*," Ricardo said. "He said he did not know where the arrows came from. He did not see anyone either."

"So it could be anybody then, not necessarily the *Itnegs*," *Don* Manuel said.

"The Ilocanos don't use the bow, *Capitán*," Tiago said.

"Not that we know of, Tiago, not that we know of, but there may be one or two out there who may have learned from the *Itnegs*..." the *Capitán's* voice trailed as he remembered that the Ilocanos were likewise skilled in stick fighting same as the *Itnegs*. It may be a remote possibility but it would not be a big step for an Ilocano to learn how to properly use a bow. Anything was possible.

"Maybe, maybe that was possible, but I still think the *Itnegs* are involved," Tiago said emphatically. Both Lorenzo Ajel and Ricardo nodded in agreement.

Don Manuel did not say anything as he calmly looked at his soldiers. 'They may be right,' he thought. And inside him a seed of apprehension started to grow.

Was the mysterious *Itneg* who showed up innocently fishing in the river by the fort somehow involved with the killings? How about Gabriela's *Itneg* uncle? He was seen around town just a few days ago and no one had seen him since he visited the fort looking for his sister. Was he hanging around, unseen, and causing all this? Was he somehow blaming them for his sister's disappearance? *Don* Manuel wished he had answers to his questions but as he looked at the men before him, he was as dumbfounded as they were.

"So let's say they were *Itnegs*," *Don* Manuel finally said, "but why? Why do they want to start trouble with us?"

Lorenzo and Ricardo looked blankly at one another but both remained silent.

Tiago shrugged. He knew why but he was not about to say anything. He wondered though how the *Itnegs* had found out that Awad was killed in their custody. Had they somehow gotten hold of Miguel and that *bastardo* had talked? Or his dead friends maybe? Were they killed by the *Itnegs* also?

And had they talked before they were killed? So many unanswered questions and Tiago seethed inside, wishing once again that he had not listened to Cortez or Miguel in the first place. *'¡Bastardos!'*

"Maybe they have decided to help *La Generala, Capitán*," Tiago found himself saying instead. "Remember her mother was *Itneg*."

Don Manuel looked quizzically at Tiago. "*Was*, Tiago? Is she dead?"

Tiago was taken aback, silently cursing himself for the slip. Did the *Capitán* somehow suspect something?

"No, no, no, *Capitán*," he said recovering quickly. "I meant, she's missing, isn't she?"

Don Manuel looked at his *Sargento* as if he was in deep thought, then he sighed and leaned back in his chair without saying anything, looking up at the ceiling. Then he rolled his neck, relishing the popping sounds as he felt the tension he was feeling easing up a bit. He hunched his shoulders and leaned forward, placing both arms on his desk.

"Perhaps," he said, "perhaps she had gone back to Abra and convinced her people to help her daughter, and now these damn *Itnegs* are involved."

Tiago nodded, relieved. "Yeah, perhaps that was the case. Maybe that's what happened."

"I don't like it, Tiago, I don't like it one bit." *Don* Manuel contemplatively said but there was an edge in his voice that Tiago felt was somehow directed at him. He wondered again if the *Capitán* knew of his involvement. 'But it's not possible,' he thought.

"Me too, *Capitán*, me too," he mumbled. "What do we do now?"

Don Manuel thought for a moment. "Let's bury our dead first thing in the morning as soon as *Padre* Joaquin shows up. Then I want you to send someone up to Cagayan and another down to Pangasinan and Pampanga. I want reinforcements. I want more soldiers here, Tiago, soldiers who can fight, the more, the better."

"Why, do you think all the *Itneg* tribes will lend a hand to the Ilocanos, *Capitán*?"

Don Manuel answered with another question. "How many men do we have in the fort, Tiago?"

"Nine hundred, maybe a thousand or so, *Capitán*, nine hundred fighting men, more than enough I would say to take care of the rebels, aided by the *Itnegs* or not!"

"You have seen them fight, haven't you?" *Don* Manuel said calmly like a patient teacher talking to a troubled student. "Even just a tribe of those we have encountered in Abra a few years back would cause enough trouble for the nine hundred or a thousand of us, make no mistake about it."

Tiago reddened around the ears as he remembered how easily that *Itneg* by the river had bested both him and the *Capitán* in their mock duels, and both of them undoubtedly the best swordsmen hereabouts if not in the whole of His Majesty's army in the archipelago.

"And how many rebels are there now, a thousand, two thousand maybe?" *Don* Manuel continued. "Then let's just say five hundred or a thousand more *Itnegs* join them, how many do we have? We need more men or they will run us out of this town again like Diego did before, and this time, it may be for good. God help us!"

Tiago shook his head, but he said, "*Si, si, Capitán*. Alright, we'll send for reinforcements. I'll see to it."

"Do that, Tiago. I heard the *Capampangans* are good fighting men and many of them are serving in His Majesty's army. I want them, but I want the *Ybanags* from Cagayan more. I heard that they're as skillful with the bow as these damn *Itnegs*, maybe better if that was even possible." *Don* Manuel. "At least, I hope they are," he added softly like a wish.

"Of course, *Capitán*, of course," Tiago said rising from his chair. "Is there anything else?"

"I want them to send at least a couple of thousand men," *Don* Manuel shook his head and waved a hand in dismissal.

Tiago surprised at the numbers thrown at him saluted and the two soldiers did likewise. Then they all turned around and went single file out of the room, Tiago leading the way and Lorenzo and Ricardo bringing the rear.

Don Manuel sighed. There was more trouble ahead, he could sense it, and he was not looking forward to it. Not for a bit at all. And he had a feeling he would need every man he could get.

Early the following morning, the emissaries seeking for reinforcements left the fort.

Chapter Forty Four

"Why did you bring them along?" Akash said as he looked at the two young Chinese again who were facing him in the living room of Ilang's house.

"They wanted to come and join us fight the soldiers. They said they can fight," Kulas said, "besides they no longer have a house. The soldiers burned it down."

Akash looked the two young men over, up and down, assessing their funny clothes, rounded hats made of cloth, and especially their long hairs braided into pigtails. He was not impressed.

"Fight? They can fight?" he asked incredulously.

"That's what they said," Kulas said defensively. He turned to the brothers, "You can fight, right?"

Both brothers grinned and nodded their heads vigorously.

"I wonder if they even understood what you are saying," Akash said. Despite himself his face showed a hint of amusement. "So, show me," he said to the brothers.

The two young men exchanged glances then at the two *Itnegs* with a questioning look.

"What?" Akash said. "Can you fight? Do you understand?" He clenched his hands into fists and shook them towards the brothers.

The brothers vigorously nodded again.

"So show me!" Akash's voice rose a bit.

The brothers shrugged their shoulders, then Ming stepped forward, but Ding Hap raised a hand and laid it on his brother's shoulder, stopping him. He pulled Ming back and stepped forward in his brother's place.

"I show you," he said, pointing at Akash. "I fight you."

Akash's eyes grew big with surprise and looked at Kulas who was trying hard to stifle a grin.

"Well, you asked," Kulas said.

"Here?" Akash turned his face back to Ding Hap, "with what?"

Ding Hap shrugged and raised his empty hands.

"Well, there you go," Kulas said. "You wanted to find out if they can fight, go ahead."

Akash looked around the living room, shook his head, and stepped forward toward Ding Hap, who took a bow, then spread his feet apart, one slightly at an angle to the other, his hands raised as if poised to stop Akash from afar. Kulas watched interestedly but with amusement in his eyes.

Akash raised a fist half-heartedly at Ding Hap when he was close enough just to see the young man's reaction, but to his surprise he felt himself being pulled forward and he was flying in the air his wrist firmly held in a vise-like grip by the young Chinese. He landed on his back on the floor with his wrist still firmly held by the young Chinese who was kneeling on one knee now and before he could move he saw a fist coming fast to his face. He closed his eyes to wait for the impact but it never came. Akash opened his eyes and stared at the fist that had stopped right by his nose, barely touching it as he instinctively shrank away from it and felt the floor at the back of his head. Beyond the fist, he saw the grinning face of the young Chinese who was looking down at him.

"Whoaaa!!" they all heard Kulas exclaim. "That was so fast I did not see what happened. You have to show me that again, but slower this time!"

Ding Hap did not say anything as he rose. He opened his fist and extended it to Akash who grudgingly took it and the young Chinese pulled Akash up to his feet. Akash was shaken but he was feeling good and looked at the young Chinese with admiration in his eyes. The Chinese did not see because he was bowing his head again toward Akash.

"How did you do that?" Akash asked.

"*Kung-Fu*," Ding Hap said. "We practice *Kung-Fu*, my brother and I."

"What the heck is *Kung-Fu*?" Kulas said.

"Martial arts," Ming said. "We learned it from our father. He was a great master, a *sifu*."

"*Martial* what? Oh, whatever," Akash said, exasperated. "Maybe you could teach him that," he pointed to Kulas who was still grinning, "he can't fight with his hands."

"I can't fly either," Kulas said, "and land on my back."

Akash ignored his friend. He turned to the brothers. "Alright, you can come with us." Then he looked back at Kulas. "We have to get out of this town as soon as night comes and go back, see if they are ready. If they are, they may be coming down the mountain any time soon. Perhaps we can meet up with them."

"Don't worry they know where to find us. I spoke with Ittok before we came down," Kulas said.

Akash raised an eyebrow at his friend.

"What? You think we'll just get out of sight without telling anyone?" Kulas said. "You know they need us when they march down to battle. Ittok will send someone for us if we don't show up when they're halfway to here."

Akash did not say anything, appreciating the fact that his friend had just not joined him without making any arrangement with the tribe. Kulas headed to the kitchen to look for food and a drink of water. He gave Akash a playful punch on the shoulder as he walked past his open mouthed friend. Akash was not expecting the punch and he winced in pain. Kulas always had a heavy hand and even his playful punches hurt.

"Can you walk?" Kulas asked the brothers as they moved apart to let him pass.

"Yes, I can," Akash answered from behind thinking the question was directed at him.

The brothers looked at one another and shrugged then followed Kulas to the kitchen.

Behind them Akash looked at the floor where he fell and tried to figure out what had happened. The young Chinaman, who was almost half a head shorter and definitely lighter, had simply caught his wrist then he was flying and landing on his back.

How the hell did he do that?

Akash could not figure it out as much as he thought about it. *Kung-Fu*? What the hell was that? Flabbergasted, he finally shook his head and followed the others to the kitchen.

They left town by nightfall, keeping to the shadows until they were well out of sight of the houses. The air was dry and there was a half-moon that gave them enough light and they made good time. They reached the foot of Mount *Bullagaw* after about three hours of walking. Akash and Kulas were ahead and the brothers trudged behind them about fifty paces away. They were walking together as a group when they started but the brothers gradually fell behind as the trail became steeper. Sensing the brothers lagging farther, Kulas and Akash thought it was a good time for them to stop and rest. Just a few steps ahead was the spring where Akash usually stopped for a drink the times he traveled to town and that was where they decided to camp for the night, but when they looked behind them the brothers were no longer in sight.

"Where did they go?" Akash said.

"Damn, maybe they got lost or perhaps they turned back to town," Kulas said dismissively.

"Let's go find out," Akash started forward then suddenly stopped. From beyond the bend of their back trail came the sound of someone hacking at something, no make that two someones hacking. Akash and Kulas looked at one another.

"That's probably them," Kulas said. "What are they up to now?"

Unarmed and empty-handed as they were when they walked in with Kulas at Ilang and Diego's house, Akash had told the brothers to pick a bolo each from the stash of weapons that Diego had in a big wooden chest. Akash and Kulas had watched with interest as the brothers hefted and balanced each of the weapons in their hands finally picking one apiece with satisfaction and a big appreciative grin in their faces, bowing a dozen times it seemed toward Akash and Kulas in gratitude.

Akash and Kulas hurriedly walked back around the bend and under the moonlight they saw the brothers at a copse of straight saplings a little bit off the trail. They had each cut a long straight growth sapling and both were intently trimming the branches off. Akash and Kulas stopped and watched with interest and curiosity.

"What are they making, spears?" Akash asked.

"Probably walking staff," Kulas said. "They are not pretty good walkers. They can't ride either."

"What do you mean they can't ride? Did they tell you they can't?" Akash said.

"No, but have you ever seen a Chinaman on a horse?" Kulas said smugly.

This time Akash swung a playful punch at Kulas but his friend was expecting it and quickly stepped out of reach. Akash flailed and tottered to keep his balance on the steep trail. Kulas reached out and grabbed a flailing hand to steady his friend.

"You're getting slow, old man," Kulas said.

"Yeah, I know," Akash said as he steadied himself. They stood side by side and looked back at the approaching brothers who now had come up the trail, each one holding a straight pole that was almost twice as long as their height.

"Those are pretty long walking staffs," Kulas said as the brothers stopped before them. "Wouldn't it be better if you cut them this high?" He raised a hand to the side of his waist.

"This is not a walking staff although you could use it as one," Ding said. "It's called a *chang gun*."

"A 'chang' what?" Kulas said.

"A *chang gun*," Akash said looking at Kulas as if he knew what the words meant.

"I heard, yes, a *chang gun*," Kulas said. "What the heck is a *chang gun*? Is it a spear? If so, you have to make a sharp point off the top."

"No, no, no, not a spear," Ming said. "It's a fighting staff."

"Ohh, a fighting staff," both of the *Itnegs* said then looked at one another as if they understood.

The brothers ignored them.

Akash turned around and walked back up the trail. "*Chang gun*," he muttered, shaking his head.

"We'll camp around here for the night," Kulas said to the brothers and likewise turned and followed Akash. The brothers shrugged and fell behind him using their poles as walking staffs.

Akash stopped by the spring and picked up several pieces of dry wood that were lying around underneath a tall shrubbery. He arranged them at an open spot where obviously fire had been built before. As he built a small fire, he looked over the brothers who had gratefully sat down opposite him with growing fondness and a little admiration. Although they were a bit slow in walking, the little Chinamen had never complained the entire time. They surely were tougher than they looked. He was glad he let them come along. He smiled as he bent down and blew on the small flicker of flame that came off his flint, feeding it with dry grass until it caught and pretty soon he had a good fire going.

Kulas was looking at his friend as he glanced at the brothers and he followed his gaze and likewise ended up giving the brothers an appreciative look. Then he turned toward the spring for a quick drink and to wash the grime off his body.

If the brothers noticed the attention they were getting, they did not give any indication. They were too tired. They patted the grass where they sat close to the fire and nonchalantly lay down, their long poles by their side. It was a good thing they ate a big dinner before they left town, both of them thought, but then again they were too tired to eat. The night air was colder and they were grateful for the heat that came off the fire.

They were snoring softly when Kulas finally walked back and sat for a few moments by the fire, studying the two Chinamen and wondering what a bunch of them, in their funny clothes, would look like, lying side by side, on and on until he could not see the last man. But damn they were something else.

Then he looked at his friend who was sleeping peacefully at the other side of the fire. He knew that Akash was closer to Awad than Allong and he wondered what his friend had felt when he learned of his sister's death. Whatever it was, he was glad he had tagged along, knowing that Akash was going to avenge his sister the only way he knew how. Kill as many of those he suspected responsible as he could. And he was glad, either one of them had not come into harm in their little foray into the town.

He dozed off for a moment while sitting down, enjoying the soft glow of the campfire. Then as if on command, he opened his eyes and slowly got up. He stretched, looked his sleeping companions over one more time, then turned around and walked away from the fire into the darkness of the trees.

He found a tree to his liking, sat down underneath it leaning his bare back against its massive trunk. He looked back at the camp but he could no longer see the fire. He was not worried of them being followed this far so he settled down, fidgeting a bit until he found a good spot and felt comfortable then he closed his eyes.

It seemed like just a few hours later but he woke up to a grey dawn with the smell of roasting chicken and the rhythmic sound of thwacking poles followed now and then by grunts and occasional yelling coming from the direction of the camp.

Kulas stretched his arms and legs while he was still seated, then he stood up grudgingly feeling his legs had gone to sleep and he stretched again, stomping his feet to put the circulation back into them. He felt the pricks of tiny needles in his legs as he gingerly walked towards the camp. His stomach growled as the smell of roasting chicken became stronger and he walked faster.

He stopped suddenly as he rounded the tree line and finally saw the camp. Akash was sitting by a new fire over which four birds impaled two apiece in two green poles roasted, but his friend's attention was not on the birds. Akash was looking at the two Chinese youth who were in a furious combat using their long poles at a wide open space by the spring.

Kulas walked closer toward the camp, his eyes likewise glued to the dueling Chinese who were grunting and yelling at times, moving and twirling their poles in a blur that was too fast for the eyes to follow yet somehow neither of the poles seemed unable to land on flesh. However fast one of the youths wielded his pole the other one was just as fast in blocking it with his own pole or simply moved out of the way.

The young men jumped over a pole aimed like a sweeping scythe to the feet or ducked when the target was the head. A strike to the body was always blocked with the opposite pole or evaded by a quick yet fluid bending forward or backward, the pole thrust like a spear harmlessly gliding past an impossibly contorted body.

To the two mesmerized spectators, it was a display of pure agility until their similarly trained eyes and ears familiar with the nuances of stick fighting detected the measured cadence of the moves, the steps and techniques memorized and perfected through innumerable practice sessions, probably since the brothers were small children. Nonetheless, both men knew that those smoothly measured and practiced moves were deadly in actual combat.

Akash looked up at Kulas as the latter leaned down and turned the roasting birds over and their eyes locked and both smiled with satisfaction in a silent agreement that their decision to let the two young men tag along was a wise one.

"Yes, they could fight," Akash said grinning.

292

"I hope they could kill too," Kulas said as he straightened up, "if it came to it."

"They will if it came to a choice between theirs and the enemy's life."

Kulas did not answer. He looked down at the roasting birds and rearranged the firewood underneath them.

"Where did you catch these?" he said.

"Not me," Akash said, moving his head toward the practicing brothers. "They had them all cleaned up and in the skewers when I woke up. They are not always that noisy. They could move silently too. I swear they could have killed both of us in our sleep. I never heard them get up."

Kulas looked at his friend thoughtfully. He had not heard the brothers move about either.

"How?" he asked.

"How did they move without us knowing? How do I know? Like us when we want to maybe?" Akash said as he turned his head back toward the brothers who had suddenly stopped. He watched them as they ceremoniously bowed toward each other. "Hey, how do you like that?" he said to Kulas.

Kulas grinned shaking his head as he saw the boys courteously bow at one another and then approached each other and grasped each other's arm. Then laughing and talking incessantly, they both turned and walked toward the campfire.

"I'll be darned," Kulas said. "They're something else. But these birds, how did they catch them?"

"Up the tree, they said," Akash shrugged casually, "they climbed and took them off the tree while it was still dark. They said birds sleep with their heads tucked under their wings and they don't move in the dark because they can't see. Go figure."

Kulas nodded. "Maybe they did that. We never knew."

"How would we know? Who the heck hunts in the dark?" Akash said.

Chapter Forty Five

"I thank you all for coming and showing your support and helping us in our time of difficulty," *Apo* Kagaid said to the tribal leaders gathered by the center of the village. The leaders of the tribes from Bangilo, Cayapa, Bacooc, Paganao, Libtek, Laguiben, Lagben, Licuan and of course, La-ang, were all there, smoking their *pinadis*, their favored rolled, long cigars, and drinking *tapuy*. They had just finished their communal meal where everyone shared cows, pigs and chickens butchered and grilled and stewed for just the occasion.

By the river, its bank closer to the village was lined with tents and makeshift lodgings not only for the Ilocanos but also for the various tribes who had arrived with their contingents, some three hundred strong, others four to five hundred. Bangilo, led by Biktol, had the least number at a hundred but all the other tribes deferred to them because of their fearsome reputation, except for the warriors of La-ang who thought they were equal to any man. It was said that a single man from Bangilo was equal to five men but this of course was taken in stride by the men of La-ang who were reputed warriors themselves.

"This is my grand-daughter, Ilang, my daughter Awad's daughter," *Apo* Kagaid extended a hand toward Gabriela who was seated to his right. Gabriela bowed her head in deference to the tribal leaders. "She leads the Ilocanos in their fight against the Spanish soldiers. She will also lead us."

The tribal leaders looked at one another in surprise. Most of them had expected either one of the sons of *Apo* Kagaid or *Apo* Dalalo to lead them.

"Wait a minute, *Apo*," Biktol said. "With all due respect, how could a woman lead us?"

Apo Kagaid was about to respond when he felt his granddaughter's hand on his arm.

"Let me speak, *Ama*," Gabriela said and she stood up before *Apo* Kagaid could say anything. *Apo* Kagaid wisely did not object and let his granddaughter takeover. This was her fight. Let her convince the rest to follow her.

"Most of you, perhaps all of you with the exception of the elders of this village, don't know me. All you see before you is a woman who is asking you to join her, me, in battle. I understand your concern." Her voice was clear and full of passion. She scanned the faces of the tribal leaders, meeting their gaze not as their equal, but as their leader.

"You have seen the Ilocanos camped by the river, in fact some of them are here," she pointed to her Uncle Nicolas and Sebastian and Nardo who were standing at the back of the tribal leaders who each gave them furtive looks. "They don't look much now, in fact they look like hell because they have been through hell and they had fought their way out at every step. These men and women, for the women with us are not just here to cook and take care of the wounded, they too fight and they have fought well for they are still with us bruised and wounded but alive and not dead in the battlefields. They have been to more battles with the Spaniards, much more than me because they were with my late husband, who had led them, since they started this fight against the Spaniards, the *Kastilas*. And these men and women, battered they may be, are all tested veterans of many bloody encounters with the *Kastilas*. They are all warriors just like you all are, and perhaps may also be as good as anyone of you, and yet they have chosen me, a woman, as their leader. And I have led them for a good half of the year now.

"Yes, I am a woman," she continued, her voice trembling now with emotion but it came out clear and strong, "and yes, we have not exactly defeated the Spaniards yet, but we have had small successes against them. I am a woman and their leader and yet, yes, the Spaniards have not conquered me yet." She paused and let her eyes roam around the crowd again meeting and holding for a brief moment each pair of eyes that met her gaze, then finally settling on Biktol who looked back at her with interest. She looked at Biktol and continued to speak as if she was addressing him alone. "If anyone of you has more experience than I do in fighting the *Kastilas*, I will be happy to step down as the leader. We need your help, but we cannot fight and expect to win against the *Kastilas* if we are not united under one leadership."

Biktol held her gaze for a moment, then he finally nodded, with a hint of reserved respect in his eyes as if he was saying, 'Alright you can lead but you better be good or I'll have your ass!' Gabriela perceptively nodded back acknowledging their unspoken conversation then she turned around and sat back down beside her grandfather.

There was a hush in the crowd as Gabriela settled down on the bench beside her grandfather who sat erect with a stoic face while Gabriela spoke, but deep inside him, he was beaming with pride. Then the silence was broken with a single soft clap that became louder as it was repeated. Everyone looked at Biktol who was clapping by himself and was now rising to his feet as he continued to clap. Then someone else stood up and joined in the clapping then in a moment the gathering was on its collective feet with the exception of Gabriela and her grandfather, and clapping so loudly that the people by the river gave each other puzzled looks wondering what was happening in the gathering of their leaders.

Apo Kagaid finally stood up and raised both arms signaling for the crowd to settle back down. The clapping slowly receded then stopped as everyone who was previously seated on the few benches finally sat back down.

"Thank you. Thank you," *Apo* Kagaid said. "Unless anyone still has any objection, then I think that's settled, so please speak now before we go on."

Nobody spoke.

"Very well then," *Apo* Kagaid said, "with all your permission, let me have Ilang take over."

Ilang stood up again as *Apo* Kagaid sat back down.

"First, let me show you some things," she caught the eyes of her Uncle Nicolas and she nodded her head briefly. Nicolas turned around and signaled to Nardo who had retreated to a nearby tree with a blanket-covered bundle by his side. The boy picked up the bundle and hurried forward, straining under the weight of the bundle he carried. He went around the benches and the crowd parted as he walked toward Gabriela. He carefully put his baggage down and untied the rope that held it together. The tribal leaders watched with interest as Nardo opened the bundle, spread the edges of the blanket and exposed its contents.

"These," Gabriela said as soon as Nardo had arranged the contents of the bundle on the blanket that was used to wrap them, "these are some of the weapons of the *Kastilas*. I want you all to see them so at least you know what kind of weapons you may be going against. These may not be much to look at but remember, in the hands of the expert, and make no mistake, those *Kastilas* and the local soldiers that they have conscripted are all experts in their use, all this are deadly and will cause great harm and death."

She signaled at Nardo who handed her a dagger and a sword. Gabriela took each in her hands.

"You all know what these are," she said. She raised a hand that held the dagger. "This is what they call *daga*, a dagger. It is similar to your short knives. And this other one is the *espada*, a sword, just like your long knives, but notice that this is double-edged unlike our *bolos* and *kampilans*. It can cut as easily from either side."

She paused and looked around and noticed a length of bamboo pole leaning against a nearby hut. She whispered at Nardo who stood up and ran and returned shortly with the bamboo pole. Gabriela put the dagger down and took the pole in her left hand. The crowd was silent as they watched eagerly, each one curious at what she was going to do.

Gabriela waved Nardo away and the boy stepped back as Gabriela walked to the open space in the middle of the gathering. She stood the pole on one end then she quickly stepped back as the pole teetered to stay upright. As it was about to fall sideways, Gabriela, holding the sword in both hands, made a swift downward slash so quick that all everyone seemed to see was the top half of the pole falling down beside the lower half as it split in two.

The warriors looked at one another in amazement then clapped and whistled with glee as they realized what Gabriela had just done.

Gabriela raised a hand and the noise subsided. "This sword could do that as easily with your necks," she said as she tossed the sword down on the blanket. Then she picked up what seemed to be a funny looking hammer to some of the tribal leaders.

"This is a pistol. This is rarely used by the Spaniards except for their officers, their leaders. They have them and use them mostly in close quarters. It shoots and does a lot of damage even death." She looked around and pointed to a basket that contained various fruits to Nardo and mouthed 'melon' silently to the boy. Nardo got a small melon the size of a man's head then looked questioningly at Gabriela as he held the melon in his hands. There was a nervous uncertainty in his eyes. The tribal leaders looked perplexedly at one another. 'Surely the woman was not thinking of shooting the melon while the boy held it, would she?' they thought collectively.

Gabriela smiled. "Stick that on one of the poles and stand it under that tree," she said to Nardo, indicating the pole that she had just cut in two and gesturing at the tree where Nardo was previously sitting under. Then while Nardo was doing what he was told to do, Gabriela checked and loaded the pistol from a packet in the bundle. As Nardo walked away from the tree, the crowd parted to make an open space between Gabriela and the pole leaning against the tree with the melon on its tip. The distance was a good twenty five paces at least.

'Too far,' Nicolas thought as he figured out what Gabriela was intending to do. As good a shot as Gabriela was, Nicolas knew that the Spanish pistol was not reliable at that distance even in the hands of an expert. He let out a sigh of relief as Gabriela started walking toward the tree and half-way through, casually raised the hand holding the pistol and pulled the trigger. A chunk of the melon was torn to pieces as the pole swayed a moment then toppled down to the ground.

The warriors, surprised at what seemed to be a booming sound from the pistol, nodded and clapped in awe and appreciation, some of them later on digging their fingers into their ears, trying to rid them of their ringing.

"That could be your head," Gabriela said casually as she walked back and laid the pistol on the blanket. "But that damage is nothing compared to what this can do," she said, raising a rifle. "This is stronger and louder and can shoot a lot farther with more accuracy than the pistol. Trust me. I am not going to show it to you because we don't have much ammunition." She laid down the rifle and picked up a musket ball and priming powder, raising them in her hands as the leaders craned to look at them. "This is what goes inside the rifle, its ammunition, and when it comes out it makes a lot more damage than the pistol. And yes it is accurate at longer distance."

"And then there's this," she said raising a body armor that was made of metal then as an afterthought, picked up a pointy helmet. "This is a helmet," she said putting it on her head. "It is to protect the head as you may have already guessed. You can whack at it with your long knives and you may not get a blood out of the enemy's head. So, aim for the neck instead."

She took it off, and tossed it down on the blanket then she put on the body armor. It was big and it hung loose on her trim body, but the warriors nodded their heads as they deemed what it was for.

"As you can see, this is to protect the body. The Spanish soldiers have them but not all of them use them anymore because of the heat. They also have leather vests that they wear underneath their uniforms. So when you hit them and they don't fall down and they don't bleed, don't think that they are invincible. Cut their necks and their heads will roll, same as anyone else. This protects them from arrows also, so when you shoot, pick an open spot on their bodies."

The warriors grinned. Now the woman was talking their language. The tribal leaders on the other hand all nodded with understanding and growing respect for their woman leader. 'What else is this witch of a woman has in her possession?' some of them thought.

And Gabriela did not disappoint them.

She took off the body armor and gently laid it down on the blanket then as she rose, she held the dagger back in her hand.

"And by the way, when an officer, one of the leaders, points that pistol at you," she said pointing down at the pistol, "use this." She held the dagger, gripping it on its tip then she swirled and threw it towards the tree, a good twenty five paces away. The dagger quivered for a moment then kept still as almost half of its blade went deep into the trunk.

The crowd erupted in cheer and clapped each other's back. *Apo* Kagaid smiled proudly. Behind him, Allong beamed shaking his head in disbelief.

'This could not be that little girl who ran to me crying every time the other children teased her,' he thought. He secretly wished his brother Akash and Kulas were there to see what he had just seen.

Allong again shook his head as he stepped away from the gathering. He had seen enough.

It was time to look after his own weapons.

Chapter Forty Six

Padre Joaquin got back into town late in the night but he woke up early and celebrated the morning Mass at the usual time. He was pleasantly surprised to see the *Capitán* was in attendance. He wondered if the *Capitán* had suddenly seen the light, or there must be something that was bothering him so much that he was seeking divine intervention. *Padre* Joaquin made a mental note to talk to the *Capitán* after the Mass.

But he did not have to worry about seeking out the *Capitán* after the mass ended because the *Capitán* was looking and waiting for him outside the sacristy.

"*Don* Manuel, what a surprise!" *Padre* Joaquin said. "*Buenos Dias!*"

"*Buenos Dias a usted tambien, Padre,*" *Don* Manuel replied. "I need to talk to you."

"But of course, *mi'jo*. Come, come to the convent and join me for breakfast."

"*Gracias, Padre*, but I have to decline. I need to go back to the fort, and I need a favor."

"What is it? What's so important at the fort that you have to miss breakfast?" *Padre* Joaquin asked.

"*Padre*, you probably haven't heard yet, but three of my soldiers had died, killed actually, it seems by the *Itnegs*."

"Oh my God! Killed by the *Itnegs*? What happened?"

Briefly, *Don* Manuel told the priest what had happened while he was away.

"We need to bury them today, *Padre*. I wanted to bring them to church but Cortez and Catriz are so bloated and rotting so badly and that smell, well I would not advise bringing them here to the church. I had them covered with lime powder but they're not of much help. You may not be able to get rid of the smell for a good two weeks or more. We can do the burial rites at the fort."

"Of course, of course, if you think it would be best that way. We'll offer Mass and do the Rites for the Dead right there at the fort then you can bury them at the plot that you have there for the soldiers." *Padre* Joaquin said aware of the existence of the small cemetery just outside the fort, where the remains of Spanish soldiers who died mostly from tropical sicknesses, were buried. "I will ride out, *Capitán*, as soon as I have breakfast. We'll get those good Christian men buried before noon."

"*Gracias, Padre.* I'll be going then and prepare for the ceremony," *Don* Manuel said and turned away before the *Padre* could insist again for him to join him at breakfast. He actually had not eaten breakfast yet but he had no appetite and with the way the day was shaping up, he had the feeling that breakfast would take a long time if he joined the *Padre*. The man of the cloth could talk and breakfast might stretch on nigh to the noon meal.

Don Manuel had been in the fort for the better part of two hours when *Padre* Joaquin finally showed up. The sun was up midway in the morning sky, blazing hot and unchallenged over a clear cloudless day. There was not even a breeze to ease the discomfort that the *Padre* endured in his short travel from the town which was just less than ten kilometers away. He rode soaking wet with his own perspiration through the gate in a two-man open carriage driven by his young Ilocano *sacristán*, Monico.

When the carriage stopped inside the fort by the open courtyard, *Padre* Joaquin took out an oversized handkerchief that looked more like a bandanna from inside a sleeve of his cassock. He took two corners, shook the kerchief open then grabbing it with both hands pressed it to his face wiping as much sweat off as he could in one pass. He slid it off his face and down to his massive chin and neck and behind it. Then he crumpled the cloth and tucked it back into his sleeve. Slowly, he got off the carriage which groaned in protest and listed precariously to one side under his tremendous weight. Monico grabbed the edge of the carriage bench to avoid sliding off to the direction of the disembarking friar.

The *Padre* looked around and was impressed that the *Capitán* had seemed to have everything ready. There was a canopy at the far end of the courtyard and underneath it he saw the three wooden coffins, each one draped in a yellow blanket decorated with the emblem of the Spanish flag. Before the canopy, uniformed soldiers stood at ease. There was no chair and no one was seated.

"Poor souls must be sweating like pigs," *Padre* Joaquin uttered under his breath. He saw the *Capitán* and his officers were at the front of the soldiers standing like honor guards although a couple of pairs of soldiers were at each side of the canopy doing the honors. He hurried toward the assembly hoping the soldiers had not been waiting for so long. He felt a twinge of embarrassment and guilt. He had dawdled on his breakfast and time just slipped by and Monico was too scared to remind him of his appointment at the fort.

Monico tied the horse to a rail by the stables without unhitching the carriage when he saw the friar walking off in a hurry. He grabbed the friar's satchel that contained his vestments and kit for the Mass and ran off after him. They walked side by side as they approached the canopy. Monico gagged when he smelled the rotting smell of the corpses. *Padre* Joaquin glared at his *sacristán* but he himself started blowing and breathing through his mouth.

'*Por Dios*,' he thought as he looked over the soldiers, 'how do they stand the smell and this heat?' He would try to make the ceremony as fast and short as he could but it would be a torture every second with that smell.

Don Manuel peeled off the formation and met the *Padre* and his *sacristán*.

"You can change in my office, *Padre*," he said without ceremony and led off toward the nearby building. The friar and his *sacristán* followed without any hesitation. They wanted to get as far away from the caskets as possible even just for the briefest time. The smell was overpowering and utterly unbearable.

Padre Joaquin went through the Mass and the Burial rites in record time to the relief of Monico and the soldiers. *Don* Manuel himself was pleasantly amazed at the shortest homily that he had ever heard from the *frayle*. It was a short walk to the soldiers' cemetery just a few meters outside the fort but by the time they got there, the poor *Padre* was already soaking wet with sweat.

Everyone sighed with relief when the final '*Amen*' was said. Ceremonial shots were fired in the air then everyone went back to the fort leaving the four Indios conscripted to bury the dead to their task.

The four poor unpaid peons whipped out their bandannas and tied them tightly around their mouths and noses as soon as the soldiers left. The stench was so bad that they only dared to take the bandannas off when the coffins were well under at least a foot of covering dirt. Yet somehow the putrid smell lingered in the air even well after the graves were filled.

"White or brown, damn bodies smell the same when they're rotting dead," Basilio who was shoveling dirt over Catriz's coffin said. The others looked at him like the village idiot that they thought he was instead of a philosopher with his astute and often misunderstood observations and opinions. 'Brainless twits,' Basilio thought noticing his companions' derisive looks. He tamped the dirt then pounded the makeshift cross with Catriz's name on it into the mound without further talking to his companions. What was the point? They could never be at his mental level anyway.

After *Padre* Joaquin and Monico had left, *Don* Manuel called for Tiago.

"What do you think?" Manuel said.

"About what?" Tiago said, his brows furrowed, unsure as to what was in his *Capitán*'s mind.

"The *Itnegs*. Do you think they have joined *La Generala*'s force?"

301

"Hard to say but I hope not," Tiago said sincerely. "Perhaps they're just on a little rampage on their own. Maybe it has something to do with the *tneg* mother."

"Why? You think they are blaming us for her disappearance? Where did she go by the way? Have you found out anything?"

"No, no, no! Nothing! I haven't heard anything!" Tiago said hastily which was not lost to the *Capitán* who gave him a quizzical look.

"Well, the men that I sent to look after those who disappeared did not have any relevant information at all," he added defensively.

The *Capitán* nodded. "But I wonder why the *Itnegs* are targeting us?" he mused. "Do they know something we don't?"

"What could that possibly be?" Tiago asked, getting nervous at where the conversation was headed.

"I don't know, Tiago, but maybe Gabriela's mother had not showed up back home. Perhaps she had befallen into harm and somehow the *Itnegs* knew and are blaming us for it. It's crazy but I just have this feeling that something was off and it's bothering me," *Don* Manuel said.

Tiago took a deep breath. He had known for a while now how intuitive the *Capitán* could be and he was nervous his intuitions might lead him to his doorsteps. 'Don't be foolish,' he thought to himself. All the people who had known about his involvement with *La Generala*'s mother's disappearance were all dead except Alfonso and he trusted Alfonso. Then he thought of the one other who knew that was still missing. 'Except that damn *bastardo* Miguel,' he thought. He wished he knew where Miguel was then he could take care of his little problem.

"I have no idea why they would think that," Tiago said. "That's preposterous!"

"Then why are they killing us? Our soldiers? We just buried three of them, all dead with arrows. Coincidental? The Ilocanos don't have bows and don't even know how to use one if they did; they could not have done it. I'm convinced it's the *Itnegs*, Tiago, and I'll be lying to you if I say that I am not worried. These *Itnegs* are nothing like the Ilocanos. They're skilled and fearless and I'm afraid would die to the last man. It would be very difficult to actually conquer and defeat them."

Tiago did not answer for he knew the *Capitán* may just be right.

"I'll send some scouts out to shake some trees and let's see what falls down," Tiago finally said. "Let's find out if the *Itnegs* are really involved and see what their plans are."

"Very well. Give them a couple of days. How long have the men you sent out for reinforcements been gone?"

"Three, four days. It shouldn't take them over a week to get there if they travel fast. They took extra horses," Tiago said. "The reinforcements should be here in a couple more weeks, maybe week and a half."

"I hope so, Tiago. In the meantime keep the men on alert. They are not to go out unless in groups, at least six to a group," *Don* Manuel said. "I don't want to bury any more of them."

"Of course," Tiago said, "I'll let them know. If you don't have anything else, I'll send the scouts out, two groups at six men apiece." He gave *Don* Manuel a short but sharp salute and walked away.

Don Manuel looked at the back of his *Sargento*. Again the feeling that something was off that he could not put his finger on and bothered him no end came over him.

Perhaps a little time with *Señora* Dela Cuesta's niece, Isabella, would ease his mind. He stood up and went to the stables. He would eat the noon meal in town, preferably in the company of the *Señora's* niece.

He was determined to go rebel hunting as soon as the reinforcements arrived. He figured he had at least a week and a half, or two to three weeks most probably, before the reinforcements got into town if the messengers did not dally someplace else. Sometimes one never knew with these *bastardos* once they were away from the fort and out of supervision. But he was not going to worry about it. The damn *rebeldes* were not going anywhere. With the help of the *Itnegs* or not, it did not matter. The mighty Spanish army had more firepower and experience even in this remote part of the world.

He was going after those pesky *rebeldes* with full force as soon as the reinforcements arrived.

But until then, he was going to enjoy the civilized company of a beautiful woman.

There was a noticeable spring in his steps as he walked toward the stables, and despite the somber start of the day, his face was actually beginning to entertain a trace of a smile.

Chapter Forty Seven

The eyes of the two Chinese brothers opened wide and they cast bewildered looks at one another as the throng of tents and people that made up the sprawling campsite that stretched for, it seemed, as far as their eyes could see, appeared before them by the riverbank. They had seen the smokes from the campfires when they were still far off in the distance after crossing Mount *Bullagaw* yet they had no idea how many people were there or how big the campsite was.

Along with Kulas and Akash, they had followed the river when they came to it after coming off the tree line from the foot of the mountain, and after another two days of walking, they had rounded the bend of the river and there were the tents and the people moving like toy figures in the distance. And beyond them were the huts that comprised the village.

"You have all those people in your village?" Ming said.

"You mean do they live there all the time?" Kulas asked.

"Yes, all of them live there?" Ding said.

"No, no. The people by the river are Ilocanos. Rebels," Kulas said.

Again the brothers exchanged bewildered looks.

"Rebels? Here?" Ming said.

"Yes," Akash said. "Like you. You're going to be rebels too. Like me and him," he pointed at Kulas. "We're joining them. We're all going to be rebels."

"We fight the Spaniards?" Ding said.

"Yes, we fight the Spanish soldiers," Kulas answered. "Are you alright with that?"

The brothers exchanged another glance at one another.

"Yes, yes, alright, we fight soldiers," they said and nodded their heads in unison. "Yes, alright with us. We are rebels!"

They were spotted when they were still way beyond shouting distance and Kulas who had the vision of an eagle, saw Allong coming out to meet them, walking away from a group of warriors from another tribe. He realized that the people along the riverbank were now a mixture of Ilocanos and different *Itneg* tribes.

"It looks like help from other villages have arrived," he said to Akash.

"Yeah, either that or the Ilocano camp had grown four or five times since we left," Akash replied.

They hurried their steps and remained silent until they met Allong halfway.

"Everyone has arrived. We will move out in two days." Allong said in their dialect. "Give the warriors from Bangilo time to rest. They were the last to come in. They arrived just a few hours ago."

"Alright," Akash said. "We need to rest ourselves."

"Friends," Kulas said in answer to Allong's quizzical look toward the Chinese brothers. "Ming and Ding Hap. They're brothers. Chinese tribe."

The two brothers exchanged glances at hearing their names mentioned and bowed their heads toward the bewildered Allong.

"Chinese tribe?" Allong said, his eyes locked on the bowing brothers.

"Chinese tribe," Kulas said casually. "From far away. Very far. They can only send these two."

Allong shrugged, looking at Akash who seemed uninterested in the conversation, ignoring the lighthearted banter of Kulas.

"They're from Vigan. Chinese merchants," Akash said then he turned to the young Chinamen in the Ilocano dialect, "My brother, Allong."

The Chinese brothers bowed again.

"Merchants? With just the poles?" Allong said in *Itneg*. Then, "Funny faces, funny clothes," he added.

"The Spaniards burned their store," Akash replied.

"Don't let their appearance fool you. They can fight. Ask Akash," Kulas said, grinning.

"Yeah, they can," Akash said grudgingly.

"With those poles?" Allong said.

"Especially with those poles, *chang gun* or something, but even without them," Kulas said. "That little one put Akash on his back with just one hand."

"That I would like to see," Allong said.

"Later, after we have eaten and rested," Akash said, ignoring his brother's incredulous look and walked ahead of the group. Allong looked at his brother, aware that he did not deny nor argue with what Kulas had said. He looked at the young Chinaman that Kulas had pointed to and all he saw was a smiling face that showed almost no eyes at all. He tried to smile back but he could not get himself to do it so he gave the young man a brief nod then turned quickly and hurried after his brother. The Chinese brothers looked at Kulas, who simply shrugged his shoulders and they followed him as he likewise moved fast after Allong and Akash.

Then together, they all walked through the camp and into the village with everyone gaping in awe at the sight of the two young Chinamen with their long poles and pigtails who were trying their best to ignore the curious stares. But they were aware after a while that they were walking with men of importance in the village from the reaction of the villagers to their *Itneg* companions so they likewise held their heads high.

Over dinner at Akash's hut, Kulas and Akash relayed to Allong what they had done. Allong had not said much, but afterwards as he left for his own hut, he had a feeling that perhaps what the two did was not good at all.

But he did not care much about it and certainly did not give it further thought. He simply kept his troubled feelings to himself. What was done was done.

But there were three soldiers dead by their hands and that was good enough. Yet he feared that now the soldiers were pretty much on edge and would be ready when they got to town.

The following day was spent with further discussions between Gabriela and her lieutenants and the rest of the heads of the tribes where plans of attack and rules of engagements were finalized while the rest of the warriors and rebels saw to their weapons and provisions. By the end of the day, jars of *tapuy* were brought out and before long all of the troops were all primed and fired up and ready for battle. Barely a soul slept that night, except perhaps for Kulas who had walked away into the foothills, sorting his thoughts about Gabriela and what the men down by the river were about to do, the thought of many of them probably not returning alive not lost amidst the raucous noise that could be heard from where he sat. But he ignored everything and by the time the bright star showed up clearly above, he was sleeping like a crocodile that had just eaten a whole deer.

They marched out early the next day under a bright early morning sun. Akash and Kulas led the way, retracing their path a couple of days before. Beside them walked the two young Chinamen. They had developed a close affinity to the tall *Itneg* who walked with ease and had an easy way of carrying himself and his friend who seemed serious but likewise seemed to be so much in control.

Although they were different, they felt that both of the *Itnegs* were the same in the sense that they seemed not to be easily bothered by anything.

And most important of all, they did not look at them, the brothers, as if they were strange people. And the two Chinamen walked with pride beside their two *Itneg* friends, holding their heads up high. Just a few feet behind them were Aklang, Bagit, Lang-gi and Dagyo with their bows slung across their shoulders. Kulas had personally asked them to join them at the front. He had a special task for them.

And after them came the ragtag army of mixed Ilocanos and *Itnegs*, marching with no rhythm or cadence, each to his own beat, at ten to twenty abreast and strung out to more than a kilometer long. Disorganized as any newly minted fighting force they may be, Gabriela hoped that their number would make up for their lack of military bearing and precision. She sighed with a refreshed sense of hope as her eyes swept over the throng of unlikely fighters that comprised her army from atop Petra her favorite steed.

They were indeed an awesome and impressive sight but they were not traveling fast enough for Akash. He was wound so tight that he barely slept since he, Kulas and the Chinese got to the village. Not even the presence of Pol-looy by his side in the night was enough to loosen him up. He could find no rest until Awad's spirit was at rest when those responsible for her death likewise lay dead at his feet.

It would take four days before they would even reach the vicinity of Vigan. And by that time, unbeknownst to anyone, the Spanish reinforcements were also getting closer to the place.

Chapter Forty Eight

Aklang squatted to make himself small knowing that he would be silhouetted against the sky, easy target for someone who might happen to look up and take a potshot at him from below. He heard that the Spanish *fusils* were not accurate at that distance and on top of that, the soldiers could not shoot straight but someone might get lucky. He would not be too happy if that happened.

He was on the rampart of the fort's southeastern perimeter wall before dawn, along with four other archers, each holding a span of the pentagonal fortress. To his right was *Ama* Kulas, and to his left crouched his cousin Bagit, then there was Lang-gi who always walked around the village with his bow slung across his shoulders, and rounding it off was another one of *Ama* Kulas's friends, Dagyo who had been intently trying to sort out the shadows below and seemed to have no success for he had not seen him make a shot yet. Just like the rest of the archers, Dagyo did not want to shoot a friend by mistake.

Out east, the grey of dawn was beginning to chip away at the black of night but down below, the fort was still swaddled in darkness despite the presence of a few lanterns that were sporadically placed and so far apart that all they did was create more shadows that danced along the walls and bushes and trees and added to the confusion of identifying a friend from foe.

So they watched patiently as the fighting below slowly spilled into the open space of the courtyard, and likewise soon enough, the darkness of dawn faded into grey providing adequate light to figure out the protagonists. Then the archers started shooting, keeping in mind that any Spaniard or anyone in a soldier's uniform was fair game, for there were natives from the Ilocos and nearby provinces who were conscripted to fight for the Spaniards. That was anyone, except, according to the instructions of Kulas and *Ina* Ilang, the big Spanish officer with the fancy uniform, the *Capitán* himself, *Don* Manuel. *Ina* Ilang wanted to kill him herself, foolish it might be.

"Is that prudent?" Kulas had asked when she made known her intentions.

"Perhaps not," Gabriela replied, looking him in the eye as if she wished he had not raised the issue nor question her intent and would just let go. "But he ordered Diego's death. I want him to die in my hands," she added as an afterthought, not really wishing to explain her reasons.

"You loved him." It was not a question but merely a statement of a fact.

"Loved him?" Gabriela paused as if in deep thought. "Perhaps, I did. But to be honest, I really don't know, Kulas. He was kind to me. He was gentle, and I miss him. And he did not deserve to die the way he did."

Kulas did not answer. He regretted asking the question. What was he thinking? He felt Ilang's hand on his arm.

"You have to understand, he was my husband. Sometimes, love doesn't have anything to do with it."

Kulas smiled shyly. "I wouldn't know," he said truthfully.

Gabriela pulled her hand back and looked away. She always had felt comfortable in the company of Kulas when they were little but now she was not too sure of her own feelings. She wanted to walk away but then again she wanted to be close to him. Then she heard Kulas speak.

"But what if you die instead?" Kulas had hated to ask the question but he felt he needed to voice out that possibility, which, knowing the *Capitán* had a real likelihood of it happening. He cared for this woman so much that he did not want her to get hurt. He loved her, there was no denying the fact, he was certain now. Perhaps he had been in love all along.

Gabriela looked away and said, "Then so be it." And she turned around ending the conversation. "If that happens," she added as she walked away without looking back, "then you can do whatever you wish."

Kulas did not answer. He merely shook his head. He never could understand women, and for a moment, despite the love he was feeling, he was glad that he was not married.

"So be it," he muttered and went to instruct the chosen archers who were going with him.

Aklang and Bagit were surprised, yet absolutely delighted when their *Ama* Kulas picked them as members of his raiding team. The fact that Kulas would rather have them as archers in their first taste of battle, but in effect putting them as far away as possible from the reach of a soldier, did not dampen their enthusiasm and excitement. Besides, they knew that they were picked primarily for their skill with the bow and arrow. And they were fast and agile.

The walls were about thirty feet high, with five guard towers where the walls joined. Each tower was manned by a guard who regularly marched his assigned span. They did their walk at almost the same exact time, so once they were out of the confines of their towers they could see each other in the open and know that each span was secure. But being out in the open simultaneously also had a tactical weakness.

Kulas was aware of this fact and totally exploited it. They dispatched the night guards in short order, five guards manning the five spans taken down by five straight-shot arrows as they walked out of the safety of their towers.

The guards never knew what hit them. Approaching undetected under cover of the pre-dawn darkness, the archers seemed to have timed their shots so perfectly that the guards went down almost at the same instant as each approached the midsection of his assigned wall.

Picked for not only their shooting prowess but also for their ability to free-climb cliffs that were higher and steeper, the archers made easy work of getting on top and over the thirty foot walls. They opened the gates to the fort without much of a resistance, with the exception of a soldier who had the runs and was on his way to the outhouse. The poor soul managed to put out a single cry of alarm before he was silenced by a well-placed arrow to the throat courtesy of Kulas. The rest of the raiding rebels led by Gabriela and the *Itneg* warriors with Akash at the front, all told almost eleven hundred strong entered the fort unmolested.

Another two hundred or so of the rebels remained a few meters outside the fort, ready to jump in as reinforcements if needed or to guard against any attempt of outside help. The warriors from Bangilo had volunteered to take on the *Municipio* and the *Guardia Civiles* in town.

Some light sleeping soldiers awoke to the unfortunate soldier's scream but they promptly went back to sleep when no further commotion followed. They assumed it was just someone having a bad dream while others were unsure of what they actually heard that woke them up momentarily. Besides, all of them thought that no crazy Indio would dare enter the fort, drunk or not. So they muttered a curse, rolled over and closed their eyes hoping to get back to their own disrupted dreams. But their intended return to deep slumber was not to be as more screaming, yelling and groaning came about shortly thereafter when the raiders went into the barracks and started methodically attacking the soldiers where they slept.

It was a sudden and precise raid that resulted in an almost completely one-sided rout, as the element of surprise was on the rebels' side.

But the Spaniards were disciplined and seasoned veterans of battles and sieges. They quickly regrouped and in a matter of minutes ably engaged the marauding rebels into scattered and bloody skirmishes within the fort. Many of them fought in whatever they had when they went to bed. There was no time to put on their uniforms although most of them, especially the veteran soldiers, disciplined as they were, managed to do so.

The fighting initially raged inside the barracks, then spread to the hallways and halls and to the perimeter of the walls, until seemingly by chance which in truth was driven by the subconscious desires of the adversaries to fight in open ground where they can better wield their swords, spears and bolos, the skirmish slowly spilled into the open courtyard.

And that favored the two young Chinamen who were in the thick of the fighting with their long poles. They fought together, one back against the other's back, attacking, bashing, thrusting, twirling and rotating as one smashing heads and legs and arms that sent weapons flying in the air and their owners writhing in pain on the ground. The soldiers, both the Ilocano conscripts and the *Kastilas,* as well as the rebels, were bewildered and awed at the same time by the amazing display of martial skills that they had never hitherto witnessed and the unfortunate adversaries were rewarded with ample bruises as they tried to test the mettle of the brothers.

And the open courtyard favored the archers as well who were up on the ramparts on top of the walls watching the melee below, and who were finally rewarded with the faint light of dawn to clearly see their targets. With most of them caught off-guard and not having time to put on their protective equipment, the soldiers were easy victims for the shooters on the ramparts. Uncannily adept at hitting smaller and faster-moving prey, the archers let loose their deadly arrows at will. And at that close quarters, there was no question of anyone of them missing. It was like shooting at a caged game. But this was battle and they took whatever advantage given them without much of a thought on the morality and fairness of it. There was no time of feeling remorse either.

That would come later if it ever did.

So they watched as the fighting went on below and they shot at will, their arrows flying with lethal accuracy, but with Ilang's request not to shoot the *Capitán* hovering in the back of their minds.

Then as if on cue, their eyes drifted to the middle of the courtyard.

What drew and held their collective attention was the seemingly unintended face-off between two combatants right in the midst of the chaos. The two were a man, a very big man in a very fancy uniform, executing a gentlemanly salute with his sword toward a woman taller than most of the rebels around her but seemed small compared to the man's length and girth. Two unlikely opponents, yet there they were, their arms on the ready, taking each other's measure, as if they were alone.

Then the big man attacked and the archers heaved a collective sigh and whooped when the woman swatted his sword away and he lost his balance in the process. Then they shook their heads in disbelief when the woman did not kill the man while he was down. She instead merely tapped the fallen man on the back with her *kampilan* then strangely she stepped back.

There was no doubt about it, Ilang had found her *Capitán* but what was she doing? But then the two resumed their fight and the archers likewise went back to their deadly shooting yet at the same time they held a curious attention to the duelers. Despite their disparity in size, the two appeared to be evenly matched in their skills. And there was no doubt about their superb expertise in swordsmanship.

Gabriela and the *Capitán* fought as if they were alone and the rest of the fighters, soldiers and rebels alike seemed to have agreed to leave them on their own.

Aklang watched the two fighters intently yet his eyes, without much movement, also took in most of the scene below, subconsciously picking where to put his arrow next. He did not want one of the rebels to get unexpectedly on the path of his arrow when he let it loose. He gripped his bow in his left hand, his right casually holding the arrow that was already nocked and poised on the bow. Patiently, he scanned the chaotic scene but his eyes floated back to the couple dueling in the midst of the carnage. How long had it been? Two hours? Three? It seemed longer but it could not have been more than an hour for the sun had barely risen up in the east and they had entered the fort at false dawn.

He fought the urge to take his eyes away from the courtyard and look to his left where the sun had just peeked at the top of Mount *Bullagaw*.

He watched with awe as the couple fought seemingly unaware of the chaos around them. He saw *Ina* Ilang leap gracefully to avoid a fatal slash from the *Capitán* and slashing back quickly in return causing the man to back down and almost slip in the process. The courtyard was now getting slick with spilt blood.

Aklang's lips curled to a smile, his eyes lighting up in admiration and pride at Gabriela's skill and agility. He had heard about her fighting prowess but he had dismissed it as merely talks for he did not believe a woman could fight as well as he was seeing now. In his heart, he had wished the man had gone down but at the same time he did not want the duel to end. For a duel it was.

And it was a sight to behold.

Then suddenly Aklang changed position, his left knee dropping to the ground in a flash and his right foot placed at angle for balance, as a blue form caught his eye rushing towards the duelers. He drew the bowstring effortlessly and loosed the arrow in one fluid motion even before his foot found solid anchor. The blue form below stopped in its tracks, the arrow grotesquely stuck on a tanned neck, now beginning to color in crimson.

It wasn't the first arrow that he had released that morning and the soldier below wasn't the first who went down from his bow.

He had lost count when the first quiver of the four he brought along was half empty. He was halfway through the second and he was aware that he had yet to miss, although that was not the thought that occupied his mind. At this distance and with the soldiers fighting in tight clusters, there was a slim chance of him missing a target. His shots, like the rest of the shooters, were precise and methodical, honed from long practices in the mountains hunting for game or just plain shooting at targets for fun with the boys.

But what nagged on the back of his mind that for a while caused him to hesitate a bit was the realization that when this was over, more men would have died from his arrows than the deadly long knives and spears of anyone of the warriors of his tribe below. Perhaps even *Ama* Akash who was in the middle of the fighting, cutting and dropping any soldier he came up to like a madman. And he was the youngest of all the fighters, and this being his first taste of battle. Again, he thought of the old man's words and was surprised that he was feeling neither remorse nor pity for the men that fell from his arrows.

Ama Dalalo had taken him aside before they left the village and warned him of how he would feel when he knew he had taken another man's life. Their conversation flashed briefly through his mind with the first arrow that he sent flying that morning but the excitement of the moment prevented him from dwelling on it, or his feelings. And after the first one, there was no going back and no time to think. The soldiers kept coming and he kept shooting, cutting them down with deadly accuracy like they were the banana trunks behind his house, standing close together waiting for his arrows to find home among them. And he obliged, without emotion, like it was the only rational thing to do. But now with the fighting taking its toll on both sides, oddly the old man's words came back to him.

"You will feel sick to your stomach and confused when you see a man go down from your arrow," the old man said emphatically, *"for taking another person's life is different from killing a deer or a wild boar. It is alright to feel bad, cry, or even throw up. There's no shame to it. Even the bravest of the braves felt the same thing after their first kill. But remember that in battle, killing is something that must be done. If you hesitate, you will end up dead for the enemy is there only with the intent to kill you."*

He didn't answer the old man for he could not force himself to speak as his mind and heart raced in anticipation of the uncertainty that faced him in his first foray into a fight where he could be killed, so he merely nodded in acknowledgement. He could not even look at the old man in the eyes.

The old man nodded in return and raised a hand to his shoulder. He felt the rough palm tentatively squeeze his shoulder then gently turned him toward the gathered warriors of the tribe, all ready to move out, everyone heavy with their weapons and ready for war.

Kulas was at the west end of the rampart, to the left of Aklang, early on in the battle. On his other flank, was the young warrior, Lang-gi, who had an uncanny way of handling a bow. On the other side of Lang-gi was the squat and chubby but silently deadly Dagyo who was so focused that his eyes never left the scene below his wall. And then Bagit, just over by Aklang, excitedly shooting at anyone that caught his attention.

Kulas had emptied his first quiver furiously as the soldiers emerged from their barracks when the alarm was raised a few moments after the rebels entered the fort. Hitting a target in the ensuing chaos was easy to do as the soldiers were massed together initially, like ghostly images in the pre-dawn light, their dappled shadows eerily dancing with them, thrown by the few lanterns strategically placed around the courtyard. They massed around in confusion, most of them not even aware that the rebels were already inside the fort. Kulas could have caused more damage as a shooter but it was not like him to be far away physically from a fight. He felt the urge to go down and join the hand-to-hand fighting below. He had accomplished his aim to breach the walls with the archers anyway. So as he emptied his second quiver, he moved quickly from his place and ran towards Aklang, unmindful of the threat that might have come from below.

But he assumed correctly that the protagonists on the ground would be paying attention to those around their immediate vicinity and would not bother looking up at the wall.

As he got closer to Aklang, Kulas pulled off the remaining two full quivers hanging from his back and dropped them by his nephew's side.

"Make them last," he said. "I'm going down there. And keep your eye on Ilang."

There was no need to remind Aklang not to waste an arrow. Kulas knew that at this distance, Aklang could hit anything even with his eyes closed. He turned around and was gone before the young archer could say a word.

Aklang watched with envy and pride as Kulas made his way down the wall, jumping off when he was halfway to the bottom, and brought out his two long knives as soon as he landed on his feet. He decapitated a soldier who foolishly rushed toward him as he was spotted, and disemboweled another who followed right behind the first one. And so his bloody trail toward the center of the fort began.

'Maybe he had finally decided to help *Ina* Ilang fight the *Capitán*,' Aklang thought as his eyes followed his uncle's bloody trail.

And for the longest time that morning, no arrow flew from the Aklang's bow as he watched with awe and pride Kulas rhythmically swinging his two long knives as he moved, felling everyone in his path. He was in constant motion, his arms moving in frenzy yet in total control of the weapons they wielded which seemed to unerringly find a mark or deflect a blow. They flashed briefly in the air, their tips scattering droplets of crimson as Kulas yet again executed a deadly thrust. He was a fearsome sight to behold with his bare chest and shoulders now splattered with blood from his victims. His was a fearful visage, exacting terror on the eyes and hearts of the soldiers in his path. They were dead before he got to them, frozen with fear and awe where they stood. The knives cleaving their flesh were just a symbolic formality.

And close by Kulas, *Ama* Akash and *Ama* Allong fought side by side, causing as much damage, blue clad bodies stained in crimson lying in heaps by their feet. And the two young Chinamen were there too in the midst of them causing as much havoc as they could with their long poles.

It took all of Aklang's discipline to avert his eyes from the warriors and look back after *Ina* Ilang.

And not a moment too soon as another man in indigo blue got a little too close to Gabriela. Aklang quickly shifted and released the arrow which flew yet again unerringly into the straying soldier. The soldier gasped in surprise and fell a few feet behind Gabriela.

Aklang let go a sigh of relief. He nocked another arrow into his bow keeping his eyes at the two duelers below. His face brightened suddenly when he saw the big man seem to lose his balance. "Finish him off, *Ina*!" he excitedly blurted, but was surprised when Gabriela stopped and waited for the *Capitán* to regain his balance. Then his expression turned to puzzlement as he noted that Gabriela seemed to be talking to the *Capitán*. And then his face showed total confusion as he realized everyone had stopped fighting, even *Ama* Kulas who seemed transfixed in his spot, knives dripping with blood, intently looking at the middle of the courtyard. The Chinese twins, fighting back to back and surrounded by soldiers grimacing from bruises all over their heads and bodies, also stood silently, their long staffs held firmly in front of them holding their opponents at bay.

The archers likewise stopped and waited but with their arrows on the ready.

Then the big man yelled something and lunged ferociously at Gabriela and as if on cue the fighting resumed again. And the archers released their arrows, each fighting the urge to shoot the big man, orders or not.

Then Aklang heard Bagit to his right yell in pain, his voice lifting above the clamor of the fighting below. His heart fell to his stomach as he saw Bagit double over and vanish from his sight. He quickly stood up and ran to his cousin unmindful of his own safety. He went through the guard tower that joined the spans they were holding and as he came out of it, saw Bagit sprawled on the rampart with half of his head and face bloodied.

"Bagit!!!" he cried, as he darted and knelt by his cousin's side. He lifted Bagit's head carefully and gingerly cradled it on his lap, his hands and arms and legs getting wet and stained by his cousin's blood. But he was unaware of it. He felt relieved when he saw his cousin's chest heaving in regular breathing.

Aklang checked the wound and noticed that the bullet only grazed his cousin's head, taking a chunk of skin and hair. But the wound was bleeding profusely. He took off his head band and Bagit's head band that fell off to his side and wrapped them around his cousin's head to staunch the bleeding. Bagit stirred as he tightened the makeshift bandage.

"You're alright. You're alright!" Aklang said as he pushed Bagit's hand away as the latter instinctively raised it to touch his throbbing wound.

"What happened?" Bagit asked.

"You got hit on the head, but it's just a scratch. You can thank the gods for giving you a thick skull," Aklang said. "You'll be fine."

"I thought I was dead and went to hell and have seen the devil as those Christians say when I saw you," Bagit tried to grin but came up with a pained wince instead.

"Shut up! You just fainted when you saw your blood, you wimp," Aklang said, glad that his cousin was alright. "Sit up against the wall and don't move."

He helped Bagit ease himself up to a sitting position, scoot backwards toward the outer side of the rampart's wall, and rest his back against it. He gathered Bagit's bow and arrows and placed them by his cousin's side. Bagit tried to grab his bow but Aklang caught and gripped his hand.

"No, leave the shooting to me. You rest until your vision clears and you can stand on your own," Aklang said.

"I'm alright," Bagit protested.

"No, you might hit one of us by mistake. Rest." Aklang took his own bow and nocked an arrow as he turned around to the fighting below. It took him a moment but he saw that Kulas was already at the middle of the courtyard, close to the dueling man and woman, and keeping an open space behind the woman's back.

"He's letting them fight," Aklang said aloud. He had hoped that his *Ama* Kulas had finally decided enough was enough and he was going to fight and kill the *Capitán* himself.

"What?" Bagit said.

"*Ama* Kulas. He's behind *Ina* Ilang but he's not helping her fight the big white man!"

"Why not? He could just finish the fight," Bagit said with a puzzled look on his face. Like Aklang he had assumed that Kulas went down there to help Gabriela in her fight.

"I don't know," Aklang said. He was also bewildered. He can see that Kulas could easily fight his way behind the big man and take him down with a quick cut. "I don't know why he is not helping her out."

"Shoot him," Bagit said. "Shoot the big man."

Aklang raised his bow and pulled the string until he felt the guiding feather of the arrow softly brush his neck, the string taut and firm against his chin. He sighted down the arrow's length but somehow something held him back. Then slowly he lowered the bow down.

"What are you doing?" Bagit said. "Why aren't you shooting?"

"No. He's letting them fight," Aklang replied. "*Ama* Kulas is letting them fight."

He watched and did not notice that Bagit had crawled by his side until the latter spoke.

"Yes, it seems that he is letting them fight. Perhaps he is respecting *Ina* Ilang's wish."

"Yes, maybe that is the man who killed *Ina* Ilang's husband."

Bagit did not respond.

For a while neither cousins said anything as they watched in awe, their silence broken only by the clanging of swords and bolos and the occasional grunts, yells and moaning from the wounded down in the courtyard.

After a while, Bagit said, looking at Aklang, "Are you alright?"

Aklang looked back at his cousin, puzzled by the question.

"You're bleeding," Bagit said. "There's blood all over you."

Aklang looked down at his arms and chest and legs, his eyes ending at the small pool of blood by his feet. He did not remember getting hit, but he dropped his bow and arrow and patted himself down. He did not feel any pain, but as he looked at his upturned palms covered in blood, he felt a surge in his chest. He leaned over the outside wall and watched as he let go of what he ate the night before.

After a while when he was just gagging air, he gathered himself then faced back the grinning Bagit.

"I think it's my blood," Bagit said impishly, then winced as another wave of pain went through his head.

It took all of Aklang's self-control not to hit his wounded cousin.

"Go with Dagyo," he finally said. Dagyo was the strongest of them all. He could help Bagit get down from the wall.

As Bagit grudgingly made his way toward Dagyo, Aklang hurried back to his place on the wall where he had a better view of watching the fight below. He had not reached the place too soon when he had to hastily make another shot as a man in uniform made his way past Kulas who was busy fighting two soldiers at the same time, and was able to get close behind Gabriela.

'Don't jump,' he thought as he realized the arrow would travel so close by Gabriela's head. He breathed a sigh of relief as the arrow found its mark and the man in uniform hit the bloody ground. Once more, Aklang released another arrow, flinching involuntarily for a moment as he realized it would travel so close to the woman's head again. He hoped she wouldn't decide to leap at the wrong time.

Despite the chaos, Gabriela felt the buzz of the arrow as it whipped past her head and she heard the unmistakable sound of it hitting flesh and a body falling down behind her. That was too damn close, she thought, but she dared not look up or around. She could never explain it but her senses were sharper and keener when she's in a fight. Was it the thrill of putting her life on the line? She ruled out fear for she did not feel scared at all. She was excited yet at the same time she felt a sense of detachment that bordered to indifference that it did not matter if she would live or die. But she kept her focus. Her eyes remained glued at the *Capitán* who was backing down to regain his balance after Gabriela slashed back at him.

'Kulas,' she thought, as another arrow flew by that even seemed closer than the previous one. She heard the gasp of the man behind her as the arrow yet again produced that distinctive thumping sound as it found its mark. She sensed the man fall behind her followed in a moment by the unmistakable clanging of bare sword hitting the cobblestone. 'Kulas' her guardian angel, she thought, 'still looking out for me after all these years.' She stopped briefly as she noted with amusement the surprised and bewildered look of the *Capitán*'s face. He had likewise seemed frozen in his place.

Up on the wall, Aklang stood up, another arrow ready on his bow, the notched end loosely held, nocked on the string. Then he did an exaggerated bow when he saw the *Capitán* turn around and look up at him. Why he did what he did he never knew later on when he thought of it. It was just a spur of the moment thing. Yet he never loosened his grip on his arrow and he stood on the ready. He noticed the other archers on the wall were standing likewise as there seemed to be a lull in the fighting below.

Aklang waited. He heard words spoken below but he could not make out anything of what was being said. He stood, with his arrow on the ready, as did Dagyo and Lang-gi. Bagit had stopped to catch his breath and sat with his back against the wall, unseen from below.

Then the silence was broken by the rapid sound of hoof beats.

Chapter Forty Nine

So there they were in the middle of the courtyard of the garrison, face to face at last, the hunter and the hunted. *Don* Manuel was amused at the incongruity of it all. He was supposed to be the hunter but here she was, the hunted, standing erect and defiant right in the center of his fort, his own lair, surrounded by his soldiers. He almost affected a smile at the boldness and irony of it all but his face remained impassive in deference to the bleeding and dying men around him. Most of them his men he realized, as his peripheral vision, sharp as ever like the seasoned hunter that he was, noted the bloody indigo uniform on most of the bodies lying on the ground.

And *Don* Manuel seethed inside, yet his demeanor remained calm and composed, seemingly unconcerned of what was going on around him. It was this cold calmness in battle that had drawn awe, fear and admiration from both his men and his enemies. And he felt more than a tinge of annoyance now as he saw that the woman defiantly facing him from across the courtyard showed neither fear nor concern.

Then a shadow crossed his face as suddenly it occurred to him that the woman facing him was not a stranger. He had seen her before, garbed entirely differently, in fact with nothing at all, not anything like the amazon-warrior standing before him. The woman canted her head as if in reaction to the changing expression in his face, and Manuel knew then that this was the same woman. For a moment he hesitated as Isabella's beautiful face entered his mind. They looked so similar, he thought. He gave a barely perceptible shrug as he banished the thought away. His mind and body fully attuned to the fact that any distraction was fatal in a fight. He had seen the woman fought her way inside the fort and she could handle the *kampilan* as well as he had seen a skilled native wield one.

There was chaos around them, soldiers and rebel Indios and now *Itnegs* also, all intensely engaged in frenetic combat, thrusting, slashing with impunity and abandon, parrying with their swords and bolos with all their might and skills, intent in killing one another, oblivious to the prospect of getting killed themselves. Nobody thought of dying. There was no time for it. All that mattered was the intent of inflicting grievous harm to the enemy, killing him, and surviving in the process. Death, if it came, was of little relevance. So they fought with abandon, everyone all tangled and bound together by the lust of battle and drunk with the color and smell of spilt blood. In their frenzy, there seemed to be no definitive line to distinguish a foe from a friend. Everyone and everything was in a feverish turmoil. The training to fight and defend as a unified force all forgotten and abandoned in the craziness of the moment.

But to Gabriela there was nobody else as she met the gaze of *Don* Manuel over the fallen bodies, ignoring the rest of the soldiers and rebels who were still standing and fighting like mad dogs. It was just her and the *Capitán*. She was so focused on *Don* Manuel that to her time stood still. She looked back at *Don* Manuel, her eyes unflinching, almost languid, showing neither fear nor anger, just an emotionless look at an enemy who was about to die and whose death did not matter to her now one way or the other. The thought of avenging Diego was no longer of importance, almost meaningless. To her, *Don* Manuel was like a stone statue, with no soul. Yet he represented everything that her beloved Diego fought against and died for. So he too must die, she thought, but strangely she did not feel any hatred or anger in her heart.

Then a flicker of hesitation crossed her face as she noted the *Capitán* looking at her in a strange way as if he just remembered something profound while their eyes met. Puzzled, she stood her ground, waiting for the *Capitán* to make the first move.

She watched calmly now as the *Capitán* seemed to have dismissed whatever thought had entered his mind and made his way towards her, stepping over bodies and swatting away thrusts and slashes directed his way, slashing and thrusting back in return, always with deadly outcome, and yet his gaze and direction never wavered away from her.

Gabriela waited patiently, almost disinterestedly, yet her attention was entirely focused now at the *Capitán*, the sequence of moves that she was going to make when her opponent showed his hand playing in her mind. And the *Capitán* kept coming until they were just a few feet apart with nobody finally between them. *Don* Manuel stopped and dipped his head curtly, a non-verbal gesture from a gentleman meeting a lady for the first time. He then raised his sword and saluted, as he was trained to do before a duel.

Gabriela's eyes flashed with amusement and her lips twitched for a fleeting moment as she suppressed a smile, gesturing with her left arm that held her shield by her side, spreading it slightly as if she was saying clearly, 'You're looking for me, here I am.'

The *Capitán* completed his gentlemanly salute with his sword, blade pointed upwards, the hilt to his lips, but his face remained inscrutable, as if he did not see Gabriela's gesture but he had noted every nuance coming from the woman before him. Gabriela noted as well her opponent's impassive demeanor and at that exact moment as the *Capitán* kissed his sword, she thought of him as a statue of a gentleman, well-mannered, yet a soulless, rigid, and cold piece of stone nonetheless.

Then the statue moved, as *Don* Manuel made a swift downward slashing motion with his sword, flicking his hand quickly, completing the salute. The sword made an ominous swishing sound in the air and it quivered dreadfully as *Don* Manuel sharply stopped its descent, locking his arm stiffly. Then as quickly he raised the sword back up, horizontally this time, pointed menacingly at Gabriela, and lunged forward closing the gap between them in a single step.

'Pity,' he thought as he moved, 'for such a young and beautiful woman to die for a lost cause.' He had totally forgotten the woman in the river. All he saw was an opponent that needed to be subdued and conquered. And most preferably, killed.

It was a quick, sudden and decisive move, one that the *Capitán* had practiced and used countless of times, resulting almost always in a quick end to the encounter. The *Capitán* did not believe in gauging the enemy. He believed in a quick first strike and end any fight as quickly as he could. There was no point in breaking a sweat if it could be helped. He expected the same result, although he felt a slight tinge of disinclination for the act, bordering to pity for this woman who they called *La Generala*. For despite the title and the warrior garb and bearing, she was still a woman, and there was something inside *Don* Manuel that grated against the thought of hurting a woman.

But he had committed to the act and he tried his best to ignore his conscience.

The *Capitán* was fast but to Gabriela he seemed to be moving so painstakingly slow. She waited patiently as *Don* Manuel stepped forward with his sword, and held her ground.

Don Manuel was surprised when Gabriela simply stood still, not moving, not even taking a step backwards perhaps, or raising her shield or *kampilan* in defense. The *Capitán* almost held back his thrust but he was committed and propelled by momentum with his sudden lunge and he instinctively locked his arm for the impact of his sword piercing Gabriela's body. But his eyes grew wide with surprise when at the last instant Gabriela quickly pivoted and at the same time flicked her wrist, and her broad-faced *kampilan* deftly swatted his sword away from her body.

Outbalanced by his momentum and the sudden impact of Gabriela's heavy *kampilan*, the *Capitán* desperately scrambled away, as the tip of the *kampilan* came inches to his breast when Gabriela followed through with a swift slash of her own after deflecting the *Capitán*'s initial thrust.

The cobbled courtyard was slick with blood and the *Capitán* found himself falling as he evaded the *kampilan*. He found himself landing on a dead rebel. Before he could get up and recover, *Don* Manuel felt the flat face of Gabriela's kampilan whacked his back. Surprised and confused, he turned around to see Gabriela taking a step back with an amused grin on her face, her *kampilan* pointed to the ground, waiting for her opponent to stand up.

Don Manuel's faced reddened, deeply embarrassed, and totally taken by surprise with how fast the woman had reacted. He braced himself up and stood erect and tall, gathering himself with as much dignity as he can muster. He faced Gabriela, giving her another salute with his sword, this time as acknowledgment for her honorable deed. His face, still crimson with embarrassment, also showed admiration and newfound respect for the rebel. He nodded briefly toward his opponent, locking his eyes on her eyes that showed no fear just a hint of amusement, almost taunting him, he thought. He felt the anger in him grew and his embarrassment gave way to the rush of the all too banal emotion of avenging his masculine pride from being trampled by a woman almost half his size. Yet in the back of his mind a thought nagged at him. Perhaps he had underestimated this woman.

Gabriela again waited, impassive and immobile like before, but she noted the change in the *Capitán*'s demeanor. He was more determined and calculating this time. Briefly she wondered if she had made a mistake in not killing the *Capitán* when he was down as she also saw the unmistakable killing rage in his face.

Don Manuel made his move, slashing and thrusting with his sword furiously, trying to overcome his opponent with his powerful and rapid attack. For a moment Gabriela was taken aback by the ferocity of the *Capitán*. She retreated as she deftly parried each furious thrust and slash by *Don* Manuel, careful not to stumble over the dead bodies or step on the slick blood that permeated the cobbled garrison floor, dancing her way gracefully out of the *Capitán*'s reach.

Don Manuel kept the pressure, his body now purely relying on all the practiced movements of previous fights and friendly engagements. But his admiration for his opponent grew as Gabriela deftly avoided his attacks, and seemed to have an answer and countermove for everything that the *Capitán* threw at her. She skillfully extricated herself out of tight situations, gracefully stepping out of harm's way. She counter attacked every now and then to check the *Capitán*'s advance, breathing easily while the *Capitán* felt himself tiring, encumbered in part by the breastplate beneath his uniform. He slowed down for a moment to catch his breath, which was a mistake as Gabriela initiated the attack this time, preventing him from taking a much needed rest. She moved in, slashing with her heavy *kampilan*, backing the *Capitán* close to the wall. But the *Capitán* was not a veteran of many wars and duels for nothing. He backed away wisely, as he caught his breath and likewise thwarted Gabriela's attack with equal skill.

So they fought vigorously and recklessly it seemed, but somehow there was rhythm in their movements, like they were two performers engaged not in a deadly fight but in a beautifully synchronized dance. Neither one seemed to gain advantage over the other, with only nicks and scratches as proof to the gravity of their encounter. *Don* Manuel felt as if he was in a dream where he did not want to be, a part of his psyche abhorring the idea of pitting his skills against a woman, regardless a very skilled one. But the fighter in him felt exhilarated at the same time with the prospect of finally meeting a very worthy opponent other than Tiago.

Don Manuel feinted and followed through with another thrust that was again deflected deftly by the big *kampilan* wielded with uncannily easy dexterity by Gabriela's dainty hand like it was as lightweight as a foil, yet there was no mistaking its heavy deadliness as the *Capitán's* sword swerved yet again to a harmless arc. Her *maestro* had always insisted on her using a heavier *kampilan* that the men favored during their practices and Gabriela silently thanked him seeing now the astuteness of that decision. The favorite *kampilan* she used now was lighter but no less deadly.

Then suddenly *Don* Manuel seemed to have lost his balance again, and Gabriela paused briefly as she was sure there was no cause for it.

Don Manuel ignored the reproach of his conscience as he broke his promise not to ever resort to Tiago's tipsy sword trick, steadfast in his belief that it was unworthy of a true gentleman. Of course, Tiago laughed at him when he voiced his opinion and he could hear the old soldier laughing now. But he blocked the laughter off his mind. He needed to finish this fast as he felt himself tiring again. He doubt if he could get a third wind. He wobbled as if he was going to fall down and waited for Gabriela's attack, expecting her to take the bait.

But the attack never came. *Don* Manuel was surprised as Gabriela held back, not attempting to rush her opponent to take advantage of his apparent loss of balance. He turned his face toward her, looking at her eyes. She looked back and smiled, shaking her head.

"There had been no *basi* available around these parts for a long time, *Capitán*, not since you've tripled the tax and your soldiers have drunk the rest. And the men who knew how to make the wine have been busy dying, fighting your soldiers."

The old man, he must have taught her, the *Capitán* thought as he was now aware that Gabriela was familiar with the ruse, remembering how the old *Itneg* was silently studying Tiago when he was engaged in a mock duel with the young warrior back in Abra and Tiago went through his drunken fighting trick.

As if reading his thought, Gabriela shook her head. "I have watched *Don* Tiago use that trick to defeat an Ilocano *maestro* in *Arnis* who was beating him so badly using only a pair of sticks. He would have shredded Tiago to tatters if he used the long knives instead. The *maestro* recovered from that encounter and he never forgot the lesson. That *maestro* taught me well, with the sticks, the knives and the *bolo* and *kampilan*. He also showed me that drunken trick. But thank your *Sargento* for me for sharing his technique."

"My pleasure, *Señora*. My only regret was that I had not personally taught you that move." Tiago's voice, filled with pride, rang clearly from behind the *Capitán*. Gabriela and *Don* Manuel had been so focused with each other that they had not noticed that the remaining rebels and soldiers in the courtyard had ceased fighting among themselves, becoming engrossed to watching them as they fought one another, so far to a stalemate.

"I am sure you are a good teacher, *Don* Tiago, as the *Capitán* learned something from you." Gabriela spoke without taking her eyes off *Don* Manuel.

"Ahh, I wish I could take the credit, *Señora*," Tiago said, "but the *Capitán* was already a better swordsman than I was and already knew that trick when we met although he vowed not to use it as he is a gentleman, or unless, I'm afraid, he was pushed to his limits. Pardon me, *Capitán*, for being truthful for once."

"That's kind of you to say, *Señor* Tiago. I wish your kindness extends also to my countrymen, or are you only kind and a gentleman when you are not drunk?" Gabriela said.

"That is a foul thing to say to a gentleman, *Señora*, but I will let it pass today, coming from such a beautiful and accomplished woman as yourself," Tiago said.

Don Manuel lowered his sword and shook his head in consternation. He did not know if he was amused or irritated by the exchange between Tiago and Gabriela. He looked around him at the fighters who were standing around, both the rebels and soldiers, who now had seemed to have abandoned the will to fight relegating themselves to mere spectators, fascinated likewise now at the verbal exchange between Gabriela and Tiago.

'This is unreal,' *Don* Manuel thought. 'How in damnation was this friendly banter happening right in the middle of a battle nonetheless?' he wondered.

But he remained silent. He looked at Gabriela as if waiting for her next words.

Noticing his quandary, Gabriela said, "You have a glib tongue, *Don* Tiago. You should find time to teach that to your *Capitán*. He seemed to have lost his ability to speak as well as his courage."

Her words seemed to have lit a fuse in the *Capitán*. "Fight you idiots!" He yelled to his soldiers as he rushed furiously toward Gabriela. And so the fighting resumed, fiercer and deadlier than before.

'No more tricks,' *Don* Manuel thought as he put to bear all the skills he knew as a swordsman. 'This foolishness must end now.' That he was fighting a woman had completely abandoned his mind. Gabriela was just another Indio or another Carib that needed to be taught a final lesson.

Sensing *Don* Manuel's renewed anger and determination, Gabriela's demeanor likewise turned serious and grim. She parried and deflected *Don* Manuel's attack calmly and without wasted effort, countering vigorously at every opportunity. She felt the side of her dress rip as she sidestepped a slashing sweep of *Don* Manuel's sword, its razor sharp tip barely touching her skin but drawing blood. She slashed back quickly with her *kampilan* connecting with the *Capitán*'s protective vest underneath his uniform, just below his left shoulder where it glanced off and down to his backside, its tip leaving a crimson mark on the Captain's unprotected lower side. *Don* Manuel took a couple of steps back, catching his breath, quickly assessing the damage done yet not feeling anything, adrenalin blocking all the pain from the wound.

Gabriela stood back herself, and took a deep breath. She was still breathing easily but her arms were getting heavier. She shrugged off and threw aside the hard leather covered wooden shield from her left arm and pressed a hand to her side where her dress was ripped feeling the wetness in her fingers. She wiped her hand in her skirt and started forward initiating the attack this time.

The *Capitán* waited and watched and his eyes grew wider as a *Guardia Civil* rushed behind Gabriela with his saber raised, intent on giving a deadly blow to the Generala's unguarded neck. But before the sword came down, the *Capitán* saw with astonishment the soldier stopping in his tracks, a surprised look on his face as his eyes lowered to the arrow that had seemed to have sprouted from his chest. The soldier dropped his sword harmlessly to the ground, both hands futilely grasping the arrow as he fell dead over his sword.

Gabriela saw the expression on *Don* Manuel's face as she sensed the soldier falling behind her, his sword noisily clanging against the cobblestone. She stopped but she did not turn around. 'Kulas,' she thought. It was not the first time that an arrow had passed by her head that morning causing no doubt a death around her. Her attention remained focused on *Don* Manuel but in her peripheral vision she noted the familiar figure of an *Itneg* archer rising on the wall from behind the *Capitán*'s back. Her eyes squinted a bit as it struck her that the figure did not look like Kulas at all. It did not matter and she dismissed the thought quickly, eyes never wavering from their intense gaze at the *Capitán*.

Don Manuel likewise stopped from advancing to meet Gabriela. He slowly turned around, bewildered, his eyes scanning the walls behind him, searching for the archer. He saw a young bare-chested *Itneg* rising from the top of the wall, giving him an exaggerated bow, bending to his waist, and a friendly wave with his bow despite the arrow nocked to it. He scanned the top of the fort and saw a couple more *Itnegs* and nobody else, armed likewise with bows and arrows. The guards on the ramparts were nowhere in sight.

The *Capitán* suddenly felt sick with the realization that the *Itnegs* were simply playing with his life. He would have been dead a while back if the archers had so wished. He had heard about the unrivalled skill with the bow and arrow of the warriors from Abra and knew in his heart that the *Itneg* behind him on the wall was as good as they come. And no doubt the other archers were as skilled as well.

He looked at Gabriela who remained immobile. She simply stood there like she was waiting for him to understand the situation and make a decision, leaving his fate to his own hands.

Don Manuel turned his head and looked back at the *Itneg* on top of the wall. There was not a doubt that he and his companions had dispatched off the assigned guards. He noted that he had another arrow in his bow but it was pointed to the ground.

He looked around at his soldiers and the rebels, suddenly aware that they had again stopped fighting, as if an unspoken truce had been called. The silence was eerie, broken only now and then by the soft moans of the injured and the sporadic fighting beyond by the stables and at the other end of the fort. His eyes roamed around the courtyard, taking in the lifeless forms that littered the place, brown and white skinned men, covered in dark red pastel turning to black under the unrelenting sun, and noticed for the first time that so many of the dead had arrows in them. *Don* Manuel winced involuntarily as he felt the tiredness and pain creeping in his body, aware for the first time how hot and dry and dusty the day had become. Above them, the sun shone like a fiery white disc in the cloudless sky.

Suddenly the silence was shattered by the persistent sound of a horse in a hurry, its hooves clattering against the cobbles. Every eye turned toward the main gate where the noise was coming from as a uniformed soldier burst forth from it, his horse frothing in the mouth, ridden mercilessly in a great hurry. He was one of three messengers and somehow with pure luck he was able to get through the rebel forces outside the fort that inexplicably seemed to be moving out. The soldier dismounted even before the horse came to a full stop, glancing around quickly, bewildered at the sight of soldiers and rebels standing around, and rushed toward the *Capitán* as his eyes fell on him. But before he could say a word, a young Indio rebel atop a chestnut horse that was about ready to fall, rushed through the smaller back gate, its doors busted open by the rebels when they entered the fort, his woven coconut leaf hat anchored by a long hemp string, flying wildly behind his head.

"*¡Soldados! ¡Soldados!*" he shouted at Gabriela. "Less than an hour away. Many *soldados!*" Abruptly, he turned his horse around without waiting for any answer and rode out the back gate as fast as he had arrived.

Gabriela took a deep breath as she heard the Spanish messenger likewise say the same thing to the *Capitán.*

"The reinforcements will be here within the hour, *Señor,*" he said, "perhaps *trenta minutos,* maybe less."

Don Manuel listened silently then dismissed the messenger with a wave of his hand. He looked at Gabriela then back to the archer on top of the wall. Nobody moved from where they stood. The archer watched him silently with his bow and arrow held steadily and ready in his hands.

Don Manuel turned his eyes back to Gabriela, then he lowered his sword when he realized that he still held it poised as if ready for battle.

"Go," he said, looking into Gabriela's eyes who met his gaze blankly. "*Por favor,*" he added as Gabriela still did not move. There was no doubt in his mind that the next arrow would be for him if the fighting continued yet he wondered why they had not shot at him when he was fighting with *La Generala*. Did these savages follow an honor code somehow? He looked without expression at the woman, yet deep inside wondering what drove her and her people to face uncertain odds yet adhere to a standard of honor.

Gabriela finally gave a barely perceptible nod toward the *Capitán*. She raised her left hand to her face, folded her lower lip between her thumb and forefinger and let out a sharp whistle that startled the soldiers and rebels alike, waking everyone up from their battle weary induced trance. Some of the soldiers started to get their swords ready to resume fighting but *Don* Manuel likewise raised his left hand above his head, a silent command for his soldiers to hold their ground.

Gabriela in turn raised her *kampilan* and waved it in a circle over her head then pointed it toward the back gate. The rebels hesitantly backed out of the fort, the able picking up the dead and assisting the wounded, as everyone headed out through the back gate. The soldiers warily watched them retreat, not making a move as they waited for the *Capitán*'s orders.

"Don't anybody move. Let them go," *Don* Manuel said, noting that the *Itneg* archers remained standing silently on top of the wall with bows and arrows still held on the ready. He would not miss, Manuel thought, of the archer behind him.

Gabriela waited until the last of her men was out of the gate, then she backed out slowly, her gaze locked on *Don* Manuel's face.

"*Señora*, we shall meet again, you can be sure of that," *Don* Manuel said, "and when we do, one of us will die."

"Then go to confession, *Capitán*, and have yourself ready to meet your Maker with a clean heart," Gabriela replied.

"I advise you to do likewise, *Señora*, for the next time I will not be a gentleman."

"I never thought you were, *Capitán*. A gentleman does not let his men beat helpless men and children, nor let them rape and abuse their women."

Don Manuel felt his blood rising to his face like he was slapped, but he checked his temper. Finally he said, "*Bueno. Vaya*, go before I change my mind."

Gabriela simply smiled as she took a quick glimpse at the top of the wall behind the *Capitán* where the archer still stood and was surprised to see the young Aklang. She looked quickly around and noticed Kulas for the first time, standing silently and serenely by the back gate with her uncle, *Ama* Akash, watching and waiting for her to move. Both men stood together casually, their serenity belied by the mean looking knives that they held loosely in their hands, dripping with blood. Their bodies were soaked and glistened with blood also yet neither appeared to be hurt at all.

Kulas gave her a barely perceptible nod urging her to get out as their eyes locked briefly. Gabriela turned around and backed out warily toward the back gate. She stopped when she reached Kulas and Akash. Standing by their side, she sheathed her *kampilan* then looked back at the *Capitán*.

"Until then, *Capitán*, practice every day," she said. "I don't want to have an advantage the next time we meet." With that she turned quickly, and side by side, she, Akash and Kulas ran out of the fort to where her men waited with her horse, Petra, ready and prancing and raring to run. She mounted swiftly, bounding on top of the horse without stepping on the stirrup, the handle of her *kampilan* ominously protruding over her head where it lay snugly in its sheath tied across her back. Kulas and Akash ran

328

past her and joined the other *Itnegs* who were already grouped together and making their own hasty retreat on foot toward the river, the twin Chinese brothers and Allong in their midst.

"We shall meet again, *Señora*, we shall meet again, of that, you would be certain," *Don* Manuel whispered as he heard the rebels move away hurriedly in a clatter of hooves. His eyes glinted in a soft glow as he subconsciously wished in his heart that their meeting would not be as enemies for the woman had earned his respect. But he knew with certainty that it would be but nothing else. "One of us will die. T'is a pity we had not met in a different time and place. Perhaps it would not have to be so."

Don Manuel did not like the prospect a bit and he tried to banish it from his thoughts. He looked around the courtyard and his grim face turned grimmer. He had more bodies to bury. The fury in his chest against the rebels flared back up with greater passion.

On top of the ramparts, the young archers made a deferential bow toward the preoccupied *Capitán* then they went down their walls, vanishing from the sight of the soldiers below.

The *Capitán* did not notice their departure. The ramparts were empty when he remembered to finally look back up. He issued a quick command to search the vicinity of the fort for the archers but no one found any trace, nor were they certain of how they got up and off the ramparts without ropes. Nobody would have believed that they were ever there if not for the arrows that they left behind, all embedded in the dead guards and the dead and wounded soldiers below.

"Tend to the wounded and bury the dead," the *Capitán* tiredly ordered Tiago. "Give the reinforcement time to rest when they come in and make preparations to ride out in two days. We'll hunt the bastards down and we're not coming back until we get all of them."

He turned around and went to his quarters. He heard Tiago bark his orders as he walked away.

Don Manuel sat alone in his quarters for a long time. He had finally cooled down and he rationally reviewed the recent events and their possible trends in the future. Try as he did, he could not come up with an outcome to his liking. He finally gave up. He felt tired. He felt weary. And most of all there was a feeling of heaviness in his heart that he could not explain. Deep inside, a tiny seed of perhaps the truth grew; the truth that he was subconsciously trying to suppress. His heart was no longer into the pursuit and the capture of *La Generala*.

Then barely half of the hour had elapsed, the reinforcements came.

329

Capitán Manuel reluctantly rose from his chair to meet the new arrivals. Despite what his heart felt, he had a promise to keep and a Royal duty to fulfill. He was, after all, a soldier; and not just a soldier.

He was an officer of His Majesty's Army, and as such, sentimentality had no place in his heart.

La Generala must be caught and hanged at all cost.

And her death would be a lesson to all Indios that they would not soon forget.

Chapter Fifty

"So what does an *Alcalde* do?" Biktol asked Ampit as he sat down again on the big leather chair behind the grand desk of the Mayor of the municipality of Vigan.

"I have no idea," Ampit said.

"I think I know," Ambit said, grinning and showing his toothless front gum in the process.

"What?" Both Biktol and Ampit asked simultaneously. Ambit was not known for his ideas and both were curious to know what he had this time.

"Grow his big fat ass sitting in that chair!" Ambit laughed, his mouth made larger by his missing front teeth, as he pointed to the portrait of the Mayor hanging on the wall behind the desk.

Both his brother and Biktol gave him baleful looks but they turned and looked at the portrait of the Mayor. The Mayor indeed was fat. They looked at one another and also broke up laughing. Several of the Bangilo warriors came rushing into the Mayor's office to find out what the laughter was all about.

"What's going on?" Kulang asked.

Ampit stopped laughing and his face grew serious.

"Shut up and pay respects to the new Mayor of Vigan!" he said sternly, pointing to Biktol who was grinning behind the desk then he burst out laughing.

Kulang and the other warriors who followed him looked at Biktol, then to the brothers, Ambit and Ampit, in consternation.

"You all are nuts!" Kulang said.

"Hey, who's going to say he's not the new Mayor?" Ampit said. "The Spaniards or the Ilocanos?"

Kulang thought a bit then silently nodded with a smile in his face. Who indeed? They just took over the town.

As agreed with Ilang and the other tribal leaders up in the mountains the day before they came down to the land of the Ilocanos, Biktol and his warriors from Bangilo were to simultaneously launch the attack on the *municipio* and the jailhouse guarded by the *Guardia Civiles* when Gabriela and her joint forces attacked the Spanish fort.

"Do what you have to do and leave the town and the *Guardia Civiles* in the *calaboso* and the *municipio* to us," Biktol had said, waving a dismissive hand. He did not anticipate a formidable resistance from the *Guardia Civiles*. Besides, his select force of battle-tested warriors was ready and raring for war. There had been too long of inactivity up there in their village and they were getting fat, bored, and restless.

And as Biktol predicted, there was not much of a resistance. His warriors basically ran over the measly and undermanned guards in the jailhouse. The dozen or so guards initially put up a brave effort to defend the jail, but they were simply overmatched. When the little skirmish was over, half of the guards were dead while the rest meekly surrendered, nursing their wounds and egos.

The municipal hall itself was practically empty. The clerks ran off as soon as they saw the heavily armed and almost naked *Itneg* warriors, leaving the Mayor who was too fat and too scared to run, cowering behind his desk inside his office. Biktol and Ampit found him there, shaking with fear, the front of his trousers dripping wet. He appeared so pathetic that even Ampit had not the heart to cause him any further harm.

"Go," Biktol told the trembling man, "Go outside and tell your people, *La Generala* is taking over Vigan. You are free."

The Mayor literally ran all over himself to get out of there, stumbling a couple of times before he was outside the door. Then suddenly he came back running and crying in fear, a pack of howling warriors behind him. He was fast for a man his size as he sought refuge behind Biktol who was studying the overstuffed leather chair behind the big desk.

"Stop!!!" Biktol raised a hand, and the warriors skidded to a stop in their bare feet, making screeching sounds on the waxed wooden floor. "Don't anybody touch him. Let him go. He has a message from me to deliver to his people."

The warriors looked at one another, shrugged their shoulders and grudgingly left to look for fun someplace else. This raid was beginning to be a letdown. They had barely broken sweat. They went out of the *municipio* and started roaming around the town in groups. They came back a short while later, empty handed, dejected and unscathed. The town was as peaceful as it could ever get. No one dared to come out and show any kind of resistance to the *Itnegs*. The sight of the dead bodies of the *Guardia Civiles*, unceremoniously dumped in a row in front of the *municipio,* was enough deterrent to any sort of intended resistance.

The locals had never seen such a show of *Itneg* force before and everyone literally cowered in fear behind tightly shuttered doors and windows.

The Mayor left and hurried to his house without talking to anyone. He locked the doors as soon as he got there, gathered the whole family, and together they knelt before the image of the Madonna. She had never failed them in their times of need.

At the Mayor's office, Biktol had settled down in the stuffed chair, his feet up on the desk.

"You need a cigar in your mouth," Ampit said from the chair across the desk.

"I don't smoke," Biktol said.

"Then you can't be Mayor. See?" He flicked his wrist, letting go of the dagger he was playing with. He moved so fast that he was on his feet and walking halfway to the framed painting of the Mayor hanging behind the desk to retrieve the knife that he had just thrown before Biktol showed any reaction.

Biktol slowly removed his feet off the desk and swiveled his chair around in time to see Ampit reach up and pull his knife off the painting of the cigar that was dangling from the Mayor's mouth. He had not noticed the picture of the cigar in the portrait before.

"I guess not," Biktol said, rising up. "And I can't let my ass grow fat and big anyways."

Ambit stopped from studying statuettes, documents and contents of cabinets around the room and looked at his brother and Biktol and the painting.

"That really is a fat Mayor," he said. "I wonder if you have to be really fat to become a Mayor."

Ampit and Biktol looked at one another. Ambit always came up with the weirdest thoughts.

"Yes, you do," Biktol said, "so you burn better when they burn you if you messed up."

Ampit grinned while Ambit gave them a bewildered look.

"Alright, enough of this. Let's go outside and see what the others are up to," Biktol said as he led the way out. The brothers followed willingly as usual.

They did not have far to go. The rest of the warriors were standing and sitting around bored and talking loudly, occasionally erupting in raucous laughter, at the stairs and the plaza in front of the municipal hall. They stopped for a moment and looked up when Biktol and the twins appeared through the door and dramatically paused on top of the stone steps leading down to the street level as if they had an important announcement.

Biktol did not disappoint. He raised a hand and everyone fell silent. He uttered three words, turned and went back up to the Mayor's office. The twins followed, willingly and silently as usual, both grinning like satisfied cats.

"Now we wait." Biktol had said. Then he turned around and went back up into the Mayor's office. He was growing fond of the big, stuffed leather chair.

So they waited for word from the raiders of the fort and the messenger that never came. After galloping off the fort, the boy was so excited and scared that he rode straight back and joined the back-up force that was gathered off the fort and rode with them as they retreated ahead of Gabriela's main force toward Mount *Bullagaw*, and on to Abra.

The warriors from Bangilo were forgotten and had not been notified about the retreat and the anticipated arrival of the Spanish reinforcements. Thus they were left behind loitering by the *municipio* as everyone else made their way toward Mount *Bullagaw*.

Akash, Kulas, Ilang and the rest of the leaders of the tribes only became aware that Biktol and his warriors were not with them when they finally stopped to take a rest at the foot of Mount *Bullagaw*. Everyone else thought that they were out there somewhere in the throng of retreating forces. But by then, the Bangilo warriors were cut off from their force by the reinforcements from Pampanga, Pangasinan and Cagayan who were then marching between them on their way toward the fort and the town.

"I want a hundred volunteers," Kulas said. "I'm going back after them."

"It will be suicide," Gabriela said. "There are too many of them."

Kulas looked her in the eye.

"Then so be it," he said and turned away. He could not let the Bangilo warriors alone by themselves in the midst of enemy territory.

"Wait! I'm coming with you!" Akash shouted as he ran after his friend.

The two Chinamen looked at one another, shrugged their shoulders and followed.

Dagyo looked at Lang-gi, Aklang and Bagit, and without saying a word ran after the Chinese. The archers followed without any further discussion. So did the rest of the warriors from their village.

Gabriela and Nicolas and the rest of the tribal leaders shook their heads, looked at one another and collectively turned their heads toward the *Itnegs* who were walking away, gratefully talking with other *Itnegs* who were falling in ranks behind them.

One of the tribal leaders spoke and someone else answered and slowly they walked away from the Ilocanos and followed the group that had rallied behind Kulas and Akash.

Gabriela looked at her Uncle and Sebastian and the rest of her leaders without saying a word. Nicolas looked back at his niece and simply nodded his head. It was an unwritten edict. They will follow whatever she decided.

Gabriela turned and walked toward her resting rebels.

334

Chapter Fifty One

Biktol looked up at the Mayor's portrait on the wall. Ampit had cut off the cigar from the Mayor's mouth and there was a rectangular hole where it used to be. He nodded his approval and swiveled his chair back and faced Ampit who had gone back to his seat across the desk. He pushed back his chair, put his feet up on the desk and leaned back contentedly. "I could get used to this," he sighed.

"You still need a cigar," Ampit said.

"I'll get that portrait replaced as soon as I find someone who can paint," Biktol said calmly and closed his eyes. He was really beginning to like being the Mayor. Yes, he definitely could get used to sitting in the stuffed chair with his feet up on the desk. But there was no way he'd let his ass go fat.

Ampit shook his head and stood up. He looked around the room and noticed that his brother was missing. Sensing that he was up, Biktol opened an eye.

"What?" he asked.

"Ambit," Ampit said. "Where did he go?"

"Check the Vice Mayor's office," Biktol said, grinned, leaned back on the stuffed chair and once again closed his eyes. "Don't worry. You can be the judge," he added.

Ampit grunted a guttural reply and walked out of the room to search for his brother. He went to the next room but Ambit was not there. He walked around and on to the east side that overlooked the road toward the fort. He stepped to the open window and suddenly stopped even before he got there. He looked out again and stared for what seemed a long time, then he turned around and hurried back to the Mayor's office. Ambit was already there, shaking Biktol's shoulder, waking him awake.

"I'm awake," Biktol growled, putting his feet off from the desk. "Wha...?"

"¡¡Soldados!!" The brothers blurted out. "They're coming this way!"

Biktol stood up and together they hurried out to the balcony facing the fort and for a moment studied the Spanish force headed their way.

"It only means one thing," Biktol said the unspoken thought of the brothers. "They had failed to take the fort."

"And perhaps everyone's dead or taken prisoner," Ampit said.

Ambit did not say anything.

Then somberly, they walked out the door toward the town hall's front balcony facing the plaza below where most of their warriors were loitering around.

Biktol walked to the edge of the balcony flanked by the brothers. The warriors below saw them and stopped talking, focusing their attention to Biktol and the brothers.

"Listen!! Gather up quickly!" Biktol yelled. "The soldiers are headed this way!" He pointed to the east where they had seen the soldiers. "Their presence means the raiding force at the fort had failed. We have two choices. We can run and go back home now, or we can stay and fight! Which will it be?"

The warriors looked at one another then yelled in one roaring and boisterous whoop. "We fight!!!"

"I guess that's it," Ampit murmured, speaking loud enough for both Biktol and Ambit to hear. "We fight."

"Yes, we fight," Biktol said with a wry smile, remembering the sight of the horde of soldiers heading their way, their pointy helmets, rifles and lances gleaming in the distance, "and perhaps to the death."

"To the death," Ambit said.

"There are too many of them!" Biktol yelled again as the crowd below settled down to listen. "We cannot fight them in an open field. If we stay and fight, we will fight them from inside these walls!" He indicated the stonewalled municipal hall.

"We don't have much time, they're coming fast!" Biktol continued. "We may die if we stay, so those who want to leave, go now and head that way!" He pointed to the opposite direction from where the soldiers were coming. "And for those who are staying behind and fight, gather around and inside the town hall. I want the archers behind those stone walls! The rest of you, get inside and we'll defend this hall as if it's ours!!!"

As a response, the warriors gathered their weapons and those who had knives and spears went inside the municipal hall while the warriors with bows and arrows positioned themselves behind the stone walls around the perimeter of the building.

Nobody left. With grim faces, they waited for the soldiers to arrive.

At the balcony, Biktol watched his warriors with pride, a trace of a smile flitting across his face yet he was worried inside. Many of them would probably be dead by the end of the day, including him.

"Damn," he said softly, "and I was just beginning to like being the Mayor."

He turned around and went once more inside the Mayor's office. He looked longingly at the stuffed chair behind the desk then raised his eyes up to the portrait of the Mayor on the wall.

"I guess you can have your chair back after today, Fat Man," he said to the portrait. The portrait stared back at him without any change of

336

expression, missing cigar and all. Biktol turned around and went out of the Mayor's office to the balcony facing east where the brothers, Ampit and Ambit, stood side by side looking stoically at the approaching Spanish army that was a lot closer now that they can see the colors of their flags and horses.

"They don't look so many," Ambit said. "Maybe we could just go and meet them."

"There're more of them than us," Ampit said, "but not that much. It should be fun." They both looked at Biktol who did not say anything.

Biktol looked at the approaching soldiers and his eyes twitched as he realized there were actually more of the soldiers than he initially thought.

"Ten to one, at least," he said to the brothers. "They outnumber us ten to one, maybe more."

"Like I said, not much more," Ampit said. "We can go out and meet them, then come back here if necessary."

"We don't have too many archers," Biktol said speculatively, "and they have guns."

"So we get closer then we can use our spears and knives," Ambit chimed in. "Let's go."

"No, we wait," Biktol said as he noted something. "There's something in the way they move that tells me they may not know that we're here."

Ampit gave him a quizzical look. "How so?"

"They don't seem to be in a hurry."

The brothers looked out at the oncoming soldiers then at one another and nodded.

"So let's go out and ambush them then," Ambit said excitedly.

Ampit and Biktol exchanged glances. 'Maybe the fool has a point,' they both thought.

"Let's go!" Biktol said without giving it further thought. He did not like waiting and much more hated the idea of being cornered regardless if it were behind thick stone walls.

It was easy enough to gather the men and spread the word out about their spur of the moment plan.

Everyone yelled their agreement. They came down from the mountains to fight and they were raring to meet it head-on. What was the point in waiting? It was not in their nature. If there was fighting to be done, the warriors of Bangilo had the reputation to meet it head on and get it over with fast. Mano-a-mano and out in the open. They did not relish fighting indoors. Numbers did not matter.

The road toward the municipal hall narrowed to where it went through a bridge that spanned a small creek that flowed on to the river. Biktol and his men positioned themselves at the mouth of the bridge. As he surveyed his men at both sides of the road and by the creek banks, a story told by an Ilocano trader who once reached Bangilo and became friends with *Ama* Lum-kang came to Biktol's mind. It was a story about a small band of soldiers in a far away land and how they all died protecting a small pass against an army that was over so many hundred times their number. This will be their pass to defend, Biktol thought, but they will not die here. They have better odds than those men in the story. They were not outnumbered over a hundred to one.

"Let their front get to the middle of the bridge then shoot," Biktol said to his archers, "and don't stop shooting until you're out of arrows! Shoot until no one's left standing! If they manage to get pass the middle of the bridge, we'll meet them head-on before they can get to this side! No retreat! We fight to the end!"

The Bangilo warriors grunted and nodded not daring to yell and let their presence known.

A few moments later, the soldiers who were the reinforcements from Pampanga and Pangasinan, turned a corner and appeared at the far end of the road. They marched casually with no sense of urgency, although their leader, *Teniente* Villar, was wondering where all the people were, not that he was expecting a welcoming band. The streets and the whole town seemed deserted and it was the middle of the day. Cautioned by too many battles, he slowed the troop down as they approached the bridge. They were going to the Municipal Hall to call on the Mayor as was planned, hoping also that the *Capitán* would be there then they would proceed to the fort and rest. The *Teniente* hated ceremonies but it was the protocol to call on the *Alcalde* first where he came from whenever they got into a new town. The other reinforcement from up north in the Cagayan valley had proceeded to the fort. They were not much for protocols. Barbarians, *Teniente* Villar thought when someone informed him of what the other group was doing.

The *Teniente*, at the head of the column, paused by the opening of the bridge. He looked across at the deserted road and at the shrubs and tall grasses by the creek banks but did not see anything suspicious.

Seasoned hunters, the warriors of Bangilo were well hidden from view and the ones by the grasses could stay immobile for a whole day if needed. Biktol, hiding behind a tree where the archers could see his signal had a hand raised. They would start shooting once the hand went down. They waited patiently as if they were waiting for a herd of deer to get close enough where they could literally touch them. It was a game everyone had played when they were small children.

338

Hesitantly *Teniente* Villar nudged his horse forward. The horse responded and walked steadily toward the middle of the bridge then its ears pricked and shook its head as if agitated by something, which was not lost to its rider. But the *Teniente* assumed it was because of the water below. The poor horse had traveled so far and must have had gotten excited by the water underneath the bridge. Then he was at the middle of the bridge.

Biktol dropped his raised hand and in a moment *Teniente* Villar was falling off his rearing horse, an arrow sticking from his neck. The soldiers behind him, riding four abreast, likewise followed their *Teniente's* fate. And the silence of the day was shattered by the raucous cawing and yelling of warriors who had seemed to have risen up from nowhere and were now pouring arrows and spears into the massed soldiers and horses caught on the bridge. Somewhere a bugle sounded for retreat and the soldiers who could manage backed out of the bridge. They left behind more than a dozen dead and wounded on the bridge including the *Teniente*, the bodies forming a soft barrier between the opposite sides.

Ampit and Ambit stood by Biktol in the middle of the road with raised hands, yelling in defiance at the regrouping soldiers who were now out of arrow range.

Then they stopped and looked at one another, perplexed at what they saw. A group of soldiers had dismounted, huddled together then started approaching the bridge on foot. They held long shields against their bodies, and as they neared the bridge, they shifted their shields to the front then they closed ranks, leaving no open space between themselves and their body length shields, the soldiers on both ends of the row kept their shields to the sides. The soldiers behind raised their own shields over the heads of the front soldiers as well as their own heads thus effectively providing solid covering from all sides.

"Damn, like a turtle!" Ambit voiced out what his companions were thinking. The soldiers moving forward were indeed moving like a turtle with their shields like a protective shell.

"Let them come through the bridge and we'll break their shell when they get across," Biktol said. "Have the spearmen ready," he said to Ampit.

Ampit waved a hand and a score of heavy set warriors armed with long spears moved forward to join them.

"Wait until they get past those bodies then attack them. Run through the shields if you have to but get through them. Break that wall! We'll be right behind you!" Biktol raised a hand and more warriors came up with long knives drawn.

The human turtle approached slowly then it moved to a lance formation as it entered the bridge. The soldier in the middle of the formation had moved a full body ahead and the soldiers flanking him shifted positions until the formation looked like a tip of a spear.

"Shoot!" Biktol yelled at the archers. He wanted to see if at least one of the arrows could somehow slip through the shields and find a mark that would cause an opening if the soldier fell down fast enough. Arrows flew but they bounced off harmlessly against the protective shields. Then as the formation reached the bodies at the middle of the bridge, it stopped then shifted form once again, this time forming a line that circled the dead bodies. A group of empty-handed soldiers following behind them pulled the dead bodies and put them on their shoulders. Then the formation started to slowly back out of the bridge.

The warriors from Bangilo were so mesmerized at the scene that they failed to notice another group of soldiers armed with lances and crossbows approaching behind the shielded formation. Biktol was about to order the spearmen to attack when he realized the shielded soldiers were not going across when he caught glimpse of arrows and spears flying over the top of the retreating soldiers.

"Take cover!!" Biktol yelled instead as he ran for cover. A few of the Bangilo spearmen were not so lucky. They fell where they stood, pierce with short bow arrows and wooden steel-tipped spears.

"Damn!" Biktol yelled, as he sidled close to the archers. "Shoot high like they did! Go!"

And so the shooting match began causing minor casualties and irritation on opposite sides of the creek.

Then the shooters from the soldiers' side retreated as the bridge was cleared off of dead bodies and the shielded soldiers had rejoined the main group.

A trumpet sounded from somewhere behind the troops and a cavalry of soldiers came charging down the road.

"To the bridge!! Don't let them come through!!" Biktol yelled at the spearmen but they were slow to respond, startled as they were with the sudden rush of horsemen who were pouring into the bridge before anyone could throw a spear. The first group of horsemen came through, followed by more, as the archers resumed shooting. Bodies fell and kept falling from the horses as the archers emptied their quivers, but the soldiers, a combination of a score or so of Spanish mixed with conscripts of loyal *Capampangans*, had ran through the bridge. Thus the order of engagement turned to hand to hand, all-out fighting that the warriors of Bangilo preferred and they went at it like mad men.

There was no rhythm to an all out, hand to hand encounter between two battle crazy groups. There was no allotted time to group or re-group, or formulate and execute a plan of attack. And that was what happened at the bridge that day. Weapons flashed in the air, they found their marks, splattering blood and breaking flesh and bones; bodies fell and living breath forced out of them. And thus it went for a good part of the afternoon, one group pushing for a moment then being pushed the next. Despite their superior number, the soldiers could not seem to break through the rampaging warriors from Bangilo.

Bodies of soldiers littered around Biktol, Ampit and Ambit who fought side by side, assisting and covering each other's back as often as they could. They were bloodied, wounded and weary-armed but they were oblivious to all pain, totally desensitized and fueled by the raging fever and lust of battle.

When the *Itnegs* led by Kulas and Akash finally came to the scene a good three hours later, it was all over. The bridge was silent except for the soft rustling of the creek below. Above it were dead bodies of soldiers and *Itnegs*. And there were more mixed corpses of uniformed soldiers and bare-chested *Itnegs* on the road and by the creek banks. Here and there, horses with empty saddles roamed about, shying away when approached by any of the men.

Kulas walked warily among the dead bodies wryly noting that there were more soldiers than *Itnegs*. Akash was looking around for survivors and finding no one, looked for signs of what happened instead, studying the tracks and how the bodies were spread out on and around the bridge.

"They met the soldiers here," Akash said pointing at the bridge.

"They were outnumbered, totally outnumbered," Kulas said.

"Yes, but they fought well," Akash said.

"Yes they did, but I don't see anyone alive, Akash. They're all dead. We should have been here."

"We did not know, Kulas. We tried. We were late. Let it go."

Kulas did not answer. "Look for *Ama* Lum-kang's son," he finally said. "Tell the men to look for Biktol."

"I was looking for him and the twins who hang around him. I haven't seen them. But look at the tracks here," Akash pointed at the ground off the bridge. "There were survivors. They have just left, that way, towards the fort, on horses, so soldiers most likely. Perhaps Biktol and the twins were taken prisoners."

"They would not surrender," Kulas said matter-of-factly. "Not those men. They would have fought to the end."

"We'll look for them then. I'll spread the word," Akash said and left.

Kulas walked around and noted that there was a trail of bodies going toward the municipal hall. He caught Akash's eyes and gestured toward the hall, moving even before Akash reached where he was standing. Akash caught up with him and together they walked through the open space between the stone walls that served as a gate to the grounds of the municipal hall. They stopped as they saw more bodies on the grounds and up the stairs to the hall. And among the blue clad corpses just beyond the main door were the bodies of the twins from Bangilo, Ampit and Ambit.

"They made a stand here," Akash said. "And look at all these dead soldiers!"

"Yes, they did not go down easy; they wouldn't have had," Kulas said as he regarded the dead twins with respect and deep regret that he was not there for them. He started up the stairs to the second floor, following a trail of blood on the steps, through a large hall room where more dead soldiers lay. The trail of blue-clad bodies led them into a big room beyond the hall room. The sign above the door, 'Oficina de Alcalde' indicated that it was the Mayor's office.

Inside, Akash and Kulas found Biktol seated behind the Mayor's desk, head resting on the high back of the stuffed leather chair. He was looking at them with wide open but unfocused eyes. Around him, sprawled all over the room, were at least a dozen more dead bodies of soldiers, some of them headless.

"He killed all of them then he sat down and died," Akash said casually reading the signs from the positions of the dead bodies and the blood trails. He noted the wounds on Biktol's body and knew that the man had simply bled to death.

Kulas nodded then shook his head silently expressing his respect for the Bangilo warrior and his growing frustration and regret for not arriving in time to lend a hand. He stepped over the dead bodies and put a hand across Biktol's face and closed his eyes.

"I am sorry, my friend," he murmured softly, "rest in peace in the land of the ancients."

Silently they reverently went out of the room. They looked into the other rooms but they found no one else, dead or alive. Akash, sensing a renewed hub-bub outside, stepped out to the balcony facing east that overlooked the bridge where the noise was coming from.

"They're moving out," he said. Kulas joined him and together, they watched as Gabriela and the Ilocano rebels, rejoined by warriors from the other tribes, massed together and started to march back toward the fort. The warriors of Bangilo had to be avenged.

"Let's go," Kulas finally said. "We're not going to miss out on this one."

At the bottom of the stairs, the Chinese brothers stood up from where they sat waiting, and followed the two *Itnegs* as they headed out toward the bridge.

The rest of the warriors, some of them now mounted on the stray horses of the slain soldiers, followed grimly behind, the sight of the dead Bangilo warriors freshly embedded in their minds. It was a scene they would not soon forget and it strengthened their resolve to follow Kulas and Akash.

They may meet the same fate at where they were going, but so be it. To them there was nothing more honorable than dying in battle.

Chapter Fifty Two

"We got here as fast as we could, *Capitán*, but it looks like we missed the fun," *Teniente* Percival Tabieros said. He had traveled with his troop from Tuguegarao for the past two weeks, spending some time in Isabela where the messenger from Vigan had found him. After sending word back to the fort in Tuguegarao, they had proceeded right away south to Vigan. He saw the blood in the courtyard and the bodies of dead soldiers as they marched into the fort and he was feeling a tinge of regret for not making his troop move faster. *Teniente* Percival Tabieros was a fighting man and he hated missing out on a good fight.

He and his troops had just finished eating and most of them were resting now, but he had stayed with Don Manuel, sharing stories, cigars and a bottle of good Spanish wine that the *Capitán* kept in his private stock.

"I wish we got here earlier," the *Teniente* said as their conversation returned back to the recent attack of the rebels.

The *Capitán* waved a dismissive hand. "What's important is you're here, *Teniente*," he said. "Thank you again for coming promptly, although we could have had surely used your help earlier. Perhaps, our casualty would have been a lot less."

"Ahh, and more of theirs, I would assure you," *Teniente* Percival Tabieros said confidently.

"Don't worry you'll have your chance as soon as the reinforcements from Pampanga come in. They should be here today or perhaps tomorrow."

"Ahh, it totally escaped my mind with all the excitement that I forgot to mention it, but they're here, *Capitán*, however they veered the other way and they went to the town first. I heard the *Teniente* from Pampanga, Villar, I believe his name is, has the habit of paying respects to the *Alcalde* first in every town he visits. Come to think of it that's almost two or three hours ago. Perhaps, they're having a little fiesta! Maybe we should have gone there too. We're missing all the fun! Hah-hah!" Percival Tabieros slapped his thigh at his joke but the *Capitán* did not even crack a smile.

"Ohh? They're here?" he said, genuinely surprised.

"Oh yes, we almost came in at the same time. I had a messenger go back to meet them and he came back to report on their intention to go to the *municipio* first. In fact, they assumed you may be there. But as for me, my men and the horses needed a good rest so we came straight to the fort," the *Teniente* sighed. "I just wished we had arrived sooner. Tired or not, we would have routed those damn rebels right here and would have been on our way back home in a day or so."

Don Manuel nodded wearily. He wanted to tell the *Teniente* about the *Itnegs* but he was finally feeling exhausted. And in addition, there was a sense of foreboding building inside his chest that was nagging at him yet he did not exactly know why. And it bothered him because try as he did he could not get rid of it.

"*Bueno*, go rest then also, *Teniente,* and we'll talk again later. I have ordered one of my men to see that the stable boys will look well after your horses, but if there's anything you or your men need, please let *Don* Tiago or me know. Again, I thank you for coming here in so short notice." *Don* Manuel extended a hand which the *Teniente* took with a firm grasp and they shook. *Don* Manuel turned around and went back to his quarters deep in thought. Perhaps he should ride out to town, he thought, but decided against it. There was much to do in the fort. He had to see to the wounded and they had bodies to bury. He'll have to send out for the *Padre* again.

He walked back out and went to the stables where he found one of the stable boys, Gabon, busy tending to the horses of the soldiers from Cagayan.

"When you're done giving them water, Gabon, ride out to town and get *Padre* Joaquin. Tell him to come and to bring plenty of Holy Water as well as his prayer book for the dead."

"*Si, Capitán,*" Gabon replied and he moved faster, spilling water from the pail he was carrying. He could barely contain his excitement from the anticipation of telling his friends in town about the raid at the fort and the arrival of more soldiers from Cagayan. He had hidden in the stables, behind the bales of hay throughout the fighting and had not exactly seen anything, but then his friends did not know that.

He finished filling the last trough with water then he hurriedly saddled and rode out. It was about a half-an-hour ride to town but he planned on being there in less the usual time. He had been barely out a quarter of an hour when he came galloping back into the fort, his horse sliding into a sudden stop in front of the officers' barracks. Gabon jumped off and started for the *Capitán*'s quarters without bothering to tie his horse to the hitching rail.

"¡*Capitán!* ¡*Capitán!*" he yelled.

Don Manuel hurriedly appeared on the door. "What now, Gabon?"

"¡*Soldados!* ¡*Soldados!* They're coming from the town. Many of them wounded!" Gabon cried excitedly.

Don Manuel cursed silently and rushed out to the courtyard, Gabon hurrying behind him. The gate was wide open and groups of soldiers had

:ome out in the courtyard looking out at the bedraggled soldiers approaching the fort.

"The *Capampangans*," said *Teniente* Tabieros who had come up to walk beside *Don* Manuel. "It looks like they had been in a fight!"

"And lost," *Don* Manuel sighed. "They did not flee. The damn rebels went to town and took it instead."

He should have known. He cursed bitterly, regretting the fact that he had let them go because of the *Itneg* archers' implied threat to his wellbeing. He felt the rage building in him. They could have missed he thought although he knew they would not. He stopped in the middle of the courtyard and waited anxiously for the soldiers from Pampanga to get into the fort.

When they got into the fort, the new arrivals stopped at the edge of the courtyard. An officer slowly moved out of the group and approached the *Capitán* and *Teniente* Tabieros. Wounded as he was, he slowly got off his horse. He grimaced in pain, yet straightened up as best as he could and executed a crisp salute toward *Don* Manuel.

"*Sargento* Adolfo Pilor de Aveño, *mi Capitán*! I am sorry for the condition that we are presenting but we were ambushed!"

"At ease, *Sargento*," *Don* Manuel said after quickly acknowledging the salute with a perfunctory brushing of his hand to his temple.

"We went to the *municipio* to see the *Alcalde* and you, with *Teniente* Villar assuming that you would be there also. And they were waiting for us at the bridge before the *municipio*. *Teniente* Villar was among the first ones to die. They were savages! Naked savages!" *Sargento* Adolfo said pausing for a moment to take a deep breath to ease the pain from his wounds.

"*Itnegs*, *Sargento*, they are not savages. You have encountered *Itneg* warriors," *Don* Manuel said. "Go on."

"*Itnegs*, *Señor*?" *Teniente* Tabieros said.

"Yes, *Teniente*. Natives of Abra. They have many tribes, all of them warriors like you have never seen."

"Better than my *Ybanags*?" said the *Teniente*.

"I have not seen your *Ybanags* fight yet, but I would venture a yes," *Don* Manuel said looking at the *Teniente* squarely in the eye. He had heard that the *Ybanags* were very adept with the bow and arrow, but other than that he knew nothing of how they fared in hand to hand fighting.

"That I would like to see," said *Teniente* Percival Tabieros cockily. "I would like to see that indeed."

"I am afraid you will, *Teniente*, and soon," *Don* Manuel said gravely, his voice tired and so filled with sadness and pity which was not lost to *Sargento* Adolfo.

"I pray that you don't personally find out for yourself, *Teniente*, for your own sake. I am afraid the *Capitán* speaks the truth. We outnumbered those savages at least ten to one, and yes, we killed all of them, but this," *Sargento* Adolfo waved a hand towards his men, "this is all that's left of us. There were close to two thousand of us just a few hours ago."

The *Capitán* and the *Teniente* looked at the surviving soldiers, most of them wounded and almost ready to fall off their horses, and those who were able to get off, were standing like men who had just gone through hell. There could not be more than seven hundred left of them.

"And how many did you say there were of the *Itnegs*, *Sargento*?" *Teniente* Tabieros said.

"A hundred maybe, perhaps less," *Sargento* Adolfo said wearily.

"Just a hundred? All *Itnegs*, no Ilocanos?" Don Manuel said. Was there another *Itneg* group, he thought, or had some of them stayed behind to raid the town? Had *La Generala* split her forces?

"Yes, they all look like *Itnegs*, *Capitán*, they did not look like Ilocanos at all," *Sargento* Adolfo Pilor said then he fell down to his knees, his strength finally giving way to sheer exhaustion.

Don Manuel and *Teniente* Tabieros rushed forward to help him, getting to the *Sargento* just in time to catch him between them as he started to fall to the ground. They raised him up to his feet, supporting him, each man taking an arm across his shoulder. The *Sargento* groaned in pain then his whole body went limp as he passed out. A couple of big bodied soldiers who had come out from their barracks to see what was going on stepped forward to help the officers.

"Bring all the wounded to the infirmary!" *Don* Manuel commanded as he handed the *Sargento* over to one of the soldiers. The other soldier relieved the *Teniente*, and they half-carried, half-dragged the unconscious *Sargento* Pilor toward the infirmary.

"Tiago!" *Don* Manuel beckoned to Tiago who was ordering the fort soldiers, including the soldiers from Cagayan, to look after the wounded soldiers from Pampanga. Tiago mouthed an order to a big soldier who was standing by his side, who nodded then he hurried toward the *Capitán*.

"*Si, Capitán*?" Tiago said as he faced the *Capitán* and the *Teniente*.

"Get fifty men, no get a hundred, a hundred fifty maybe, and go to the town and take care of the dead. They would be by the *municipio* according to the *Sargento*," *Don* Manuel said, trying to sound as calm as he could.

"A hundred, a hundred and fifty men, *Capitán*, just to look after the dead?" Tiago said incredulously, looking at the *Capitán* as if he had lost his mind.

347

"Yes, Tiago, perhaps more if what the *Sargento* said is true," *Don* Manuel said ignoring the look in Tiago's eyes. "Get the townspeople to help. Have them dig mass graves if needed. And get the *Padre* later to pray over them when they're buried."

Tiago was about to say something flippant but something in the *Capitán*'s eyes made him hold his tongue. He realized the man was serious.

"And as for the dead *Itnegs*, drag them to a nearby field and burn them!" *Don* Manuel continued in a cold even voice yet his eyes were burning with rage.

The *Teniente* and *Sargento* Tiago looked uneasily at one another then *Teniente* Tabieros spoke.

"If you don't mind, *Capitán*, I would like to go with the *Sargento*," he said. "I'll bring some of my men."

"Of course, of course, *Teniente*, as you wish," *Don* Manuel said and turned to go back to his quarters. Gabon who was standing behind him quickly stepped aside.

"Should I still go get *Padre* Joaquin, *Capitán*?" Gabon asked.

"No, no, there's no need, Gabon. He would be busy in town. We'll bury the dead we have out here and we'll do the praying ourselves. Tell Mariano and the rest of the stable boys to start digging. Let me know if you need help. I want the dead buried by the end of the day." The *Capitán* walked away in a rage, muttering to himself. "How many more had to die?" he said softly and he was afraid to answer his own question. *La Generala* was still out there. The *Itnegs* that *Sargento* Pilor and his men had encountered were just a small renegade troop.

The healthy soldiers, Spanish, and *Ybanags* alike, helped the wounded from Pampanga and Pangasinan and led them to the infirmary which turned out to be inadequate for all of them. They brought out cots and made makeshift beds out on the ground. The fort doctor conscripted able soldiers as assistants, mostly veterans who had been wounded themselves in battle and in the absence of a medic had attended to their own wounds. They knew what to do and pretty soon, they had most of the wounded soldiers bandaged up and resting.

What they could not help with was the distant and vacant looks in the soldiers' eyes like they had been through a nightmare and they had not woken up.

Tiago ordered pick axes, crowbars and shovels loaded into the flat bed carriage, picked big bodied forced volunteers and together with *Teniente* Percival Tabieros and a hundred of his *Ybanags* rode out of the fort, almost two hundred and a half strong.

"Damn too many men for a burial detail," Tiago muttered as he surveyed the troop.

"If the *Sargento* was right, *Señor* Tiago, we would be burying more than ten hundred bodies, including the *Itnegs*," *Teniente* Tabieros, who was at his side and heard him, said grimly. "Perhaps more, but personally, I think the *Sargento* was just delirious from his wounds."

"Ahh *Teniente*, I hope you are right. It's preposterous to think that a hundred *Itnegs* could manage to kill even a hundred soldiers of His Majesty's army, never mind if they were *Indios*. I think we train them well enough to deserve a uniform."

"True, *Sargento*, very true. Look at my *Ybanags* here. Each one of them deserves the uniform he wears. Sometimes I think they are as good as we are, God forbid. And I expect the same from the *Capampangans*."

"Well, we shall see soon enough, *Teniente*, we shall see soon enough. I hope to God though that the *Sargento* was delirious as you said. I am not looking forward to hauling dead bodies the rest of the day," Tiago said as he kneed his horse to a trot. He looked toward the town and suddenly reined up, the *Teniente*'s horse shying away as it almost bumped into his horse.

"Wh-what now, *Sargento*? Why did you stop?" *Teniente* Tabieros said, looking at where Tiago's eyes were fixed at and finding the answer to his question. He saw a huge dust cloud from the direction of the town. "Coming this way or going away?" he asked.

"I am afraid they're coming this way, *Teniente*," Tiago said without taking his eyes off the cloud of dust that seemed to grow bigger by the moment. There was only one reason for the presence of a dust cloud that big. It would be from a large group of either people or animals, and as far as he knew, no one around these parts had any large number of animals. The rebels had returned, he was sure of it and said so to the *Teniente*.

"Ahh, now we'll see if the *Capitán* was right, *Sargento*," *Teniente* Percival Tabieros said.

Don Tiago lowered his head from looking up at the dust cloud and gave the *Teniente* a perplexed look.

"He said the *Itnegs* are better fighters than my *Ybanags*," *Teniente* Tabieros said. "I hope those are *Itnegs*." He gestured with his head toward the town. There was a glint of wildness in his eyes.

Tiago stared at the man. He shook his head. "Be careful of what you wish for, *Teniente*," he said sadly. "Be careful of what you wish for." He pulled his reins and turned his horse around. "We're going back to the fort!" he yelled.

"Wait!" *Teniente* Tabieros cried. "Why don't we go meet them? There are more than two hundred of us!"

"*Teniente*, we would all get killed," Tiago said calmly.

349

"We can't live forever, Tiago," *Teniente* Tabieros said. "Go back if you must but me and my men are going to town. And please do me a favor and send the rest of my men from the fort to follow us."

"As you wish, *Teniente*, but I must go back and warn the *Capitán*."

"Of course, Tiago, go!" *Teniente* Tabieros gave the *Sargento* an impish look. "Perhaps I heard wrongly that the soldiers of Vigan are not scared of anything or anyone!"

Tiago was about to spur his horse forward but abruptly reined back and turned toward the *Teniente*. "Scared? No, I am not scared, nor any of my men is scared, *Teniente*. We only have more sense because we know who we are facing."

"Sense has got nothing to do with being a man, *Sargento*. It's what's in here!" *Teniente* Tabieros struck a fist to his breast. He turned away from Tiago, faced his men, raised himself up on his stirrups and yelled, "Follow me! We're going to town!" Then he nudged his horse and moved forward ahead of the column.

Tiago looked at the officer's back in disgust, trying to quell the anger that was rising in his chest.

"Valentin! Rafael! Leoncio! And you, Fernando!" he yelled. "Take that carriage and ride back. Tell the *Capitán* the rebels are coming and be ready to defend the fort! The rest of you, follow me! We're going to hold those *bastardos* up as long as we can!" Tiago then kneed his horse and caught up with the *Teniente*.

Teniente Tabieros cast a side glance at the *Sargento* and gave him an approving smile.

"Who wants to live forever, eh, *Teniente*?" Tiago said smugly. He was not going to have this *peon* from Valencia think that the men of Compostela had no balls!

"That's what I always say, *Sargento*, that's what I always say," said the *Teniente*.

And together, the two Spaniards rode forward, heads held high to the wind, leaving their fates to the Man above.

The two forces met halfway between the town proper and the fort, where the dusty road was flanked by flat open fields. They stopped about three hundred yards from each other and calmly surveyed one another out, taking the other's measure from a safe distance.

The Spanish force, disciplined as they were, maintained a precise military formation, their sabers and swords out, their mounts prancing on their feet raring to go to battle as their riders who calmly sat on their backs reined them in, waiting for the command to attack. The *Ybanags* who never ventured out without their bows and arrows, had their weapons out and ready, arrows firmly held in place against bowstrings. Even without an audible command, they had positioned themselves at the front of the formation where they could shoot without anyone blocking their aim. Yet seasoned fighters as they were, there was hesitance in their movement. They knew, as they looked at the force in front of them, that they were severely outnumbered.

Opposite them, the mixed force of Ilocanos and *Itnegs* seemed to mass together in a big lump at the middle of the road and thinned as it spread out to the open fields by its flanks. Behind the big mass in the middle of the road, the force of Kulas and Akash and the warriors of their village slowly inched forward and stopped a few yards away.

Kulas motioned for the archers to position themselves on and beside the road then signaled for the others to evenly spread out. Akash moved forward to find out what was going on. They had seen the soldiers as they approached, and there were not too many of them, and he and Kulas wondered why Ilang had stopped. In their thinking, if one had the advantage of numbers, it should be used in an immediate all out attack and not wait for the smaller group to think and come up with a plan.

Akash made his way up through the mass of bodies until he got to the front. He gazed at the soldiers for a moment then he walked up to where Ilang sat on her horse, reining it firmly as it pranced about.

"Let the men spread out into the fields," he said to Ilang as she looked down at him. "They're too crowded in the middle of the road. There would be too much confusion when those horse soldiers ride in."

Ilang looked at her troop and then turned her eyes to Nicolas who was listening. Nicolas nodded his agreement. Then Akash spoke again and turned around and made his way to the back as Nicolas barked an order for the rebels to spread out.

Akash ran the few steps of the open space to where Kulas stood with the archers on the middle of the road. They conferred and Kulas motioned for the archers to move to the side and Akash ordered a group of warriors armed with long spears to take their positions on the middle of the road. He spoke to them and they waited.

A shout came from the front, followed by the sound of thundering hooves and the clamor of battle began. Although acutely aware that they were outnumbered, *Teniente* Tabieros firmly believed that his smaller force was far too superior over a bunch of ignorant *Indios* and he had no qualms about ordering an all out attack. He was anticipating the idiot rebels to run off and scatter in fear at the magnificent display of precise horsemanship and bravery of his well trained soldiers. With a cry that resounded in the open field, he had ordered his force to attack, with him in the lead.

Ilang patiently waited in the middle of the road, a hand raised over her head. Nicolas sat silently on his horse a few feet away. Then as the soldiers were almost a hundred yards off, Ilang dropped her hand and the rebels on the road parted and *Itneg* archers from the other tribes stepped up and quickly loosed arrows at the charging cavalry, moving to the sides of the road while another group of archers moved up in their place. The *Ybanags* themselves started shooting and arrows started flying from opposite sides, indiscriminately hitting human targets. Riders and running rebels fell down from opposite sides.

Despite the chaos upfront, Kulas and Akash waited with their force patiently in the back.

Then the road seemed to have cleared up in front of the attacking cavalry. Pushed by the momentum of stampeding horses, some of them now riderless, *Teniente* Tabieros, miraculously unharmed so far, found himself charging at another band of *Itnegs*, spears poised and calmly standing in the middle of the road, blocking his path. He yelled and spurred his horse forward, his right arm wildly waving his saber. He saw a tall *Itneg* calmly looking at him by the side of the road and the *Teniente* headed for him. 'Let's see how good you bastards really are,' the *Teniente* thought and he started to yell again but was surprised when no voice came out from his mouth. Bewildered, he tried yelling again but still no sound came out except for a soft gurgling noise down his throat then he felt his raised sword getting heavier and he was powerless to keep it in his hand. It fell clattering on the ground, then *Teniente* Tabieros, with eyes glazed found himself falling as he desperately looked down at his sword. He tried to grab the pommel of his saddle but his fingers would not respond. He was dead before his head hit the ground, two arrows sticking out so close together from the base of his throat.

Aklang calmly strung another arrow as he watched the big man waving a saber drop from his horse and shot another soldier, this one armed with a bow and the arrow aimed at Kulas who stood at the side of the road like an innocent spectator. The soldier who did not look like a Spaniard dropped his bow and arrow as he clutched his chest and fell hard to the ground. His now riderless horse charged then reared backwards with a spear on its neck. Another one followed, and then yet another, and the charge screeched to a halt with dead, wounded and riderless horses mingling and jostling each other around.

Tiago, who was caught near the middle of the charge, sensed the commotion upfront and tried to rein in and control his mount, lying low in the saddle as he saw soldiers falling around him, systematically dropped by arrows from the *Itnegs*. And those whose mounts fell under them were now engaged in hand to hand fighting against the *Itnegs*. *Don* Tiago tried to ride out but he could not.

"Dismount!!" he yelled as he realized they were sitting targets, for the rest of the rebels had closed up the gap where they had ridden through. He worked himself to the edge of the confused troop, most of them now fighting furiously on the ground and he found himself looking at a familiar face, his hands holding two knives dripping with blood.

"You!" *Don* Tiago mouthed, as the face looked back at him and smiled in recognition. *Don* Tiago moved forward and the smiling face likewise moved to meet him. Then they stopped a few feet apart.

"We meet again, *Señor*," *Don* Tiago said calmly.

The face continued its amused smile and the head behind it bowed a little but the eyes remained on *Don* Tiago. Then the hands raised his two bloodied long knives.

"These are not sticks anymore, white man," Kulas said in *Itneg*. He hoped his raised hands holding his knives were enough for the man to understand. He had recognized the old soldier who had toyed with Bel-leng a long time ago during the hunt.

Don Tiago nodded. He understood. He understood too that he was about to die. Somewhere he heard the tolling of the bells of the Cathedral of San Tiago and he could see its towers faintly in the distance, and beyond, the rolling hills of Compostela beckoned. *Don* Tiago smiled. Perhaps it was time to go home.

He charged.

'I have to do the *camino de los peregrinos* when I get home,' *Don* Tiago thought as he stared at the bare feet of the *Itneg* beside his face. He wanted to look up at the man but he could not move his head and for a moment he wondered why, then the night came.

Kulas bent down and brushed a bloody hand across the Spaniard's face and closed the dead man's eyes. Whatever he may had been, the old soldier had faced his death well.

It was a total rout.

The victors looted the vanquished of their weapons. And they caught the horses that were unharmed and rode them toward the fort.

Biktol and his *Bangilo* warriors could rest in peace. They had been avenged.

Kulas and Akash walked in front this time, right behind Ilang and Nicolas who wisely slowed down their horses. And beside them were the Chinese twins with their long poles.

There was no hurry. The fort was not going anywhere anyways.

Chapter Fifty Three

Capitán Manuel scanned the rows and rows of rebels facing the fort through his spyglass, Ilocanos and *Itnegs*, not a few of them vulgarly dressed in his soldiers' bloody uniforms. He panned to the left then all the way to the right, then back again. Then suddenly he stopped and readjusted the focus on the glass and was rewarded with a sharper image of a familiar horse. He took a deep breath. The only way somebody else could ride that horse would be if its owner was dead.

He turned to the soldier who stood by his side on the rampart. "What's your name, *soldado*?" he asked conversationally.

The soldier, caught off guard, stammered, "*¿M-m-m'llamo, Señor*? My name?"

"Yes, your name. You have a name, don't you?"

"*Si, Capitán*. Yes. My name is Roberto."

"*Bueno*, Roberto. And your family name? What is it?"

"Roldan, *Señor*. My name is Roberto Roldan, from Zaragoza." The soldier beamed proudly.

"See those rebels, *Sargento* Roldan?"

"*Si, mi Capitán*, I see them, but *Sargento*? I am not a *Sargento*!"

"You are now, *Sargento* Roldan. And now listen up. When you see those rebels come within that tree line, that's about two hundred, maybe two hundred and fifty yards from here, I want you to order the cannons to be fired, but not at the same time. Space them out, one after the other. I don't want those damn rebels to get too close to the walls. You understand?"

"*Si, Capitán*. Yes, fire the cannons, one after the other when the rebels get to the tree line. I'll take care of it," the newly minted *Sargento* Roldan said emphatically.

"Good, good, *Sargento*. I'm relying on you."

"But, *perdon Capitán*, begging your pardon, how about *Sargento* Tiago when he comes back?"

Don Manuel looked at Roberto with sadness in his eyes. "*Don* Tiago won't be coming back, Roberto. You are the *Sargento* now."

"He won't? You mean he..?" Roldan could not make himself say the word.

"Yes, Roberto, he's dead. The rebels killed him and probably the rest of the burial detail that went out, including *Teniente* Tabieros and his *Ybanags*.

Do your job, Roberto and I'll make you *Teniente* as soon as those rebels are on their knees. Don't fail me now..." *Don* Manuel's voice trailed.

"I won't, *Capitán*, you have my word," Roldan said gravely. "And I thank you for your trust."

"Go, spread the word, *Sargento*. Get your men ready. I want those cannons aimed at different sections of those rebel lines." *Don* Manuel waved Roberto off.

Roldan saluted sharply and hurried on to the soldiers who were manning the five small cannons they had positioned on top of the wall that faced the rebels. They were placed about fifteen feet apart.

"Listen up! Per the *Capitán*'s orders, fire the cannons when those rebels get to about two hundred yards, that's by that tree line," Roberto said, pointing below. "Don't fire at the same time. Space them out starting from that end," again he pointed to the southernmost cannon. "And aim at the mass," he paused, and then added with emphasis. "For *Don* Tiago!"

The soldiers collectively gave Roberto a surprised look. "What do you mean 'for *Don* Tiago?'" the soldier nearest him asked.

"The *Capitán* said the rebels had killed *Don* Tiago, along with the *Teniente* from Cagayan. He just made me *Sargento*," Roberto said.

The soldiers looked at one another then looked down at the rebels who were slowly advancing toward the fort. "*Bastardos*," one of the soldiers mumbled. "Let them come." He fed a ball to the cannon. The other handlers did the same.

The nearby soldiers who were lined up on top of the wall had heard Roberto and pretty soon the word went down the line that *Sargento* Tiago had been killed. The news stirred fury in the hearts of the soldiers who were collectively fond of the old soldier. Now they had one more reason to hate and put down the rebels.

"Just say the word, and we'll bring the fury of the Crown on these *Indios*!" the soldiers said to Roberto as he walked back beside the *Capitán*.

"They're ready, *Capitán*. We're ready. Just say the word," Roberto said as the rebels got closer to the tree line.

"Hold it, Roberto. Wait, wait, let them come closer," *Don* Manuel said. He noted some of the *Itnegs* had their bows drawn and were ready to shoot their arrows. 'Too far still,' the *Capitán* thought.

But then an arrow flew from one of the *Itnegs* and the *Capitán* watched in wonder as it arched far and high up in the air then as if it had a mind of its own, headed downwards right on top of the wall. And down the line from where the *Capitán* stood, a soldier grunted in pain. Then more arrows started flying up in the air and falling down on the soldiers. *Don* Manuel was dumbfounded.

355

"Fire, Roberto, fire the cannons!" he hurriedly said.

Roberto turned toward the cannon handlers. "Fire cannon one!!" he yelled as loud as he could and he was answered with a loud booming sound a moment later that caused havoc on the rebel line below. Yells and groans of pain reached up to the soldiers on top of the wall. Then another cannon spat its deadly load and more yells and groans could be heard amidst the noise. And then another one followed until all five had shot their first load. While the advancing rebels retreated and tried to regroup at the lull of the cannon fires, the other soldiers could not contain their eagerness to join in the melee and they started shooting their rifles, ineffective they may be at that distance.

"Hold your rifle fire! You're just wasting bullets, *cabrónes!*" Roberto yelled. "They're too far!" *Don* Manuel smiled. It looked like he made the right choice with Roberto.

"Resume cannon fire, one more round! Give it to those *bastardos!*" Roberto added and the smile on the *Capitán*'s face grew wider. He nodded. Tiago would have had approved.

And the cannons roared again.

"Get back! Get back! Retreat!" Gabriela yelled. The command was repeated down the line and the Ilocanos and *Itnegs* alike scrambled back from as far away from the cannon fires as they could. No one had counted on the cannons. They had to regroup.

"We will lose too many men. We can't attack the fort this way. We're too open," Kulas said.

Nobody argued. It was too obvious.

"We have to lure them out," Akash said. The other tribal leaders agreed. They'd rather fight in the open. They were willing to face the single shot rifles but the cannons were too much. But as everyone knew, that was easier said than done. It looked like the Spaniards were all set to stand pat inside the fort for now. Kulas wondered if they were waiting for more reinforcements.

Gabriela and the Ilocano leaders exchanged glances, seeking a decision which seemed no one was willing enough to come forth with. The Spaniards had sustained big casualties, in the town and down the road. There could not be too many of them left in the fort, reinforcements or not. The rebels hated to let go now while they have the advantage in numbers. But how long would the *Itnegs* stay with them if they kept having considerable casualties?

"We have to take the cannons out," Gabriela said.

"Agreed, but how?" Nicolas said. The rest expectantly fixed their eyes on Gabriela.

Gabriela sighed. "I wish I know," she said looking up at Kulas and then to her uncle Akash.

"Let's move back away from the reach of the cannons and set camp around the fort. Make sure no one comes out and ride away for more reinforcements. We'll find a way to get in but not out in the open like this, perhaps in the night, but not tonight," Kulas said. The Ilocano leaders had seen what the tall *Itneg* could do in battle and there was something in his manner that discouraged any effort of antagonizing him that no one dared to speak up. Besides they thought he had a valid point, and no one really had any good idea on how to neutralize the cannons.

Every one silently nodded their agreement, except for Gabriela. "Why not tonight?" she said.

"Because they would be expecting us," Kulas said. "We can wait. We have water, the river's out there, and we have food. Send some men to town and get more provisions. Just get them anywhere you can. I don't think anyone would object."

"I'll see to that," Sebastian said.

"Ask for what the people can afford and are willing to give," Gabriela said to Sebastian. "We are not thieves."

Akash and Kulas and the other tribal leaders exchanged glances. No one among them would have thought of asking for needed provisions for battle. They simply took what was needed to advance the course of battle.

"You can ask but make sure we have enough food to last us for at least a week," Kulas said.

"Why a week?" Nicolas asked, beginning to understand that the *Itneg* was preparing for a siege on the fort. "They may have enough provisions inside the fort to last them for a month. They have horses and cows there that they can eat. And they have a well for water."

"I am not giving them a week. I am giving us a week," Kulas said. "If we can't take the fort within a week, then we will never take it. We're going back up to the mountains after a week." He scanned the faces of the leaders, *Itneg* and Ilocano alike, and nobody spoke. He had made a decision without consulting any of the elders, including Akash, yet no one dared to oppose him. His eyes finally settled on Gabriela and their eyes locked, exchanging unspoken thoughts which the other understood as if they were said clearly in the open.

'I care for you a lot, perhaps even love you a lot, but I can't sacrifice any more of the lives of my people for you to pursue your vengeance or the cause of your dead husband, whichever it may be your reason now. I am giving you a week, because yes, I care about you, even perhaps love you.'

'I understand, and thank you. I care for you too, perhaps more than you'll ever know and I care to admit, and I am sorry I dragged you and our people into this. I am truly sorry, although I am also disappointed because I had wished that you would be with me to the end.'

And nobody spoke for a while.

Akash finally broke the silence. "Let's move then and start setting camp. Let them know we're not going away," he said.

"And spread out, surround the fort as much as possible, including, no I mean, especially by the back gate along the river," Kulas said. "Nobody gets out."

"Nobody gets out," Nicolas echoed and everyone nodded that they understood.

"Alright, let's move," Gabriela said, but she looked at Kulas and signaled for him to stay.

"Look after the men," Kulas said to Akash. "I'll follow and talk with you later."

Akash grunted, turned around and signaled to the Chinese brothers who were hanging around the impromptu gathering of the leaders, and they walked away toward the warriors of the village who were assessing the damage that they sustained from the cannons. Like most of the other tribes, and especially the Ilocanos, they had suffered some casualties.

"What happens after a week?" Gabriela asked when she and Kulas were finally alone.

"Either this will be over or like I said, the warriors will go back home," Kulas said.

"And you? Are you going back with them?"

"I don't know, Ilang. Perhaps," Kulas paused. Then, "Do you want me to stay?"

Gabriela looked up at him with soft tender eyes. She did not have to say a word. Then she lowered her face.

"I don't have the right," she said softly. "I have no right to make you stay."

"What if I say I have no place else to go?" Kulas said. In his heart, he was speaking the truth.

"Then I want you to stay. With me. With this," she waved a hand to the rebels and warriors who were setting camp, "or without them." She looked back up at Kulas.

Kulas' chest swelled and he was lost for words. He reached out and held a gentle hand on Gabriela's shoulder, gave it a soft squeeze, let go then turned around without saying a word. He walked towards Akash and their warriors with gladness in his face yet somehow with a heavy heart.

He did not know what was happening to him. He would sort things out when this was over.

They set camp around the fort, well beyond the accurate reach of the small cannons. They kept the campfires going all through the night, letting the soldiers know that they were not going away anytime soon.

Sebastian and his crew came back with pigs, chickens and several cows that he swore were voluntarily given, and during the day, they openly cooked, ate and loitered around, singing songs and making no attempt whatsoever to breach the walls of the fort. That second night, they did the same thing again, the flames from the campfires flickering throughout the night like eternally vigilant sentries in the dark. And the singing continued, fueled with *basi* that somehow found its way into the camp. The leaders let the men drink and have their fun.

The soldiers responded with cannon fire now and then, the balls falling harmlessly a few hundred yards short away. The *Capitán* was not worried. They have enough provisions for at least a good month. He had been in a siege before and he was determined to win the waiting game.

Then on the third night, Kulas made his move. He asked for volunteers from the other tribal leaders, to join him and Akash and the select village archers that included Aklang, Lang-gi, Dagyo and Bagit. It was way past midnight, yet they made some groups in the camps stay up and make noise as much and as long as they could. And with the diversionary noise and under cover of darkness, they made their way unnoticed to the foot of the walls of the fort. There were five groups of ten warriors in each group. The plan was simple, just like they had done successfully before by the river. Breach the walls, get in, and open the gates, or help other warriors get over the walls. If they could not manage to open the gates, then do as much damage as they could and get out.

"Five groups," Kulas figured. "One of us should be able to get through."

"We will," Akash said. "I'll have the gates open."

"Remember, the back gate first. That's where most of them will be coming in," Kulas said.

Akash grunted. Ilang and the Ilocano rebels were by the riverbank, well hidden in the dark by the trees, ready to break out and charge as soon as the signal was sent that the gate was open. 'I hope those Ilocanos are not too drunk to fight,' Akash thought as they waited. Each of them had figured out where to get up and over the wall. The thirty feet high walls were not much of a challenge for them who had made a game of climbing sheer-faced cliffs with just their bare hands and feet.

"Wait until you hear yelling from inside the fort," Kulas had said to his men.

359

"What yelling?" Akash asked.

"One of the groups, maybe two or even three will be spotted as soon they try to scale the walls assigned to them," Kulas said. "That's when we make our move. I hope they'd be able to get away unharmed when they're spotted."

Dagyo smiled. He knew Kulas expected the other groups to be spotted. "Sneaky bastard," he said, his smile spreading into a wide grin.

"Better them than us," Bagit said.

"Yeah, and we have better chances of getting through and doing the job," Kulas said. "We've done it before and we'll do it again."

Everyone turned serious and nodded.

The yell came followed by a barrage of rifle shots from the north side of the wall that was assigned to be breached by the warriors of Bacooc.

"Let's go!" Kulas said and he scrambled up the wall. All ten warriors made their pre-determined paths up the wall without any incident. The surprised guard that Kulas came up to when he got to the top was so focused at the commotion from the north wall, that he never got the chance of even turning his head to the sudden noise from behind him when his neck was twisted and broken. The other guards fell from knives and arrows shot at very close ranges. Not one of the guards was able to shoot a rifle or raise an alarm. The guards by the back gate below met the same fate, falling from Akash's arrows.

Akash opened the back gate, waved a torch hanging by the gate and watched as Ilang and the rebels poured out of the darkness and headed toward him. He did not wait for them. He turned around and went inside and joined the other warriors who were spread out, facing the courtyard, bows and arrows poised and ready in their hands.

'Looks like I was wrong about giving it a week,' Kulas thought as he let his arrow fly. It struck a soldier who happened to turn around and was about to yell and shoot at seeing the rebels coming through the back gate. The rifle of the falling soldier rattled on the pavement and the other soldiers refocused their attention from the northern wall to the rebels rushing into the fort thru the wide open and unguarded back gate. Harried shots were fired, some luckily finding targets among the onrushing mass of bodies, yet the rebels came hurling bamboo spears and yelling at the top of their lungs in an adrenaline filled state of craziness. And again, the deadly arrows of the *Itneg* archers wreaked havoc among the soldiers who bewilderedly looked at one another as men beside them kept falling. Thus the battle inside the fort started again for the second time that week.

'I wish Tiago was here,' *Don* Manuel thought as he found himself in the midst of a skirmish in just his night shirt. He had no time to put on his uniform which, unbeknownst to him at the time, was a very lucky thing because Aklang and not just a couple of the other archers were separately and actively looking out for the big man with the fancy uniform. They had no orders not to shoot him this time. As far as they were concerned, he was fair game.

But at the moment, the *Capitán* was not in any of the archers' sights. However, they were not lacking for targets as the soldiers, roused from their sleep, came out from their barracks in confused groups, and unsure where the attackers were coming from, paused for a moment out in the open to get their bearings and the archers shot at will, not missing much of any one they aimed at.

Then suddenly rebels were falling from arrows themselves. For a moment, some of the Ilocano rebels thought that the *Itnegs* were mistaking them for soldiers since most of the soldiers were fighting without their uniforms, most of them having been roused from their sleep. Then they realized that the arrows were coming from inside and around the buildings where the soldiers were coming from. They had not figured out on the rest of the *Ybanags* left behind by *Teniente* Tabieros who were now methodically mowing down the rebels with their arrows in an impeccable show of mastery of their bows.

Kulas saw what was happening and caught Akash's attention. He signaled and pointed at the shooters from the barracks. Akash nodded and together they moved away, crouching as they sprinted to position and engaged in a shootout with the *Ybanags*. Aklang, Lang-gi and several of the other archers saw what Akash and Kulas were doing and also shifted their attentions to the *Ybanag* archers, leaving the soldiers armed with rifles and swords to the similarly armed rebels and warriors.

It was a stand-off for a while, with neither group gaining any significant advantage, but soon the superior and disciplined experience of the soldiers, especially the cold accuracy and control of the reinforcement soldiers from Cagayan tipped the balance in favor of the defenders. Their *Ybanag* archers stayed well covered inside the barracks, shooting in rotation through the windows and the doors, presenting not much of a target for the rebels. The spears and long knives of most of the rebels were useless against the rifles and arrows of the soldiers who now were fighting behind the safety of walls.

And the occasional rebel who was brave and foolish or drunk enough to venture a rushing attack to get into the barracks was felled by either an arrow or a bullet before he could get past the open space. The rest, including Gabriela and Nicolas and the rebel leaders were held down in their place opposite the barracks, unable to push forward without exposing themselves.

"Let's burn the place down," Akash said to Kulas as they conferred together to assess the situation.

"Place is mostly made of stone," Kulas observed. "Fire wouldn't do much."

"Then we'll smoke them out," Akash said. "Then we can attack under the smoke."

"Or get out," Aklang chimed in as he had sidled by and overheard their conversation. The two older warriors looked at him. "Look," Aklang continued, pointing to the barracks where the *Ybanags* had not stopped shooting their deadly arrows. "We cannot get through that open space. Those shooters are too good. They have not been missing much."

Kulas nodded and watched as another rebel cried in pain then followed by silence. The boy had a point. And the soldiers were too disciplined to leave a position which was to their advantage.

"Let's give the fire and the smoke a try anyway," Akash insisted. "I'm going into the stables. Wait for the smoke then do what you need to do. I'll see you inside or outside, whichever plays out."

"Go. I'll warn Ilang," Kulas said. He turned to Aklang. "Stick with the others. If the rebels and the others attack, stay back and cover them. If they move out, get out also, you and the other archers. I'll find and meet you outside."

Kulas and Akash went their separate ways without waiting for Aklang to say anything.

A few moments later, the horses from the stables came running out in droves as the bales of hay inside burned fast sending clouds of smoke drifting up and into the nearby buildings inside the fort.

"Fire!!" someone yelled. And some of the soldiers attempted to get out from where they were hiding and tried to contain the growing fire but they were met by either arrows or rebels emboldened anew by the sight of the fire that they knew was started by one of them. A group of rebels and *Itnegs* rushed into the open trying to break through and get into the barracks but they were repulsed by the soldiers inside. Wave after wave of attempts was handily repulsed by the disciplined defense of the soldiers. The *Itneg* archers tried shooting into the barracks with flaming arrows, but they were easily doused by the soldiers inside.

And then the grey of dawn loomed in the east. Kulas and Akash gave each other a knowing look, and both without saying anything stood up from where they sat, resting, and worked their way toward Ilang and the rebel leaders. Somehow along the way, the Chinese brothers showed up, their long poles held uselessly in their hands.

"Go, wait for us by the river," Akash said to them. They looked at one another and at Kulas who nodded, then they scampered away in the dark toward the back gate. Aklang and the other archers saw them and catching a wave from Kulas, promptly followed the Chinese.

"It will be light in a moment," Akash said to Ilang. "We'll be too open out here, too vulnerable. It's time to move out."

"We've lost too many men," Kulas added. "We're going to lose more come daylight."

"They're right, Maria," Nicolas said. "Let's go while we can."

Gabriela sighed. She looked at the barracks which now and again was lit up from rifle fires and knew the men were right. "Spread the word then," she said. "We'll fight another day."

Kulas waited until Gabriela was out through the back gate before he moved out. Akash was waiting by the gate when he reached it. They were the last to walk out.

Inside the barracks, *Don* Manuel watched as the rebels left. He ordered his men to stay put. He did not want them walking into a trap.

Besides they had a fire to put out and wounded soldiers to attend to.

And they had more dead to bury.

Then two weeks later, fortified by more reinforcement, Don Manuel, Captain of His Majesty's army in the north of *Las Islas Filipinas*, led a formidable force of mixed Spanish, Ilocano, *Pangasinense*, *Capampangan* and *Ybanag* soldiers out of the fort of Vigan in the pursuit of *La Generala* and her remaining forces. It was the biggest military undertaking the Spanish had ever staged in the north and yet it took them the better part of over a month before they finally captured Gabriela and what was left of her rebels who were by that time were mostly made up of Ilocanos.

The Chinese brothers had gone down south hoping to get to Binondo where there was another uncle who ran a store and a restaurant there.

The *Itnegs*, never comfortable of running away from a fight, and the memory of the Bangilo warriors in the back of their minds, most of them secretly wishing that they had also gone to meet their ancestors in such an honorable manner, had gone back home to their tribal villages. Except for one who was back up someplace roaming around again in the mountains, the people from his village assumed.

But he was not.

Kulas saw when the soldiers went back to Vigan with their prisoners. He witnessed them leave behind rows of hanged bodies of the captured rebels along the shoreline from the coastal *pueblo* of Santiago all the way up to Vigan.

By the time the soldiers and their prisoners reached Vigan, only eight of the rebel leaders were left alive, including Gabriela. The *Capitán* thought that it would be most fitting for them to die, especially *La Generala*, in the place where it all began.

He planned to display their dead bodies there, grotesquely hanging in the gallows, as a reminder to the rest of the Indios of the foolhardiness of questioning His Majesty's sovereignty over them and testing the patience of His Royal army.

Kulas watched from a safe distance, unseen, well away behind the throng of curious spectators many of them roused from their homes and forced in attendance, as the guards walked Gabriela up the steps to the gallows where the hangman ominously waited. All the other leaders had been hanged before her, including Sebastian and Nicolas, and their dead bodies now dangled in a row from the scaffold, swaying gently in the wind. But there was nothing gentle in their deaths and neither the dark hoods that mercifully covered their faces could hide the tortured anguish and pain that they endured, especially the ultimate humiliation of being paraded and executed as nothing but despicable and common criminals.

Even the thought that they died for a noble cause did not lessen the agony and pain in their hearts as the unforgiving rope snapped their necks and finally gave them the freedom from the Spaniards that they sought.

There was only one empty noose left, reserved for the last of the rebels, their leader, Maria Josefa Gabriela, *La Generala*.

Don Manuel, with Isabella by his side, watched solemnly as Gabriela walked past him at the foot of the stairs going up the gallows. But before she placed her foot on the first step, Gabriela turned and met her captor's eyes. For what seemed a long time prisoner and captor looked at one another, not with anger or hatred but with respect and regret in their eyes.

But *Don* Manuel saw something else in his prisoner's eyes that made him wince and caused an eye to twitch involuntarily. There was pity in *La Generala*'s eyes, and it was for him.

Tersely, *Don* Manuel signaled for the guards to move the prisoner on.

"Pardon me, *Señora*, but I am only doing my job," the hangman whispered as he shook loose the last of his black hoods. He started to raise and slip it over Gabriela's head but stopped as the prisoner spoke.

"Keep the hood for your next victim, *Señor*," Gabriela said without turning her head to look at her executioner. "I would like to see the faces of my people as I die and I would like them to see mine."

"It will not be a pretty sight, *Señora*."

"I have never been known for being pretty, *Señor*, so don't worry about it."

364

"As you wish, *Señora*, but I want you to know that yes, you are no[t] pretty," the hang-man dropped the black hood on the platform floor an[d] slipped the noose down Gabriela's neck. "You are beautiful and I say tha[t] with all sincerity and honesty. Again I am sorry. Please forgive me." He whispered as he tightened the noose. Then he walked the few steps to the lever that triggered the trapdoor on the floor to open underneath.

"T-thank you," Gabriela whispered as the hangman put his hand on the lever and pulled and she found herself floating in the air.

In that fleeting moment when the noose tightened around her neck, Gabriela's eyes swept the faces below and then she caught sight of a figure way back, far away from the crowd that made her smile.

"Wait!" She cried, raising a hand as the figure turned away, but no voice came out of her mouth and she could not move her hands for they were tie[d] tightly behind her back.

Don Manuel felt a lump in his throat as the body jerked spasmodically then finally became still. He stared grimly at the face of the dead woman who had caused him so many sleepless nights and was surprised to see that she seemed to be smiling. He shivered and reflexively stiffened up, startled by the sudden grip of a cold hand on his arm. He looked down and gently patted the hand of Isabella who nervously clung to him. 'Perhaps I should have not let her come,' he thought but it was too late now. Gently, he put an arm around the frightened woman and turned her around, away from the gallows.

"Post a couple of guards through the night," he said to *Sargento* Roldan as they walked past him, "and don't let anyone move the bodies until I say so."

"*Si, Capitán*," *Sargento* Roldan said. He knew that *Don* Manuel wanted the people to see the hanging bodies to put fear in their hearts and he wondered how long the *Capitán* would want to keep them up this time. He pitied the poor *peons* that he was going to designate as guards. But *Sargento* Roberto Roldan was a compassionate man.

'Twelve soldiers, two guards in two-hour rotations to make it easy on them especially when the bodies begin to smell,' he thought. 'Yes, that should do it.'

The plaza finally cleared as darkness fell. The two guards designated to take the first watch stood rigidly at first at the foot of the scaffold fearful that the *Capitán* may be watching from his *casa* that was right across the plaza. But as the hour wore on, they relaxed a bit. The flickering light from the couple of lamps placed nearby played shadows against their stolid faces. They cast a glance now and then at the swaying bodies on the platform

365

thankful that it was dark enough for them not to see the face of *La Generala*. They were relieved when the next pair of guards came up to replace them.

"It's peaceful," they assured the new guards. "Everyone's gone to sleep. It looks like they had enough excitement for the day."

And so it went with the next two pairs of guards. And the following pair, as well as the next. All was quiet and peaceful. Even the stray dogs and cats stayed away from the plaza. It did seem indeed that the Indios have had their fill of excitement for the day and were just contented on sleeping the night away. The two guards who had the luck of getting the two o'clock hour past midnight wondered why they even had to be there at all. They did not have to wonder long.

When the guards assigned to relieve them came two hours later, they found one empty rope hanging from the crossbeam of the gallows. And underneath the platform were the two guards, dead as the other bodies left hanging above them.

Both of them had their throats slit and their horses were gone.

And *La Generala* was gone as well.

Epilogue

Three days later, Pedro Becbec and Miguel Vicos met at *Ina* Andang's *carinderia*. They had not been seen in town for a long time and their presence caused a minor point of curiosity among the regular customers.

"They finally showed up now that *La Generala* is dead," one whispered.

"Yeah, I wonder what hole these two snakes crawled into when she was riding about," another one said.

"I heard Pedro went with his wife to her province up north, in Isabela, I think, but as for Miguel, I don't know. I thought he was roasted when his house went up in smoke, but I guess it's true what they say about bad grass. Rumor is he's living in an abandoned hut out in the fields," their drink mate chimed in as they cast furtive glances at Miguel and Pedro.

But Miguel and Pedro were oblivious that they were the topic of the conversations around them. Or they were getting good in ignoring the curious glances and gossips directed their way since they turned against Diego. They dined and drank as if they were unaffected from it all.

"Well, I hope we can finally live in peace, *amigo*," Pedro said to Miguel, raising his glass of *basi* in a toast to his friend.

"People like us, Pedro, will never find peace," Miguel said gravely as he lifted his glass to his lips, ignoring Pedro's toast, and kept it there until it was empty. His hand shook uncontrollably when he put the glass down.

And up by a cave in the Cordilleras where an underground spring gurgled softly inside, Kulas put the final big boulder in place at the entrance, completely sealing it. He stepped back and surveyed his handiwork. Not satisfied, he picked up a hefty piece of driftwood lying about and used it to topple dirt and loose pebbles from above the cave's mouth finally burying it completely from view. Then he broke some densely leafed bushes and branches off the nearby undergrowth and brushed away the tracks of what he had done. He placed the branches on the caved-in dirt then he went down the slope and turned loose the two horses that he had taken from the dead guards.

Perhaps they will find their way back down to town, although he doubted it.

But it did not matter.

They had brought Ilang home.

§

Made in the USA
Lexington, KY
09 December 2018